A NEW BEGINNING

ALSO BY CHARLES RUSSELL

FAITH AND FAMILY SAGA
    A Year to Remember
    Making Memories
    Lasting Memories
    Faith and a Fast Horse

Coming Home

TWO BOOK SERIES
    When the Cactus Blooms
    My Country God's Country

TWO BOOK SERIES
    A Silver Lining in Every Cloud
    A Cloudless Sky

The Gathering Storm

A NEW BEGINNING

CHARLES LYNN RUSSELL

Copyright 2024 by Charles Russell
All rights reserved
No part of this book may be reproduced in any form or by any electronic or mechanical means, including informational and retrieval systems, without written permission from the author except for brief descriptions in a book review.

ISBN: 979-8-9873351-9-2

Published by Texas Star Trading Company
174 Cypress Street, Abilene, Texas 79601
www.TexasStarTrading.com
(325) 672-9696

Design by Lauren Monsey
Monsey Creative LLC

Published in the USA

Dedicated to my wife, Patricia, sons Kelly and John and grandson Charlie. A small family but one filled with love.

ACKNOWLEDGMENTS

My wife, Patricia, continues to provide the encouragement that keeps me moving forward, both in my writing and everyday life.

A special appreciation to Susan and Bob Nethery, Doyle Russell, and Mary Danna Russell for proofing the book, which is no easy task considering the challenges I face with my limited spelling and grammatical abilities.

Finishing out my team of proofreaders and, batting in the clean-up spot, is Glenn Dromgoole. His ability to copy-edit a book must be second to none and is only rivaled by his patience with me. I appreciate the support he and his wife Carol have provided me in writing eleven books in as many years.

AUTHOR'S NOTE

I enjoyed writing this book. It is fiction, but like my other novels some of the characters are based on people that did exist. The book could be labeled historical fiction because there is a great deal of actual events included. Since I am a history major, the research I did for the book was interesting as well as informative.

Two characters in the book, Charlie and Leta, were my great uncle and aunt.

They were born in the late nineteenth century and spent their lives in Texas. Of course, their lives do not coincide with the story, but their physical traits, personalities and mannerisms do. It was fun remembering my experiences growing up around them. Uncle Charlie was a constable for a time, and when he passed, Aunt Leta gave me his pistol.

The setting for most of the story is Coleman County which has a rich and well documented history. I was surprised to learn that John Chisum had a ranch in the southeastern part of the county before he became famous for his cattle drives and part in the Lincoln County War. He established a store that later became the beginning of a community named "Trickum," which is another story in itself.

Another surprise in my research was the Comanche chief Quanah Parker. I had always envisioned him as a diplomat for his people and was not aware, in his youth, that his name struck fear in the settlers. His band was the most ferocious of any of the tribes on the plains, yet he was able to live in the world of the white man in his later years.

I have no idea how the book will be received by readers, but it was one of my favorite stories to tell.

Inside of me there are two dogs.

One is mean and evil and the other is good and

they fight each other all the time.

When asked which one wins, I answer,

the one I feed the most.

Sitting Bull, Chief of the Lakota

PART 1

THE MORNING SIDE OF THE MOUNTAIN

1879
ROSWELL, NEW MEXICO

Leta

On my way to work, two cowboys blocked my way on the narrow boardwalk. One was taller than me but the other smaller. The little one smiled and moved closer. "Well, little lady, where are you going this morning all by yourself?"

I was seventeen and used to the attention and enjoyed it. Smiling, I said, "To work for Captain Lea at his store." I tried to step around him, but he moved and blocked my way.

"You sure are a pretty little thing. Why don't we go somewhere and get to know one another a little better?" He took hold of my arm.

I jerked away. "I'll be late for work. Please get out of my way."

His grip became tighter as he pulled me toward stairs that led to a building. "Please let me go. You're hurting me."

"You're a little tease, aren't you? I've seen you flirting with all the cowboys. Just relax, and we can have some fun."

Suddenly, he let go of my arm. I turned and saw him flung to the ground with someone kicking him. He was trying but couldn't get away. The larger man tried to help him, but he ended up on the ground being pummeled in the face by the assailant. Someone came to the rescue of the larger man and pulled my savior off him. "Whoa there, little guy. You don't need to kill him."

It happened so fast, and then I saw the man who had saved me—or the small boy. The big gun on his hip looked out of place. How could this guy do so much damage? He started walking away. "Wait, wait. Come back."

He stopped and turned. "What is it?"

"I need to thank you. Those terrible men scared the daylights out of me."

"You shouldn't be presenting yourself the way you do. You got what you deserved."

He turned and started walking away.

His comment made me furious. "Wait just a minute, cowboy. What did you mean by that?"

He continued without stopping. I caught up with him and grabbed his arm. "Wait a minute! I deserve an explanation for what you said." When he turned, I realized, even with his boots, I was taller than he was.

His gaze went from my head to my feet. "I've seen how you smile at all the men. You're advertising like one of those saloon girls. The dress you're wearing comes halfway to your knee. What do you expect these men to think?"

By now I was so mad I couldn't put together a sentence. I stomped my foot. "Y-you are t-terrible! Why d-did you h-help me?"

He hesitated and then laughed. "Because you're so damned pretty." He turned and walked away again.

This time I didn't stop him. On the rest of the way to my job, I stared straight ahead when meeting anyone.

It was a Saturday, which meant a busy morning. People were shopping for a week's supply of food, and it was noon before I had a few minutes for a break. I had just sat down when a man came through the door who looked familiar and came directly to me. He took off his hat. "Miss Payne, my name is John Chisum. I have a ranch just outside of town. I understand that two of my men were rude to you this morning. I want to apologize and tell you that those men do not work for me any longer. I'm terribly sorry. That is not usual conduct for the men who work for me."

No wonder he looked familiar. He was already famous. "That's all right, Mr. Chisum. No harm was done. How did you find out what happened?"

He smiled. "Bad news about me or my men has a way of getting out fast." "The man who helped me was not nice. In fact, he was rude and said ugly things to me."

At least I could tell someone who would understand.

He burst out laughing. "You mean Charlie? He works for me, also. Would you like him fired, too?"

"He said some really mean things to me. Is he always like that?"

Another big smile. "Well, I don't know what Charlie said to you, but I've known him a long time and never known him to lie. He's quite a little man. He came up the trail with me from Texas when he was only twelve in '72."

Now, I really messed up. I insulted a boy who had worked for him for years. "I'm sorry, Mr. Chisum. I was simply confused. He came to my rescue, stopped those terrible men and then scolded me. Maybe I better just shut up. The more I talk the more trouble I get into."

"I tell you what, Miss Payne—I'll send a buggy to get you tomorrow evening. I would consider it an honor if you would have dinner with me. Maybe we can get this all straightened out."

What should I do? I couldn't refuse the most respected person in Roswell, maybe even New Mexico. "Okay, I guess so."

"Good. It's settled. Someone will pick you up about four in the evening." He left, and I regretted my decision to accept his invitation for the rest of the day.

"I don't understand why John Chisum would invite you to dinner," my dad said as we were eating supper Saturday evening.

I had not told them about my encounter with the cowboys on my way to work. Maybe the least I said the best. "He was just being friendly to new people in the territory." Hopefully, that would satisfy my dad.

My mom and dad ran the general store for Captain Lea. We had come to New Mexico two years earlier from Ohio for that purpose. I was still confused about why we would leave a state to come to a territory like New Mexico.

"It still doesn't make sense. He may be wanting to court you. I won't have that. He's too old for you. I don't care if he is rich."

"Dad! John Chisum is the most respected person in this part of the country." Should I go ahead and tell him what happened?

He stopped eating and put down his fork. "Just the same, I want to have a talk with him before you go out to his place."

That left me no choice. I started from the beginning and told them what happened, leaving out the lecture from the cowboy who rescued me. "I think Mr. Chisum feels badly about his men being rude to me. This is just his way of making it up to me."

"Well, that makes a lot more sense. Why didn't you tell us that in the first place?" He went back to eating.

"What about the cowboy that protected you from those terrible men?" Mother asked.

I shrugged. "I thanked him, and he left without saying much." Maybe that would be enough of an explanation—hopefully.

"I would like to meet him. You said he worked for Mr. Chisum. Why don't you invite him for dinner some evening? Your dad and I need to thank him."

Why couldn't they just let it be? I didn't want to ever see that rude person again. What would my mother think if I told her he compared me to one of those girls who worked in saloons? "I probably won't ever see him again. Mr. Chisum's ranch is huge."

"You were fortunate that he came along when he did. I feel

we owe him something," Mother continued.

I excused myself and went to my room. I sat down on my bed and thought, *I'm seventeen and ready to leave home. I was bored working in the store that my dad ran and wanted some adventure in my life. Besides, my parents were beginning to wear on my nerves.*

I began trying to decide what to wear to the ranch. I had several nice dresses since we could order them at a discount from the store. It was pleasant weather for April, but that could change. My choice was conservative. I certainly wasn't going to be compared to a saloon girl.

I waited anxiously until, a few minutes before four, a one-horse buggy stopped at the front of our house. An older man came to the door and asked if I was ready to go. Within a few minutes we were on our way to the headquarters of Mr. Chisum's ranch, which was only three miles from town. In an attempt to make conversation, I asked my driver how long he had worked for Mr. Chisum.

"Only about four years. I hired on after he came to New Mexico from Texas. He's a good man and fair to everyone."

"Do you know one of the cowboys that works for him, whose name is Charlie?" I couldn't resist asking about him. Surely, he was detested by the other hands.

He chuckled. "Sure, everyone knows Charlie. He's something else—always joking and cutting up. Everyone likes him. He's a top hand—can ride about anything. He's a favorite of Mr. Chisum."

I kept thinking someone would have the same opinion as me about this rude little cowboy. We arrived at the ranch headquarters and were greeted by a middle- aged man, who introduced himself as Jock and said he was Mr. Chisum's foreman. "Miss Payne, welcome to the Jinglebob. Mr. Chisum thought you might be more comfortable with some female companionship. My wife is waiting for you inside and can keep you company until supper. We'll eat around six."

Adeline met me with a smile and a hug. "When they said I was to entertain Miss Payne, I expected someone much older."

"Just call me Leta. This Miss Payne thing doesn't fit. I am glad to find a woman among all these men."

She laughed. "We're few and far between around here. It's not that bad though to feel special."

I liked Adeline at once. She was probably in her late thirties or early forties, a pretty lady, and a little on the plump side. Conversation came easy with her, and I found myself enjoying my visit to Mr. Chisum's ranch.

She leaned forward and whispered. "Do you know who's going to eat with us tonight?"

"No. Mr. Chisum came into the store yesterday and invited me to dinner." I explained what had happened on my way to work and his apology for the conduct of his men. "I think he just wanted to do something for me."

She leaned closer and spoke more quietly. "Lew Wallace will be here—the governor of the territory. He is a guest of Mr. Chisum this week. Can you believe it? I'm nervous as a cat. What if I say the wrong thing or get choked. I know we'll have Mexican food. He has a wonderful cook. The problem is spicy food gives me gas. What if..." and she started giggling, which turned to laughter.

I joined in the laughter but was interrupted when her husband came into the room. "What's so funny?"

Adeline wiped away tears, she had laughed so hard. "Honey, you don't want to know."

His confused look transformed into a smile. "You're not going to get Miss Payne into trouble, are you? We eat in fifteen minutes if y'all want to freshen up."

After he was gone, Adeline said, "Well, Leta, pray for me."

"You have me nervous. I had no idea we would be in such company. Have you ever met the governor?"

"No. I have been told he's writing a book about the Bible. I'm sure he will be a gentleman. Well, time's a wastin'. Let's wash up and get in there amongst them."

We entered the dining room, and the five men who were seated rose. I felt like some kind of queen. After we were seated, Mr. Chisum made the introductions. "Miss Payne, I'll begin with you. You have already met my foreman Jock and his lovely wife, Adeline." He gestured to his left. "These men are my brothers—Jim and Pitzer." He looked toward the end of the table. "This is my distinguished guest, the Honorable Governor of New Mexico—Mr. Lew Wallace. Lew, you haven't met Jock's beautiful wife, Adeline. The other pretty lady is Leta Payne, who I only met yesterday, under unusual circumstances."

"It is a pleasure, ladies," the governor said, nodding in our direction.

Adeline and I stayed quiet as the men made small talk about the weather and cattle prices until the food arrived. I had never seen so much food. There were a dozen large bowls. All I recognized were the beans, enchiladas, and tortillas. The bowls were presented to us by two young girls. I took a small helping of several dishes, being careful not to get too much on my plate. I noticed that Adeline did the same. With everyone eating, talk ceased until the dessert was served. It was some kind of pudding and delicious. I gained the attention of Adeline who smiled and nodded, showing all was going well.

Jock, Adeline's husband, broke the silence. "Governor, how is everything going in Lincoln? I know you have your work cut out for you."

The governor hesitated with his spoon halfway to its destination. "It varies day to day. Sometimes I'm encouraged—other days I think it's a hopeless situation. I tried the amnesty route, and it didn't work out."

Mr. Chisum interrupted. "Miss Payne, what do you think about our cook?" It was clear he wanted to change the subject.

"The food was so good. Do you eat like this every meal?"

He laughed. "No, just on special occasions. We do have good meals every day though—just not as extravagant as this." He turned his attention to the governor. "Lew, Miss Payne had a disappointing issue with two of my men yesterday. Fortunately, Charlie Barlowe intervened, and the situation did not get out of hand. You remember Charlie. He came with me to Lincoln the last time we brought some cattle up there."

"Sure, the little guy. You and Charlie have been together a long time, I understand."

"Correct. His dad worked for me in Texas. When he passed away Charlie was twelve. His mother had died when he was only a few years old. I sort of adopted him, and he came to New Mexico with me."

"He's the best hand we have on the ranch," said Jock, the foreman. "Don't let his size fool you. He's not afraid of anything."

"I just love him. He's so cute, I just want to hug him," Adeline said. "If I was single and ten years younger . . ."

Jock interrupted, laughing. "Don't you mean twenty years younger, Adeline."

Now, I understood why the invitation to Mr. Chisum's ranch. He wanted me to hear all these good qualities of Charlie Barlowe, whom I despised. Well, I wasn't going to change my opinion of him.

After the meal was finished, the men vanished to another room, leaving Adeline and me to ourselves. "That was a wonderful meal."

"Leta, I'm glad it's over. I ate too much and was scared to death my stomach would start acting up." She rose. "Let's go sit on the porch. It's a nice evening, especially for April."

I had brought a coat, and it felt good. The sun had already gone down but the colors still remained, and it was beautiful. "I noticed that Mr. Chisum changed the subject when Lincoln was mentioned to the governor."

"Jock should have known better than to bring it up. I know you've heard of the trouble in Lincoln. That's the reason for the governor coming here. There's been a war going on there for over a year in which a number of men have been killed. Mr. Chisum has tried to stay out of it—especially the violence. He does support one of the groups from a financial standpoint."

"I've heard of the Lincoln County War but don't know the details. People come into the store talking about it. I only hear bits and pieces and am usually too busy to make sense of it."

Mr. Chisum came out on the porch, interrupting us. "We better get you home, Miss Payne. I hope you enjoyed your visit to the Jinglebob Ranch."

"I did and thank you for the invitation."

"It's dark but not far into town. The buggy will be around to pick you up in a few minutes. I'm sure we will see you again." He left, going back into the house.

"Adeline, I'm so glad to get to know you. You made the evening pleasant. I feel like I have a new friend. Come into the store when you're in town." I heard the buggy coming around the house.

"Oh, Leta. I will come to see you. You can't believe how lonesome it is without a woman to talk with."

I hugged her and made my way to my ride home. It was dark. But I recognized the little man standing beside the buggy.

THE BUGGY RIDE

Leta

I couldn't believe it. I stepped back. "Just what are you doing here?"

"Boss's orders. Take you home—unless you want to walk."

I backed up another step. "I'm not riding with you!"

He climbed back into the buggy. "Suit yourself." He slapped the reins on the horse, and the buggy pulled away.

Now what? I couldn't walk three miles in the dark. I couldn't go back inside and tell Mr. Chisum I refused to ride with him. That would be rude. I yelled, "Wait a minute!"

The buggy came to a halt and waited, giving me time to catch up. I climbed in and sat as far as possible from him. It wasn't easy since it was one of those hug-me-tight seats. He popped the horse on the rear, causing him to jolt forward throwing me up against him. I moved over and grabbed the rail. "Slow down! What's your hurry?"

He pulled up on the reins, brought us to a stop and turned toward me. "You want to drive this rig? I didn't ask for this job. What is your name anyway?"

"Miss Payne."

He extended his hand. "I'm Charles Kimbrough Barlowe. You can call me Charlie—most people do."

Now, I felt like a prude. I accepted his hand. "It's Leta."

We started off again, slower this time. Nothing was said for the rest of the trip. When we stopped in front of my house, I thanked him for bringing me home.

"No problem." He waited until I was at my door before leaving.

My mother and father ambushed me before I could get to my room. I told them about eating at the same table as the governor and named the other guests present.

"You mean the governor of New Mexico?" Mother asked.

"Yes, I was a little nervous, but it went fine." I described the meal and told them about making a new friend. The questions came fast and furious about everything from what we ate to what the others were wearing.

"Did Governor Wallace talk about the Lincoln County War?" Father asked.

"He tried, but Mr. Chisum changed the subject."

"Did you see the cowboy that came to your rescue?"

"He brought me home, Mother. I don't think he's a nice person. I didn't tell you before, but he was rude to me. It's hard to explain. He saved me from those men and then said some ugly things. Please don't ask me for details. It doesn't matter anyway. If you will excuse me, I'm going to bed. It has been a stressful but interesting evening."

I left before they could ask me any more questions. I didn't light a lantern and sat in the dark in my room, thinking. *Why was I so angry? I had never been criticized before by anyone—period. I had no brothers or sisters and was probably a little spoiled, or maybe protected would be a better description. Why did everyone like him? Mr. Chisum said he never lied, yet he told me I resembled one of those girls who worked in the saloon. How did he know about saloon girls?*

The week following my visit to Mr. Chisum's ranch, I was back to my everyday routine of rising at six and getting to work by eight. My father opened the store at seven but generally had few early customers. Weekdays, we were busy at times but not anything like Saturday.

I was surprised and pleased that Adeline came into the store just before noon on Friday. She held up a sack she was carrying. "Lunch. You ready for a break?"

"Absolutely. I'm starved, as usual." She followed me into a backroom with a table and chairs. "You saved me from a walk home."

She took two wrapped sandwiches out of the sack. "How long do you take for lunch?"

"If we're not busy, an hour. My dad doesn't take a break. He'll grab some crackers and cheese when there are no customers. I'm not nearly that dedicated. How was your week?"

She handed me a sandwich. "Boring—cook, clean, wash, and repeat. Jock's leaving for four days in the morning. Rustlers have been hitting us hard the past several months. I worry when he's gone. It's a dangerous business."

I took my first bite. "This sandwich is delicious."

"We eat lots of beef, but Mr. Chisum is particular, and everything is always cooked just right."

I chewed slowly, enjoying the sandwich. "We eat mostly pork. Beef is so expensive it's a treat when we have it. Does Jock have to be gone from home often?"

"Yes, that's been the case lately. It's hard to cover the ranch and stop the rustling. The effort takes all the hands."

"How big is the ranch?" I asked.

"It goes 150 miles along the Pecos River on the east side and 60 miles on the west. There are about 100 cowboys that work for the Jinglebob."

"Mr. Chisum owns all that land?"

Adeline laughed. "Not hardly. He actually owns forty acres where the ranch house and outbuildings are located. The rest is open range that he grazes. Of course, it is understood that the rest of the land is his for grazing. Woe to anyone who tries to move cattle onto the ranch." She finished her sandwich, wadding up the wrapper. "Changing the subject, but who drove you home last Saturday?"

I hoped to avoid this discussion. "Charlie Barlowe." Maybe that would be enough.

She giggled. "Did you enjoy the ride?"

Now, how do I answer that question? "It was better than walking."

She looked confused. "You mean you don't like Charlie?"

Was I going to have to tell this story to everyone in Roswell before they'd leave me alone? If we were going to be friends, I couldn't keep things from her, so I told her the entire story including Charlie insulting me.

She jumped and started clapping her hands. "He likes you, Leta. If he didn't, he wouldn't have rescued you. He also said you were pretty. I can't believe it! A romance in the making—right before my eyes. Listen! He will be coming around soon. I guarantee it!"

"I don't think so. He compared me to a saloon girl. Besides, I'm taller than he is."

"Leta! You don't know Charlie. He thinks he's seven foot tall. You can't believe how full of himself he is. You being tall is not going to make him any difference. And he said you *dressed* like a saloon girl, not that you looked like one."

"Aren't those girls pretty?"

She made a face. "Heavens no. If they were the least bit attractive, they'd be married. I feel sorry for them. Don't you think Charlie's cute? He's only nineteen, you know."

"I don't know. I was so mad at him for what he said, I didn't think about how he looked."

"Leta, the thing about Charlie that makes him attractive is his confidence—and he has plenty of that. I need to warn you though—he smokes cigars. That's better than Jock. He chews that nasty tobacco. I make him wash his mouth out before he kisses me."

There was my opening. "How long have you and Jock been married?"

"It will be twenty years in June. Jock is a good man, and I wouldn't trade him, even with his tobacco chewing."

Lunch lasted more than an hour. "I'm sorry but I must get back to work. Thank you for the sandwich and the visit. Please come back again."

"I'm supposed to give you an invitation to a party at the ranch a week from Saturday. You'll have a wonderful time. All Mr. Chisum's parties are fun. It starts at dark but come early."

"Okay, I accept and look forward to it."

She rose to leave. "Now it's my time to get a visit from you. Spend the day with me this Sunday. I'll be lonesome since Jock is leaving tomorrow. If you don't have a way out to the ranch, I can get one of the cowboys to pick you up and take you home."

I picked up the sandwich wrappers and stood. "That sounds good. We actually keep a rig at the stable. I take advantage of my day off and don't get around early. I can be at the ranch by ten if that's okay."

"Perfect," she said. "I look forward to our day together. I can show you around the ranch and still have plenty of time to visit."

Adeline left, forcing me to go back to work. It was usually slow this time of day, which gave me time to restock items. We sell groceries as well as dry goods and keep a surplus in our supply room in the back of the store. Not having to wait on customers gave me time to think. I had paid more attention to the talk about Lincoln, which generally came from the men. I became familiar with words such as Tunstall, McSween, and Dolon. Mr. Chisum's name is mentioned often. I did put together enough to know that the war in Lincoln began when Tunstall was murdered last February, almost a year ago. I kept hearing the name Bonney who, it seems, was an important figure in the war.

I tried not to think of Adeline's infatuation with the little cowboy. Why did I keep thinking of him that way? His name is Charlie Barlowe. But he is a little cowboy. I'm 5'8" and he is at least an inch, maybe two, shorter than me. It was more than clear that both Mr. Chisum and Adeline were determined that I be impressed with him. Granted, there were not that many women available for single men in Roswell. Maybe I thought he was not good enough and it wasn't just that he'd been rude to me. Anyway, I wasn't even convinced that he was interested in me.

I knew that I was attractive by the attention I received from the boys and even the older men. Being tall didn't seem to discourage them. My reddish-brown hair and the high cheekbones with full lips seemed to attract them, also. Maybe it was the dimples when I smiled that gained attention. I did nothing to discourage it, which had gotten me into trouble with the two cowboys. I did not have any serious suitors. Oh, there were young men who had asked me to go with them to dances or picnics, but that didn't amount to much.

Several customers came in at the same time and my personal thoughts ended. I approached one of the ladies and asked if I could help her. "Yes, I need some cloth for a new dress."

I pulled a couple of bolts of cloth from under the counter. While she was examining them, I overheard two men talking. "I don't know what's going to happen up there. They keep killing one another. Wallace hasn't been governor but a couple of months. Maybe he can do something about it," one of the men said.

The other man said, "I don't see him stopping it. There's already been over twenty killed. I think it's going to take the military. Fort Stanton is close, and it looks like to me they might be the solution."

"I'll take five yards of this one."

"Huh," I asked, distracted by the men's exchange.

She frowned and raised her voice, "I said—five yards of this one."

"Oh, sorry." I measured out the five yards, cut, and wrapped it. "The cloth is 22 cents a yard, which makes the total $1.10."

She dug around in her purse and came up with the exact amount. She still looked angry. "You might pay better attention to your customers." She took her package and left.

She was right but didn't have to say it. I guess she was having a bad day and needed to take it out on someone. That was the thing about waiting on the public—you never knew what to expect.

My thoughts returned to the two men I overheard. Over twenty men had been killed. I hadn't been interested until my visit to the Chisum ranch and getting to know some of those affected by the war. No wonder Adeline was worried about her husband. It was clear now why Mr. Chisum didn't want it discussed at the dinner table. Was Charlie Barlowe involved?

TRIP TO TOWN

Charlie

I was low on smokes. That meant a trip to town, didn't it? The truth of the matter was, I had cigars for at least another week. But what if something happened that kept me away for two weeks? "Damn," I muttered. What am I doing lying to myself? I want to see her again. I hadn't even been in the store where she worked. I always got my cigars at the other store. I should spread my business around. Why was I trying to justify something so simple?

There were several of us who had the day off, lounging around the bunkhouse. There was a poker game starting up, which held no interest for me. I washed up the best I could, shaved what few whiskers decorated my face and put on some good smelling stuff that I saved for special occasions. I studied myself in the mirror—satisfied, not overly impressed. I put on my best shirt, some clean jeans, and polished my boots.

"What you gettin' all spiffed up for, Charlie? Goin' somewhere?" asked one of the men at the poker table.

"Yep. Need to see a man about a dog." I needed to get out of here.

Laughter broke out around the table. "Let us know if the man has more than one dog," said another one of the men.

I left, knowing more wisecracks would follow. I selected my best horse and pointed him toward Roswell. It was a short ride, but it gave me time to plan. I would just saunter into the store and look around, hoping she would ask if I needed help.

I would politely ask her how she was doing. One thing would lead to another and before leaving I'd ask her to go with me to the dance next week. What could go wrong?

When I rode up to the store it was obvious that it was busy. Several buggies and three horses were tied to the hitching rail. I found an open spot, tied my horse, and went in. There were at least a dozen shoppers. I scouted out the place and saw her behind the counter weighing something in a sack for a man. I moseyed around, trying to look like I needed help finding something. This went on for at least fifteen minutes and she never looked my way. My plan wasn't working. "Be patient," I said, under my breath. Another fifteen minutes passed and only a few customers remained.

"Can I help you find something?" The man had come up behind me.

"I-I need some cigars."

"You won't find them over here. I hope you're better at finding cattle." He started toward the counter.

I was already frustrated, and his smart remark made me mad. I turned, went outside, and sat down on the steps. I might as well give up. I'd already made a fool out of myself.

"What kind of cigars do you want?"

I turned and there she was, looking down at me. "Well, what kind of cigars do you want? That's what Daddy said you were looking for."

"Cheroots," I mumbled.

"How many?" she asked.

"Twenty, I guess."

"Would you like for me to bring them out here, or are you going to come inside like the rest of our customers?"

I got up, wondering if it wouldn't be best to leave and forget about the whole thing. I decided against that and followed her back inside. She went behind the counter and produced a box of cigars, counting out twenty. She wrapped and tied them in brown paper. "Sixty cents."

I dug around in my pocket and came out with two quarters and a dime. I gave her the money, took my cigars and turned to leave, wanting to run rather than walk.

"Is that all?" she asked.

"Yeah, I guess." I got halfway to the door, stopped, turned around and came back. She was still standing behind the counter. "I came in here to ask you to go with me to the dance next Saturday. It didn't go as planned. I made a fool out of myself."

She smiled. "For the first time, Charlie Barlowe, you said something that impressed me. Are you asking me to go with you to the dance or have you backed out?"

"Will you? Will you go with me?" I asked.

"Yes, I accept your invitation. I understand it starts at dark. Adeline wants me to come early. I'll be ready about an hour before dark. Is that satisfactory?"

"Good. I mean that will be fine."

"I have customers waiting. I'll see you next Saturday."

I left the store, embarrassed and humiliated, but happy.

The next week I finally accepted the fact that my visit to Roswell on Saturday was a complete disaster. She must have gotten a good laugh describing my behavior to her friends. I had to be pretty stupid to go through that humiliation in order to ask her to go to the dance with me. I can never remember being that unsure of myself. She was the prettiest girl I had ever laid my eyes on though. Maybe that made all the humiliation worthwhile.

I spent most of the week repairing corrals that were close to the outbuildings on the ranch. I realized, along with everyone else, that Mr. Chisum kept me close to headquarters. No one said anything to me, but it was too evident for them not to notice. I didn't like the setup and had talked with him about it but always received the same response. "Charlie, I need you close. You are the most loyal and dependable man I have on the ranch." The truth of the matter—he was protecting me. There had been several of the hands killed while confronting rustlers, which continued to be a problem.

We arrived in New Mexico from Texas in '72 and established headquarters at the Bosque Grande, about thirty miles south of Fort Sumner. The problem was the Indians. Mr. Chisum became frustrated with the heavy losses over a period of several years and sold his holdings to a St. Louis beef company in 1875. He then moved his headquarters to South Spring River, a few miles out of Roswell, thinking there would be fewer Indian problems there.

One set of problems was traded for another. Mr. Chisum went in with Alexander McSween to establish a store, which included a bank in Lincoln, a community about seventy miles northwest of Roswell. James Dolon and Lawrence Murphy, up until that time, had the only store and bank in the area and a monopoly. They wouldn't stand for the competition and violence followed. John Tunstall, a wealthy Englishman, joined with Mr. Chisum and McSween. Both McSween and Tunstall, Mr. Chisum's partners, were killed in '78. Somehow, Mr. Chisum had stayed out of the actual fighting. Being seventy miles away probably had a lot to do with that; however, he was a careful man with a lot of experience, which also helped him stay away from the violence.

The conflict or Lincoln County War brought riff-raff from all over the Southwest. That led to rustling, which was a lucrative business, since the Jinglebob ran around 80,000 head of cattle. When we came to New Mexico, Mr. Chisum used the long rail as his brand. This could be changed easily to other brands by rustlers. He created the Jinglebob, which had become famous and was impossible to change. It was a slit on the cow's ear with one part standing upright and two-thirds of it bobbing. I'd heard him say, "Those ears won't jingle, but they sure will bob."

The war was supposed to have ended last summer when McSween was killed. What followed was one revenge killing after another. A guy about my age, who went by several names, the most recent being Billy Bonney, kept the rustling and violence going. He and Mr. Chisum had been on the same side at the beginning but had a falling out over some money that Bonney claimed Mr. Chisum owed him. Long story short—Bonney promised to get the money by rustling Jinglebob cattle.

That wasn't the only problem between them. Mr. Chisum's niece, Sallie Chisum, who was a favorite of his, lived on the ranch. She was a daughter of his brother. No one seemed to know how it came about, but Sallie and Billy Bonney became friends or maybe it was something more serious. Mr. Chisum had made it known that Bonney was not to set foot on the ranch. Everyone knew that he and his bunch were rustling cattle from the Jinglebob. Sallie wasn't that much of a looker and, in my opinion, Bonney just encouraged the relationship to get back at Mr. Chisum. Of course, I didn't know that for sure.

I was twelve when my dad, who worked for Mr. Chisum, died. My mother had died when I was only five. With no one to look after me, Mr. Chisum became sort of a parent, or maybe a guardian is a better term. I lived in the bunkhouse with the other cowboys, and by the time I was fifteen was doing a man's work. When he moved his cattle operation to New Mexico from Texas, of course I came with him. The other cowboys treated me well, probably because Mr. Chisum wouldn't have allowed it any other way.

I did learn that he had another family in East Texas which included two girls. The mother of the girls was a slave who he later freed. They stayed in East Texas in a house provided by him along with other necessities. I was aware that on several occasions he went back to visit them. It didn't seem quite right that he would go off and leave them, but I had no right to question the man who had done so much for me.

I stood in front of the mirror and saw what was lacking—a tie. I had never owned one and none of the other cowboys had one either. There was only one thing to do.

When I knocked, one of the house servants opened the

door. "I need to see Mr. Chisum."

She had not worked at the ranch but for a short time. "Mr. Chisum has guests and is not available."

"Just tell him Charlie needs to talk to him."

"Mr. Chisum has guests and is not to be disturbed." She left before I could object.

If he had guests that meant he was in the den, probably having a drink with some of them before the party.

I was correct, and he saw me before I had a chance to speak. "Charlie, come in and let me introduce you to some friends of mine."

"I need a minute with you, Mr. Chisum."

"Sure." He rose and came over to where I was. "What is it, Charlie?"

"I need to borrow a tie."

A big smile broke out. "Is it the young lady that was so angry with you?"

"Yes."

"Well, Charlie, it looks like I raised you right. You certainly have good taste. Come with me."

We met the house servant in the hall. I smiled at her and tipped my hat.

A half-hour later, I left the house feeling properly dressed with the string tie that Mr. Chisum had selected and helped me tie.

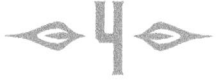

THE PARTY

Leta

My parents had demanded that they meet Charlie. I knew what that meant— questions. I was watching from the door when Charlie drove up. He sat in the buggy for a few minutes until he realized I wasn't coming out. I could tell by the way he looked and the way he carried himself that he had gotten his confidence back. His hat was cocked to one side, and the way he strutted reminded me of a rooster. His pants were tucked into his boots. He even had on a tie.

He stopped before coming up the steps. "You ready to go?"

"My parents want to meet you." Thank goodness he wasn't wearing his gun.

"Is that necessary? You asked me to pick you up an hour early. We might be late."

"We have no choice, Charlie. It is customary for the parents to meet the man before he takes their daughter off to a party."

He strides into the house and follows me to the living room where my parents are waiting. They stand when we enter. "Mom, Dad, this is Charlie Barlowe, the man who rescued me." I turned to Charlie. "Charlie, this is my mom and dad— Mr. and Mrs. Payne."

My dad stepped forward and offered his hand. "Good to meet you, Charlie. Sit a few minutes and visit with my wife and me."

Oh, my. I was afraid of this. I wasn't going to let it last long before insisting that we leave. My dad leaned forward like he was going to pounce. "Tell us about yourself, young man."

Charlie had taken off his hat and his hair looked like it was pasted down with grease or something because it had stayed in place. "There's not much to tell. Both my parents died before I was a teenager. Mr. Chisum kind of took me in, and I've been with him ever since."

My dad cleared his throat like something important was coming. "Have you been married or involved with another woman?"

I glared at my dad, hoping he would look at me.

Charlie looked confused for a second. "Well, no, I reckon not. There're not many women in these parts. The men outnumber them about a hundred to one. I'm only nineteen. Most of my time is spent horseback, miles from women. I saw those men harassing your daughter and knew I had to do something about it. She's about the prettiest girl I've ever seen. She's sassy, too. I like that."

Charlie Barlowe grew several inches with that response.

Dad leaned back and looked somewhat satisfied. "Do you have any bad habits, young man, that Mrs. Payne and I should know about?"

I continued the brutal glare at my dad. He's bound to feel it.

Charlie moved around in his seat like something was sticking him. "I don't know exactly what you mean."

Again, my dad leaned forward, almost coming out of his chair. "Smoking and drinking the devil's brew. That's what I mean."

I noticed Charlie tighten up and take a deep breath before answering. "Sir, you know I smoke Cheroots since that was my reason for being in your store last week. Actually, that's not true. You almost caught me in a lie. I came in hoping to see your daughter. I usually do my business at the other store in town. As far as drinking—the man who raised me, who I have great respect for, told me that he wouldn't trust anyone who didn't have a drink occasionally. So, if you consider smoking and drinking bad habits, you have found me guilty of having bad habits. Mr. Chisum also taught me that the key to living good is moderation in all things."

I had enough and bolted up. "We're going to be late. Let's go, Charlie!"

We were out the door before my dad could fire off another one of his questions. We were in the buggy about to leave when my mom came out the door. "Wait just a minute." She put her hand on the buggy and looked up at Charlie. "Thank you for saving Leta from those terrible men." She moved her attention to me. "I'm sorry, Leta. You know how he is." She stepped back. "Charlie, I know she's in good hands. Y'all have fun."

Thank goodness that was over and even worse than I expected. As we drove off, I noticed Charlie's gun in the bottom of the buggy. I apologized for my parents asking so many questions.

"No problem. They just wanted to know more about me. Your dad didn't get the answers he wanted."

It was still light when we reached the ranch, which was a busy place. Men were putting up lanterns on the porch, which circled the long house divided into two sections with a breezeway in between. Wood was being stacked for a large bonfire, and several men were shoveling dirt and removing large sacks. I pointed to them. "What are they doing, Charlie?"

"A hole was dug two days ago, and a fire was built in it. When there were enough coals, meat was put in sacks. The sacks were placed in the hole and covered up, allowing them to cook. They are removing the sacks. The meat will be tender and delicious."

I told Charlie if he would take me to Adeline's house, I would come to the party with her and meet him there, since we were early. Her house wasn't but a few hundred yards from Mr. Chisum's.

She was sitting on the porch when we arrived and came to meet us. "Leta, you look beautiful. And Charlie—how handsome you are!"

Charlie came around to help me get down. It was the first time we'd been that close. I felt the strength in his arms and gloated a little at this gentlemanly gesture in the presence of Adeline.

"Do you want me to come back for you in an hour?" he asked.

"Don't bother, Charlie. We can walk. It's not that far," Adeline said.

"Did Jock get back?" I asked, after Charlie left.

"Yes, but he had to leave again this morning. He really hated missing the party. They received word that a group out of Lincoln was going to be here within the next few days to rustle more Jinglebob stock. Now to something more important. What do you think about Charlie? Isn't he cute with that string tie and all?"

"So far so good. He was interrogated by my parents to the point I was embarrassed. He did well. I don't understand why he has to have that big old gun all the time. It looks like he could do without it on nights like this."

She shook her head. "Leta, with the current situation we have, it would be taking too big a chance. Violence can break out at any time."

"But I noticed that Mr. Chisum doesn't wear a gun," I said.

"I know. He never has, to my knowledge. I assume he relies on his cowboys. Jock never leaves the house without his gun." She laughed. "I probably wouldn't recognize him without it. About Mr. Chisum—he kinda does things his way. He rides a mule rather than a horse. He doesn't care what people think. He also dresses like all the other cowboys when he's on the ranch. I've seen him dressed to go on a trip and he looks totally different—like you would expect a southern gentleman to look."

"I've never been to a party out here. Tell me what to expect."

"There will be tons of food including all kinds of pies and cakes. Of course, there will be drinks. Liquor for those who want it but tea, coffee, water, and lemonade, for those who want something without alcohol. Oh, yeah, there is always a gigantic bowl of punch. Mostly people just sit around and visit. The breezeway is large enough for a dozen or so couples to dance. It is so seldom that we have an event where people gather just for fun, there will be a large crowd. They will travel as far as fifty or sixty miles to attend. A large part of the crowd will stay the night and into tomorrow. There will be friends that I haven't seen for six months or more. Mr. Chisum usually has two or three parties a year."

We talked until it was almost dark before joining the party. Charlie had been watching for us because he met us before we reached the house. He took my hand, and we went the rest of the way as a couple. The amount of light was amazing with all the lanterns burning. There must have been at least a hundred on the porch and inside the house.

It didn't take long to realize how popular Charlie was with the crowd. We had trouble getting anywhere with people stopping him and wanting to talk. Most would ask him how he was doing. He would respond and then introduce me. When we finally got through the crowd and had a few minutes to ourselves, I said, "These people are so nice. They all know you."

"Most are Jinglebob employees and have seen me grow up. A few are frequent visitors to the ranch." He smiled. "These are my people."

He took my hand. "Let's go get something to eat." There were tables set up at the back of the house loaded with beef, beans, and potatoes in one section with a choice of bread or tortillas. Another table was loaded with desserts. A third table had drinks. After filling our plates, we found seats at one of the tables. The beef was unbelievable, much better than what we'd eaten when I came out for dinner a couple of weeks ago. Charlie went back for seconds, but one plate was enough for me.

As we finished, I heard music coming from the breezeway. "That's a fiddle. Someone is incredibly good."

Charlie took my empty plate. "Let's go take a look. Maybe we can get close enough before it's too crowded."

The area the music was coming from was already packed,

but we managed to squeeze in. I couldn't believe it. Mr. Chisum was the one playing the fiddle. I whispered to Charlie. "I had no idea he could play the fiddle."

"Very few people outside the ones that are here tonight know it either. He's really good and enjoys entertaining."

"Any request?" Mr. Chisum yelled, when he stopped playing. "Arkansas Traveler," someone spoke above the rest.

It was amazing watching him play and the reaction of the crowd. He took requests for the next hour and played popular tunes, such as "Cotton Eyed Joe," "When Johnny Comes Marching Home," "Soldiers Joy," "Dixie," and "The Battle Hymn of the Republic." After each tune ended, the applause was deafening. He ended with "Nearer My God to Thee."

Charlie whispered, "Let's get out of this crowd."

We found a place in the front yard that was not as well-lit and with fewer people. "That was wonderful."

"A lot of people misunderstand Mr. Chisum. He's a kind and caring person. When you are responsible for so many people, it's necessary to make tough decisions. Some of these decisions seem harsh, but I've never known him to cause grief or hurt to anyone intentionally."

We talked about our past and what we would like to do in the future and seemed to be in a world all by ourselves. I noticed the crowd began to thin out and saw it was later than I realized. A man appeared out of nowhere. "Charlie, there could be trouble at the back."

He touched my arm. "Wait here."

No way was I going to wait. I followed him through the house and stopped at the door to the back porch. It was light enough to see Mr. Chisum standing by one of the lanterns. I could easily hear him. "I told you, Billy—you're not to set foot on this place."

I could see the figure at the other end of the porch but not as well. He moved forward and stopped. "I came to see Sallie. You can't stop me and if you try, I will kill you right here in front of all your friends."

"I'm telling you to leave, Billy. You've been rustling cattle from all of us. You're not welcome here."

"I'm not leaving. What are you going to do? You're not even wearing a gun. Go get one."

My breath hung in my throat when Charlie stepped into the light and stood by Mr. Chisum. He spoke so softly I could barely hear him. "You heard Mr. Chisum—you need to leave."

"Who the hell are you to be giving orders, little boy?"

I had to strain to hear what he said. "Just a Jinglebob Cowboy. But I am wearing a gun. Now, get off this ranch."

I held my breath expecting the other man to start shooting. The silence seemed to go on and on . . .

In a voice that could be heard by everyone, the man said, "Your time's coming, Chisum." He took a step closer and pointed at Charlie. "I'll get you, too." He turned and disappeared into the darkness.

My legs were shaking and weak. I had to hang onto the door to keep from falling.

5

TRAGEDY

Charlie

I missed few days seeing Leta during May, June, and July. I would go to her house at the end of most days and spend the evening either sitting on her front porch or taking her for a buggy ride. We would tell one another about our day and sometimes talk of the future. Her dad had not warmed up to me and continued to forbid Leta from seeing me, to which she paid no attention. Before many of those visits, I knew I wanted to marry her. She was something else with those green eyes and dimples when she smiled. She was aggressive and sure of herself as shown by the third time I visited her and was about to leave. I had turned and was walking away when she said, "Wait! When are you going to kiss me, Charlie Barlowe. I'm tired of waiting."

My world changed on Friday, the first of August. I was working with some colts when I saw several of our cowboys riding to the house, leading a horse with someone tied over the saddle. I knew what that meant and went on to the house. Mr. Chisum came out, and one of the cowboys was telling him what happened.

"We were about twenty miles up the Pecos late yesterday afternoon when we came upon rustlers. I recognized some of them. It was the Seven River Warriors. They ran, and we followed them for several miles. They set up an ambush, and we rode right into it. Jock was in the lead and was shot and killed. We were stupid for being led into a trap. Who's going to tell his missus?"

Suddenly, I was sick and felt like throwing up. Jock was a good foreman and a friend.

Mr. Chisum saw me standing off to one side. "Charlie. You need to go fetch Leta. Adeline is going to need her."

I hitched up the buggy and was at the store within a short time. Leta was behind the counter waiting on a customer. She saw me come in and smiled. I walked to the counter and interrupted. "Leta, you need to come with me."

At first, she looked confused and then realized something was wrong. "Excuse me, I have to leave. My dad will wait on you."

I didn't explain until we were in the buggy on the way out of town. "It's terrible news. Jock was killed last night. Mr. Chisum sent me to get you. He said Adeline would need you."

"Oh, no," she cried, grabbing my arm. "How? Why?"

"Seven Rivers bunch. Caught them rustling. A gun battle. I'm sorry, Leta."

She didn't speak the rest of the way. When I stopped in front of her house, Adeline ran out into Leta's arms. I knew there was nothing I could do except get in the way. All I could think of was Jock lying over his horse—dead. I went back to the colts' pen and tried to get my mind off how fragile life was on the Jinglebob.

I spent the rest of the morning trying to stay busy with the colts I was riding. At noon I checked on Leta. She came out of the house, giving us some privacy. "Charlie, she's suffering. It was so sudden but not something she hadn't thought about. She had mentioned to me several times how much she worried when Jock was gone. Why is there so much violence and men being killed?"

"It's not easy to explain, Leta. This Seven Rivers group started out as a bunch of small ranchers who were mad at Mr. Chisum because their cattle got mixed up with his. They felt justified in stealing Jinglebob cattle. This attracted rustlers who joined the group as a way to make easy money. Probably at least half of the Seven River Warriors had no cattle to begin with. Rustling is serious business—a hanging offense. Killing is bound to follow when men are stealing your property."

"I still don't understand. I need to get inside with Adeline." She started back inside but stopped and turned. "Oh, I nearly forgot. Would you go into town and tell my parents where I am and not to expect me back tonight?"

That evening, after supper, I fixed two plates and took them to Leta. She came out on the porch again. "She still doesn't want to see anyone. Several people have come by, and I feel bad not asking them in."

"People grieve differently. Some want a crowd to be there with them—others want to be alone or have a friend with them. That is what Adeline is asking and should be respected. It doesn't matter what anyone thinks during a time like this. The only one who matters is the person who is suffering. Try to get her to eat something if she can."

The bunkhouse was quiet with no joking, laughing, or card games. Several of the men who had brought Jock in were talking quietly. I didn't join them, only sat and listened.

"It's not worth it. Trying to stop men from stealing a few scraggly old cows. It's not worth it," one man repeated. "Giv'em the damn old cows. A good man died for nothing." The man talking, took a long drink from a bottle and passed it around.

Another man said, "I keep asking myself—why in hell did we follow them and ride into an ambush? We should have been smarter than that. We stopped them from taking any cattle. Why weren't we satisfied?"

I stayed quiet as long as I could. "Let me answer your questions. You ride for the Jinglebob brand. These men were stealing our property. If you hadn't gone after them, they would have come back. They may anyway but not with as much confidence. You not only did the right thing—it was the only thing to do. If Jock was sitting here with us, he would tell you the same thing. Now, I'm not as old as you, but I've been here longer than most. The Jinglebob means something more than just a name. It's our home and way of life. When threatened we must defend it. You're feeling guilty and angry, but you did nothing wrong. Now, pass that bottle over here and get some cups. We're going to drink to a good man who died doing his job and who we will miss."

I went to bed but couldn't sleep. Finally, after laying in my bunk for hours, I got up and went to see about Leta and Adeline. The house was dark, so I sat down on the porch and leaned back. Maybe they were sleeping. I sure didn't want to disturb them. The night was clear with a full moon—a Comanche moon Mr. Chisum called it. He explained that settlers on the plains had been terrified when there was a full moon since that is when the Comanches liked to raid. We had Indian problems at the Bosque Grande before we moved here. Mr. Chisum never let me go with the cowboys that pursued the Indians. He had protected me then just as he does now. But Billy Bonney was coming after both of us. I wasn't afraid of meeting him. We could have it settled once and for all. I wasn't going to let him get to Mr. Chisum.

Sometime during the night, I went to sleep, leaned against the house. Something pressing against my lips woke me. I looked into those green eyes and thought, *maybe I'm dreaming.*

"Wake up, Charlie, I'm hungry. What are you doing out here anyway?"

I wasn't dreaming. "I couldn't sleep. I came over here and since the house was dark, I thought you might be asleep. How's Adeline?"

"She passed out about an hour ago. She's accepted the fact that Jock's gone. We talked about her future. They had no children even though not by choice. She has family in Kansas, including a sister and brother. She will probably move there and try to start a new life. Oh, Charlie, it is so sad. Why do things like this have to happen?"

"I don't know, Leta. I do know she's fortunate to have you."

"What will happen now? Will Mr. Chisum want revenge against this group that killed Jock?"

"No, I have never heard him mention revenge. Life on the Jinglebob will just go on as normal. Of course, a new foreman will be selected."

She kissed me again. "Thank you, Charlie, for sleeping on the porch to be near me."

The funeral for Jock was held on Sunday, the third of August, at ten in the morning on the ranch. It was a graveside service with the only preacher in town conducting it. Mr. Chisum said a few words after the service and then played "Nearer My God to Thee" on his fiddle which brought out the handkerchiefs from many of the cowboys, including myself.

At the conclusion of the service, he invited everyone to the house for lunch. It seemed that the answer to sadness was a meal together. Adeline didn't want to take part, so she and Leta went back to her house.

After I had eaten, I took plates to them. This time Leta asked me to come in. Adeline sat at the kitchen table with a cup of coffee. "It was a nice service, wasn't it, Charlie?"

"It certainly was. Mr. Chisum said some wonderful things about Jock—all which were true. We will all miss him, and I am so sorry."

"I always worried but still didn't expect it to happen. That doesn't make sense, does it? Nothing seems to make sense anymore. Three days ago, when I told him bye if I had only known . . ." Adeline broke down.

When I started to leave, she stopped me. "Wait, Charlie. I'm sorry. I wanted to ask you something. What are your plans for the future?"

"Jinglebob is my home, Adeline. I don't plan on leaving here. Mr. Chisum has been good to me."

"What about the threat from this Billy Bonney? Aren't you afraid?"

"No, not a bit. I won't let him get close to Mr. Chisum, either."

She looked away as if talking to herself. "I wish Jock and I had left and gone somewhere there was no killing."

I knew it was time for me to leave. Leta followed me outside. "Charlie, I don't know how she's going to do it. To recover will take a long time. Can you take me home? I need to change clothes, then I'm coming back. She doesn't need to be left alone."

"Sure. I'll get the buggy and be back in a few minutes. Something else, Leta. Mr. Chisum wants to talk with me in the morning. He told me to bring you, also. It's strange. I don't have any idea what he wants."

6

A CHANGE OF PLANS

Leta

"You don't have any idea what he wants?" I asked. We were walking from Adeline's house on the way to see Mr. Chisum.

"No, what's strange is that he asked me to bring you. How is Adeline this morning?"

"She slept more last night. I'm going to need to get back to work. I hoped Mr. Chisum might have one of the girls who work in the house stay with her today."

When we arrived, I was surprised that Mr. Chisum opened the door. "Good morning, Charlie, Leta. Come in and join me for coffee."

We followed him into the den where he motioned for us to sit down. Immediately, a girl appeared with two cups of coffee. "I know you must wonder about the reason for my request to speak with you. I put it off as long as I can. I'll get right to the point." He spoke directly to Charlie. "Three months ago, Billy Bonney showed up at the party and confronted me. You intervened and possibly saved my life. Bonney left but threatened both of us . . ."

Charlie interrupted. "I'm not afraid of Bonney."

Mr. Chisum raised his hand. "Let me finish, Charlie. I know you're not afraid of him. That's not the point I'm going to make. In a fair fight, I would put my money on you. But, let me tell you a little about Bonney. He changed after Tunstall was killed. Maybe it just brought out the worst of him. He swore vengeance on the men who killed Tunstall. To a large extent he was successful. His group executed several of the men they caught who were involved. Billy and his Regulators, as they called themselves, ambushed Sheriff Brady and four of his deputies as they walked down main street in Lincoln. Brady and one of his deputies were killed. Brady had nine bullets in him. Billy and thirteen Regulators penned Buckshot Roberts down and killed him at Blazer's Mill. Roberts was with the group that killed Tunstall. Do you see what I'm trying to tell you Charlie? Billy Bonney does not give his enemies a chance. You are one of his enemies as I am."

"I won't let him get close to you," Charlie said.

Mr. Chisum frowned and shook his head. "You just don't get it, Charlie. Billy kills me, he won't cheat me out of many years—maybe four or five—ten at the most. You have your whole life ahead of you."

Charlie jumped up. "I'm not running from Billy Bonney or anyone!"

"Sit down, Charlie, and listen to me. I have two grown daughters back in Texas. You are the closest thing to a son I will ever have. I buried a foreman yesterday. I don't want to bury you. I have a plan, and it's a good one. Just listen until I finish, then you can have your say."

Charlie sat back down. "Okay, but I won't run!"

"Seven years ago, we left Texas. I have regretted that move many times. I wanted access to more land that would allow me to own more cattle. I have that now, except the land is not mine. It's open range and people are moving in. The men that killed Jock are part of that movement. The time of John Chisum and open range is coming to an end. I currently own forty acres and run thousands of cattle on land that belongs to anyone who comes in and settles on it. Oh, I may hold on another five years or maybe longer. But there is no future for my kind.

"The country we left, Charlie, is better than this country. The water is better—the grass is better. I want you to go back to

Texas and grow with that country. The railroad will be selling land soon. You can buy it cheap. Put a fence around it, and it will be yours and later your children's and then their children's. Build something that will last."

Charlie had calmed down but hadn't finished his argument. "I don't want to leave here. When is all this going to take place?"

"As soon as possible. Within days," Mr. Chisum said.

"Everything I care about is here." He looked at me.

Again, shaking his head. "Mercy, Charlie. Surely, you're not that dense. You have been spending more time with Leta than the ranch."

Mr. Chisum looked at me. "Tell him, Leta."

"He means for me to go with you, Charlie."

Charlie squirmed around in his chair. "But-but . . ."

Mr. Chisum nodded at me. "Go ahead, Leta. Spell it out to him. He's not as smart as I thought. All he knows is cattle and horses."

"He means for us to get married, Charlie. Well, are you going to ask me or go by yourself to Texas?"

"Sure, I want to marry you. It's just so sudden. Will you marry me, Leta?"

"Yes, I will marry you, Charlie Barlowe."

Mr. Chisum stood. "That's enough to put on you for now. Talk about what I've told you and come back for supper tonight. I have more plans for you."

"Could you have someone stay with Adeline, today?" I asked.

"Yes, of course," he said, as he left the room.

"You have not known this boy but a little over three months, Leta. How can you even think about marrying him?"

Charlie had taken me home, giving me a chance to break the news to my mother without my dad's presence since he was at work. I thought it might be better this way. "Mother, I love him. I won't love him any more or any less if I know him for three more years." I hadn't even mentioned Texas yet.

"What will your daddy think?"

"I know what Daddy will do. He will forbid me from marrying Charlie just like he forbids me from seeing him. That didn't stop me, did it? I would like your approval, though. I will never have his and have accepted that."

Tears rolled down her face. "You always had a mind of your own, Leta. There is no use trying to stop or even postpone your plans." She got up and hugged me. "I will accept your plans and pray that you are making the right decision."

Should I tell her about going to Texas? No, that could wait until later. "Please tell Daddy. There is no use me trying to reason with him. You have more influence on him than anyone. Charlie is going to pick me up, and we are going back to the ranch."

My mom left the room. I imagine she didn't want me to see her cry. Charlie should be back by now. I told him not to be gone for long. I was a coward for not wanting my dad present when I told her. I didn't want to see his anger and feel his wrath. The sound of the buggy interrupted my thoughts.

"How'd it go?" he asked, as I climbed in.

"Better than I expected. Of course, my dad wasn't home. You changed your mind about marrying me yet?"

He reached over and pulled me to him. "Not a chance. Mr. Chisum just moved things up a bit. I was going to ask you, anyway. It's going to Texas that troubles me. People will think I'm running away."

"Does it matter to you what people think, Charlie? I thought you were bigger than that."

He didn't respond for several minutes. "I don't know. I'm confused. I feel like I'm running from Bonney. I've never run from anything."

I was getting tired of this male thing. "Mr. Chisum tried to explain it to you. I'm not going to argue. You do what you think is best for you—no one else really matters anyway. You need to know this, though: I trust Mr. Chisum. I am not marrying you unless we leave New Mexico and go to Texas."

He stopped the buggy. "Just how are we going to make a living in Texas? The area he is describing has no town. There is a little store and that's all. I might get some work with the area ranchers, but it will not be enough to support us."

"I don't know, Charlie. Maybe we will find out tonight when we see him again. I know that he cares deeply for you and has thought of everything. Of all people, you should trust him." We were already acting like we were married—arguing about everything.

Nothing was said on the rest of our trip to the ranch. Charlie let me off at Adeline's and left, going who knows where. I sent the young girl who was staying with Adeline back to the ranch house, saying I would stay with her.

I told Adeline about Mr. Chisum's offer and Charlie's response. It was good for both of us. Adeline could think of something besides the death of her husband, and I could relieve some of my frustration.

"He's just a man, Leta. To them it's just fight or flight and nothing in between. After he thinks about it awhile, he will accept Mr. Chisum's plan."

"What if he doesn't?"

"I hope you meant what you said when you told him the marriage would not happen if he stayed here rather than going to Texas. I am a widow because of the situation that exists here. Just killing and more killing—no end in sight."

I didn't know if I could do it or not. Maybe I was bluffing when I gave him no choice as to where we would live. I changed the subject. "Have you thought about when you might leave for Kansas?"

"Yes. I have been trying to write a letter to my sister but haven't gotten but a few lines. Could you help me? When I start to describe what has happened, I break down. I am going to leave as soon as possible. I want the letter to get there before I do. Mr. Chisum came to see me while you were gone today. He said when I left, he was going to give me six months of Jock's wages to help me get started in Kansas. It was a relief to know I wouldn't have to depend on anyone until I could find a job."

"Mr. Chisum did the right thing, but many would not have. It shows what we already know about him—he is a kind and considerate man," I said.

We spent the next several hours writing a letter to her sister. She would tell me what to say, and I would write it down. After finishing the letter, I copied it again to improve my writing and eliminate the mark-throughs. Adeline had a tough time telling about Jock's death. We finished the letter, both being satisfied, and prepared it for mailing.

"Do you feel any better about leaving New Mexico?" We were on the way to eat supper with Mr. Chisum. I was hoping that given some time to think about it, Charlie would come to terms with leaving and not consider it running away.

"I guess it depends on what else Mr. Chisum has to tell us. I can't see leaving a job with security and traveling hundreds of miles to a place where all we face is uncertainty."

It disappointed me that Charlie did not have greater trust in the man who had done so much for him. I would learn that this was a trait that would create conflict between us in the years to come.

MORE PLANS

Charlie

I wasn't interested in my food, wanting to finish and hear the other plans Mr. Chisum had for me and Leta. He and his two brothers were the only others at the table besides Leta and me. We were having Mexican food. Any other time I would have enjoyed the delicious offering. I had been in a foul mood all day. This was my home and had been for seven years. It was like Mr. Chisum wanted to get rid of me. I thought we would always be together. Deep down I knew the reason but didn't want to accept it—he was afraid if I stayed Bonney would kill me. I wasn't afraid of Bonney and wished he would come after me. I had never backed down from any man.

I paid little attention to the talk between Mr. Chisum and his brothers. I glanced at Leta who was sitting across from me. She was the prettiest girl I had ever laid eyes on. I had said that before and stood by it. She was almost skinny but not quite. I smiled and she caught me looking at her. Thank goodness she couldn't read my thoughts.

"Let's move out onto the porch. It's a nice evening. It's probably just my imagination, but I thought there was just a touch of fall in the air this morning." We followed Mr. Chisum outside and found three chairs waiting for us, which was not a coincidence. It was so calm we could hear laughter coming from the bunkhouse, which was several hundred yards from us.

"Have you discussed the plans I gave you this morning?" Mr. Chisum asked.

Leta looked at me to answer. "It disturbs me that I will have no way to provide for us. All we are going to face is uncertainty. I'm not as excited about that country as you are. Of course, I was only twelve when we left Texas."

He smiled. "Charlie, what an adventure it will be. You and your beautiful bride starting out fresh in a growing area. You would be part of building something in Texas. You would be getting away from this mess in New Mexico, which is not even a state and probably won't be for years.

"I have more information for you that should help relieve some of your fears. I have been accumulating some quality heifers to use for breeding stock. I am going to send fifty of them with you as a wedding present. My ranch in the southeastern part of the county is still open range. A friend of mine runs a few hundred cows there. I'll send a letter with you to give him, explaining everything. There is also a small house on the ranch. It's not much but will do as a place to start. I had a store there but sold it before coming to New Mexico. It did good business and is still open. I will send a letter with Leta to give to the owner. I am sure she will be able to work there for some extra income." He looked at me, waiting for a response.

"I appreciate your offer, but the Jinglebob can't spare the men to drive the heifers to Texas."

"I agree, Charlie. We never have enough cowboys. That's not going to be a problem since you and your new bride are going to trail the cattle to Texas. I have one hand who can help you. He is an older cowboy that wants to go back to Texas, where he has family. He has already given me notice that he's leaving. Pete is a good, dependable hand. The three of you should be able to make the drive. I can give you a chuck wagon and supplies for the trip. I figure that you can do at least eight miles a day. I would bet that you could be in Coleman County between forty and forty-five days from the time you leave— maybe even sooner. Most of the heifers should be bred and calve in early spring." He looked at me again.

This time I stared at Leta. "Sounds good to me," she said.

"When do we leave?" I asked.

Mr. Chisum broke into a smile. "Today is the fifth of August. Ten weeks from now would get you to Texas and settled in before winter. Let's have the wedding a week from today. Will that be okay?" This time he looked at Leta.

"Yes. That will be fine, Mr. Chisum, and thank you." She glared at me, with a warning.

"That will be good. Thank you. Will you come to see us?"

"Of course, Charlie. The first time I come to Texas, I will make a point to put you on my route. I hope you will become as excited about this adventure as I am. I will also write and let you know what is going on here."

He turned to Leta. "We will have the wedding here at the ranch, if that is satisfactory with you?"

"Yes, of course," she said.

He stood. "I know this is a lot to digest. I will leave you alone to discuss it. Please forgive me for being so authoritarian. I didn't know of any way to go about it."

"He left us out of the plans. He told us what to do without having any say in the future," she said, after Mr. Chisum had left. "Has Mr. Chisum always been that way?"

"No, of course not. He's never tried to control my life. I've lived in the bunkhouse with the cowboys since I was this high." I held my hand about four feet off the floor.

"Why do you think he's doing it now, Charlie?"

I looked off in another direction, thinking.

"Look at me, Charlie. Tell me the truth as to why Mr. Chisum is acting this way."

I looked at the floor and muttered, "He's afraid Bonney will kill me. He's protecting me." Our gaze met, and this time I spoke up. "I don't want anyone's protection. I can take care of myself."

"I bet Sheriff Brady was thinking the same thing as he lay dying in the street with nine bullets in him. What would you say he was thinking, Charlie? Did you catch the part where Mr. Chisum said at the time he was killed there were four deputies with him? You're talking like a child! If you don't start making sense, you can stay here by yourself and be part of the bloodshed. But it will be without me by your side." She got up and left, heading back toward Adeline's.

Now, I had really messed up. I was only expressing my feelings. It looks like a guy could do that without getting chewed out.

I knew the man that Mr. Chisum was sending with us. I wondered if he even knew about it. His work was close enough that he came in every night.

"Pete, I understand you are leaving the Jinglebob and going back to Texas." I caught Pete as he was putting his horse up and feeding him.

"Yep. You should know since I'm going to be traveling with you. Mr. Chisum's paying me a month's wages to help you get your heifers to Texas. It sure helps me out. I believe he said we would be leaving on the fifteenth, which is only ten days."

I was surprised but shouldn't have been. Mr. Chisum was so sure of himself that he had already told Pete. "Pete, why do you want to go back to Texas? Don't you like working here?"

"Sure. It's a good place, and Mr. Chisum is a fair man. I have family in Texas and, right now, this is a dangerous place. I was with Jock when he was killed. I made up my mind to leave then. I don't see an end to this stupid killing."

I needed assurance of something else. "Do you think we can trail the heifers three hundred miles?"

He laughed. "You having doubts about the cattle or getting married? We can get the heifers to Texas. Your missus can drive the wagon, and we can handle fifty head without any problem. Mr. Chisum is going to lend us a lead steer, which will help."

Everything was wrapped up and tied in a neat little package. What made me mad was, I'd had nothing to do with it. It was presented to me to take without question. I left Pete to his feeding and went for a walk to do some thinking. *Did I really want to marry Leta? Yeah, no doubts there. Did I want to leave Jinglebob—maybe- maybe not? Could I marry Leta and stay at Jinglebob? Absolutely not. She had made that as plain as the nose on my face.*

I had made my decision. I was going to marry Leta and drive fifty of my heifers, which would calve in the spring, to Texas and begin a new life—but I still had doubts.

8

THE WEDDING

Leta

It was the twelfth of August and my wedding day. I was getting dressed at Adeline's and becoming more nervous by the minute. It had been a busy week with one stressful event after another. Charlie didn't hold out long. After I gave him my speech and left him on the porch, Adeline took me home. He woke everyone up in the middle of the night banging on the door. I thought sure my dad was going to shoot him. He promised not to say anything else about staying in New Mexico and facing the danger. I finally convinced my dad to put up his gun and go back to bed. Charlie and I sat outside and talked until dawn.

Of course, when I told my parents they threw a conniption fit, threatening me with everything from taking me out of the country to having Charlie arrested. My dad screamed, hollered, and stomped around telling me what a terrible daughter I was and how I would be sorry for disrespecting my parents—even quoting the Bible. My mother cried and cried until she was exhausted. I held my resolve and won. I was able to withstand the onslaught longer than they could dish it out. I didn't know whether they would show up for the wedding or not. I hid out at Adeline's for the past week to avoid my parents. If my dad didn't show up, Mr. Chisum graciously said he would give me away.

One good thing about the wedding was it had given Adeline something else to think about.

Three days after the wedding we planned to leave for Texas. Several days during the week, Charlie gave me lessons on how to drive a wagon pulled by mules. Since I had been driving a buggy for years, I learned quickly. I had limited experience riding a horse though and spent one entire afternoon with Charlie, giving me some much-needed instruction. The next day my sore rear made me wonder how the cowboys stayed in the saddle for hours at a time.

I looked at the clock and then in the mirror. I was ready. The wedding was at six and it was only four. I asked Adeline what we were going to do for the next two hours. "Just sit down and relax. I'll get us something to drink." She came back a few minutes later with two long-stemmed glasses and a bottle. "Jock and I were saving this wine for a special occasion. This is the only special event I will ever have on this ranch. A half glass of wine will relax you."

She handed me a glass and poured the wine. "I've never drank alcohol before. You think it's all right?"

She waved a hand. "Of course. It's only a small amount. You need something to relax you."

I took a sip, and it was actually good. "I'm nervous about the honeymoon, too. We have a room in the only hotel in Roswell for tonight. We have to finish getting ready for our trip, so one night is all we have time for."

She smiled. "Leta, you will honeymoon all the way to Texas and then for the rest of your lives. Honeymoons take care of themselves when two people love one another."

I took another drink of wine. "At least thirty days without taking a bath. I can't imagine that." I noticed half of the wine was gone. Such an unwelcome thought, but I smiled anyway.

"Oh, I bet y'all find a stream to bath in—probably several between here and Texas. I think it is so exciting! It will be an adventure that you will remember for the rest of your life."

A few minutes later, I finished my wine and felt much better. I wasn't nearly as nervous. I looked at the clock and it was still only five.

"Would you like a little more wine?" Adeline asked.

"Maybe just a little." She poured more into my glass. I sipped the wine as we talked, conversation became easier and easier. I was no longer worried about anything. I was sure that I could handle everything, including my wedding and honeymoon. I noticed that it was 5:25 and time to go. I stood and had to grab the arm of the chair to keep from falling. I straightened up and stood still for a few seconds.

"Are you all right?" Adeline asked.

"Jush a little zizzy. I mushita sit too wong."

"We better go. The fresh air will do you good. I shouldn't have given you that second glass of wine."

I still felt great but was not steady as we made our way to the big house for the wedding. Adeline had to hold onto me to keep me moving in a straight line. The first people we saw when we reached the house were my parents. I didn't expect them to come.

"Leta, let's not stop and talk to your parents. We'll just go by, pretending we don't see them."

I agreed and stared straight ahead. It didn't work.

"Leta, wait a minute. Aren't you going to talk to us?" My dad asked.

Adeline still had hold of my arm. "We're sorry, Mr. Payne, but we're late. Please excuse us." We kept walking.

My dad stepped in front of us. "What's going on, Leta? We came to your wedding, against my wishes. You are refusing to talk to us."

"Shorry, Dad. We're swate."

He stepped closer. "Leta, you been drinking!" He turned to my mother. "Look at your daughter—she's drunk. I told you this whole thing was a mistake. Now, maybe someone will listen to me."

Mother just stood there, looking confused.

Adeline realized it was hopeless to try and explain to my dad. "Mrs. Payne, I gave Leta some wine. She wasn't used to liquor. It was my fault. I should have known better. Please don't blame her. I am so sorry."

I wasn't worried about my parents. I wasn't worried about anything. "It's no shuse, Adelsim." I started forward without Adeline's support and stumbled, almost falling. "Opps, got to be scarful." Adeline took my arm and guided me inside the house.

"It's still twenty minutes until the wedding, Leta. Let's wait in this vacant room. I'm going to get you some coffee. Wait here."

After she left, I sat down in a soft chair. Suddenly, I was sleepy. The next thing I know, Adeline is shaking me. "Wake up, Leta! This is no time to sleep. Here, drink this coffee."

I took the cup, which wasn't hot, and drank it. Adeline got me up and told me to walk around the room. I was steadier after the coffee and made several rounds without help. The door opened and someone said, "It's time."

We went out into a hallway and my dad was standing there. "Your mother demanded I go through with this. Can you stand up by yourself?"

I straightened up to my full height. "Yes. I fhink show." I made it to the preacher, holding on to my dad's arm. The ceremony was short and even though I weaved a little, I made it.

The honeymoon was a difficult matter. I had to have Charlie stop twice and let me throw up on the way to the hotel. I kept apologizing, and he kept laughing. At the hotel, I continued to be deathly sick. I would never touch liquor again. I kept apologizing, and he stopped laughing. I finally collapsed across the bed and didn't wake up until the next morning. Charlie was gone! Our marriage ended before it ever began because of the liquor. I began to cry—softly at first and then bawling like a baby.

The door opened and Charlie came in. "What in the world is the matter?"

It took me a few seconds to tell him. "I thought you left me."

He handed me the cup of coffee. "It took me some time to

find a cup of hot coffee. I finally found it in a saloon. You better be careful—it may have some whiskey in it."

I sipped the coffee. "I am so sorry. I made a fool out of myself. How can you ever forgive me?"

"I can think of several ways." That mischievous grin appeared that I would come to know so well.

"Hold it tight against your shoulder. It has a little kick."

Charlie was giving me a shooting lesson. Mr. Chisum had presented me with my own rifle—a Winchester 73 as a wedding present. Charlie already had one, but Mr. Chisum said we needed all the firepower we could get. I was lying on my stomach with the gun resting on a rock. When I squeezed the trigger, the sound was deafening, leaving a ringing in my ears. The kick as Charlie called it wasn't that bad. The bucket I aimed at stood proudly, like it had won the shootout.

"You shot too high. That's a common mistake which probably accounts for three-fourths of the missed shots. Take a finer bead on the gun site and try again."

I took careful aim and squeezed the trigger—nothing. "What's wrong?"

"I'm glad that bucket wasn't an Indian. You have to work the lever to put another shell in the barrel."

I took aim again, this time with a shell in the barrel, and squeezed the trigger. The blast seemed to shake the earth. I heard the clang as the bucket jumped about three feet. I looked up at Charlie who was smiling. "That's more like it. Now, all you need is practice."

We were leaving early tomorrow. We had spent the last two nights in the covered wagon that was going to be our home for the next thirty to forty days. I smiled thinking, *that wagon was plenty sturdy.*

We had carefully packed our supplies in the wagon to allow room for our bed. I was worried about my cooking skills. I had done little of the cooking at home. The open fire was going to present a challenge, even for an experienced cook. I was hoping that Charlie had done some campfire cooking.

Tomorrow was August 15, 1879. We were starting to Texas and a new life.

9

MOVING CATTLE

Charlie

The east was red with the promise of another day. "Move 'em out!" I yelled. We were pointed toward the rising sun, with Pete on one side and me on the other. Leta was driving the wagon from behind. Moses, the steer that Mr. Chisum had loaned us, was leading us toward Texas. How appropriate that we were being led to the promised land by Moses. Mr. Chisum had told me to follow his earlier trails, which meant turning back south and following the Pecos River to Horsehead Crossing. From there we would turn east toward Fort Concho. That seventy miles would be the toughest part of the trip due to lack of water until we reached the Concho.

I looked over at Leta in her hat, long-sleeved man's shirt, and pants. It wasn't going to be easy keeping my attention on the cattle. She had gone from being pretty to the cutest thing I'd ever seen. She refused to wear a bonnet, instead choosing one of my old hats.

The wagon had enough supplies to get us to Texas, including plenty of Arbuckle coffee, or axle grease as the cowboys called it. Staples also included dried meat which consisted mostly of smoked beef jerky. It could also be used to make stew. Some hardtack was included as a last resort. It was dense unleavened bread which would last forever but was hard as a rock and had to be soaked in coffee or water to eat. Of course, beans and potatoes were included. The dried beans would last, but the potatoes had to be eaten within a short time. Mr. Chisum's cook also included a sourdough starter. A large slab of salt pork was included as well as canned peaches and tomatoes. The supplies packed tight against the wagon sides enabled Leta and me to have a place to sleep.

I was fortunate to have Pete, one of the best cowboys on Jinglebob. I would guess he was in his mid-thirties. Tall and thin, he was a good shot with either pistol or rifle. I didn't expect trouble since most of the Indians were on a reservation, but there were always a few that would leave the reservation and present a danger. Mr. Chisum insisted that 200 rounds of ammunition for each of us be included in our supplies.

The first part of our trip was about 150 miles along the Pecos River. We would keep the herd at least a half mile from the river until it was necessary to water them. It was the middle of August which meant we could expect hot weather.

We made such good time the first day, we didn't even stop for dinner. We grabbed a slab of jerky and kept moving. When we stopped at dusk, I figured we had traveled at least twelve miles. Then we turned the cattle and drove them to the Pecos to drink. We were fortunate enough to find a few cottonwood trees to make our first camp.

"I'll water the mules, Leta, if you'll start a fire and put the coffee on." I took the harnesses off the mules and let them water. It took me some time to hobble them and get back to camp. The fire was going, but there was no sign of the coffee pot.

I approached Leta, but she only stared into the fire. "I have no idea how to make coffee."

"No worries. We'll grind enough beans for tonight and tomorrow. I'll show you—it's not hard." By the time Pete got there the coffee was boiling.

"What's for supper?" Pete asked. "I'm starved."

"What about fried potatoes and fried salt pork?" I asked.

"Sounds good to me," Pete said.

Making coffee was not the only thing Leta couldn't do. I

showed her how to peel the potatoes, how much lard to use, and how hot the grease needed to be. "Pete and I need to check on the cattle. Can you handle the rest? After the potatoes are done, cut off a couple of slabs of salt pork and fry them."

She nodded and eased the potatoes into the grease.

The cattle grazed close to the river and were calm. "Pete, I'll take the first watch until midnight. They're quiet now, but I don't trust them."

When we returned to camp, Leta was frying the salt pork. The potatoes were set off to one side on a bench—or were those potatoes? It was a gob of something black. I noticed Pete looking at them, too.

We drank our coffee until she removed the salt port from the skillet. She took two plates and filled them with the black stuff and salt pork. Both of us thanked her when she presented them to us. A closer look revealed the black gob as potatoes. The salt pork looked good, so I decided to start with it. The first bite I tried not to gag but had to spit it out. "Did you wash the salt pork?"

"No, I just cooked it. Is something wrong?"

"It's got to be washed. It's cured in salt—a lot of salt. You can't eat it until the salt is washed off."

"I didn't know." She left, going off into the dark.

I followed, and found her crying softly. "I'm sorry. I can't do anything. And I'm filthy from eating dust all day. You should have married someone who could cook." She continued to cry.

"Aw, you can learn to cook. I'll help you. We've got plenty of water. Can you swim?"

She stopped crying but still sniffled. "Sure."

"How about going for it." I pointed toward the river. "You mean.."

"Yep. That's what I mean."

She giggled. "What if somebody sees us?"

"Who? I have first watch tonight. Pete is probably already asleep. Besides, it's dark."

She plopped down and started pulling off her boots. "You're bad, Charlie Barlowe."

I forgot all about supper.

When I got up the next morning, Leta and Pete were sitting by the fire drinking coffee. Pete nodded at Leta. "She had the coffee made when I came in from my watch. It's good coffee, too."

It was still an hour before daylight. I helped Leta with breakfast, which consisted of fried potatoes, eggs, and several thick slices of bread browned in the skillet. The ranch cook had included a half dozen loaves of bread that would stay good for a week. After that, it would be biscuits from the sourdough batch.

We had two barrels of water tied to the wagon but took advantage of the river to wash our dishes. We had our little herd moving before the sun was up good.

The next several days went so smoothly I was beginning to worry. Moses was doing his job, and the heifers had behaved themselves better than I expected, plodding along like experienced cattle. Pete and I still took turns at night on watch. One day he would take the early watch and the next day the late watch. I felt bad about having a nice bed in the wagon while he slept on the ground.

Leta was making a hand. She learned quickly, and within a few days was cooking the meals. Since she did most of the cooking, we washed the dishes. It was good traveling along the river. I couldn't imagine what it would have been like to take a straight line to our destination, trying to find water along the way. I kept dreading the time when we would have to turn back east and leave the river.

On Sunday, August 22, we had been on the trail six days and by my calculations had gone about sixty miles. I know it was not the norm, but a day of rest would be good for everyone, including the cattle. We camped last night in a grassy area with a good pool of water in the river. I discovered that Pete was religious and prayed before each of our meals. Resting on Sunday would appeal to him. I had put some fishing line in with our supplies, hoping to find the time and the spot to add to our menu.

While the heifers grazed contentedly and Pete read his Bible, I decided this was the time and place. With Leta, I picked out a good spot, baited my hook with a huge grasshopper and tossed my line out about fifteen feet. "We may have fried catfish for supper."

Leta sat down beside me. "I've never fished before. I haven't ever eaten catfish. Why do they call them that?"

"Because they have whiskers like a cat." This was my chance to impress her. I couldn't believe she'd never fished.

"How long do we have to wait before you catch one?"

"It depends on how hungry they are. Sometimes you don't catch any, other times the action is fast."

"Could you make me a line so I could fish?" she asked.

I had plenty of line. I cut off about twenty feet and tied a small rock on the end with a hook about a foot above it. "You need to catch a grasshopper."

"Will you put it on for me? I couldn't stand to put a hook in one."

I laughed. "Nope. You going to fish—you bait your own hook. Besides, I'm getting a bite right now. Watch the line in my hand. See it bump?" I jerked the line back. "Got'em." I pulled in a catfish that was about six inches long.

"Are we going to eat that little fish?"

Disappointed, I took him off the hook and threw him back in. "He's too small. I'm going to catch another grasshopper. You want me to get you one?"

"No, I'll get me something else to use." She went off toward the wagon while I searched for another grasshopper. I found one and was putting it on when she returned with a slab of salt pork the size of my hand. "What in the world are you going to do with that?"

"Put it on my hook."

I was amazed at how dumb women could be. "It's too big. A fish couldn't even get his mouth around that. Besides, that's enough meat for a meal. You're going to waste it. Tear off a little piece and save the rest."

"Nope. You won't bait my hook. I'm going to do it my way." She threaded the hook through the meat.

"Do you want me to throw the line for you. I can get it way out there?"

"No, you wouldn't bait my hook. I am going to do everything myself." She threw the line out about eight feet.

"That's not far enough out. Bring it in and let me show you how to get more distance."

"Nope. You wouldn't bait my hook. My line is fine where it is."

Talk about stubbornness. I should have baited her hook. She will never let me forget it. I felt a bump on my line and jerked. This time it was a good eating size catfish, about a foot long. A dozen of those would make a nice meal for us. "See, that's how you do it. You sure you don't want me to throw your line out further where the fish are?"

"Nope. You . . ."

I interrupted. "I know. I wouldn't bait your hook."

Three hours later I had caught two more fish. It was getting hotter by the minute. "I've had enough. The four fish is not enough for a meal." I had made a stringer for the fish, which were still alive. I'm going to throw these back. No use wasting them.

"I'm going to fish some more," she said.

"Suit yourself. You'll burn up. You're not going to catch anything that close to the bank, especially with that pound of meat on your hook."

I went to the wagon to get a cool drink of water and find shade. I checked on the heifers and then lay down under the wagon trying to catch a cool breeze. Pete leaned back against a wagon wheel, still studied his Bible. I had the late watch last night and was bone tired. A blood curdling scream woke me. My first thought was Indians. I reached for my rifle—fully awake. I looked around but saw nothing. Pete held his rifle, looking around.

The scream again. It was coming from the river. Leta! I'd forgotten about her. I ran and hollered, "I'm coming, Leta!" The Indians must have her! I went over the bank, tripped and fell, rolling the rest of the way to the water. I looked up and saw Leta smiling. Beside her was the biggest catfish I had ever seen.

10

TROUBLE

Leta

We had been on the trail for fifteen days, not yet halfway to Coleman County, according to Charlie. I studied a map, which showed us taking the long way. Charlie said it was because of the water, or lack of it if we took the shorter route. Driving the wagon was boring. I learned to move back to avoid so much dust. Charlie warned me several times that I was lagging too far behind. He wouldn't admit it, but he was still upset because of the gigantic fish I caught. The fish provided several meals, and Pete went on and on about that being the biggest catfish he had ever seen.

The boring job gave me plenty of time to think. Three days after my wedding, my dad softened up a little. Maybe because he realized I was leaving for good. He stopped trying to talk me out of leaving and even was civil to Charlie. My mother cried every time I was around her. It was a relief to get away, but the last few days I had missed them. They had been good parents and, as time went by, I would realize it more and more.

Late in the afternoon, I saw three riders coming from the east. It would be the first people we had seen since leaving. I urged the mules to get closer to the cattle. Evidently Charlie and Pete saw them since they came back to the wagon.

"Get inside the wagon," Charlie demanded, not taking his eyes off the men. I peeked through a small opening in the canvas.

"Howdy," said one of the men, who rode forward ahead of the others. Charlie nodded. "Hello."

The man had a creepy smile, like more of a sneer. "Where ya' headed with those heifers. You don't see many shorthorns in this area. Floppy ears—Jinglebob, huh?"

"Yeah. Going to Texas." I noticed Charlie glancing at Pete.

The man looked around at his friends. "Yeah, those are nice heifers. Must be worth $10 each at least, maybe more."

Charlie eased his horse closer to the man. "Look, fellow. We don't want any trouble. We need to be moving along."

The smile disappeared. "Sure. We're just trying to be friendly." They rode off toward the north.

"Come on out, Leta. They're gone. I doubt that's the last we will see of them though." He got off his horse. "Let's sit a spell."

Pete joined us. "What'd you think, Charlie? The guy doing the talking looked familiar."

Charlie lit half a cigar he'd been chewing on. "Probably saw him on a wanted poster. They're up to no good. We're going to have to be on a sharp lookout. Leta, would you get us some jerky? Let's move out of here and put as much distance as we can from those guys."

We didn't stop until it was almost dark. After gathering some buffalo chips, I started a fire. We seldom found wood on our route. Buffalo chips were plentiful along the river and were easy to start. They also gave off little smoke. It was difficult at first using manure to cook with but isn't a problem anymore. I put the beans in and included some jerky. Now, I started my specialty—coffee. I had a pot that held two quarts. I filled it two-thirds full of water from one of the barrels tied to the wagon. I put it on the fire until it was hot but not boiling. I added a cup of ground coffee and brought it to a boil. I let it boil for about five minutes, being careful not to let it run over. I moved it off the fire and added another half cup of water, which would settle the grounds to the bottom.

When Charlie and Pete returned from checking on the cattle their coffee was ready. It had taken some time to get it just right. It pleased me when they bragged on it, which they did often. They drank coffee with every meal except, of course, when we ate on the move.

While the fast-moving forks hit their plates the talk turned to the strangers. "When do you think we might see them again?" Pete asked.

Charlie set his empty plate down. "I don't expect them to be patient. Probably within the next couple of days—at night."

Pete got up and refilled his plate. "Do you think we should both stay up tonight?"

"No. We need to get our rest. Just be careful and expect trouble any time."

We had three good days, and Charlie announced that we were over halfway. The fourth day in late afternoon we ran into a thunderstorm with lightning and heavy rain. The cattle handled the storm well, thanks to Moses, who just turned his back to the storm and stood. We all huddled in the wagon until it was over. Charlie decided that since we only had a couple more hours, we would camp there for the night.

The weather had cooled, making for a pleasant evening. We had a small celebration of our halfway mark with our meal consisting of fried salt port, canned tomatoes, leftover biscuits, and gravy made with canned milk. We splurged and opened canned peaches for dessert. Charlie and I went to bed early, and Pete took the first watch.

Charlie was rummaging around in the wagon getting dressed to take his watch at midnight when we heard the first shots. Charlie grabbed his rifle and jumped out of the wagon in his long underwear. I dressed as quickly as possible but could see little in the dark. I heard the cattle running and men yelling. I didn't know what to do except to get my rifle and wait. When Charlie didn't come back, I panicked. Maybe he was shot and killed. Finally, I started off in the direction of the shots. Before I had gone far, I heard Charlie. "Leta, over here." I followed his voice and found him with his arm around Pete helping him. "He's been shot. I don't believe it's serious. We need to get him to a light."

I supported Pete's other side, and we were able to get him back to the wagon. "I'll get the lantern." When I returned, Pete was lying on the ground.

"I took a bullet in my leg," Pete mumbled, pain reflected in his voice.

Charlie used his knife to cut away Pete's pants to reveal the wound. "I hate to ruin a good pair of pants, Pete." Charlie examined the wound. "Looks like it went through and missed the bone. Leta, get the medicine chest."

The box I brought Charlie held bandages, camphor, resorcin and a bundle of clean cloths. Two bottles of laudanum were also included.

I watched as Charlie cleaned the wound. Before he started, he had Pete drink some of the laudanum. "Damn, Charlie, that stuff is terrible. Don't we have some whiskey?"

He laughed. "Sure, Pete. But we're saving that for something better than patching you up."

The bullet had struck the outside of Pete's left thigh, right below his hip and exited on the other side. After Charlie finished cleaning the wound, he applied the resorcin in and around it. "It's a clean wound, but the problem will be keeping it from becoming infected. We have to keep it clean and let it heal from the inside. I'm going to put a light bandage on it and change it every day. There's no way you can ride or walk for some time."

"What about the heifers, Charlie? We can't just let those guys take them from us without a fight."

"They can't travel fast. I'm going after them when it gets light. It won't be hard to follow the trail."

"You can't go by yourself. There's three of them. I can drink some more of that laudanum and be able to travel by morning."

"No! Forget it, Pete. If you don't take care of that wound, you'll not be around to help anyone."

The words came out before I realized what I was saying.

"I'm going with you."

Charlie stared at me. "You got to be kiddin'. You'll stay here and take care of Pete and do exactly what I tell you to do."

We left at daylight the next morning. We had argued, and he had even threatened to tie me to the wagon, but I prevailed. The rustlers knew that water would be a problem if they stayed east. They turned back south four or five miles from our camp. Charlie pouted for the first couple of hours before he said a word. "You're the hard-headiest woman I've ever known. What if you get killed? I would never forgive myself for letting you come with me."

"Don't flatter yourself, Charlie. You didn't let me come with you—remember? These heifers are our future. Not just your future. I'm not going to get killed. You can just forget that. You would probably marry someone that was prettier than me and did exactly what you said. I couldn't stand that!"

He actually smiled and shook his head. "That reminds me why I married you. Anyway, when we find these guys, you stay back out of the way."

He should know that demand was useless. "Do you have a plan when we catch up to them?"

"I will when the time comes. They'll take the heifers back to the river to water by nightfall."

Late that afternoon we saw the dust before we could make out the cattle. They were at least a mile ahead of us. "I want to make a wide circle and get ahead of them before night. They will not be expecting us to come from the south," he said.

We stayed far enough away so as not to be seen and by dusk were in front of the cattle. We stopped and waited for it to be dark enough to advance closer. "What's your plan, Charlie?"

"Don't rush me. I'm still thinking."

"I have a plan. You want to hear it?" I asked.

"I guess but be quick."

After I finished telling him how we should go about getting

the cattle, he exploded. "No! No! That's the dumbest idea I ever heard. You would be in too much danger. I won't allow it! Forget it!"

A half hour later, I stumbled toward the cattle, my shirt torn and face dirty. The rustler guarding the herd saw me, but it was too dark to see me clearly. "Stop right there. Put up your hands."

"Please don't shoot me."

When he was close, he lowered his rifle. "What in the world are you doing out here, girl?"

"I need help. My daddy has a place southeast of here about ten miles. I was out riding, and my horse threw me. I was close to the river, so I stayed because I was afraid of walking back in the dark. My daddy will come looking for me soon, but I'm scared. I saw you and thought I could stay with you until my daddy got here."

A big smile appeared. "You sure can. We'll take good care of you. Come with me."

I followed him back to the camp where the men had a fire going and something cooking. "Look what I found." He explained to the other two what I had told him.

The looks I received were frightening and sent chills up and down my spine. I had to be brave. After all, it was my idea. "Could I have some coffee and something to eat? I'm hungry."

There was a scramble by two of the men after my request. The man who had brought me to camp won and presented me with a plate of food and coffee.

"Jed, you need to get back on watch," one of the men said. "We can take care of this little lady."

"Not a chance," he replied. "You can take my watch. After all, I found her."

I forced down the food, which was terrible and drank the coffee, which was worse. "I feel much safer here than wandering around in the dark. My daddy might not be here until sometime tomorrow." The stares become bolder. I began to shake and realized that could give me away. I took some deep breaths. "Where are y'all headed with the cattle?"

The third man who had said nothing spoke up. "We're delivering them to a ranch up the river. What did you say your name was?"

I couldn't give them my real name. "Mary." Now, I needed a last name. "What is you daddy's name?" he asked.

"Jim Fowler." I was becoming more frightened by the second.

"Funny, I've never heard that name before. I thought I knew most of the ranchers around this area."

"W-We haven't been here long." *Hurry, Charlie,* I thought.

The man who brought me to camp asked, "What's going on, Red? Why all the questions? You can see she's just a girl and scared."

The man he called Red, who seemed to be the leader, stood. "Something just doesn't seem right about this whole thing." He started toward me...

11

QUITE A LADY

Charlie

I followed Leta and the night guard back to their camp, careful not to create any sound that would give me away. By now it was dark, and I knelt far enough out of the light from the fire and two lanterns not to be seen. I could hear what was being said and questioned my sanity for allowing her to go through with this, but I had to admit it was the only way to get all three men together. So far it was going the way we intended. I watched as she ate the food she was given and thought how difficult that must have been. The three men were staring at her, and I could imagine what they were thinking. My sweaty hands were gripping the Winchester. I had to decide when to make my play. Should I use my pistol since it would be close range or rifle? I decided on my rifle which was more accurate. Should I demand they surrender or shoot from the dark without a warning? I recognized the man at our wagon who had done the talking. I assumed he was the leader.

He was questioning Leta, and I could tell she was getting nervous. He raised his voice and walked toward her. My decision was made for me when he reached and grabbed her. I fired, the bullet hit him in the throat and he spun halfway around still holding on to Leta and fell face down on top of her, with her screaming.

"Drop your guns!" I yelled.

They hesitated only a second and began firing into the dark. I heard the hiss of bullets coming close. I fired again and the man closest went down. The last man dropped his gun and held up his hands. "Don't shoot! Don't shoot!"

I walked out of the dark to Leta. "Are you hurt?" I never took my eyes off the one man still standing.

I could hear the fear. "N-No. I d-don't think so. Blood a-all over."

I glanced at her and saw that her shirt, hands, and even face were covered in blood. "Can you help me?" I asked.

She moved over close to me. "I'll t-try."

"Gather up all the guns and bring them over here." She did as I asked.

The second man I shot struggled to get up. "Help your friend," I told the man who wasn't wounded. "Then see about the other guy."

The wounded man held a hand to his bloody shoulder. The other one knelt beside the first man I shot and turned him over. He stood and said, "He's dead."

"What are you going to do with us?" asked the wounded man.

"They hang rustlers, don't they? The problem is there are no trees. I guess the only thing left to do is shoot you. You'll be just as dead."

The begging started with the wounded one. "Please, mister, it was Red's idea. We just went along with him." He looked at the other man. "Isn't that right, Joe?"

"Please, mister, we don't want to die. We should've never got mixed up with Red." The one who wasn't wounded kept on pleading.

I finally grew tired of it and stopped him. "Here's what I am going to do. You can take one horse and leave." I nodded at the wounded one. "He can ride. You won't need water since you can follow the river. You better not be here when we return with our wagon. If I see you, I will shoot you on sight, no questions asked. You bury your friend the best you can."

"Leta, you still up to another task?"

"Yes. What do you want?"

"Take their guns and throw them in the river. Make sure you get them far enough out to be in deep water." She had to make two trips to get it done.

I took several steps toward them. "Now we're leaving. I figure it's about ten miles to our camp. We'll probably be back by mid-morning at the latest. Remember what I told you."

"Are you sure you're all right?" I asked as we rode off into the dark.

"He would have hurt me, wouldn't he, Charlie? Did he have to die? Couldn't you have just wounded him like you did the other man? I mean he probably had people who loved him somewhere." Then she started crying. "I still have his blood all over me. At first, I thought I was shot."

We rode a little while longer before I stopped and helped her off her horse. I took her by the shoulders. "Listen to me, Leta. In situations like we have just been in, there is no hesitating. You have to shoot to kill. I wasn't trying to wound the man. He was just fortunate that the bullet struck where it did. I was aiming for the largest part of his body and hit his shoulder. To answer your questions—yes, the man would have hurt you, and if I hadn't shown up it would have been worse. These were bad men, capable of anything. The most dangerous of the men was the one who I killed. I'm sorry that it happened, but it wasn't our choice. Remember that."

We were back by ten the next day, and there was no sign of the men. The heifers had scattered somewhat to find grass but, with Leta helping, we had them back together by mid-afternoon. With the night travel and everything that had happened, I thought we should camp here.

Leta disagreed. "I don't want to be around here a minute longer. The further we can get away, the better."

We moved down the river another five miles and didn't set up camp until dark.

Pete's wound was doing fine. I had changed the bandage before we started this morning. He drove the wagon with Leta taking his place moving the heifers.

I helped Leta build a fire and make coffee. We didn't cook and ate jerky for supper. We sat by the fire with full stomachs, talking about the rest of our trip. "Pete, how is your leg?"

"It's not bad—just stiff. There's not much pain unless I bump it on something. I hate it that I'm no use to you with the cattle, especially at night."

"That's no problem. I'm going to help Charlie," Leta insisted.

I started to argue but decided against it. I'd already found out how much my objections meant and didn't want to be embarrassed in front of Pete. I needed to assert my authority somehow, so I laid out our sleeping arrangements. "Pete, Leta and I are going to trade places with you tonight. You sleep in the wagon, and we'll sleep outside. We want to keep that wound clean."

Pete started to object. "Remember, Pete, I'm the boss of this outfit and what I say goes. Don't argue." He didn't say anything else. I felt better, being in control of someone at least.

"Charlie, could I take the first watch tonight? I'm afraid I couldn't wake up at midnight."

What was this? Asking my permission was a little out of character. Maybe she felt bad not respecting my orders and doing whatever she wanted. "That will be fine, Leta. I appreciate it. Just be sure and stay on your horse. The cattle are used to a person on horseback but would get skittish of someone on foot. If you need a break for personal business, ride out of sight." She just nodded. Maybe I was going to be a trail boss again. I decided to give some more orders. "If you see anyone, fire a warning shot. Don't worry about the cattle. I'll be out to relieve you at midnight."

"Could we get a late start in the morning—say at least an hour? I'm going to be tired and will need to cook breakfast."

I wasn't about to disagree. "Yeah, that's a good idea. An extra hour will help us both."

After Leta left, I brought out a bottle of whiskey and uncorked it. Pete held out his cup and smiled. "I wondered when we were going to have us a real drink." He took a sip and clinched his cup like he thought someone might try and take it away. "She's quite a lady, isn't she?"

"Yeah, I guess so. Sometimes, I wish she'd listen to me a little better. I didn't realize she was so headstrong."

"What has she done that was not the right thing to do, Charlie? I mean, could we have gotten the cattle back if not for her idea? You could not have taken those men if they hadn't been all together, distracted by Leta."

I took a sip of my drink. "No, I reckon not. But it wasn't necessary for her to tear her shirt that much and show so much skin. More important, she could have been hurt or killed."

Pete held out his empty cup. "Didn't you think of that when you brought her on this trip? Surely, you knew of the danger we would face. There's probably going to be more, since we're only a little over halfway."

I poured him another two fingers. "Take it slow. That's going to be all for tonight. To answer your question. Yeah, I knew of the danger. She's just more fearless than I thought. You know, being a female, I thought she would be afraid and cower in the face of danger. Instead, she meets it head on. It just confuses me."

He pointed his cup at me to make his point. "Let me tell you something, Charlie Barlowe. You have gotten yourself a jewel. You know what they say—even a blind hog occasionally finds an acorn. That's about as plain as I can put it."

I didn't know whether that was meant to be a compliment or a put down. I don't guess it mattered. He was right. She was a jewel.

12

INDIANS

Leta

It was torture to sit in the saddle, my rear was so sore. I had ridden yesterday morning and the day before in Pete's saddle without adjusting the stirrups. He was at least four inches taller than me, and I bounced every time my horse moved out of a walk. My legs were also raw. Charlie finally noticed the problem and fixed my stirrups.

The thing about being alone at night with the heifers, it gave me too much time to think. I washed my hands until they were raw, and I could still feel his blood on them. I threw the blouse away. When he was on top of me, I struggled to get up but once free, stayed on the ground, until the shooting stopped. It was over quickly but those few seconds will stay etched in my mind forever. For the first time I had doubts about going to Texas. I was safe in Roswell and this kind of danger never entered my mind. Then I scolded myself, whispering, "Charlie wouldn't have been safe though, if we had stayed."

What confused me most was Charlie's reaction to killing the man. I expected him to be upset, even though he was justified. He seemed not to give it a second thought. I felt guilty for my part. It would have never happened if I had not used my appeal to distract the men. In the past I had enjoyed and encouraged the attention of men but never for this dark purpose. I kept thinking—*why didn't we just let them keep the cattle and go on to*

Texas? Were fifty cows worth risking our lives and taking a man's life, even if he was a terrible human being? As I look back, it was clear that doubt never entered Charlie's mind as to what we were going to do.

There were all kinds of night sounds: coyotes were howling in the distance; an owl was screeching; a rustling in the brush revealed a raccoon, not ten feet from me, with several babies following. To break the boredom, I rode around the small group of cattle, wondering what they were thinking. I had heard Pete and Charlie sing during their watch. Maybe it would be a good idea. I smiled—that might start a stampede.

"You asleep?"

I jumped and nearly fell off my horse. "Charlie! Don't sneak up on me like that."

"What if I'd been an Indian?" he asked.

"Well, you weren't! What are you doing out here this early? It's not twelve."

"I felt bad lying in my bedroll while you were out here. I've had enough sleep. Go on in. I'll take it the rest of the night. Since we're going to take an extra hour in the morning, maybe we can have fresh biscuits."

I got off my horse. "Come down here, Charlie. Hold me a little while."

"What's the problem, Leta?" he asked, his strong arms wrapped around me.

"I don't know. It's just been so much—so fast. It doesn't seem real. Maybe it's only a dream."

He chuckled. "No, it's real. We're on our way to Texas for a new beginning. We'll have a few problems on the way, but together nothing will stop us."

By the fifth day, my sores had healed, and I actually enjoyed my new job. I came to realize how important Moses was. The heifers followed him, stopped when he did, and were content to plod along after him at his speed like small chicks following their mother. My hat kept blowing off since it was too big. tCharlie fixed it by putting two small holes in the brim and running a string through them. The ends came together under my chin allowing me to tie the hat on. It would still blow off but only as far as the back of my neck. I grew tired of putting it back on and left it off much of the time. The result was my hair bleached out to a lighter color and my face tanned. Charlie teased me and said I could be mistaken for a Mexican.

The ninth of September marked the twenty-fifth day we had been on the trail. Charlie said we were close to Horsehead Crossing where we would turn back east toward our new home. At mid-afternoon I noticed a dark cloud in the north, which produced no lightning or thunder. The closer it got the blacker it became with blowing dust along the bottom. I was riding on the left side of the cattle when Charlie motioned for me to come over to where he was.

"We better stop here. That's a blue norther coming. A change in weather is going to make the heifers nervous. You stay here while I ride around to stop them. We'll hold them here until they settle down."

No sooner had Charlie stopped them than the wind started blowing from the north. It continued to blow and each time I thought it couldn't get stronger, it increased. The dust stung my face forcing me to turn my back to it. My horse became uneasy and hard to control, moving first one way and then another. The temperature must have dropped thirty degrees in a few minutes. I began to shiver and became as cold as on a snowy day in mid-winter. I was occupied with my feisty horse, but I was able to head off some of the restless cattle who were trying to leave the herd. They finally quieted down. About the time I thought there was no way to take any more of the wind, sand, and cold, Charlie motioned me toward the wagon. I could barely hear him when he hollered, "I think they'll be okay now. You go ahead and get into the wagon."

I was glad to follow his order. I joined Pete inside, still shivering. "What's going on, Pete? I've never seen anything like this."

"A norther. Not unusual but a little early this year. Out here there's nothing to break the wind. It's been picking up dust all the way from Colorado."

I went through our clothes and found a coat. "It got cold so quick. I'm freezing."

He laughed. "We're used to 100-degree days and suddenly it drops to fifty. Your body doesn't have time to adjust. It'll blow itself out sometime tonight or tomorrow depending on how strong it is. After that, we'll have several beautiful days with little wind and cooler weather. Then it's back to being hot."

It would have been impossible to build a fire, so we had a cold supper of jerky, substituting water for coffee. Charlie took the first watch, saying that maybe the wind would lay by midnight. After he left, Pete insisted I stay in the wagon and no amount of arguing would change his mind. I have to admit my argument might have been a little feeble. Exhausted, I went to sleep at once. I woke up to Charlie shaking me.

"Wake up. It's midnight. What are you doing in the wagon?"

I was still groggy but managed to respond. "Pete insisted I sleep here."

"The wind's not blowing as hard but it's cold. You better bundle up," he said.

Still half-asleep, I managed to get dressed. Charlie had my horse saddled, and I was on the job within a few minutes.

Time seemed to stand still. It didn't help that I couldn't get warm even with the heavy coat and gloves. The wind continued to blow; riding away from it was bearable but turning around and facing it was brutal. By five o'clock I gave up and went in. The trail boss would just have to chew me out. I'd had all I could take.

The wind calmed enough that I chanced a fire. I got coffee-makings out of the wagon without waking Charlie. Pete crawled out of his bedroll beneath the wagon and helped me get a fire started. I got as close to the fire as possible to drink my coffee, getting warm for the first time in hours.

Charlie joined us as the sun was coming up. "Coffee smells good." He shivered. "Amazing that it can go from hot to cold in one day." He looked at me. "Any problems with the heifers last night?" He got his coffee and sat down.

"No. If they were as cold as me, they couldn't have run off if they wanted to."

"The way I figure it, it's time to turn back east. I've dreaded it since we left. That will be the toughest part of the trip. We have about seventy miles until we reach the Concho. It's doubtful if there'll be any water before then. We're going to push them hard and try to make it in four or five days. It's been seven years since I made the trip with Mr. Chisum, but I remember it well. We were driving over a thousand head, and they stampeded twice between the Concho and Pecos. Once it was a storm that set them off—the other time it was just plain thirst. Of course, we don't have to worry about a stampede, but with these young heifers, it's just keeping them moving. I hope the weather will stay cool, but that's just dreaming.

"I believe it would be best if we stayed here for two days. With the rest and full bellies, they'll be in better shape to make the Concho. It'll be good for the horses, also—not to mention us."

I felt better after two days of rest as we pushed the heifers east away from the river and toward our new home. Evidently the rest helped them, too, since they moved out without encouragement. By mid-afternoon they had slowed considerably and required some prodding to keep them moving.

The flat terrain held little vegetation and no trees. I was surprised when they appeared as if they just came up out of the ground. There were six of them and they stopped the herd. It was the first wild Indians I'd ever seen. Charlie went forward to meet them, and I rode back to the wagon to join Pete, who was holding his rifle.

"What's going on Pete? Why did Charlie go out to them?

Isn't that dangerous?"

"It looks like they want to talk. I imagine they'll demand one of the heifers. I'm guessing they left the reservation to hunt and didn't find game. It's hard for the Indians to believe that the buffalo are almost gone. Indians admire courage. Charlie going out to face them will gain their respect and maybe prevent a fight. I'm not sure but from here I don't see any rifles." He reached behind him and brought out my Winchester and gave it to me. "Prop it up on your leg so they can see it. Three of these rifles will impress them as much as anything."

"What kind of Indians are they, Pete? I mean what tribe?"

"Comanche. The best horsemen that ever lived and the most feared by white men and other tribes."

We watched as they cut one of the heifers out and chased her away from the herd before shooting arrows into her. She struggled to stay on her feet until one of them drove a lance through her. I looked away, sickened by the sight.

Charlie rode back to the wagon. "It looks like they may be satisfied with the one heifer. Let's move on away from here and put as much distance between them as possible."

We didn't stop until dark and then Charlie stayed with the cattle. He told me to remain at the wagon with Pete and keep my rifle handy. I took him some jerky and a cup of coffee, which he accepted before telling me to go back to the wagon.

"I'm going to keep you company for a little while, Charlie. Do you think they'll come back tonight?"

"Maybe—I don't know. If we get through the night, I believe we'll be okay. I hated to give them the heifer, but it probably saved us a fight. One of them had two fresh scalps hanging from his lance. I'm surprised they were this far south. They're a long way from the reservation. The closer we get to Fort Concho the safer we'll be. I hope we run into a troop of Buffalo Soldiers before too long."

"Were those scalps the men who . . . ?"

"He interrupted me. "Don't think about that, Leta. We'll never know for sure."

"Who are the Buffalo soldiers?"

"They're Negro soldiers who patrol this area and are stationed at Fort Concho. They would be a welcome sight."

"Weren't you afraid when you went out to meet those Indians?"

"Yeah, but I didn't have a choice. If I hadn't, they would have driven the herd off and forced a fight. We could have lost as many as fifteen or twenty head—not to mention the danger to us." He finished his coffee and handed the cup to me. "You better get on back to camp."

"Nope. I'm staying. Remember—we are in this together, Charlie Barlowe."

13

DESPERATE

Charlie

Four days after confronting the Indians, we plodded along not making but about seven or eight miles a day. I knew we were in trouble. It was requiring all of our efforts to keep the herd moving with several falling back and slowing the entire bunch down. On the fourth day two of the heifers lay down and refused to move, regardless of our efforts to get them up. I put a rope around the neck of one but couldn't get her to her feet. It was late in the afternoon, so I decided to camp there and hoped the two heifers, after a night's rest, would get up.

The mood was dismal around the fire that night. "What are we going to do, Charlie?" Pete asked.

"I don't know anything to do, except keep moving."

Leta had more bad news. "We're low on coffee. We need to ration ourselves to a cup in the morning and one at night. Do you have an idea how far we are from water?"

I hesitated and dreaded answering. "With the time we've been making, at least three days, maybe four."

Leta said what Pete and I were thinking. "We'll never make it with the heifers. We may get to our new home with one steer—Moses."

"The horses are beginning to suffer, also. We'll give the ones we are going to use tomorrow a little water in the morning from our barrel. It's different trailing heifers. They're not as strong as steers and, of course, younger. They've always had all the feed and water they wanted. I knew it would be harder but not anything like this. Maybe we should have waited until the weather was cooler." This was not the time to be second guessing myself.

"Are you sure there is no water before the Concho?" asked Pete.

It irritated me to get questions I couldn't answer. "I don't know, Pete. That's just what I've been told by people who have made the trip. The one trip I made, we went the whole way between the Concho and Pecos without water."

It was Leta's turn to irritate me. "Are you sure we are going in the right direction to reach the river?"

I didn't answer but got up and walked off. Right now, I wasn't sure of anything, except it was not the time to question my decisions. I said it was three or four days to water—it could be five. We were not making good time and only traveled about two-thirds the distance we should in a day.

I didn't go far from the wagon, and Leta came out a few minutes later. "I'm sorry, Charlie. I didn't mean to question your judgment. I'm scared, not just for the cattle but for us as well. It's such a desolate country with nothing you can see for miles. There's just so much time left until we run out of water. Maybe it would be best if we left the cattle and rode on. We might come back for them when we reach the river."

The stress and heat must be affecting her thinking. "No! I would never consider leaving the heifers. We're going in the right direction. We'll make it with the heifers. I don't want to discuss it anymore."

"I just suggested a possibility. You don't have to get angry."

"You said, just the other night, that we were in this together. You suggested giving up. You need to understand something about me if we're going to be together the rest of our lives—I . . .don . . .quit. I would die before leaving these heifers out here. If we're truly in this together, you better feel the same way." Leta went back to the wagon and had nothing to say for the rest of the evening.

The next morning the two heifers wouldn't get up. I tried again to put a rope around their necks and pull them up but failed. I left the herd and Leta went ahead. I stayed behind and shot the heifers, ending their suffering and saving them dying from the wolves. It was the low point of the journey.

I caught up with the herd, which was easy since their pace was even slower today. When I went by the wagon, Pete motioned me over. "Charlie, I'm ready to ride again. My leg is healing and beginning to itch. Leta has done a good job but needs to drive the wagon."

"You sure?"

"Yeah. I can help you keep them moving."

I was pleased that Pete was going to join me. His experience would be welcomed and would make a difference. I motioned for Leta to meet me at the wagon. When I told her the plans, she seemed relieved, not offering any objection. After our talk last evening, she had little to say.

Pete was more aggressive, which helped in moving the heifers along. We didn't stop at noon, afraid some more would lie down. When we made camp, it was almost dark. I figured we had made seven or eight miles.

After we finished eating, we sat around the fire and talked. "Leta, were you glad to get back to driving the wagon?"

"Yes. I was worn out trying to keep the cattle moving. Pete is better than me. I know we made more distance today."

"You did a wonderful job replacing me. We couldn't have gotten this far without you," Pete said. "I know we are in trouble. Sometimes, when all else fails, we go to the Lord for help. I have a suggestion. I would like for us to join hands and let me lead us in prayer. If you are uncomfortable doing this, I will understand."

Leta, who smiled for the first time today said, "Pete, that is a wonderful idea. Come on, Charlie. Prayer is certainly not going to hurt you."

We formed a small circle and held hands. Pete began, *"God, we are in trouble. We are asking for Your help in getting us to water and saving these poor animals. We trust in You and thank You for*

Your great love for all of us sinners. Amen."

Strange—I felt better. "Thank you, Pete."

The next morning, three more of the heifers were difficult to get up. At mid- morning they lay down again. This time I was only able to get one of them back up and moving. We left the other two and, like the day before, I went and shot them. That made five we had lost. One, I had given the Indians and four that had given up. We were moving at a turtle's pace again, unlike yesterday.

Angry, I had to take it out on someone. I returned to the herd but stopped at the wagon. "Well, a lot of good praying did."

"You have to have faith. That isn't one of your traits, though, is it Charlie?" She slapped the mules with the reins and pulled away, leaving me sitting there on my horse.

By late afternoon, according to my calculations, we hadn't made over five miles. This was the sixth day since leaving the Pecos. We might as well stop and get an early start in the morning. The weather was scorching with no wind. I motioned to Pete that we were going to make camp. He came over to me. "Tough day, Charlie. Maybe tomorrow will be better."

"Don't look like your prayer did any good," I repeated. I was upset and looking for an argument.

"Oh, I don't know, Charlie." He stopped as if deep in thought. "I think it's Psalm 35 that says, 'Be still before the Lord and wait patiently for him.'"

"Well, Pete, I'm out of patience. Let's set up camp. Maybe a cup of coffee with some whiskey will make me feel better."

I ate little of the beans and salt pork Leta cooked for supper before pouring a generous portion of whiskey in my coffee. I was surprised that Pete turned down my offer and left, saying he was going to check on the heifers.

"No use checking on them. They're too weak to go anywhere. They'll probably be three or four down in the morning." I was talking more to myself than Leta.

"Is that what you expect, Charlie?" She stood. "Maybe it's just what you're hoping for. Then you can be angry and say mean things to Pete and me. You're upset and mad at the world—plus feeling sorry for yourself. All your negative feelings won't change a thing. Now, I'm going to bed. At least I won't have to listen to you."

I poured more whiskey in my cup without adding coffee. What was wrong with her? She just didn't understand. These heifers were our future, and I was having to kill them. Prayer—it was a waste of time. I'd thought it might actually help. Our situation was worse today than it was yesterday. Was I really willing to stay here and die with these heifers, like I said? I might have to make that choice tomorrow.

I had just poured myself another drink when Pete came back. "Heifers are okay. Most are lying down. I'm not giving up, Charlie. I've been praying about it some more. Sometimes the Lord just takes His time."

"You keep on praying, Pete. I think you're wasting your time, but it's your time." I drained my cup and staggered to the wagon. My bedroll was on the ground at the back of the wagon. The canvas to the entrance was pulled together and tied. I stood there and stared. So that's how it is.

I woke up the next morning to someone shaking me. Leta was standing over me with a cup of coffee. "Brought you some coffee. Feel bad, don't you? That's what liquor does to you. I know from experience. Drinking all that liquor didn't change a thing, did it? Here drink this—maybe it will help."

I sat up and took the coffee. The last thing I needed was a lecture. My head was killing me and felt as big as a five-gallon bucket. At least she was talking. "Thank you."

"Breakfast will be ready soon—biscuits. Enjoy your coffee. That's all you're going to get today."

I didn't know she had that sharp a tongue when I married her. I saved half my coffee for the biscuits and struggled to my feet. I was so focused on my headache I hadn't noticed Pete. "Have you checked on the heifers this morning, Pete?"

"Yeah. We have a couple of them down. We do have a little south breeze this morning that makes it better. We need to get started as soon as we can to take advantage of the cooler morning. It won't last long."

I knew he was right. When Leta gave me my biscuits, I thanked her and then bragged on how good they were. I didn't get much in return except, "Glad you liked them."

Pete had saddled my horse, anxious to get started. I felt closer to normal, but still had a headache. The sun wasn't up when we started to drive the cattle. The two that were down got up and moved with the herd. We hadn't gone but a few hundred yards when Moses turned back south. "What's the matter with him, Pete? Is he out of his mind?"

Pete rode up and turned him back east. As soon as Pete rode away, he turned south again. This was repeated several times. Pete rode over to me. "What should we do, Charlie? He's decided to go south."

"It looks like we don't have a choice. Maybe he knows more than we do. Let him go." The herd turned south, and we followed.

After at least a mile, I hollered at Pete. "This is stupid. He's out of his mind. Let's try to turn him back." When I rode to the front to turn him, he broke into a trot and then began to run. The heifers were trying to keep up. Then—I saw the water.

14

PRAYER ANSWERED

Leta

After reaching the water, Charlie and Pete were furiously trying to keep the cattle from drinking too much. It looked like it was going to be an impossible task, but they kept them away from the water for a half-hour before letting them drink again.

The water was only knee deep to the heifers and became muddy almost at once, which didn't seem to bother them. Pete said that evidently a recent storm had dumped several inches of rain in a low spot with some runoff—the result being a good-sized pond. It probably had not been here two weeks ago and would be gone in a couple of weeks. Regardless—prayer answered.

By noon, the cattle had drunk their fill and were grazing on the recent growth of grass. Charlie came over to the wagon. "We'll stay here tonight and tomorrow. We all need the rest. I will never question Moses again."

I couldn't resist. "What about prayer? Are you going to question it again?"

He opened his mouth, but nothing came out before riding off to join Pete.

I thought a celebration was in order, so I gathered buffalo chips, built a fire, and put on a pot of coffee. When Charlie and Pete saw what I was doing they came over.

"A cup of coffee would be mighty fine," Pete said. "What

about one of those left-over biscuits? My appetite has improved since breakfast."

"Charlie, you want a biscuit?" I asked.

"Yeah, that sounds good. The heifers are going to be okay. It's amazing how fast they've recovered after drinking. I doubt if we could have made another day. I'm thinking that we can make good time and reach the Concho in two days."

Pete took the biscuit I offered. "You know, we only lost five head. That's not bad under the circumstances. Of course, they've lost a lot of weight. Maybe the fall grass will be good where we're going. This time of year, the grass cures out and has a lot of strength to it."

Charlie ate his biscuit and drank his coffee, staying silent. I was curious as to what he was thinking. I had learned two things about Charlie Barlowe in the brief time I'd known him—one, he didn't like to be told what to do—the other, he didn't like to admit making a mistake. "What are you thinking, Charlie?"

He drained his cup, looked at the ground and said the one thing I didn't expect. "I was wrong to talk to y'all the way I did. I took my frustration out on you. It's no excuse, but I was frustrated, maybe scared is a better word. It won't happen again." He rose, gave me his cup, and left.

I couldn't believe it, after what I had been thinking. I smiled. Charlie was more complicated than I thought. Pete sat cross-legged on the ground and finished his biscuit. "There's a lot of pressure on Charlie. A new bride and a gift of fifty head of short-horned heifers, which are the future of the cattle business in Texas. He has his shortcomings, like all of us. But he is a good man, and I'm proud to ride with him." He emptied the few drops of coffee in his cup, which were mostly grounds, got up and left.

It was my time to be thankful. I was going to my new home with two good men.

◈

Our good fortune continued when we left our water hole,

with a north wind that made it much cooler. We were on the trail before sunup, and when we made camp that evening, Charlie announced we had made at least twelve miles, maybe more. Spirits were good as we sat around the fire that night.

"I expect to see the Concho any time," Charlie said.

"Do you have any idea what the house we are going to live in is like?" I knew men didn't think about things like that, but it had been on my mind since leaving New Mexico.

"No. It doesn't matter as long as we have a roof over our heads. We can build a house later when we have the money. The first thing I need to do is find work on one of the ranches. You have the letter that Mr. Chisum gave you. When you give that to the man who owns the store, he'll probably hire you."

"Pete, what are your plans?" I asked.

"Oh, I don't know. I have family in the area, but they struggle to make a living. I'll probably hang around with Charlie. Maybe we can both get a ranch job."

You would think that Charlie was the older of the two, the way that Pete followed him. He was a good influence on Charlie. I had no doubt about that.

"I'll take the first watch tonight, Pete. The heifers are going to be feeling better and might try to wander off," Charlie said.

"How far to where we are going after we reach the Concho?" I asked.

Charlie hesitated as if calculating. "Probably about sixty miles. We should make it in about five or six days. We should be settled into our new home by the first of the month."

I wanted more information. "This place we're going to will not be our permanent home. Is that right?"

"Yeah, Mr. Chisum said the best part of the country was about twenty miles north, along a creek. That was his choice for us to buy the land for our ranch. He said the grass was good and water plentiful. Of course, the railroad has not put that land up for sale yet. That will come later when, hopefully, we have the money to buy land."

Still not satisfied, I pushed. "And when will all this take place?"

"You ask a lot of questions, Leta."

"That's the only way I know to find out anything. You sure don't volunteer much information. I trust you, Charlie, but I'd still like to know our plans for the future. That's not asking too much, is it?"

"I don't know when land will come up for sale. I hope it's far enough in the future that we have some money saved."

I offered to take a share of the watch later that evening, but Charlie insisted it wasn't necessary.

Charlie took the first watch, leaving Pete and me to visit. Pete admitted that he knew something about the house where we would live. "I've seen the house, Leta. It's pretty bad but livable, I guess. I mean it beats nothing—but not by much. I'm telling you this, so you won't be disappointed. I doubt if Charlie has seen it or didn't remember it, since he would have been only about twelve."

"I don't guess it makes any difference, but thanks. I'll know what to expect, at least."

Late the next afternoon, we saw the trees in the distance. The cattle picked up their pace, anxious to reach water—the Concho. It wasn't necessary this time for Charlie and Pete to limit their drinking. The water was clear, much different from the last watering hole. We made camp among some large oak trees.

I walked down to the river and thought how wonderful a bath would feel. Charlie joined me. "It looks good doesn't it. This is actually the head of the Middle Concho, which is the reason there is so much water. There's a north and south branch, also. They come together later to form the main river. Mr. Chisum gave me a geography lesson when we came through here before."

"How long are we going to stay here?"

"Just tonight. I'm anxious to get settled in our new home. Water won't be a problem now, and we should be in Coleman

County in four or five days."

"I'm going down the river a few hundred yards and bathe. That water looks so good and clean. Will you and Pete get a fire going and the coffee on?"

Charlie smiled. "What about going with you? There could be Indians around?"

"I just need a bath, Charlie. I have never been this filthy in my life. Just give me a little while alone, to bathe in private. I deserve that."

He looked down, mumbling, "I know you deserve it. I was just hoping." He perked up. "I might do a little fishing. Wouldn't catfish be a welcome change?"

"That would be nice." I went to the wagon and found a towel and some clothes that looked close to clean. When I started down the river, Charlie was already baiting his hook with some salt pork. I smiled, remembering him making fun of me for using salt pork for bait. I went at least a hundred yards before finding a spot shaded by large trees. A beautiful spot with lush grass down to the water.

For the next half-hour I wallowed in luxury. The water wasn't over my head, only coming to my shoulders. I actually had brought several bars of soap on the trip. I washed my hair and for the first time felt clean. I had not felt this good and this clean since leaving Roswell. I would have to reward Charlie for giving me this privacy. I laughed out loud. I hope he caught a fish bigger than mine.

I was reluctant to get out but knew they would be hungry, and supper wouldn't fix itself. I waded out and started toward my clean clothes, which I had hung on a tree limb. I stepped on something that moved and at once felt the pain in my ankle. I heard myself scream—kicked my foot once and the snake hung on. The second effort he went flying off into the grass. I examined my ankle and saw the two small punctures. "You have to stay calm," I said aloud. Was the snake poisonous? I quickly got dressed, not knowing if Charlie and Pete had heard me scream. How loud was the scream? I had no idea.

I started walking to the wagon, trying not to rush, knowing

that would make the poison move through my body faster. Charlie met me smiling, holding up two large catfish. "Look what we're having for supper."

"I've been snake bit." I pointed to my ankle.

His reaction would not have been any more alarming if we'd seen a hundred Indians coming toward us. He started moving around like his pants were full of ants. "Where! How! When! Let me see! It was a cottonmouth! They're poisonous! Pete—come here quick! Hurry! Bring your knife!"

Now I really was frightened. What was he going to do with a knife, especially in his state of mind? I was ready to run when Pete arrived carrying his knife. Charlie took the knife. "Okay. I'm going to have to cut an x on the bite."

I backed up several steps. "Charlie, you're not going to get near me with that knife in your condition. Give the knife back to Pete. Do you know what to do, Pete?"

"Yeah, I've seen it done on rattlesnake bites. I need to sterilize the knife." He went over and lay the knife down on a rock with the blade in the fire. "Charlie, get the whiskey."

My ankle had begun to burn and swell. Was I going to die? Suddenly, I was dizzy and nauseated. The next thing I knew, Charlie had his mouth on my ankle, sucking on the wound. "What are you doing, Charlie?"

Pete answered him. "He's sucking the poison out of the wound."

Charlie would rise occasionally and spit. When he thought he had sucked enough and spit enough, he poured whiskey over the wound. *I must be important to waste their precious whiskey*, I thought and then passed out again.

When I came to, Charlie gave me a cup of whiskey. I was too sick to object and downed it. That was the last thing I remembered until morning when I woke up hungry. My ankle was swollen to twice its size, but I felt fine.

Charlie presented me with a cup of coffee. "How're you feeling?"

"Not bad." I took a sip of the coffee, which was terrible. "We moving out today?"

"Not till you feel like it," he said.

I tried to sit up. "I'm okay. What are we having for breakfast?"

"There was so much going on last night we skipped supper. We still have those catfish. How does that sound for breakfast?"

"Wonderful," I said, glad to be alive this morning.

15

TRICKUM

Leta

"Why in the world would they name a place Trickum, Charlie?" We went past the store that Mr. Chisum had told us about where I might work. Since it was Sunday, the store was closed.

"I don't know. I guess you can ask when you talk to them about a job. We still have several miles before we reach our home. I don't remember where the house is. Pete will have to show us."

I tried to lower my expectations to the point where I wasn't going to be disappointed. When the house came into view, I had not lowered my expectations enough. It was a shack, which was a compliment to its appearance. It was not painted, and the porch had fallen halfway down, being held by one post. I could see holes in the roof before we even reached the house. Coming closer, sacks covered the two windows in the front. When we reached the house, Charlie came over to the wagon. "The grass is better than I expected for this time of year." He looked toward the house. "House needs a little fixin' up."

I didn't know whether to laugh or cry at his observation.

The first month at our new home, we lived in the wagon

and took our meals the way we had on the trail. Charlie and Pete worked on the house to make it livable. Charlie hadn't told me that Mr. Chisum gave him three months' salary before we left New Mexico. He was able to get supplies from a town about twelve miles northwest of our new home. It was amazing what the two of them were able to do in such a short period. By the time the weather started getting colder, we were able to move into the house. Charlie and Pete were both able to get work on the largest ranch in the area.

I didn't apply for work at the Trickum store. By the middle of November, I suspected that I was pregnant. When I told Charlie he refused to let me go to work, saying we would make it fine.

Our first child was born on May 20, 1880, and was named John Chisum Barlowe. Charlie announced he would be called Chisum. I counted the days I was pregnant and thought that his name should have been Pecos. We wrote a letter to Mr. Chisum at once and told him of his namesake.

Charlie made forty dollars a month, which was enough for us to get by on and save a little. His dream had become mine—to buy a ranch on the creek that ran through the area twenty miles north of here. There was some revenue from the Jinglebob heifers that we drove from New Mexico, as cows produced calves each year. We sold the bull calves and kept some of the heifers that Charlie picked out.

We occasionally received a letter from Mr. Chisum which described the situation at the Jinglebob. A letter which came in July of 1881 said that Billy Bonney, who had become known throughout the southwest as Billy the Kid, was killed by Pat Garrett. It was a relief for us to know that the threat to Mr. Chisum had been eliminated. Of course, I was relieved knowing that Charlie would never encounter the killer again. Charlie was too proud to acknowledge that fact.

A letter came in 1883 which brought sadness. Mr. Chisum

was ill with cancer and was going to Kansas City for treatment. Charlie fretted for several days as to whether he should join him. The decisive factor proved to be the time of year. It was spring and the cows were calving, and Charlie chose not to leave.

Pete and Charlie were inseparable, working on the same ranch and spending their free time together. The ranch covered so much area that Charlie was able to live at home and work on the southern part.

I had no idea what kind of father Charlie would be. It turned out that he was crazy about little Chisum and was teaching him to ride when he was two.

In late December of 1884 we received word that Mr. Chisum had died. Charlie took it bad and wanted to attend the funeral in Arkansas but knew it would not be possible. He withdrew into himself and talked little for three days. I would learn from the experience that Charlie would not share his grief, and nothing I could do or say would change it.

For the next six years we saved and hoarded every extra penny that we could. When the railroad started selling land, we had a little over $2,000 saved. Charlie found the perfect plot of land on the creek north of town. It had 8,000 acres and was to be sold for $1 an acre. Charlie went to the bank and borrowed $7,000 and kept out $1,000 for improvements on the land, including fencing and a house.

The loan was approved, and our dream had come true. We moved our wagon for a temporary home, and Charlie and Pete started building us a house. Both had quit their jobs and devoted their time to our new ranch. It took them several months to build our house and another month to build a one-room house for Pete. By the fall of 1890 we had moved our 200 cows from Trickum to our ranch. We were home.

PART 2

THE TWILIGHT SIDE OF THE HILL

16

OCTOBER 18, 1929
NEW YORK STOCK EXCHANGE

Elliot

I stood in disbelief as stocks fell, thinking what a buying opportunity this was. The Dow had been steadily going up since the end of the war and peaked last month at 391. It would occasionally have a down day but recover quickly. I had owned a seat on the New York Stock Exchange for nine years and made more money than I could have ever imagined, even investing somewhat conservatively. Now with the stocks growing cheaper by the minute, I threw caution to the wind. I started buying, using most of the cash I had, and not slowing down, continuing to buy on margin, which only needed a small percent of the cost. All the time I calculated how much money I was going to make when the market reversed, which it would. We had elected another Republican president, and there was no reason to believe it wouldn't continue to go up.

By the end of the session, I was exhausted. I had tripled my stock holdings in one day and was margined to the hilt. Now, I looked forward to next week when the profits would become known. It was hard to believe more people had not taken advantage of the cheap stocks. Even though the stocks continued to fall until the closing bell, I had no doubt but what they would recover on Monday. It wasn't unusual for profit taking to occur on Friday, causing panic selling by those who didn't understand the market.

A cold mist fell as I waited for a taxi to take me home. I had a Rolls-Royce in my garage but didn't drive it to work. The weather at this time of year was depressing due to many days like this one. Within a few years, along with my family, I would be spending the winters in Florida. I could be doing it now, but still had not quite reached my financial goal. My acquisitions today just might put me over the top when I sold. I felt sorry for those poor souls who sold today, losing as much as twenty percent. They'd be sorry when the market shot up as we got closer to the holidays. It always happened that way.

On the half hour ride to my home, I leaned my head back against the seat and tried to relax. I needed a drink but that could wait until I was home. I wasn't going to stop at any of the speakeasy joints. Prohibition was the stupidest thing we had ever done in this country. Home was a three-story house with approximately six thousand square feet with electrical lights and indoor plumbing. The servants, an Italian immigrant family, occupied the third floor. The couple with their two daughters were all we had at the time but that would change within the next year. The woman and one of the daughters took care of the household jobs, including the cooking, while the other daughter looked after our ten-year-old son who had been stricken with polio when he was six. The father served as chauffeur and took care of the yard and, being quite the handyman, did repairs that came up. Effie kept insisting that we needed more staff.

When we stopped in front of my home, I gave the driver a five and told him to keep the change. He stuck it in his shirt pocket and said nothing. Taxi drivers had to be the rudest people on earth.

Our front door opened onto a hallway which led to a large living area. I went directly to my liquor cabinet and took out a bottle of Canadian Whiskey. I never touched the stuff made from stills. My stash was restocked the first Monday of each month. At nine in the evening a delivery was made to my front door, which I accepted with a cash payment.

I took my drink to a soft chair in front of the burning fireplace and eased down, propping my feet up on a hassock. I had just taken a sip when Effie came in complaining. "I don't understand why we stay here in the winter. We should be in Florida with my friends. The weather is miserable and will only get worse."

"Hello, Effie. How are you today?"

She glared at me. "I just told you. Weren't you listening?"

"I thought we might greet one another like most couples do after being apart all day."

She snapped back, "Okay. How was your day, Elliot?"

"Good. The market was down, and I bought more stocks. I can't believe people don't learn to buy when the market is down and sell when it's up. That's worked for me the past nine years."

"Remember, Elliot, you had some help. You could never have bought a seat on the exchange if not for my daddy."

I waited a few seconds to control the anger. "How could I forget? You remind me at every opportunity. I paid your daddy back with interest." I moved to something less confrontational. "Where's Nichole?"

"She's staying the night with a friend. They'll probably stay up all night talking about boys. That's what sixteen-year-olds do, I guess. She's already talking about leaving home and going to college. She only has one more year at Trinity, so it will happen soon. Time goes so fast." She rose and left, talking on the way out. "I need to speak with Amara about dinner."

Amara, the wife and mother of our servants, was a good cook as evidenced by my expanding waistline. The spicy Italian dishes that she put on the table were delicious. Amara and her husband, Leonardo, were in their forties. Their daughters were both in their early twenties. They had come to the United States six years ago. We were fortunate to get them, and they had become like family. They could speak English—the daughters better than their parents.

Grant, our youngest, had been stricken with polio four years ago. He struggled to walk, even with a cane. Trinity, the private school which Nichole attended, refused to admit him because polio was known to be contagious. He begged to attend school with his sister, but my efforts failed to get him enrolled, so I hired a tutor to come to the house three days a week.

The drink began to take effect, and I relaxed, closing my eyes, moving back in time. I left home at eighteen, coming to New York. I wanted to live in a city and never see a horse or cow again. That was nineteen years ago, and I never regretted it. All the people and buildings were intimidating at first, but fortune was with me. I found work at Whitlock Iron Works after only two days of looking for a job. The company produced cash registers, nuts, bolts, and all kinds of fasteners. The owner was Benjamin Whitlock, Nichole's dad. I met her at a company party, and after a two-year courtship we married in 1912.

After we married, I moved to an office position with a nice pay increase and continued there for the next eight years. Mr. Whitlock introduced me to the stock market, and with my pay increase I was able to trade stocks. He invested heavily in the market and did well. Mr. Whitlock started his company on borrowed money and prospered before investing in stocks. He was one of the new rich families in New York, unlike the Rockefellers and Carnegies who had been wealthy for years. He was generous and loaned me the money to buy a seat on the exchange, at which point I left the company.

Nichole was born in 1913, and Grant six years later in 1919. I bought our house in 1923. By then, I was making more money than I could have ever imagined. The Florentines were already with us when Grant was diagnosed with polio.

I guess we were a happy family even though we did little together, each of us having our own life. Mine was work and time at the club. Effie, with her group, played cards several days a week and took shopping trips downtown. Nichole either had friends over or was spending time at one of their homes. Grant and his little dog Rose were inseparable. Sofia, his caretaker, spent much of her day with him.

I tried to never think of Texas. I had only been back once when Chisum, my older brother, died. I stayed less than a week and didn't feel guilty about leaving. My dad was grieving so much he hardly knew I was present. Chisum had always been his favorite. My mom and dad were now in their late sixties. I was the youngest, having been a surprise when my mother was thirty, which was ancient for childbearing at that time.

I would get a letter every month from my mother, describing events in their life. I had only sent two letters this year, feeling obligated to keep in touch. They knew and accepted that I would never return to Texas. From the time I can remember, I detested that lifestyle and got away from it as soon as possible.

My dad and I had never been close. My older brother, who was single, still lived at home and worked the ranch with my dad. He was twelve years older than me. They considered me old enough to work by the time I was nine or ten. I was nothing but a hired hand from that time on. I came to resent both of them and everything about the place. Neither one of them even went with Mom and me to catch the train that would take me north.

At some point, I can't say exactly when, Effie and I drew apart. The first years of our marriage were wonderful, and we spent all the time together that was possible. The more money I made the further apart we became and now, you could almost say we led separate lives, only seeing one another coming or going. I know most of it was my fault because of my obsession with the market and making money. When I reached my goal, I would make it up to Effie.

Tomorrow, I will go to the Union Club, which I joined shortly after buying my seat on the exchange. I would spend most of the day there, playing cards and visiting about politics, stocks, and sports. Lunch would be served, and it would be mid to late afternoon before I went home.

My thoughts were interrupted by a familiar sound—a sliding noise followed by a knock. Grant was on his way. He would drag one foot and then put his cane down to take another step. I got up to meet him as he came into the room, with Rose right behind him. "Grant, why isn't Sophia helping you?"

He struggled toward a chair and plopped down. Rose leaped into his lap. "I don't need anyone to help me."

"Did you have a good day?" I asked, sitting in a chair closer to him.

"It could have been better. Sofia was going to take me to the park this morning, but the weather was yucky. My teacher came this afternoon. I wish I could go to school like other kids. It doesn't seem fair. I have no friends. Oh, there's Sophia but she doesn't count. I forgot about Rose. She's my best friend." He stroked the small, long-haired Chihuahua's head.

I always dreaded these conversations that made me feel like a failure. "I'm sorry, Grant. I've tried but failed to get them to let you attend. Your illness is contagious."

He sat up straighter. "Just tell them I promise not to breathe on anyone."

I smiled. "Okay, I'll try again next week."

He struggled to get up. "I'm going to the kitchen to see if there is anything to eat."

When I moved to help him, he objected. "I can do it."

I watched him shuffle out of the room, helpless to do anything that would make his life better.

The next morning, at the Union Club, most of the conversation revolved around the stock market and its decline the day before. Of the ones who joined in with their opinion, only one was a naysayer who, of course, was a Democrat. The predictions were positive, with the most common being, "It always goes back up— why would this time be any different?"

The one person who disagreed received dagger-like stares as he made his prediction. "Money is too easy to get. There is too much speculation, backed by little evidence. We have overproduced in manufacturing. Who's going to buy all the automobiles or the new homes being built? I know you don't want to hear it, but we're headed for trouble."

It looked as if the crowd might physically attack the man, but cooler heads prevailed until the person saw how upset he had made his colleagues and left. Laughter followed his exit as comments were made about how ridiculous he sounded.

I left after lunch, still tired from the stress and excitement of yesterday plus the fact that I drank too much last night. The club had a parking lot, so I took the Rolls. I bought it two years ago and enjoyed driving it when I had the opportunity, which was not often. I expected Effie to be home, but Sofia said she had left and would be gone all afternoon. That was strange, since she'd told me this morning that she had no plans for today.

I selected my favorite chair and relaxed, thinking of what my portfolio would look like at the opening bell on Monday.

17

1736 MILES SOUTH BARLOWE RANCH

Leta

"Leta, where're my teeth? I left them on the stand by the bed last night."

I couldn't believe he had lost his teeth. "Charlie, I haven't had your teeth. Are you sure you left them in the bedroom? Maybe they're in the living room." He was getting worse about not being able to find things. With his seventieth birthday coming up soon, I guess it was time he began to show his age.

I poured him a cup of coffee and set about cooking his bacon and eggs while he looked for his teeth. It wasn't daylight yet, and the kerosene lamps didn't supply much light. That didn't matter since I could cook breakfast in the dark after all the years of having the same menu. There was a half-smoked King Edward on the table. I stopped fussing about how much he smoked about fifty years ago. The drinking was a different matter. I still stayed on him about that and would until my last day on earth. His latest attempt to get by my nagging was to tell me the doctor had told him it was good for his health to have an occasional beer or shot or two of whiskey. I didn't believe the doctor told him that and questioned him. He stumbled and mumbled around until finally getting out something about a slight misunderstanding.

Charlie came into the kitchen and picked up his coffee.

"Somebody must have moved them. I left them right there on the nightstand when I went to bed last night."

I didn't try to argue with him but just gave him a peck on the cheek. I had to bend slightly since he was several inches shorter than me. That had never bothered me since I had loved him dearly for fifty years.

"That's good coffee, Leta. It's cold this morning. I imagine we had a freeze last night. I was hoping we'd have grass for another few weeks. I guess that would have been asking too much."

I put his breakfast on the table. "Just be thankful for what we have."

He paused from buttering his toast. "The last ten years have not been much to write home about."

"Just the same, Charlie, there are a lot of people worse off than we are."

He looked up but went back to eating. He finished his breakfast, got up, and refilled his coffee cup. "I guess you're right, but selling our calves for $6 a hundred doesn't seem like a lot to be grateful for."

He sat back down. "When's the last time you heard from Elliot?"

I always dreaded the question. "It's been a couple of months. I know he's busy."

He frowned and popped his teeth like he always did when upset. "Wouldn't hurt him to write you more often. He's not that busy. You do realize we've never seen our grandkids."

This was not what I wanted to talk about to start our day. "We've been over this many times. This wasn't a life for Elliot, and we always knew that. I just hope he's happy and doing well."

"He's probably eating our cheap beef and never thinking about us." He picked his cigar up from the corner of the table, licked it a couple of times and lit it on the kerosene lamp. "It's getting light. We're driving cattle to another pasture. I might be late coming in for dinner."

After he was gone, I sat down with a refill of coffee. So

many years had passed with so many memories, accompanied by tragedy. He continued to work for various ranchers, and we saved every penny we could. By 1890 we had enough money to make a down payment on 8,000 acres of school land in the county. The price of the land was $1.00 an acre. We were only able to put down $1,000 which left us with a huge debt. Over the next twenty years we were able to pay off the note due to good cattle prices. Once the ranch was paid for, we expected to make a good living, but cattle prices had been poor throughout the 20's, and we struggled.

So much tragedy had occurred in our years here. Our son, Chisum, died suddenly in 1915. He was buried here at the ranch cemetery. Charlie has never gotten over Chisum's death and his resentment of Elliot for leaving. Chisum had never married and loved the ranch. He and his dad were as close as a father and son could be. Our best friend, Pete, who had been with us since New Mexico, died in 1918 from the flu.

We did have blessings. Both Charlie and I had been in good health. Charlie had to get false teeth several years ago when a colt he was breaking bucked him off and knocked out his front teeth. His teeth were bad anyway, so we went to a dentist in Abilene for the procedure. The teeth never fit well, being too loose. Charlie was stubborn and refused to go back to get them fixed.

Our biggest problem was getting help. We had one full-time hand—a boy who was only nineteen. He showed up on our doorstep two years ago and asked for work. He was a good looking boy with black hair and dark skin, causing us to suspect that he had Indian blood. He talked so little that I began to wonder if something was wrong with him. We discovered he was just shy and unsure of himself. He was a hard worker and good with horses. It didn't take me long to realize what a blessing he was. Charlie was always trying to find fault with him but wasn't successful. He stayed in the small house where Pete had lived.

We still had to rely on day workers for marking our calves and roundup. Only one hand limited us to the number of cows we could run. Currently we had 200 mother cows and 93 yearlings we purchased last spring. Charlie still rode but that wasn't going to last much longer. I'd been on him to stop altogether, but he was stubborn. Our ranch most years had good grass and was not rough except for the far western part that held mountains. Charlie could cover a lot of the ranch in his 1924 Model T Ford pickup. I'd been on him to trade it in for the new Model A, but he kept putting it off. I imagine he would drive it until it quit. Charlie was not just thrifty—he was so tight he squeaked when he walked.

I was boiling water to start canning peas that were left over from my garden when there was a knock on the back door. It was Daniel, our hired hand.

"Ma'am, Charlie had an accident. I don't think it's bad, but we need the pickup to bring him to the house."

"What happened?"

"A deer scared his horse, and he took a fall."

On the drive back to Charlie, I rehearsed my 'I told you so speech,' hoping this could actually be a positive event. After all these years, he still wouldn't listen to me, even though I was right most of the time—especially about his riding. I was ready to light into him by the time we arrived, and then I saw him sitting on the ground with his head between his legs. Everything left me except pity for this little man who, when younger, could ride anything. Now he was sitting there—defeated by age.

I went to him and asked softly, "You okay?"

He looked up—dirt covered one side of his face. "My suspenders broke. The doe and fawn were hidden in the grass. They didn't spook until I was right on top of them."

The two dayworkers didn't know what to do and waited for instructions. "Help me get him to the pickup." With one on each side of him and me holding up his pants we got him to the pickup, while Daniel held their horses.

He moaned as we placed him in the seat. "I don't believe

anything's broken. I'm going to be plenty sore for several days. We got the cattle moved and were on our way back when it happened. Aren't you going to give me hell about riding?"

I smiled and reached over to squeeze him on the shoulder. "I love you, Charlie Barlowe. That's all that matters now."

Daniel went with us and rode in the back and led the horses. At the house, he helped me get Charlie to his chair in the living room before he left to take care of the horses.

"Thank goodness we have a telephone. I'm going to call the doctor to come out and see about you."

"Might be a good idea. I have a terrible pain in my left hip and leg."

Surprise! I had expected an argument. He must be hurting badly to be so agreeable. When I tried to call, Millie Shelton was on the phone. We had two other families on a party line. I knew she would talk for a lengthy time, so I went back to keep Charlie company and took him a cup of coffee and two aspirin. He wasn't used to sitting around doing nothing.

He thanked me. Charlie, even after all these years, was polite to me when I did something for him. I knew other husbands who were not that considerate.

He chewed up his aspirins, which I could never do, and sipped his coffee. "I need to face it, Leta. I'm too old to be riding. I could have been killed today and left you alone. Of course, you'd have probably found someone else much younger than me, who was rich and could buy you a new car."

He wasn't hurting so bad he couldn't joke. He was known far and wide for his wit. "Oh, Charlie, you're not so old." Now, here I was taking up for him when I ought to be saying, you should have listened to me.

"You're right. I have a lot to be thankful for. I married you and fifty years later we're still here. I saw things most men will never see. I saw herds of buffalo on the trail drives. John Chisum was like a father to me. I confronted William Bonney who later became Billy the Kid. What an adventure it was to drive cattle from New Mexico with you, my young bride! In 1929, how many men are living who can say these things?"

He paused and finished his coffee. "I miss Chisum. It's been fourteen years, and I still think of him every day and what could have been. This ranch could be so much more if he had lived. And then there's my other son. I made mistakes with him. It's not easy to admit, but I drove him away. For some reason, I stayed angry at him for not being more like his brother. Now he hates me. He didn't understand but why should he—being just a boy? It took me a long time to realize this and even more to admit it. Now it's too late."

"We should never give up, Charlie. We don't know what the future holds." I had never known him to even hint at reconciliation with Elliot. This was a first.

"It makes me sad, Leta, to think what will happen to the ranch after we're gone. I love this place. We worked hard to buy it and have put so much of our life into it. After we're gone, Elliot will sell the ranch—maybe even split it up to get a higher price."

"We just have to live one day at a time, Charlie. You're worrying about things we have no control over. We just need to keep the faith and hope for the best."

"Faith? Leta, I've never gotten over being mad at God for taking Chisum. I don't have much faith in getting help from Him."

I went over and kissed him on the forehead. "I'll try to have enough faith for both of us."

18

A FOOL

Effie

I woke up early and lay there wondering if I could do it. I'd been trying to get up the courage for the past six months. It was going to be the biggest decision of my life.

I had been unhappy for the past several years. The relationship between Elliot had deteriorated to the point it ceased to exist. It began when he left my dad's company. At first I thought it would get better. It would just take time for him to become adjusted to his new position as a holder of a seat on the Dow. It never happened and rather than pay more attention to me and his family, he withdrew even further into his work, occupied with making money.

It hadn't always been this way. The first ten years of our marriage were wonderful. We spent time together as a family, shared good and bad news with one another, and seldom had a disagreement. When he started neglecting me, I tried to talk with him about it, but his response was always the same, "We'll have plenty of time for that later after we have all the money we need."

Elliot was from Texas, which impressed me from the time we first met. I pictured cowboys with big hats like in the films. My dad also liked him, and I had always wanted to please my dad. I was surprised when Elliot refused to even talk about his past and Texas. To this day I knew nothing about his family or what he'd done before coming to New York.

Now, back to my big decision. Eight months ago, in March, I was coming out of a store downtown, carrying an armload of clothes. There had been a sale, and I couldn't stop buying. Just as I stepped outside, the packages slipped out of my grasp and went everywhere. I started gathering them up and realized someone else was helping me. When I stood, this man was holding some of my items.

"Looks like you are kind of overloaded," he said, smiling.

"I-I-tried to carry too much. Thank you."

"No problem. Where are you going with that load?" "To the nearest taxi," I said. "And home."

He looked up and down the street. "There is no taxi in sight. A coffee shop is just around the corner. I'll help you with your packages for a cup of coffee."

I had never seen this man. What should I do? It would be rude to refuse. "I guess so."

"Great." He smiled. "My name's Sidney."

"Effie." I returned the smile.

"That's a very fitting name for a beautiful lady."

That caught me completely off guard. No one had called me beautiful in years. "Thank you," I said. We made it to the coffee shop with my packages and spent over an hour visiting. He was a good listener and seemed interested in what I had to say. I discovered that his wife had died ten years ago during the flu epidemic, and he hadn't remarried. I told him about my family, being sure that he understood I was married. I enjoyed the conversation and the attention, which was a change. He was forty and really nice looking with just a little gray around his dark hair. He had come over from England when he was twenty and stayed.

When he helped carry my packages to a cab, I thanked him and was about to leave when he asked with his charming accent, "Do you come downtown often?"

"At least once a week, usually with friends." The cab was waiting, and drivers were not known for their patience.

He reached and touched my arm. "It was really nice visiting

with you. I have been lonesome since my wife passed. Could you meet me next week at the coffee shop? It will be my treat this time."

I couldn't just stand there, trying to decide. "I don't know."

"If you will make it about noon, maybe we could have lunch."

The cab driver had run out of patience. "Lady, get in, or I'm leaving. I haven't got all day."

"Please," he said.

"Okay," I said. I looked back, and he was waving.

After that we would meet each week at the little coffee shop and leave there to have lunch somewhere or go to the Talkies. At first, I justified it by thinking we were only friends who enjoyed one another's company. That didn't last but a couple of meetings. The first time we went to the theater we held hands—the next time he put his arm around me. After a couple of months, he invited me to go to his apartment. I refused, saying I wasn't ready for that. He was patient and didn't mention it again for several months. I kept putting him off until last week when I agreed. He said he loved me and if I left my husband we would get married. That put me over the edge. Why shouldn't I? Elliot didn't love me—maybe he never did. All he was concerned about was making money.

Sidney made me feel attractive again and good about myself. I was more aware of how I looked and bought nicer clothes. That was one thing about Elliot—he never complained about how much money I spent, which made me think he could care less as long as I was not a part of his life. One of my best features was my short black hair which I kept perfect by visiting a hairdresser each week. I had chosen the Boyish Bob cut which was popular with the younger women. It was perfect for my slender face. I had gained weight before meeting Sidney but now was the same size as when Elliot and I married.

Did I love Sidney? I couldn't say, but I did love the way he treated me. After meeting him I began to feel good about myself. It was already seven o'clock and would take at least an hour to get ready and then another hour for the taxi ride.

That only gave me an hour to waste. I would skip breakfast and bring coffee back to my room. Elliot and I had been sleeping in separate rooms for the past five years. His excuse had been that he stayed up late and rose early and didn't want to disturb me.

Enough of laying here. Back to my original question—could I take a taxi at ten this morning and go to the address Sidney had given me? The answer was 'yes' if I didn't change my mind. It was time for action. I had to decide what to wear today. I went to my closet, looking at my selections. I settled on a little black dress that came just below the knees that Coco Chanel had introduced several years ago. I wasn't going to wear a hat and cover one of my best qualities. I know! I'd wear a headband. Why not? I was a liberated woman. I had a simple black one without the feathers that decorated the ones worn by flappers. I slipped it on and was pleased with the effect.

At nine o'clock my taxi arrived. Amara walked with me to the door. "Ms. Effie, you are gorgeous. Wherever you are going—have a fun time."

When I got in the taxi and handed him the address, he stared at me. I knew I looked good. I asked the driver how long it would take to get to the address.

"It's across town. Probably at least forty-five minutes. Have you been there before?"

"No. This will be my first time." It really wasn't any of his business.

I became more nervous by the minute, unable to sit still. I had avoided seeing Grant this morning. He was so sweet and innocent and here I was about to do something terrible. Did I really believe it was terrible? What if I kept refusing Sidney? Would he have continued to meet me weekly? Almost certainly not. Maybe that was the reason I was on the way to his apartment.

Unlike yesterday, it was beautiful with sunshine and warm

temperatures. We went through some nice neighborhoods with expensive homes. I was anxious to see the apartment where Sidney lived.

The last part of our trip the scenery changed. The buildings were older and rundown. Trash lined the streets and people were sitting outside on the steps of apartments smoking or drinking from bottles that appeared to contain liquor. The driver stopped in front of one of the apartments that was similar to the rest.

He turned around. "Here we are, ma'am. I wasn't trying to be nosey when I asked if you'd been here before. I was surprised when you gave me the address. As you can see, this is not a good neighborhood. I'm not sure it's even safe for you. Are you going to visit someone?"

"Are you sure this is the right address?"

"Yes ma'am. I'm positive. Could it be that you were given the wrong numbers?"

Maybe Sidney had written his address down incorrectly. No! He would know his own address. Should I get out and go into his apartment? I would have to go right by unsavory looking characters. Would it be safe? Why would Sidney live here in this neighborhood? Something was wrong.

The driver waited patiently, which was unusual. "I would recommend that you reconsider, ma'am."

Now what? I couldn't get out and be left here alone. "No. Let's go back downtown." I gave him the address of the coffee shop where we had our regular meetings. Maybe I misunderstood and was to meet him there. I was grasping for some kind of explanation even if it wasn't realistic.

On the ride back I stayed confused. Sidney could not live there in that slum area. The way he dressed, talked, and carried himself didn't make sense. When we stopped in front of the coffee shop, I paid the driver and thanked him.

"I'm sorry it didn't work out. You made the right decision not to stay in that place," he said.

The little shop was busy. I found a seat in a corner and waited. The waitress, who was young and dressed as a flapper with a skirt that came above her knees and a headband with colored feathers, took my order. I had noticed, on my weekly meeting with Sidney, how flirtatious she was with the male customers.

"You meeting your friend today?" she asked when she brought my coffee.

"Maybe. I don't know. There has been some confusion."

She laughed. "That's not a surprise to me."

"What do you mean?" I asked.

"How much do you know about him?"

Why the interest from this girl? "I have been meeting him here for the past several months. He lost his wife during the flu epidemic ten years ago. He's a nice man and has been good company. He's forty years old."

She rolled her eyes. "Honey, you and I need to talk." She left before I could ask her what she meant.

I lost interest in my coffee and watched the girl as she waited on other customers. The crowd thinned out, and she came back and sat down at my table. "You are not the first or the second or the third. He works this area and has for the several years I have been here. You're younger than most and prettier. It is the same with every one of them. Weekly meetings that abruptly end and the woman disappears. And then another one takes her place. I would guess that he is at least ten years older than he told you and lied about his wife. From watching, I would say that he eventually gets money from them after he threatens to tell their husbands. Of course, this doesn't happen until—well—you know what I mean. He's as sleazy as they come. I mind my own business most of the time. But you deserve to know about him. To sum it up—he preys on lonely women. Now I have said enough." She got up and left.

Shocked, I sat there, unable to move. Could that be true? Why would she lie? Could I have been that dumb and naive? I paid my bill and left, unable to think clearly. I walked several blocks until coming to a movie theater. I bought a ticket and went in, sat down in the dark, and cried throughout the show.

19

SURPRISE

Elliot

I was reading the Journal when Effie came home Saturday. I heard the door close and looked up as she came through the living room. She didn't stop or speak and went straight to her bedroom. What was going on? Maybe I should try and find out what her problem was. It might be better for me to let her cool off and talk with her later.

When she didn't come to dinner, I went to her room and knocked. There was no response, and I continued to knock. "Effie, what's going on? Open the door."

"Go away! Leave me alone."

"Are you ill?" I asked.

"No, I'm fine. Just leave me alone."

I decided to wait until tomorrow to try and talk with her. I couldn't imagine what the problem could be. Evidently something occurred which upset her. As far as I knew nothing had happened that was out of the normal. I didn't need this now with everything that was going on in the market.

I left for the exchange Monday morning with more on my mind than the stock price today. Effie was gone yesterday morning when I went down for coffee. Amara said she left early and was going to her parents for a few days and had taken a suitcase with her. I tried to telephone her later in the morning, but her dad said she didn't want to talk to me. He was confused, also. They didn't live that far from us, only about a half hour drive. I decided not to go over, thinking it might be better to give it a few days. I wanted to avoid a confrontation in the presence of her parents.

When I arrived at the Exchange there was an atmosphere of anticipation and concern. The overseas markets had been down again this morning. Trading wouldn't begin for another hour and, hopefully, by then the optimism would take over. For the first time, doubt about my decision surfaced. Maybe I had overdone it Friday by the amount of buying I did on margin. I shouldn't be concerned since I had banked with the Bowery Saving Bank for years, and they had provided the funds for buying on margin. They had always been willing to work with me and been generous with their loans. They also charged some of the lowest interest rates in New York.

The one thing that bothered me somewhat was the amount of money I owed. When I bought my home, I could have paid cash but instead financed it to keep my savings to invest. I did the same on the Rolls, deciding to finance it rather than pay for it outright. The result was that I had substantial payments to make each month. It had not been a problem thus far since my trades had been so profitable. I bought when stocks dropped and sold when they went up. For the past nine years that had been a no-fail strategy. They had always recovered and continued to go up. I had been patient up until last Friday when the temptation to go all in was too great to resist.

At the opening bell, stocks dropped but recovered quickly and traded back and forth throughout the day. It was not a typical day since ordinarily the stocks recovered and continued to rise. By the end of the day the market was down but not by much. I was still confident that my investment would pay off within the week. I had decided to sell as soon as I had some profits and not be greedy.

Effie was still gone when I got home Monday. I was

frustrated with my day on Wall Street, which added to my anger at her just running off and not telling me why she was upset. I decided enough was enough and would go over to her parents'.

I took my car, which always reminded me how successful I was. The big Rolls and smooth ride were enough to make my problems seem less important.

Effie's dad came to the door, invited me in, and said he would tell her I was there. When he came back with her, I was surprised at how she looked. Effie had always been an immaculate dresser, but her appearance was anything but that. Her wrinkled clothes and lack of makeup didn't look like the Effie I had known for over twenty years. After her dad left, she remained silent staring at the floor.

"What's going on, Effie? We need to talk."

She turned and went into an adjoining room. She sat down in one of the chairs instead of on a couch—I assumed, to keep her distance. Before I could say anything, she blurted out, "I want a divorce!" And started crying.

Nothing she could have said would have been more of a surprise. I thought she was satisfied with our separate lives. She'd never said anything to indicate otherwise. I gave her all the money she could spend and never complained. "Why? What happened?" I asked.

She took a deep breath. "You have to ask? Maybe that is the problem. We have no life together. We live in the same house—period—that's our marriage. We sleep in separate rooms, never do anything together, never talk about our problems or dreams, and you must ask—why. What would change if we divorced? Nothing, except we wouldn't live in the same house. Maybe we could live in the same house and not be married. You could give me a weekly allowance, and everything would be the same as it is now. Would that bother you? I can't see how it would. It wouldn't change our relationship. I guess you are happy having your job on Wall Street and making money. I am not happy, and life is passing me by." She began crying again.

Confused, I didn't know what to say. She was so upset—it

probably wouldn't make any difference. "How long have you felt this way?"

She started shaking her head. "Years. You have caused me to do things that make me despise myself. You have no idea because you are so involved in the stock market and getting rich."

"I do it for you and our family. We are about to be fixed for life and move to Florida. That is the reason I work so hard." I spoke softly and tried to sound convincing.

"That is a lie! You never think about our family or me. You are obsessed with Wall Street. You will never have enough money. You like who you are. Don't you see that?"

"What did you mean when you said that I caused you to do things that made you despise yourself?" I asked.

"Never mind. I told you I wanted a divorce. We have no marriage anyway." She got up and left.

"Stop, Effie. We're not finished!" I shouted, but she was gone. I wasn't going to beg her or grovel. She was being unreasonable. Of all times for her to have a nervous breakdown, and that was what it was.

I didn't try to speak with Effie again Tuesday or Wednesday. I decided to give it some time and maybe she would come to her senses and realize what she would give up with a divorce.

The market moved little those two days. I didn't know what to think of that and considered selling some of my stock at a small loss. I decided against it, since for the past nine years it would have been a first to lose money. I was determined to hold out until the market shot up again. On Thursday the 24th, the market went into a free fall. I couldn't believe what was happening. I was determined not to sell and take a loss. By midafternoon, the market began to recover and closed down only six points. It was clear what happened—the value had gotten the attention of buyers. I was relieved and thankful that I didn't sell any of my stock.

The next day the market was stable and moved little. Since it was Friday, I had expected some to panic and sell. When that didn't happen, it proved to me that Monday would be an up day.

I had not seen or heard from Effie since Monday. When I got home Friday, Amara told me Effie had been there and picked up some of her clothes. I didn't know what to do. I thought she would have come back home by now.

When I went to the living room, Amara had put the mail in its usual place on the coffee table. As I went through it, there was a letter for Effie. It didn't have a return address, which was strange. I had never opened her mail, but she wasn't home. I used my small pocketknife to carefully open it so as to be able to reseal it and began reading.

Dear Effie,
I was disappointed that you did not come to my apartment as we had planned. I believed that you loved me. Evidently, I was wrong. I have spent a great deal of time with you the past eight months. It appears that the days with you were wasted. I am demanding that you compensate me for my company during this time, or your husband will be informed of our relationship. Five thousand dollars would be appropriate. You will bring the money to our regular meeting place at ten Saturday morning, November 3. If you choose not to comply with my demand, Elliot Barlowe, your husband, will receive a full accounting of our relationship.

My hand trembled as I placed the letter back in the envelope and sealed it. So that was what this was all about. Effie had been involved with another man for eight months. It was hard to believe. Now it made sense. She blamed me for forcing her into a relationship that caused her to despise herself as she put it. How convenient that she held me responsible. Now what? Should I confront her? Would she pay the blackmail money? Why didn't she go to his apartment? Her not going meant the relationship had not advanced further than scheduled meetings— probably weekly.

More questions, the longer I thought about it. Should I be glad she didn't go to his apartment? Was I jealous? I tried to envision what the man looked like. Was he younger and better looking? I glanced down at my protruding stomach, sucking it in. I had become less concerned about my appearance over the past several years. Effie was still attractive, and it shouldn't surprise me that other men would find her so.

Amara came into the room bringing me back to reality. "Mr. Elliot, I am sorry for disturbing you. Have you seen Nichole lately?"

"No. I've been busy this week and focused on the market." I hadn't even thought of Nichole this week. "Is she home?"

"No, she is staying with a friend this weekend. Leonardo thought I should talk to you. He is worried about her, and I agree. She comes and goes as she pleases and dresses like she's grown."

Another problem. What else could come up to disrupt my life? "I will talk with Nichole. I've always relied on her mother to look after her. Thank you, Amara, for bringing this to my attention."

She hadn't been gone but a few minutes when I heard the familiar slide and knock announcing the approach of Grant. He greeted me with a smile and asked, "Did you talk to the school this week about me being allowed to attend?"

This was the first time I had thought about it. "No, Grant. It has been a hectic week. I'll do it next week—I promise."

"Okay." He turned and left the room, as quickly as he was able.

What was wrong with my family? Why was this happening all at once when I was under such stress?" I got up and moved toward the liquor cabinet.

20

EMPTY PLATES AND FULL BELLIES

Leta

"I don't know, Charlie. I can't tell anything unless I get some pictures of it. It might be just bruised, but again it could be broken. Hips are one of the hardest fractures to diagnose. You shouldn't have even been on a horse at your age."

"Doc, I'm not paying you to give me advice about what I can and can't do. You should know by now that all I'm interested in from you is medical treatment. I don't tell you how to do surgery, do I?"

Dr. Johnson had made a house call to examine Charlie's injury. It was the same every time they were together. They argued constantly about something. Charlie and Dr. Johnson had been friends for over forty years, and each was as bullheaded as the other.

"Whether it's broken or not, Charlie, you're not going to be able to do anything for some time. I know you're not going to want to hear that, but you might as well accept it. I'm going to give you some pain medicine and recommend that you come into my office tomorrow for an x-ray."

"Are you going to charge me for the x-ray if it's not broken?" Charlie asked.

Dr. Johnson looked at him in disgust. "Now, aren't you something, Charlie Barlowe? I can't think of another person who would ask such a dumb question. Of course, I'm going to charge you for the x-ray, no matter what the results."

Dr. Johnson turned toward me. "Leta, you'll need help getting him to town. Do you have someone?"

"Daniel can help me. We'll be in to see you tomorrow, Dr. Johnson."

Charlie interrupted, "I can't afford to lay around the house. We're shipping cattle to Fort Worth this week."

"Leta, would you call me before he starts this venture? I want to come out and watch him get on his horse."

After another exchange or two, which of course, consisted of disagreements, Dr. Johnson left. I gave Charlie one of the pain pills, and he was asleep within a few minutes.

We should have about 270 head to ship—the ninety or so yearlings we had bought in the spring and the calves that had been weaned off the mother cows.

The x-rays revealed that Charlie's hip wasn't broken, but Dr. Johnson recommended that he stay off it for at least a month. This started an argument that lasted so long I left and went back to the waiting room to join Daniel, who had gone with me to help with Charlie.

A few minutes later Charlie came out in a wheelchair being pushed by a nurse, with crutches across his lap. "Let's go, Leta."

I told Daniel to take him outside while I took care of the bill. I gave a check for the five dollars and joined them at the pickup. Charlie asked me how much the bill was after we started home. "It was two dollars for the office visit and three for the x-ray."

"That's robbery. I wasn't in there but half an hour. Doc is going to get rich charging those prices."

I didn't argue with him, changing the subject. "How many rail cars did you get to ship the cattle to Fort Worth?"

"Eleven. That should be plenty."

"That's still going to be about twenty-five a car. They're going to be crowded." He always got as few as possible to save money.

"I haven't missed going with the cattle for the past twenty years. Daniel could go with me to help me get around."

"Charlie, you can't make the trip this year. You're not able. You can't even walk, so just forget it. Besides, I can't do without Daniel."

He was silent the rest of the way home. He looked forward each year to going with our cattle to the Fort Worth Stockyards where they would be sold. He still hadn't admitted that he wasn't going to be able to do anything for the next several weeks.

I called one of the dayworkers last night and told them about Charlie's injury and that they would need to get another day hand to help move the cattle to the railhead in town. It took six to make the seven-mile drive to town. The five day hands, Daniel, and Charlie would have been enough. Of course, Charlie would need to be replaced.

We parked in front of our house and helped Charlie to a chair on our screened-in front porch. He could try out the crutches later. It was a beautiful fall day and from there you could see the half mile to the road. I got some reading material for Charlie and went in to fix dinner. I was going to cook one of Charlie's favorites— fried ham and gravy. I went out back to the smoke house and cut off two large slabs from a ham. After heating a large scoop of lard, the skillet was ready. There was no need to pay attention since I'd probably gone about this task at least a thousand times. The kerosene stove that we had bought two years ago helped also. The kitchen didn't heat up in the summer, and it made it easier and quicker to prepare a meal.

We'd built a small house in 1890 when we bought the ranch. We built a tiny one- room house for Pete at that time. We constructed our current house in 1910, and Pete moved into our old house. After he died in 1918 it had remained vacant. We had offered the house to Daniel when he came to work for us, but he refused, satisfied with the one room house.

Daniel took care of our hogs, We had a pen for them far enough from the house to be away from the smell. We butchered a hog after the weather cooled off in the fall. Usually that was around the middle of November. He also did the milking. I looked after the chickens, which had a pen and roost closer to the house. I let them out during the day, but they went to roost every night. The pen was varmint proof preventing coyotes, fox, coons, and anything else that craved chicken from getting to them.

I was hoping that one day not too long in the future we would have indoor plumbing and not have to rely on the outhouse and chamber pot. Many of our friends in town already had this luxury.

Ranching had been up and down since we moved to Texas. Not only was the market unpredictable but the weather as well. We had a terrible drought in 1901- 1902 and from 1917 until 1919. During those years we sold off most of our cattle and hunkered down until it rained. The years from 1904 until 1910 were prosperous with abundant rainfall and decent cattle prices, meaning good profits. We paid off much of our mortgage on the ranch during those years.

Charlie had grieved over the death of Chisum, our oldest, but I did, also. He didn't realize how much I suffered. When Elliot left it hurt me much worse than it did Charlie. Elliot was my baby, and we had always been close. I was his refuge from his dad and his older brother. I knew he'd leave as soon as he could, but there was nothing I could do. I often dreamed of seeing him again and getting to know my grandchildren, whom I'd never seen. I wrote to him monthly but seldom received word from him. I tried telephoning him but was never able to get through.

Oops, the ham steak was burning. I quickly removed it. It was well done, but Charlie liked it that way. When I went to tell Charlie dinner was ready, he was asleep, slumped over in his chair. Evidently, arguing with Dr. Johnson had worn him out.

I shook him gently on the shoulder. "Charlie, dinner is on the table."

He opened his eyes. "What're we having?"

"I made you a large salad from my garden. If you're going

to get well, you need to eat healthy."

He closed his eyes. "I'm not hungry."

"What if I told you we were having fried ham with red eye gravy?"

His eyes popped open. "Could you hand me my crutches? I need to try them out." He needed help getting up but managed to get to the kitchen.

I was up at four to start breakfast. We were driving our livestock to the rail station in town today. They would be kept in pens, fed and watered tonight and loaded tomorrow. Five hungry men would be here before daylight, and I wanted to be ready for them.

I had a huge coffee pot used for this occasion. I brought in ham and bacon yesterday evening from the smoke house and gathered enough eggs. Biscuits would take the most time. I figured on at least four for each man.

We were fortunate to have dayworkers to help us. Without them, it would be difficult if not impossible for us to make it. Two of our dayworkers were brothers who had always been dependable. Jake and John had been good to us and called Charlie "Uncle Charlie." The big argument between Charlie and me involved their pay. Charlie insisted we didn't need to pay them much since they were like family. This time I wasn't even going to ask him but go ahead and pay them a decent wage. I was not going to allow our dayworkers to do it for less than what other ranchers paid. Sometimes I just had to put my foot down. It would take all day to drive the cattle to town and get them fed and watered. The next day they would be loaded onto the boxcars for their trip to Fort Worth.

At a little after five Jake and John arrived, followed shortly by the two other day hands. Daniel was the last to come in.

Since the table was crowded, I didn't sit down and said the blessing while standing. The men attacked the bacon, ham, scrambled eggs, biscuits, gravy and a jar of molasses like they hadn't eaten in days. Charlie, on the other hand, hardly ate anything. He was telling everyone what to do and wasting his breath. Jake and John had driven our cattle to the railhead for years. I guess, since he wasn't going, he thought it necessary to go over everything in detail.

I finally grew frustrated with listening to him ramble on and on. "Charlie! Let the men eat. They know what they're doing. Eat your breakfast. We'll go to town tomorrow and watch them load onto the rail cars." Now he'd pout for a while but get over it.

By the time breakfast was finished, it was beginning to get light. Everyone thanked me and told me how good it was. That wasn't necessary since there were only two biscuits left, no eggs, an empty gravy bowl, a slice of ham and a coffee pot with maybe half a cup left. I thought there would be leftovers but should have known better. Oh, well, it was nice to be appreciated and what better way than empty plates and full bellies.

"You want me to fry you a couple of eggs to go with those two leftover biscuits?" I asked Charlie, who was still pouting.

"I'm not worth much, Leta. Just old and crippled."

I went over and stood behind him, leaning over and hugging him. "Don't be silly, Charlie, you are still my hero. Now, let me cook you some breakfast and make us another pot of coffee."

"I'm not hungry. I want to go sit on the porch. Join me for a cup of coffee, and we'll talk about a time when we were younger."

The table full of dirty dishes could wait.

21

THE LETTER

Effie

When he handed me the envelope with my name on it, I knew what it contained. Maybe it was better for everything to come out. "It's been opened. You know what's inside?"

"Yes, you have been cheating on me for eight months. I never thought you would do that. It appears that you made a poor choice."

I opened the envelope and read the letter. It was as I had expected—blackmail plain and simple. My first thought was, *now I will not have to make a decision as to whether to pay the $5,000.* Strange, but I was not that concerned about Elliot discovering that I had a relationship with another man.

"Now what?" he asked.

I put the letter in my lap. "I still want a divorce. This does not change anything."

"I have so much going on now, Effie. Could we just put everything on hold until things settle down?"

"You mean the market is giving you concern? So what's new? You put your work ahead of everything. Sure, there's no hurry. I will not move back into the house. After you get your business in order, let me know, and we can finalize the divorce. Then I can move on with my life."

"What about the man who's demanding money?" he asked.

I held up the letter. "I will take this to the police. Hopefully, I will be the last victim of this man who preys on lonely women."

"What about Nichole and Grant? Are you going to put them out of your life, too?"

"Of course not. I'm going to continue to be a part of their lives. But Grant has Sofia, and Amara looks after Nichole. They will get along fine." I was not so sure of this. I was not going to let him put a guilt trip on me.

"Tell me, Elliot, do you feel any responsibility for our marriage ending? I mean, do you consider it all my fault?"

It took him a full minute to answer. "I don't know. This has come about so fast and unexpectedly. I thought I was a good provider and had no idea you were so unhappy. Maybe I should have paid closer attention."

"If you had known of my unhappiness, would you have done anything about it? You have been so engrossed in making money, I doubt it."

"I don't know, Effie. These are questions which I never would have expected. I've not been unhappy with our marriage. It feels like this came out of nowhere. I don't want a divorce. But it seems you are determined and are against trying to work out our problems, which I didn't know existed."

"Let me ask you something, Elliot, and be honest with your answer? What, at this very moment, is the biggest concern in your life?"

He remained silent.

"Just be honest, please," I said.

"Okay, it's the market and what will happen in the next few days. I am all-in— margined to the max. Are you satisfied now?"

"Yes. That settles it." He was still sitting in his chair when I left.

Saturday morning, I went to the police and took the letter with me. I spoke at length with a detective who was polite and attentive. When I explained everything in detail, he told me what needed to be done.

"You are going to need to meet him at the designated place and time. Take an envelope with you that will represent the money. Ask him if he will leave you alone if you give him the $5,000. When he agrees, give him the envelope. We will be close, and after he accepts the envelope, we will arrest him. If we do not go through this exchange, and just arrest him on your word, he will deny sending the letter."

"What if he suspects something?" I asked.

He smiled. "That's not likely. He has probably done this many times and gotten away with it. Most women will pay rather than face the alternative. It is brave of you to help us in putting him out of business."

"Thank you." I didn't tell him that my marriage was over anyway.

I put off going back to my parents after leaving the police station. It was no surprise that my dad took Elliot's side, or it seemed that way to me. He pointed out how well Elliot had done financially, even saying how stressful his job was. He was sympathetic when I told him how Elliot had neglected his children and me, but was careful not to offer any criticism of his son-in-law.

My mother was present but offered nothing, which was not surprising. She always agreed with everything my dad said. My first impression of her from the time I was a little girl was that she was helpless. I had never seen her angry or even disagreeable. My dad made all of the decisions, large or small. I often thought of what would happen to her if she outlived my dad.

I had two younger brothers who were in business with my dad. He did a poor job of hiding his partiality to them. I tried for years to please him, to be praised for something I did, or even be recognized as special. The closest I came to pleasing him was marrying Elliot. Now, that little bit of approval would be gone.

I knew that he and my brothers were involved in the market. When they were together most of their talk revolved around Wall Street rather than Whitlock Iron Works. I guess the stock market has made us all rich, which was supposed to make us happy.

I was going to start looking for a job immediately. I was not going back to work for my dad. I had always been interested in fashion and was going to apply at some of the large department stores, starting with Macy's. Elliot had made his fortune after we married, so I would receive a large settlement in the divorce, but I wanted to stay busy. I wondered if Elliot had even considered having to give half of his worth to me.

I would agree to let him keep Grant and Nichole and retain visiting rights. They would be better off living in the same house with care provided by Amara and Sofia. Would I marry again? It was not likely. I wanted to keep my independence and not be disappointed again.

I decided to go back home—or what used to be home—since Elliot would be at the club all day. When I arrived, the garage door was open and the Rolls was gone, which meant I was right. I needed to talk with Amara and tell her the situation and my plans. Also, it would be a good time to visit with Nichole and Grant.

It was almost noon, and Amara was in the kitchen preparing lunch. I asked her if we could talk. "Sure. Lunch is in the oven and needs another twenty minutes."

"Has Elliot said anything to you about our situation?" I asked.

"No. I suspected you were having problems."

"We are getting a divorce. It will not affect you and your family. I want you to continue to look after Nichole and for Sofia to take care of Grant. I will be visiting them often."

"Do they know?" Amara asked.

"No. I plan on talking to them today."

"Nichole is not here. She did not stay here last night. I do not know where she is," Amara said. "She comes and goes as she pleases. It is not my place to make rules for her."

Surprised at her tone, which conveyed rudeness, I didn't know what to say. "I'll talk to her and remind her she is only sixteen."

"When my girls were Nichole's age, they had rules and Leonardo was there to help me. We had few problems."

The last thing I needed was a lecture from a servant. "Well, Elliot is not Leonardo, and we have a different situation." This was getting nowhere. "Where is Grant?"

"He and Sofia have gone to the park. It is a nice day. He is a sweet boy. He wants to go to school and is sad that he cannot."

"Do you know when they will return?" I asked.

"They just left before you came. Maybe two hours."

I wasn't going to sit around here for two hours. "I will come back tomorrow or Monday." I left, glad to get away from Amara's insinuations.

I woke up Sunday morning to someone beating on my door. "Effie, you have a phone call. It's Elliot, and he said it was important." I stumbled out of bed, put on my housecoat, and made it to the telephone, thinking all the time, *Elliot is going to apologize and ask me to come home.* "Hello."

"Effie, the police called. They need us down at the station."

"What do you mean? What do they want us for? I've already talked to a detective about the blackmail letter."

"It has nothing to do with that. They have Nichole and some of her friends. They insisted that we both come," he said.

"This is crazy. What time is it, anyway?"

"A few minutes after five. Either get a taxi or have your dad bring you."

"What is Nichole doing at the police station?" I asked, becoming more irritated by the second.

"Effie! Our daughter is in some kind of trouble. Are you coming or not?"

"Okay. I'll get there as soon as possible," I said, hanging up the phone.

Evidently, my dad had been listening. "I can take you, Effie. It could be a long wait for a taxi."

I dressed in the clothes I had worn yesterday and took no time for makeup. We left soon after Elliot called. Traffic was light and we were at the police station within a short time. Elliot met me in the hallway. "What is it, Elliot?"

"Come with me," he said.

We went through a door into a larger room, which held several uniformed officers and fifteen or twenty men and women. I looked for Nichole but didn't see her. I started back the opposite direction and saw several women standing off to themselves. I gasped. It couldn't be! It was! One of the women was Nichole. She looked like a cheap—a cheap flapper. Her dress was well above the knee, a headband included feathers that resemble an Indian in one of the films and she had on enough makeup for three women.

I marched over to her and met the stench of liquor several steps before arriving. "What are you doing here, Nichole?"

She shrugged as if she didn't know and looked off in another direction. "I asked you a question, Nichole. You answer your mother!"

She remained silent and stared at the wall.

Before I tried again, a uniformed officer came up to us. He gestured toward the crowd. "Ma'am, we raided a speakeasy not far from here tonight and arrested these people. This young lady had no identification, and we figured she was underaged. It took some time, but we finally got her home telephone number and parents' name. The judge will be here shortly and decide what to do with your daughter."

An hour later our Nichole was released to us after a tongue thrashing that not only included Nichole but Elliot and me as well. I left the building feeling about as low as I had ever felt. Outside, I tried to talk with Nichole again but received the same response—silence.

"I'll talk with her when we get home," Elliot said. "I can call you later today if I get to the bottom of this."

On the ride back with my dad, questions came at me from all directions. What kind of mother was I? Had this been going on for some time or was this just a one-time incident? Why hadn't I seen it? Elliot was just as much to blame as me—maybe more.

22

PANIC

Elliot

Nichole hadn't said a word since leaving the police station. "What were you doing in that terrible place?"

It took so long for her to answer I thought she was going to clam up on me just as she did her mother. "Having fun with my friends. The three of us like to go out on Saturday night."

"That is no place for a sixteen-year-old or, for that matter, anyone. Have you been there before or was this the first time?"

"Several times," she said. "It's exciting."

"Are you not ashamed of yourself for being arrested? Does it bother you that it frightened your mother and me?"

"That's a lie. You and mother could care less. Amara may have worried but not you and mother." She didn't sound angry, only stating it as a fact.

"Your mother and I do love you, Nichole."

"Another lie. You only care about your life. You seldom talk to me, and Mother never does. I might as well be a piece of furniture. It is the same with Grant."

I didn't know what to say. It was no use arguing. What was alarming was that she was so matter-of-fact about it—like there was no doubt. Nothing else was said and when we got home, she went to her room.

I wish she had cried and been angry, so we could have had a big argument. I had so much going on now that I decided to bury it in the back of my mind. Tomorrow was Monday, a day that could make me richer than ever imagined or. . .

I arrived early, anxious to see what the overseas markets were doing. I was disappointed to find that they were down. It wasn't by much and maybe they would recover. I talked with several other guys, who were optimistic. All were of the opinion that if the market dropped by a lot, buyers would take advantage and put more money into it, causing stocks to recover. That was what happened last Thursday.

My stomach was in knots at the opening bell. The market was down and kept dropping. Trading was heavy—way above average. Should I sell and take a loss, or would it recover like it did last week? At any minute, I would start receiving margin calls. Surely, with all these bargains, buyers would start buying—reversing the slide. It had always happened that way. By noon I received my first margin call on stocks that I bought with only ten percent down. I had purchased stock that cost $100,000 for only $10,000, borrowing the rest. I lost the $10,000 plus another $10,000 because they were dropping so fast, and there were no buyers. It went from bad to worse with one margin call after another. A dozen times I started to sell everything while I still had a substantial amount of money. I couldn't make myself take that much of a loss, which took nine years of careful investing to make.

By two o'clock, I became angry, cursing the politicians and bankers who were to blame. An hour later I started praying that the market would recover before the close. "Please, God, let the stocks go up. I promise to give you ten percent of everything if you'll just save my money." My prayers were not answered, and the market continued its downward spiral until the closing bell.

I calculated my losses for the day before leaving the floor. I stopped in the men's room on the way out and threw up.

When I got home the liquor cabinet was my first stop. I

had just sat down with my drink when Grant appeared. I just wanted to be left alone.

"Hi, Dad. Did you have a chance to talk to the school?"

"No! I didn't have time, Grant. Now stop nagging me about that. I've had a terrible day. Just leave me alone."

"But you promised," he said.

"Did you hear me? I want to be left alone!"

I didn't watch him leave but heard the slide and thump of his cane. I drank and thought for the next several hours. Why did I invest so much on margin last Thursday? I already had made a fortune and could have sold and gotten out of the market—fixed for life. It was simple—I wanted more. It looked like a once in a lifetime opportunity. I was going to double or maybe even triple my investment. Why didn't I buy government bonds with my cash instead of keeping it for investments? I kept reinvesting my profits for the past nine years, not even using some of it to pay off the house and car. I kept an account for living expenses, which included payments, essentials, and salaries for Leonardo and his family. Now, half of my fortune was lost in one day. The market had to recover tomorrow.

When Amara came in and told me dinner was ready, I told her I wasn't hungry and continued to drink until around midnight.

I woke up the next morning to someone gently shaking my arm. "Mr. Barlowe, breakfast is on the table." It was Leonardo.

"Just coffee," I said, closing my eyes, hoping to ease my headache.

He came back a few minutes later with a cup of coffee. I thanked him and asked what time it was.

"Seven-thirty, Mr. Barlowe," he said, as he left.

I wanted to get to work and check the Asian markets. My clothes were wrinkled, and I needed to shave but that could wait. The bottle of Canadian whiskey sitting on the stand next to my chair was almost empty. It was no wonder my head hurt.

I called a taxi and left the house without changing clothes. On the way to Wall Street, I felt better—full of hope for what the day would bring. Surely, with the price of blue-chip stocks at such a bargain, buyers would see the opportunity. When I arrived on the floor of the exchange, my hopes sank. The overseas markets were down.

With the opening bell, stocks plummeted on big volume. Where were the buyers? I kept waiting for an upturn, but it didn't happen. I heard moans and cursing all around me. I broke out in a cold sweat and could feel my heart pounding. I began to cry just before there was a tightening in my chest and a feeling as if someone was sitting on me. The last thing I remember—was falling.

When I could focus everything was white—the ceiling, the walls, the woman's dress standing by me, and the sheet that covered me.

"You are awake. How do you feel?" asked the woman.

"Tired and weak," I managed to whisper.

"Do you know where you are?"

"No," I said.

"You are in room 414 of the New York Presbyterian Hospital—the cardiac ward. You were transported here yesterday after suffering a heart attack. The doctor gave you some sedatives to keep you quiet until more tests could be done. You have not been allowed visitors but that can change now since you're awake. Would you like some water?"

"Yes. Dry."

She gave me a glass of water and propped me up with a pillow. I drank most of it. "What day is it?"

"Wednesday, October thirtieth."

Everything was becoming clear, now. The market's freefall, my agitation, the heavy feeling in my chest. "How did I get here?"

"Ambulance. I will tell the doctor that you are awake."

After she left, I tried to sit up, but the room started spinning. I had a heart attack—impossible. I wasn't even forty.

Was I going to die? I was too young to die, or was I? I had known men who died at my age and even younger.

Who were the visitors? Did Effie come to see me? Probably not. More than likely it was Leonardo and Amara. The market—what happened after I was brought to the hospital? Maybe it recovered, and I'll have enough to start again if I live.

The doctor came in and introduced himself as Dr. Olfert. "How do you feel?"

"Weak and tired," I repeated.

He moved the stethoscope across my chest then wrapped a cuff around my arm and took my blood pressure. "You had a heart attack. We will not know for a while how much damage was done. You need rest for the time being. After a week or ten days we will do a step test, so we can determine how strong your heart is. We do have some new medicine to strengthen the heart. Generally, if you go forty-eight hours without additional problems, it is a good sign. Do you have any questions?"

"No. I guess not. Oh, I do have a question but not about my health. Do you know how the market ended yesterday?"

"The last two days were a record drop in the market. I was invested but sold at the end of last month. There was too much optimism. People were investing, who had no business in the market. Everybody was making money, and there was no end in sight. So much investment was on margin. The signs were all around, but no one was willing to look at the facts. I was glad I sold in September. It is not going to get any better either."

"I don't understand. When the market went down last Thursday it recovered by the end of the day and was stable on Friday. Why hasn't it recovered this time?" I asked.

I could see and hear the impatience. "Do you not know that the market recovered last Thursday because the big banks stepped in. They propped the market up by bidding more than the asking price and buying large numbers of shares. They have loaned out so much money for margin they need the market to remain high. People that invest in the market should be aware of the manipulation involved."

The doctor left after the lecture, leaving me feeling like a fool. I couldn't stay in the hospital. I had to get back to the exchange and see what was left of my portfolio. I tried to sit up but fell back, too weak to get out of bed. Exhausted, I went back to sleep.

I woke up and realized someone was standing by my bed. It was Ben Whitlock, Effie's dad. "How are you feeling, Elliot?"

"Tired and weak," I said again.

"We were worried about you. Effie is waiting outside. She didn't know if you would want to see her," he said.

"I would like to see her. Do you know anything about my portfolio? I'm too weak to get to the exchange."

"Elliot, I assume you are in a similar situation as my sons and me. We lost virtually everything. We still have some investments that were not bought on margin, but they are down twenty-five percent in the last two days. The stock we bought on margin killed us. If we had just stayed away from margin, we might have survived. We're going to hang in there and hope the market recovers."

"I don't know what to do, Ben. I can't get to the exchange."

"Would you like for my broker to take over your account?" he asked.

"Yeah. I do have some investments that were not bought on margin. Maybe if the market recovers, I can start over."

"Okay. I'll tell Effie you want to see her."

He left and Effie came in. It was the first time in years I realized how beautiful she was. "Thank you for coming, Effie."

"What happened, Elliot?"

"I had a heart attack. Probably brought on by stress. I've lost a lot of money, Effie. I don't know how much. The market crashed. Your dad has lost, also."

"You should be worried about yourself and not money," she said.

"What about the house, the car, the servants, the kids? What will happen if I'm broke and cannot support my family?"

"It's still about money, isn't it, Elliot? Here you are—maybe on your death bed— and you are worried about money. I feel sorry for you. We will make it whether you live or die. Money is not the answer to everything." She left.

I did not need that from my wife. Maybe I was a failure as a husband and father, but I had given them a huge house with electricity and plumbing plus servants to wait on them. That should count for something. I went to sleep, thinking everything and everyone was against me.

23

SHIPPING

Leta

Charlie decided that Daniel should go to Fort Worth with the cattle. It wasn't that he had that much faith in Daniel, but he was worried about not having someone with them to see that they were fed, watered, and looked after. Charlie didn't have a lot of trust in other people and was always imagining that someone was out to cheat him. I imagine that this was the largest town Daniel had ever visited. Knowing so little about him, I couldn't say that for sure. We had questioned Daniel about his past but received only one-or two-word responses that yielded little. He was from Oklahoma and had been gone from home for three years. We didn't know whether he could read and write. Charlie always paid him in cash, which wasn't enough in my opinion. Charlie argued that twenty-five dollars a month plus room and board was a "God's plenty," one of his most used sayings. Charlie liked to include the Lord when he wanted to sound convincing.

Charlie was convinced Daniel was at least half-Indian based on his riding and his way with horses. He was dark with high cheekbones and, coming from Oklahoma, Charlie was probably right. His black hair was long, coming to his shoulders. Regardless, he was a hard worker and a good boy. I just wished he was friendlier and we could get to know him better. He rarely ate with us but would take his meals back to his house. I constantly reminded Charlie that we couldn't do without him, and we should pay him more.

"I don't know why we have to buy him clothes, Leta. He gets a monthly salary. You act like we're rich, giving money away like you do."

We were on the way to town to watch the cattle load. I was driving since it was all Charlie could do to get into the pickup. Most women didn't drive, but I had from the time we bought a pickup. "Charlie, there's no use arguing with me. Daniel's going to Fort Worth, and he needs a new pair of pants and a nice shirt. He's so thin it will be hard to fit him. I'm going with him to see that he gets something nice."

We were at the railhead before they began loading. Daniel had taken a bedroll and stayed with the cattle. He met us as we drove up to the pens. Charlie rolled down his window. "Is everything all right?"

"Yeah."

"Have they been fed and watered this morning? I don't want them losing weight on the train ride."

"Yeah."

"Have you had anything to eat this morning?" Charlie asked.

"No."

I had expected this and made him two bacon and egg sandwiches. Charlie gave him the sack containing his breakfast.

"Thanks," he said, taking his sack and walking away.

"I wish he wouldn't talk so much," Charlie said, chuckling.

John and Jake arrived a short time later and began loading the cattle. They were driven from the pens into an alley leading to a cattle car and loaded. After one car was full, another was loaded.

With only three of the eleven rail cars left, I summoned Daniel over and told him to go with me. Charlie was leaning up against the fence counting the cattle as they went up the ramp. I drove us to one of the dry goods stores I was partial to and told Daniel we were going to get him some new clothes. He said nothing and showed no sign of approval or disapproval.

The weather was apt to be cool, so I picked out a flannel shirt a size too large since it would probably draw up when washed. I chose a pair of size 28 Levis. "You need to go in there," I said, pointing to a small closet used to try on clothes. "Put these on and let me see how you look."

He came out a few minutes later with the red shirt and pants on. There was a full-length mirror on the closet door. I pointed to it. "Look at yourself."

After standing in front of the mirror for at least a minute he turned and smiled. "Thank you very much. It is the prettiest clothes I have ever had."

I had to take a deep breath to hold back the tears. "You're a handsome young man, Daniel. Now, go put your old clothes back on, and you can take those with you to Fort Worth."

When he returned, I took his new clothes to the checkout stand. The clerk wrapped them in brown paper and tied them with a string. "We have a good sale on our boots, also."

We left the store with Daniel wearing a new pair of boots that needed breaking in and carrying the package holding his Levis and shirt. I was surprised to see the knife in his old boots that he transferred to his new pair. He was wearing his old hat, but the clothes and boots were going to require enough explaining to Scrooge. The bill came to $11.35, which I didn't think was that bad for what we got. When we returned to the rail cars, they were just finishing the last load.

Charlie crutched over and met us. He started in on Daniel at once. "You see that our cattle get hay and water when they're unloaded. Make sure they're all put in the same pen. Count them again and make sure there are 268 head. You stay with them tonight and don't go wandering around the stockyards. Your job is to take care of our cattle."

I listened as long as I could. "Charlie, that's enough instructions. He'll be fine." Since I stopped the instructions,

Charlie noticed Daniel's new boots. He started popping his teeth. "Looks like you got some boots." He looked at me. "How much did they cost?"

I might as well end this before he got started. "They were six dollars and worth every penny. His old boots had holes in the soles. I wasn't going to let him go to Fort Worth wearing those. I also bought him a new shirt and a pair of Levis. Before you ask how much—the bill was $11.35." I gave Charlie my sternest look. "And I don't want to hear any more about it."

Charlie took a cigar out of his shirt pocket, stuck it in his mouth and hobbled off. I asked Daniel if he'd brought some money for the trip. "Yeah, ten dollars."

"That should be plenty. Now, you won't be able to come back on the train until day after tomorrow. After the cattle sell tomorrow, you get a room and don't sleep outside on the ground. You should get back here about noon. We'll be waiting on you."

He thanked me again for the clothes. I watched him until he was out of sight, and mumbled a prayer, "Please look after him, God."

Before we left, I gave John and Jake a check for seven dollars each. I also gave them a check for $12 to be split between the day hands. On the drive home, Charlie had already gotten over being upset about me buying Daniel an outfit. That was the thing about Charlie—he didn't stay mad for very long.

"Leta, do you think they'll bring $5,000? That's what I'm hoping for. We can make it on that and have some left over."

It was cool but the cigar smoke forced me to roll my window down. "I have no idea, Charlie. We should be thankful we had the rainfall to take care of that many cows and stockers."

"I worry about Daniel bringing the check back. He might decide to run off. After all that would be a fortune for him."

"That is ridiculous! Daniel is a good boy and would never do anything like that," I said.

"How can you be so sure, Leta? I know he has a lot of Indian blood. We've treated them pretty bad, and he might feel we owe him something."

I rolled the window all the way down before choking on the smoke. "Just trust me. That will not happen. Daniel will get back with our money."

I was glad to get home before he came up with something else to worry about.

After I got Charlie in the house, the first thing I had to do was slop the hogs, since Daniel wasn't here. I would have to milk in the morning, too. I changed into my overalls which weren't that becoming, but I wasn't dressing for fashion.

I took a five-gallon can of maize that was in a small storage shed and had been soaking since yesterday. It was heavy, but I managed to get it over to the hog shed. The pen held a sow and a couple of hogs that weighed about 250 pounds, which had been selected and weaned out of a litter in the early spring. We had sold the rest of the litter when they weighed around 100 pounds. The sow was bred back to a neighbor's boar. We would give him one of the hogs to butcher as the breeding fee. It hadn't turned off cold enough yet to butcher.

It was a little early, but I went ahead and fed the chickens. They would return to the coop before dark. There was no use trying to drive them into the coop. You didn't herd chickens. They went where and when they wanted. We only had eight layers; however, they provided all the eggs we needed. We kept about thirty broilers in another pen. I was never good at wringing a chicken's neck to kill it. Our neighbor was an expert at that. She was a big, strong woman and her arm was just a blur as she twirled that chicken around. It would only take about three rotations until the head came off. Sunday dinner was usually fried chicken, one of Charlie's favorites.

A norther blew in last night, and it was cold. I built a fire in the living room fireplace and lit my oven to warm the kitchen. I took Charlie his coffee to the living room where he was sitting in front of the fire.

"How cold is it?" he asked.

"I'll check the thermometer on the back porch." I came back later and told him it was thirty degrees but seemed colder with the north wind.

"It'll be cold in Fort Worth, too. I bet Daniel didn't stay with the cattle. He probably slept in a warm room on a feather bed."

"I wouldn't blame him one bit if he did. That would show he had good sense."

We stayed close to the fire all morning. Just before noon the phone rang. When I answered, it was the sheriff wanting to talk to Charlie. It took several minutes for him to get to the phone. I went back to the kitchen to start dinner but was interrupted by Charlie's response to the sheriff.

"I knew something like this would happen. Damn it all to hell! I should have gone with him. Is that all the information you have?"

I'd about broken Charlie of cursing, but it had taken some doing. Something bad must have happened to set him off. When they hung up, I went back to the living room.

"Well, it's happened, Leta. The sheriff got a call this morning from the police in Fort Worth, and they've got Daniel in jail. The police didn't say why he was arrested, just that they were holding him. He probably got drunk and caused trouble. Most Indians are drunks if they can get hold of liquor. I should have gone with him. I knew it." All the time he was talking, he was hobbling around the room like a caged animal.

"Just settle down, Charlie. We don't know the details. The problem now is to decide what to do. Did the sheriff say he would get back to you?"

"Yeah. When he found out something."

"All we can do is wait. It doesn't do any good to worry. You're not in any shape to make a 150-mile trip to Fort Worth."

"What about the money? He may have lost it gambling, got in a fight, and was arrested. Without the money from the cattle, we could be in a world of hurt."

"Charlie, for crying out loud, stop imagining all those outlandish things. Now get over here and sit down while I cook dinner."

When I left, he was still circling the room.

24

BAD NEWS

Effie

I left the hospital frustrated and angry. I expected Elliot to be frightened and humbled by his condition. Instead, he was the same person—worried about money. I went from the hospital to Macy's and filled out an application for a job. The lady was positive, saying that with the holiday season coming they usually hired more people.

Now, with Elliot in the hospital, the problem was going to be paying the bills and salaries for our servants. He took care of all of that. He even gave Amara the money for groceries. When it came to money, he was in control.

It was only three days until I would take the envelope to Sidney. In a way I was looking forward to it but at the same time embarrassed. I had tried to put the entire episode out of my mind. I kept asking myself how I could do such a stupid thing. I decided to go back home since Elliot would be in the hospital for an indefinite time. I was more comfortable there and wouldn't have to listen to my dad extol Elliot's virtues. The last couple of days my dad had been unusually quiet and stayed to himself. I assumed it had to do with the stock market. My mother was gone most of the day—where she went was a mystery. To be honest with myself, I missed my house and the servants.

I went directly home from Macy's and received a warm

welcome from Amara. It could have been because of her next comment. "Mrs. Barlowe, today is the thirtieth, the last day of the month. We usually receive our pay at this time."

I should have expected this problem. "I need to go to the bank and withdraw some cash to pay you."

I waited in line at the teller's window. When it came my turn, I asked for a withdrawal from Elliot's account. He left and came back shortly. "I am sorry, Mrs. Barlowe, your name is not on the account."

I was furious. "You mean, I cannot get money out of my husband's account?"

"Yes, I am afraid that's what it means."

"Who else can I speak with?"

He pointed to an office that joined the lobby. "That man is a bank officer. He might be able to help you."

After a half-hour wait, which did nothing to improve my mood, I was invited in to express my complaint to a man sitting behind a huge desk, smoking a pipe.

"How can I help you?" he asked.

I explained my situation beginning with Elliot being in the hospital and concluding with the need for cash to run the household. "I need to pay the servants today."

He lit his pipe, blew smoke, and looked serious before removing it. "You do understand our position, Mrs. Barlowe? Your husband did not include your name on the account. To allow you access to his account would violate our policy." He examined his pipe before laying it down on his desk.

I would not have been surprised if he saw smoke coming out of my ears. "Well, sir, what must I do to gain access to my husband's money?"

"You would need to present me with a letter signed by Mr. Barlowe asking that your name be put on his account."

I was literally shaking with anger. I closed my eyes for a few seconds for calm, said thank you, and left. Within a few minutes, I was on my way to the hospital, muttering to myself. "It will not do any good to yell or scream. Just stay in control and tell him what you need. Keep your emotions under control."

I stopped outside his door and knocked before entering. I saw that he was asleep and sat down in one of the two chairs available. I studied him and saw the man he used to be—relaxed and handsome. Did success and money turn him into what he was now? Almost certainly. What else could it have been? Did I still love him? I whispered the answer. "Not the man he has become." He stirred, and I moved to the bed beside him and gently shook his arm.

He opened his eyes. "Effie."

"Wake up, Elliot. We need to talk."

"Could you get me a glass of water and help me sit up?"

I poured a glass of water from a pitcher and put a pillow behind him. He was able to get up enough to drink. He gave me the glass. "What is it?"

"We need to pay Leonardo and Amara. The bank will not let me have the money. My name is not on your account. I also need expense money for this month."

It took a few seconds for him to understand. "Sorry. I should have already done that."

"The bank officer said I needed a letter signed by you. I brought paper and pencil."

He closed his eyes, and I thought he had gone back to sleep. "Write a note. I'll sign it."

I wrote a couple of sentences directing the bank to put Effie Barlowe on the account and Elliot signed it. "I'm sorry," he repeated.

My anger vanished. He was weak and helpless, and the reality that he might die hit me. "Do you feel any better, Elliot?"

"No. I'm exhausted from signing my name. Have you seen Grant and Nichole?"

"No. But I'm going back home to stay, at least until you get out of the hospital."

"Good." He closed his eyes and this time he was asleep.

There was a fleeting temptation to kiss him but, instead, I left quietly.

I had instructed the taxi to wait on me and within the hour was sitting across from the bank officer. I presented him the note. He frowned and said, "I'll put this with Mr. Barlowe's account information." He left and was gone longer than it took to perform the simple task he mentioned.

When he returned, he was carrying a folder. Before he said a word, he filled his pipe, lit it, and blew a cloud of smoke. "There is a problem, Mrs. Barlowe. Your husband's account is depleted. The balance is zero. In fact, he owes the bank a substantial amount of money."

"There must be a mistake. He keeps enough money in his account to meet monthly expenses."

Another cloud of smoke. "Are you aware of your husband's stock investments?"

"No, not really. I know he has a seat on the stock exchange and has done very well with his investments."

"That was true until recently. A couple of weeks ago your husband made an unusual move. He doubled and maybe even tripled his stock holdings on margin, borrowing money from the bank. He had always been a solid and wise investor, and we loaned him the money. It was a big mistake for us to allow him to buy that amount of stock on margin. The last two days his losses have been tremendous. Are you familiar with margin?"

"No, I've heard him and my dad talk about it, but I don't understand it."

"Mr. Barlowe only had to put up a small percentage of the stock to buy it, borrowing the rest from the bank. That is called buying on margin. It allows one to invest a great deal more money than they have and increase their profits. The negative side is one can lose a great deal more money than they have. Mr. Barlowe's stock went down quickly and drastically, forcing the selling of his stock that was bought with borrowed money. To sum up the problem—it was necessary to sell all your husband's stock to recover our losses. It still was not enough, and he now owes the bank a great deal of money. We are carrying the note on his house and car. He has some equity in those that will be used to pay off his debt to the bank."

I sat in stunned silence and listened to this man, who seemed more concerned about his pipe than telling me we did not have any money. I got up and left, not saying anything. I knew it would do no good to tell Elliot. He was not capable of anything now. Maybe my dad would have some advice or some answers for our problem.

My dad was in his office at his business with the door closed when I arrived. The secretary said he had given orders not to be disturbed.

"Do you think that includes his daughter?" I asked.

She looked confused. "I will ask him." She went to his door and knocked. After a few seconds she motioned for me.

My two brothers were with him and, from their looks, were involved in a serious discussion. My dad didn't invite me to join them. "Dad, I need to talk with you. It is important."

"Could it wait? We're busy," he said.

"No! It can't wait. We have no money in our bank account. From what the bank officer told me, we are broke!"

My dad looked at my brothers and back at me. "We were just discussing our financial situation. It is not much better. We are trying to figure out how to save the company. The last ten days of the market's performance has ruined us. If we had just not bought so much on margin. But hindsight does not matter now. I don't have any advice to give you, Effie. We are all just going to have to try and survive."

"What should I do? Elliot is not able to deal with anything in his condition. I can't pay our servants or the bills. I have a few dollars that would buy groceries, and that's all."

"I wish I could help, but it is impossible. It is going to take every dime I can raise to save the company."

I looked at my brothers, who wouldn't meet my gaze. I got up and left, not knowing what else to say.

I thought all the way home how to address Leonardo and Amara. There was only one thing to do—be honest. It was fortunate that both were home when I arrived.

We met in the living room, and I went right to the point, telling them of our situation and that it was not possible to pay them. I saw the fear in their eyes as they absorbed the information. After all, they had been with us since arriving in the country.

"Is there no hope?" asked Amara.

"I have not told Elliot. He is not in any condition to receive the news. I doubt if he can do anything about our situation. The bank gave no sign that they would work with us. You are welcome to stay here as long as we have the house. I will continue to give you board as long as possible. I will do everything I can to find you another family. You have been wonderful, and I appreciate everything you have done for us."

"Grant is going to be devastated to lose Sofia," Amara said.

"We have a little money saved and can help with the groceries," Leonardo said.

There was nothing else to do, and I went to my room and lay down across the bed. Everything had happened so fast, it was the first time I had time to actually think about our situation. From the time I can remember, I never wanted for anything. Now we were in a totally different world. I said *we* and *our* rather than *I* or *me*. Did that mean the divorce was off? "Of course," I muttered, at least for now. My reaction to this entire day was a surprise. I was not angry or going around wringing my hands and crying. I had not shed a tear. I was frightened but not as much as I should have been. For the first time in ages, I said a prayer. "God, help me to be strong."

A representative from Macy's called me the next morning and offered me a job in the women's clothing department and asked if I could come to work immediately.

A BIG DECISION

Elliot

Effie didn't tell me about her bank visit until three days later. My reaction was to wish I had died and didn't have to face the humiliation of losing everything. I would have taken my life if I'd had a way. I stopped eating and hoped that would do it. I refused to eat or take my medicine for two days and ignored Effie's, the doctor's, and nurse's pleadings and threats. The third day Effie brought Grant to the hospital for the first time. He was aware of my intentions and with tears said he needed me and not to die. I could not resist his appeal and started taking my medicine and eating again.

My last conversation with the doctor was anything but encouraging. He was not sure how much damage had been done to my heart. His advice was to not become excited or worry and not do anything that was strenuous. He was positive about my weight loss and encouraged me to keep it off. I had lost from 185 down to 165 while in the hospital. I was still weak and became tired at the slightest exertion.

The shocking surprise was Effie. She had come to visit me every day after she got off work at Macy's. She seemed happy, which was confusing. She was making $20 a week which was enough to buy groceries and pay some bills. She had heard nothing else from the bank. That would probably come when we failed to make the car and house payment.

Nichole had been to see me once and only stayed a few minutes. It was clear that she wasn't happy. Leonardo and his family had already found another position just down the block from us. It wasn't surprising since they had become well known in the neighborhood. The result of their leaving was that Nichole had to miss school and stay home with Grant.

I had no idea what we were going to do. We faced eviction in the future and, with me unable to work, would have to depend on Effie's salary. Her dad had already made it clear that he could not help us.

Effie checked me out of the hospital on Saturday, November 16, sixteen days after I entered. The bill was $467. Effie gave them a check for $10 and set up a payment plan of $9.52 a month for four years.

I left the office in a wheelchair, too weak for the walk to a waiting taxi, pushed by my wife who three weeks earlier had been demanding a divorce.

After two weeks at home, I was able to get around the house and even take short walks in the afternoon if the weather allowed. On Friday, November 19, one month after my heart attack, I took a taxi to the bank. For the previous two days I had worked on a presentation to the bank officer for a loan. At the bank, I rested outside his office until I was able to talk with confidence and strength.

I didn't know the man sitting behind the desk. I introduced myself, sat down, and started my presentation that was leading up to asking for a loan. He held up his hand, stopping me. "We are not making any loans. We have already had an alarming number of depositors withdraw their money. After the stock market's behavior there is a feeling of panic. If we have a run on our bank, we need all the capital available."

"If I could just get a few thousand dollars. I have been a good customer of your bank for almost ten years . . ."

Again, the hand came up. "I am sorry, but we are not

making any loans— period."

I left but had to stop and rest on the way out because of the tightening in my chest. Was I having another heart attack? I had some pills that the doctor told me to always have with me. I took one of them and felt better within a few minutes. What kind of life was this going to be—hurting every time I was upset or did too much? I wished again I would have died.

On Friday, December 20, the bank sent someone to get the Rolls. I had missed the November and December payment. I knew that the house would be next. We could do without the car, but the house was another matter.

The next evening the news was even worse when Effie came home. She had been let go since the Christmas buying was almost over. It was a cold miserable day. We huddled in front of the fireplace and sat in silence for the longest—neither knowing what to say.

"What are we going to do, Effie?" I asked. "I can't work. Not even a desk job. We are not going to have a place to live. Your dad is not in much better shape than we are. How much money do we have?"

"Counting what I was paid today, a little over ninety dollars. There is no use waiting for them to take the house. We know that is coming. You had a life before coming to New York. I know it was in Texas. I think it's time you told me about your family, and if it is possible for them to help us."

I had thought about Texas for the last several weeks and tried to put it out of my mind every time. I hated my life there and swore to never go back. It didn't matter how I looked at our present situation—I was to blame. I slumped down further into my chair and gazed into the flame. "My mother and dad live on a ranch over 1300 miles from here. You burn up in the summer and freeze in the winter. You work from daylight until dark, and everyone is always wishing for it to rain. It is eight miles to town if the roads are passable. That was the life I was glad to get away from and never planned to return."

She leaned forward. "Would they help us? At the moment that is all that matters."

"Yeah, of course. That is the kind of people they are. They would help us if we were strangers." There was no use not being truthful.

"That settles it, Elliot. We will go to Texas. You might not agree, but we have no other choice. The sooner we leave, the better. I will go to the train station tomorrow and get our tickets. What is the name of the town where your parents live?"

Could I really do this? I was never going back, but Effie was right. I told her and spelled it out. "When should we tell Grant and Nichole?"

"There is no use putting it off. Nichole is home and Grant will want to see Sofia before we leave. I will go get them."

A few minutes later the three of them came back. I looked at Effie, wanting her to tell them our plans. She stood. Maybe that increased her confidence. "We are moving, far away from here. It is not a choice but necessary due to our financial situation."

"Where?" asked Nichole.

"Texas. To where your dad lived before he came here. His family is there."

"Will we see Indians?" asked Grant excitedly.

In spite of the dire circumstances, I smiled. "No, probably not."

Nichole interrupted. "I am not going! I will stay here with my friends."

This time, Effie looked at me. "No. You will go with us, Nichole. We are still a family.

"No. I will not leave here!" she screamed, getting up and running out of the room.

Effie followed her, saying, "Maybe I can talk to her."

Grant fired questions at me. "Will I get to ride a horse?"

"I wouldn't be surprised."

"Can I shoot a real gun?"

"Probably."

"Will there be cows?"

"Definitely."

The questions kept coming until Effie returned. "She continued to insist that she was not going with us. I finally told her that in two years, when she was eighteen, she could do what she pleased. But, for now, she was not going to have a choice. I left it at that. We need to notify your family that we are coming."

"We'll have to send a telegraph," I said. "You can do that tomorrow when you go to Grand Central to get our tickets. I just want to tell them we are coming to visit and wait until we get there to explain that we need help."

Effie left early the next morning to go to Grand Central to buy our tickets. I expected her to be back by noon, but it was four in the afternoon. She was tired and frustrated. It was easy to understand when she told me why it took all day.

"The tickets cost more than I had. I went to my dad's and borrowed the money from him to make up the difference. We are going to have to change trains a number of times. All we could afford was coach, so we will need to take some lunch meat, bread, and fruit. We cannot afford to eat in the dining room. It is going to be a long and difficult trip. We leave Wednesday morning at seven. That is Christmas Day, but maybe that is for the best. We have no money for gifts anyway."

"Did you send the telegram?"

"Yes. I just said we would arrive on the twenty-eighth or twenty-ninth. It is going to take us at least three days and maybe four. We only have two days to get ready. That should be enough, though, since we can only carry so much on the train. All we will be able to take is one suitcase each. We will have to make do with that. I have enough money left to buy some groceries to take and more along the way. Did Nichole leave the house today?"

"No, I made sure. It's sad that we have to keep her a prisoner in her own house."

"That is better than her not being here when we get ready to leave. I don't trust her even though she has agreed to go with us."

I kept thinking all this must be a dream. Six weeks ago, I was rich by most standards. I lost it all trying to get more, throwing caution to the wind. The market has always recovered for the past nine years. I looked at Effie who leaned back in her chair, asleep. She had a tough day, being forced to go to her dad for money. Strange, but I would have never thought she was capable of doing what she had since my heart attack. She had demanded a divorce two short months ago after an affair. She didn't give me any of the details about the set-up for the man who was blackmailing her. All she would say was, "His days of preying on women are over."

I thought about it being like the prodigal son coming home broke and asking for help. I hated my years on the ranch, but my parents were good people, like I had told Effie. They would be glad to see us and share whatever they were able to.

We were at Grand Central at six on Wednesday morning. It was not crowded since it was Christmas Day, and most had already arrived at their destination. At a few minutes until seven we began loading onto our car. Effie had to help Grant up the steps, which was even more difficult because he was carrying Rose. They were stopped on the platform by a large burly conductor. "Dogs are not allowed on the train." He reached for the dog.

Grant clutched Rose to his chest. "No!"

"The rules do not allow animals on passenger trains," he said, looking at Effie.

"Could you make an exception for my son? He is attached to his dog. It will devastate him to lose Rose."

The smirk betrayed his answer before it came. "Lady, there are no exceptions." He reached and took Rose from Grant.

She gave a cry and struggled to get away, but he squeezed her tighter until she couldn't make a sound. He stepped back and allowed us to enter.

As I went by, the conductor turned and gave Rose to a Negro porter. "Get rid of it."

"You are an evil person," I said as I passed the conductor. "Someday you will pay."

We found seats and tried to console Grant who was crying and begging to get Rose back. All the sympathy and promises to get him another dog did no good. It was only going to be a matter of time until Grant made himself sick.

The conductor came down the aisle taking tickets. When he took mine, I said, "You broke his heart."

He moved on down to the next passengers not saying anything.

After the conductor went to the next car, the porter came down the aisle, bent down to Grant, and whispered, "Yur little dog, with me. I'z take care her till yalls next change trains."

26

THE SHERIFF

Leta

I eased out of bed, trying not to wake up Charlie. He had only been asleep a short time and kept both of us awake most of the night. I started a fire in the living room fireplace and went to the kitchen to put on the coffee pot. It was already getting light outside, but hopefully Charlie would sleep late. Maybe we would hear something from the sheriff today about Daniel. I couldn't imagine what he did to be put in jail. He was not that kind of boy.

I went back to check on Charlie, and he was awake. "You didn't sleep much."

"No, my hip and leg hurt," he said.

"Probably because you walked about three miles around the house yesterday."

He swung his legs over to the side of the bed. "Leta, we're going to lose all the money from the sale of our cattle."

"You don't know that. You always think the worst."

"I should have never trusted an Indian. Did I ever tell you about the time a bunch of them stole our horses on a cattle drive back in '77? We had just crossed the Pecos River and camped there for the night. The next morning half our horses were gone."

I'd heard the story several times but didn't tell him. "Charlie, that was over fifty years ago. Times have changed. Let me help you into the living room by the fire. I'll get you a cup of coffee and some aspirin. Why don't you just leave on your wool pajamas and housecoat? It's cold this morning. There's no need to get dressed."

I gave him his crutches, and he hobbled into the living room. I went back to the kitchen and started making biscuits. One of his favorite breakfasts was biscuits soaked in molasses. Maybe that would get him in a better mood.

The phone rang just as I was taking the biscuits out of the oven. It was Pastor Kennedy, and he told me he was coming out to visit Charlie later this morning. He'd heard about his accident and felt like he needed to see him. He was the pastor of the First Presbyterian Church, where we had been members since buying the ranch.

When I told Charlie, his reactions didn't surprise me. "That's the last thing I need today, Leta. I don't feel like entertaining anyone, especially a preacher. Would you call him back, and tell him I don't feel like seeing anyone? That's the God's truth."

"No, I will not. He's coming to see you, and you'll just have to get through it. It's nice of him to visit. And you shouldn't be using the Lord's name in vain."

"I'm not using His name in vain. I'm just telling you He would agree with me. He knows I don't feel like seeing anyone today—let alone a preacher. And besides that—ten to one Pastor Kennedy gets here about time for dinner."

There was no use arguing with him. I wasn't about to tell the pastor Charlie didn't feel like seeing him.

He handed me his cup for a refill. "Now I'm going to have to get dressed."

"You have a clean pair of khakis, and I'll iron you a shirt." Charlie didn't wear anything but khakis for everyday. He hadn't worn Levi's in years, saying they weren't as comfortable. He wore boots with short tops and his pants were always stuffed in his boots. Charlie was only five-six, which made him two inches shorter than me.

"There's no need to hurry, Leta. It's still several hours till dinner."

I was hoping that we'd hear from the sheriff before the pastor arrived. Charlie was going to have trouble conversing if we still didn't know anything about Daniel. I decided to cook chili for dinner. I used pork in my recipe instead of beef, but it usually turned out good. I would make cornbread to go with it and have enough of both left over for supper.

At mid-morning, the phone rang. I beat Charlie to the phone but just barely. It was one of my friends in our Sunday school class wanting to check on me since we had missed church yesterday. We usually made it to Sunday school and church. I explained what had happened, ensuring that the news of Charlie's accident would be well known in the community by nightfall. She was a talker and the hub of communication for the area.

After we hung up, Charlie reminded me that the sheriff may have tried to call while the phone was tied up. I ignored him and went back to cooking dinner.

I had the food on the table and told Charlie it was ready when there was a knock on the front door. I looked at the clock—11:55.

Pastor Kennedy didn't stay long after dinner, saying he had several more visits to make in the afternoon. He should be okay until supper with the two bowls of chili and two thick slices of cornbread. He also didn't turn down a slice of apple pie we had left over from yesterday.

After he left, I received the expected response from Charlie after he lit his cigar, leaned back in his chair, and smiled. "Pretty predictable, huh?"

I had no answer, but instead got up and began clearing off the dishes. Charlie watched me until he finished his cigar. "Well, Leta, it's time for my nap. You know, I get tired of being right all the time."

He couldn't resist rubbing it in. I finished washing the dishes and decided to take a nap, also, to make up for last night. Charlie always napped in his chair, and I would lay on the couch. We had no more than settled down until I heard a car drive up. I was at the door and let the sheriff in before he had a chance to knock. "Afternoon, Leta. I have some news for y'all."

He followed me into the living room where Charlie was trying to get up. Before the sheriff could even greet him, Charlie blurted out, "What'cha find out?"

"Just sit down, Charlie. It'll take a little time."

"Where is he? What did he do? I was afraid something like this would happen."

The sheriff raised his hand to stop the questions. "He'll be home tomorrow. Actually, he is taking the train to Baird. He should arrive around two in the afternoon. . ."

Charlie interrupted him, "Does he have the check for my cattle?"

"Just give me a chance to explain, Charlie. I'm going to tell you everything I know."

He shook his head. "I'm sorry. I've been a nervous wreck. I never did trust that boy. Go ahead."

"Maybe when I finish, you'll feel better. The police called me from Fort Worth and told me what happened. The night your cattle arrived at the Stock Yards, your boy stayed with them. I can't imagine anyone sleeping outside on the ground this time of year. Evidently, that is what he was doing when two men attempted to move some of your cattle to another pen. When your boy discovered what was happening, he confronted them. They thought he was just a kid and attacked him— big mistake. He carved them up pretty good. For a while it looked like one might not survive. That was the reason they kept your boy—in case the man died." The sheriff chuckled. "They said it took a yard of catgut to sew them fellows up. Anyway, this had been going on for some time. Owners had been complaining about being short cattle when they sold. Your boy will be put on the train in the morning and is quite the hero at the Stock Yards. That's about it."

"Do you know anything about my check for the cattle?"

Charlie asked.

"No. The guy I talked with didn't mention it."

"Sheriff, we appreciate you coming out here to give us the news." I wasn't going to wait for Charlie to thank him. All that was on his mind was the money.

"No problem. I knew it would be hard to do on the phone." He rose. "I need to be going. Can you have someone pick up your boy tomorrow?"

"Yes, that won't be a problem."

Charlie finally thanked the sheriff as he was leaving.

"What do you think about Daniel, now?" That was my first question after the sheriff was gone.

"I was wrong, Leta. He did stay with the cattle. But I still don't have the money. He could get off the train anywhere between here and Fort Worth and be a rich Indian."

It didn't do any good to argue. I didn't have any doubt but what Daniel would have the check for the cattle.

I finally gave in and agreed for us to meet Daniel in Baird. From our house it was about thirty-five miles. We could have asked John or Jake and either would have been glad to go, but Charlie wouldn't have it. He was bound and determined to be there when Daniel got off the train. The roads were not good, and if anything happened on the way Charlie wouldn't be able to help. We could break down or get stuck and be there until someone came along to help. Our pickup was old, and we had been blessed with some recent rains.

We left the house at ten-thirty, which would give us over three hours. I couldn't go but about twenty miles an hour. I had to stay in the ruts to keep from sliding off the road. I wished several times during the trip that I had refused to drive. We made it with an hour to spare and waited inside the depot for the train.

The train was an hour late and, of course, Charlie's imagination took over. First, he thought the train might have been robbed. After that, he predicted it could have run off the rail. A few minutes after three the train rolled to a stop.

It only had a few passengers, and Daniel was one of the first people we saw. When we greeted him, I knew something was wrong.

"Have you got the check for the cattle?" Charlie asked before a greeting.

Daniel reached into his jean pocket, brought out a rumpled envelope, and gave it to Charlie. He opened it and stared at its contents. He handed it to me. It was a check made out to Charlie Barlowe for $5,805.

"You satisfied now?" I asked with more than a bit of sarcasm. Speechless, he just nodded his head and smiled.

I directed my attention back to Daniel, who stood with his head down. "Daniel, what's wrong?"

He continued to stare at the ground. "I messed up the clothes you bought me, ma'am. They have blood all over them. I am sorry."

Charlie found his voice and slapped him on the shoulder. "Don't you worry about that son! We can get you some new clothes."

Charlie was talkative on the way home. "The stockers cost about $2,000 counting the interest on the loan. Even with the feed bill that's going to leave close to $3,500. I still can't believe they sold that good. The market must have been better than I expected."

I kept thinking—*Charlie's attitude toward Daniel should change after this.*

27

A CHANGED SCROOGE

Leta

I was heating water to wash clothes when I heard a car honk. Who could that be? I wasn't expecting a visitor. Charlie had gone into town to deposit the cattle check. I went to the front and met Charlie coming up the steps with a big smile.

"What do you think, Leta?" He motioned toward the car parked in our driveway.

I couldn't have been more surprised if President Hoover had been the visitor. "It's beautiful, Charlie. I can't believe you bought a car."

"I couldn't resist it. The bank repossessed it last week from a guy who couldn't make the payments. It's not new but has less than a thousand miles on it. It's a 1928 Model A Sedan. It sells for about $500, and I got it for $325. With what the cattle brought, we can afford it. I'll drive my pickup for several more years. Come on—let's go for a ride. You can't believe how smooth it is. They say it'll run sixty- five. Of course, that's too fast for us."

I'd never have thought Charlie would be this excited about spending money, but I was pleased. I'd already thought about the three of us crowded into the seat of the pickup. We drove back to town to get it. He was right about the smooth ride after bouncing around in the pickup.

I let him out and drove the car home. I couldn't believe

how easy it was to maneuver and how much power it had. I looked down once, and I was going forty- five miles an hour. That was the fastest I'd ever driven.

Charlie had a much different attitude toward Daniel after he protected our cattle and came back with the check. Daniel realized it also and started taking most of his meals with us. A couple of weeks after his trip to Fort Worth, while we were eating breakfast, Charlie asked Daniel what he would like to have as a bonus for his Fort Worth trip. Daniel seemed confused and Charlie explained that we wanted to do something for him to express our appreciation not only for the trip but for being such a good worker.

"You got me new clothes," Daniel said.

"He means something more than clothes," I said. "Something that you would really like of your own that you couldn't afford to buy."

He stopped eating and seemed deep in thought. "It would cost too much."

Charlie pushed back from the table and took out a cigar. "No. You go ahead and tell me what you'd really like. I'll decide if it cost too much."

"My own horse."

He put a match to his cigar and smiled. "I see no problem with that. There's a horse trader in town that usually has a dozen or so for sale. We'll go in this afternoon and take a look at them."

I had never seen him smile the way he did. "Thank you."

After breakfast and Daniel left, I filled up his cup. "That was kind of you."

"He's a good boy, Leta. I want to keep him if at all possible. It's almost 1930 and word travels fast. It'll get around what he did in Fort Worth, and ranchers are always looking for good, honest hands."

"Did you see him smile when you agreed to get him the

horse?" I asked.

"Yeah, that was almost worth what the horse will cost, which brings up another point—that horse trader is not honest. We're going to have to be careful."

"Have you ever known an honest horse trader, Charlie?"

He laughed. "No, come to think of it, I haven't."

"Today's Monday, the eighteenth. It's only ten more days until Thanksgiving. We've been going to one of our neighbors for Thanksgiving. We could stay home this year if you like, and I could cook for you and Daniel. He's refused to go with us the last two years."

"I'd just as soon stay home Thanksgiving and eat a steak if you'll cook one of those peach cobblers that I like. If I remember right, it's the Beltons' time to host the dinner. The last time we ate with them the dressing was dry and the turkey was tough. We can pick up T-bones at the meat market in town. There's not a law that we have to have turkey at Thanksgiving."

"You're getting around much better. Dr. Johnson's going to be surprised when you go in for your checkup at the end of the month." I wanted to remind him that Dr. Johnson wanted to see him then.

"I'm getting around better after I ditched the crutches. I'm not going back to that money-grabbing doctor either."

I was afraid of that. "Charlie, you don't need to take any chances at your age. To be on the safe side we need to let him look at your hip." I was probably wasting my breath, because he changed the subject.

"There is something that concerns me. When I was in the bank a couple of weeks ago there were several guys withdrawing their money. I asked the banker what was going on. He beat around the bush and didn't answer my question. I knew one of the guys and followed him out and asked him why he was closing out his account. He told me he wasn't taking any chances. The stock market crash had created panic, and he was afraid there'd be a run on the banks. 'I feel better about having my money at home,' he had said. Of course, banks don't keep enough money on hand to cover all deposits, and he is correct. If there is a run on the banks, depositors would lose their money."

"Should we take our money out of the bank?" I asked.

"This bank has been good to us for a long time, Leta. I might take out a little but not all of it. I trust them and can't help but believe they'll take care of their customers."

"How much do we have in the bank?"

"Over $5,000. If I don't change my mind, we're not going to buy any stockers in the spring. We're going to wait and see what happens. We have a Republican president, and they've never been generous to us farmers or ranchers. The economy is going to take a downturn, which will affect the cattle market."

I didn't ask Charlie about the older cows we had that didn't have a calf this year. There was at least a dozen of them. I noticed they were not in the bunch we shipped to Fort Worth. It would have embarrassed him to try and explain. The truth was he didn't want to send them to the packers. They had produced calves for years, and he felt like we owed them. He would never admit that to any of the other ranchers because they would laugh at him.

After lunch, I went in with them to look at horses. We took a trailer in case Daniel found one he liked. The barn and pens were at the west end of town. When we arrived, there was no one around. The large pen held more horses than I expected—fifteen, maybe more.

"Let's go see what he's got, Daniel. Remember, he'll look you right in the eye and lie to you."

We hadn't been there but a few minutes until the owner came out. "Good afternoon, Charlie Barlowe! You're looking at some prime horse flesh. Some of the best I've ever got my hands on." He hesitated and turned toward me. "Why, hello, Mrs. Barlowe, you're looking good today."

"We're here for something that might fit Daniel," Charlie said.

He went over to Daniel, grabbed his hand and pumped it. "We can fix you up, young man. We got some gentle horses here that will treat you right." He pointed to a corner of the pen, where a bay stood with its head down, like it was taking a nap. "That little mare over there would be just right for you. She's ten years old and sound as a dollar."

"Could I get in the pen?" Daniel asked.

"Sure, but you need to be careful. I don't want you getting hurt," he said.

Daniel climbed over the fence and walked among the horses. Occasionally, he would rub one on the neck or on the rear. He came to a roan and when he reached to rub him on the neck, he tried to bite him. Daniel moved out of reach just in time before the roan whirled and got in position to kick him. He quickly moved a safe distance. He continued to drift among the horses for several minutes and then came back to where we were standing.

"I like the roan."

That set Sleepy, the horse trader, off. "Are you crazy? That horse isn't broke! He's an outlaw. He'll kill you or worse."

I admit, Sleepy was making a good point. I couldn't believe Daniel would choose the roan. Maybe he wasn't as knowledgeable of horses as Charlie thought.

Sleepy was just getting started. "I'm not selling you that horse. It would ruin my repetition as an honest horse trader. People would blame me when roany stomped all over you. Pick you out another horse—any of them. Like I said, that little bay mare would fit you like a glove."

Daniel caught me, and probably Charlie, by surprise. "That bay mare is at least twenty."

"Uh, I-I can't believe it. You, young whippersnapper, disputing my word. Me, as honest as the day is long."

Charlie had listened to it enough. I'd already heard him popping his teeth. "Bull shit, Sleepy. Get off your high horse. You'd rather climb a tree and tell a lie than stay on the ground and tell the truth. We came to buy this boy a horse. Now put a price on the roan, or we're leaving."

"Well, uh, I-I guess I'd take $200 for him. But you got to sign a paper saying you'd take responsibility if the horse kills the boy."

More teeth popping. Charlie moved right up against Sleepy. "I'm going to give you $75 for that roan, and that's my one and only offer. Furthermore, I ain't signing nothing."

"Uh, I don't know, Charlie. Let me think about it a minute."

"Let's go, Leta. There are other places to buy a horse."

We were in the pickup backing away when Sleepy came running, waving his arms. "Okay, I'll sell him. But I don't appreciate you cussing me."

"I didn't cuss you, Sleepy. I said you were a liar. And you and everyone in this county knows that's the truth. Now, I'll give you a check and get this horse loaded."

I had forgotten about Daniel with all the theatrics going on between Charlie and Sleepy and was surprised when he spoke. "I would like to ride him."

"Now?" asked Charlie.

Daniel nodded his head.

"Fine with me."

Sleepy smiled. "I'd like to see this."

Daniel took a rope, his saddle and bridle out of the back of the pickup and went back into the pen. He left the saddle and bridle on the ground inside the pen. He eased over close to the horses, holding the rope down to his side. When he was close enough, he was so quick, I didn't see the rope until it was around the roan's neck. The battle was on. Daniel dug his heels in, and the roan pulled him around the pen, snorting and bucking. I thought he would have to let go. Finally, the roan began to slow down or better yet choke down. Suddenly, the roan was lying on his side, eyes bulged out, struggling to breathe. Within a short time, I thought he was dead. I couldn't see him breathing from where I stood.

"I'm not giving you your money back, Barlowe! Your boy killed the roan. It's good enough for you!" shouted Sleepy.

For a minute, I thought he was right. Then Daniel knelt by the roan's head and loosened the rope, rubbing him on the neck. I could see the roan begin to take huge breaths. All the time Daniel stroked his ears, head, neck, and then moved to his withers. Finally, he touched about every part of roany, even his back legs. He was talking to him all the time. I was too far away to understand, but it wouldn't have mattered. It wasn't in English.

He gave a gentle nudge and roany got to his feet. Daniel then did the strangest thing. He blew into roany's nostrils and stood there, looking into the horse's eyes. He then led him over to the fence, slipped the bridle on and rope off. He placed the blanket and saddle gently on his back, tightened the cinch, led him in a circle, tightened the cinch again, and got on him. They stood for a few minutes before Daniel urged him toward the gate.

Charlie walked over to the gate without limping and opened it. "You ready to load him, son?"

"No, I'll ride him home."

Charlie came back to the pickup. "I've never seen anything like that. In fact, I've never heard of anything like that."

Sleepy was nowhere around.

Thanksgiving came and went. December flew by, and it was only a day before Christmas when we received the telegram telling us that Elliot and his family were on the way to visit and would be here a few days after Christmas. I was excited, but Charlie was suspicious. "Something's not right, Leta. Elliot wouldn't come back just to visit."

"I don't care why he's coming back. I'm going to get to see my grandchildren for the first time. We need to get set up for them. We have two extra bedrooms, but Nichole will need a room to herself. That means Grant will have to sleep in the room with his parents. We have a half-bed in our old house. You and Daniel can bring it here. We only have one extra chamber pot, so we'll need to get another one. We can get it when we go in to buy groceries."

"I tell you, Leta, something is wrong. There is another motive for them coming. I have no idea what it is, but believe me, Elliot is not coming back just for a visit."

My patience was running thin. "Charlie, listen to me! We haven't seen our son since Chisum's funeral, fourteen years ago. We have never met our grandchildren. I don't want to hear any more of your negative comments. We are going to get ready to welcome our family." Thrilled beyond words, I couldn't wait to see my son and his family.

28

TEXAS

Effie

The seats on the train were not that uncomfortable, but it was cold. The car was only about a third full. I had anticipated it being cold and brought several blankets. We left right on time and within half an hour it had begun to get warm. There were pipes bringing warm air from the steam created by the engine. I looked across at Nichole and Grant who were already asleep. Nichole was a pretty girl and on her way to becoming a beautiful woman. I only wished her attitude resembled her looks. She stayed angry after we told her about moving. She finally agreed to go with us after I promised her that when she was eighteen it would be her decision to live where she wanted without interference from us. Nichole never wanted for anything and for the past several years was allowed to do whatever she wished. It was little wonder that she rebelled against leaving the life she had created for herself.

Grant was worn out after the fright of almost losing Rose. I hate to think what would have happened had it not been for the porter. In my brief time working at Macy's, I realized that there were all kinds of people. Most were nice but a few were downright angry and mean. It made you appreciate those who treated you well. The porter saved us a world of grief by what he did, which could have, and might still, cost him his job. He was a Negro, whose grandparents may have been slaves, yet he befriended strangers at great risk. I will never forget his kindness.

Elliot sat beside me, not having said a word since we left the station. He looked terrible, and I could hear him breathing. He only had a dozen of the pills left that he took when in pain.

For the first time in, I don't remember when—maybe ever—I saw them as my family. I felt a strong urge to protect and look after them. *How strange*, I thought. A couple of months ago, I had an affair and made a fool of myself. I was determined to get a divorce and start a new life, leaving my family for someone else to look after. How quickly things change.

I brought enough food to last us several days. The sack Nichole carried on the train held bread, cold cuts, apples, and cookies. Whenever we had to change trains, I planned to replenish our food. I had gotten enough money from my dad for train fare and food for the trip. I also had a little money saved from what I made at Macy's.

I tried to visualize what Texas would be like. I had never been close to a cow. Some of the New York police rode horses, but I never touched one. It frightened me when they came too close. According to Elliot, Texas was a depressing place. Would his parents have a house big enough for all of us? Elliot wasn't going to be able to work. I would have to find a job in town to provide at least some income. Nichole would have to start school, but we couldn't afford a tutor for Grant. Maybe Elliot or his grandparents could help him. There were so many questions and few answers. I had prayed for strength and felt more capable. I would continue to pray, something I had not done for years.

<hr />

We had to change trains the next day at noon. When we exited the train, the porter took Rose out of the inside of his coat and gave her to Grant as we passed. I stopped and hugged him in front of everybody. I heard a gasp and comment from a lady behind me. "Well, I never!"

We had an hour wait for the next train, which gave me time to find a small grocery and buy more food. The weather had not improved and the depot had a stove, but a crowd prevented us from getting close enough to get much heat from it. A young man approached us and motioned toward Grant. "Ma'am, if you'd like I can take this young man over by the fire and get him warm."

"That is very kind of you." I looked at Grant, who was already struggling to get up. The result was that when we were ready to board, Grant and Rose were warm while we were still freezing.

I held my breath as we approached the conductor. He smiled at Grant. "Do you have a ticket for the dog?"

Grant clutched her to his chest. "No sir. Please let me keep her."

Another smile from the conductor. "Well, she's small, so we'll just let her ride on your ticket."

When we took our seat, I saw Elliot rubbing his chest. "Are you hurting?"

"Yeah. I need to take a pill." He leaned back against the seat after swallowing the pill.

He looked even worse today. His color was a pasty white, and the least exertion caused him to gasp for breath. I felt sorry for him and reached for his hand. How long had it been since we held hands? I could not remember the last time.

Over the next two days, we only changed trains one time. On our fourth day we were right on the border of Texas. It would be the last part of our trip, with this train going to our destination. According to the conductor we only had 300 more miles to travel.

Elliot was actually doing a little better. Grant and Rose had made the trip better than I expected. Nichole was still angry and complaining. She was appalled at the toilet facilities, which consisted of a pot over a hole in the train that emptied out onto the tracks after using it.

I sat by the window and observed the country as we traveled through Texas. The land was flat with few trees and every so often cows could be seen grazing. Grant, glued to the window, looked for buffalo. Elliot slept most of the time and Nichole was not interested.

After four days without a bath and wearing the same clothes, I felt dirty. Just to be able to wash and change clothes would help. We were about out of food and were tired of eating cold cuts three times a day. We had to make several stops as we traveled and did not arrive at our destination until after dark. The depot was well lit, which meant it had an electrical system.

Inside the depot, we used a phone in an office for Elliot to call his dad, who told him they would be here shortly. I tried to straighten up myself and the kids without success. We must have been a sad looking bunch as we waited on a bench.

It was longer than I expected before Elliot got up to meet the elderly man and woman who came in the door. They were older than I expected and looked nothing like I had imagined. The problem being that I had expected someone who looked similar to my parents. His dad was short, wearing boots and a small cowboy hat, not one like they wore in the Talkies. He had half a cigar clamped in his teeth. His mother was tall and somewhat thin yet looked capable of doing much more than a person her age.

When Elliot reached them, his mother was crying as she hugged him. I was curious to see how he would greet his dad. It turned out to be a handshake then a slight hug—nothing like the mother's. They followed Elliot over to us.

"Effie, this is my mother, Leta, and my dad, Charlie." He motioned toward each. "And this is my wife, Effie, and my son, Grant, and daughter, Nichole."

His mother hugged me, and his dad offered a handshake. His mother then hugged Grant, but when she tried to hug Nichole, she turned away. I could have pinched her head off. It did not seem to bother his mother. She turned back to me.

"Effie, we are so glad to have you. I can't believe it, but I am so happy."

His dad said, "We brought the car and pickup to give us more room. If you'll bring your suitcases, we'll get you loaded,"

We put the suitcases in the back of the pickup. Grant and Elliot rode in the pickup with Elliot's dad. Nichole and I rode in the car with his mother. As we entered the car, I grabbed Nichole's arm and gave her the angriest look possible.

We talked on the way to their home, mostly about the trip. I was afraid she was going to ask us how long we were going to stay. We made it without that happening. I wanted Elliot present when we had to answer that question.

I was surprised that they didn't have electrical lighting. The house was dark with only the kerosene lamps providing light. Leta showed us to our bedrooms and told us that supper would be ready shortly. After she left us, it gave me a chance to talk with Elliot. "Did you tell your dad why we were here?"

"No, I would rather wait until tomorrow. Maybe I'm just trying to put it off. Did you notice how rude Nichole was to my mother?"

"Yes, I am sorry. I will give her a good talking to when we are alone."

We had ignored Grant who had remained in the room with us. "I like them. They're nice. The pickup is neat."

"Grant, if you'll wait on us in the living room, your dad and I need to change clothes. After we finish you can come back in and change."

***

The meal was good. We had eaten nothing for four days but cold cuts. The fried pork chops, potatoes, and gravy were delicious. I didn't know food could taste so good. After we finished, Leta asked us if we'd like to take a bath.

"That would be wonderful," I said.

"We won't worry about the dishes now. I'll put water on the stove and get the tub. We bathe in the kitchen where we're close to the stove. Elliot, there's a bucket on the back porch. If you'll fill it up at the pump outside, I'll put it on the stove. There's nothing like a hot bath to make you feel better."

Then it hit me. They bathe in a tub right here in the kitchen with water heated on the stove. How gross. I looked at Elliot and for the first time in days he met my stare with a smile. He had known all the time how we would bathe.

Elliot's next statement was also a surprise. "Grant, you and Nichole will need to know where the outhouse is located. You are to use it in the daytime. You have a chamber pot in the bedroom that you can use at night. You'll need to empty it every morning.

The look on Nichole was priceless—somewhere between disgusted to unbelievable. "You mean there is not a water closet in the house?"

Charlie laughed. "No, honey. We just have an outhouse with a Sears and Roebuck catalogue. You can read it while doing your business and use it when you're finished."

"Charlie, don't laugh at her. She's used to life in the city. It'll take some time for her to get accustomed to the country." She turned to Nichole. "Don't pay him no mind. We need to decide what you're going to call us. I would prefer Grams if that's okay with you?" She looked at Grant.

"Sure. I like it," he said, smiling.

She turned toward Nichole, who just shrugged.

"Then it's settled. I'll be Grams. Charlie, what do you want your grandkids to call you?"

He took his cigar out. "CK will be fine with me."

"Grams and CK. Do y'all realize you're the only grandkids we have?" she asked.

Neither responded but at least Grant smiled. "I can help with the dishes."

She waved the offer away. "Not a problem. We're going back to the living room and give you some privacy for your bath. Elliot, you need to get a bucket of water."

I jumped up. "Let me do that since it is my bath water. Elliot can show me how." He could not lift anything in his condition. I followed him outside.

He handed me the bucket. "Thank you."

I assured him, "We're going to have to tell them everything tomorrow."

It was dark but he showed me the pump and how to work it. I had to move the handle up and down several times before water started coming out. The bucket of water was heavy, but I managed to get it back into the house. Leta was the only one left in the kitchen. Elliot went on into the living room.

"Well, he could have helped us put it on the stove," Leta said. Together, we lifted the bucket onto the burner.

We sat down at the table while the water was heating. Nothing was said for several minutes until she looked straight into my eyes and asked, "What's going on, Effie?"

29

PROBLEM SOLVED

Elliot

The trip to Texas was even more difficult than I expected. The pain came often and was only relieved by one of the pills. I was in poor condition and realized it even more during the journey from New York. I could do little without being out of breath and hurting.

Our reception was about what I imagined it would be. Mother cried, my dad was uncomfortable and stood back and let her do the welcoming. Mother showed her emotion—Dad held his in check. On the ride to the ranch, there was a lively conversation between Grant and my dad, involving horses, cowboys, guns, and buffalo, which let me off the hook.

It had been years since I sat down to a meal prepared by my mother, and I was reminded what a fabulous cook she was. When the talk turned to available facilities for bathing and toiletry, I couldn't help but be amused at the reaction of my family. I should have warned them beforehand what to expect. It was hard to imagine Effie or Nichole going to the outhouse.

After supper, I went to the bedroom and laid down, allowing Grant to have Dad all to himself. Effie came in later, after her bath. "Well, that was an experience. I got into this round tub that wasn't big enough to fit into. I was all rolled up into a ball sitting in four inches of water. Someway, I do not know how, I got wet all over. I actually feel better, though. Nichole refused when she saw the tub. What about you?"

"Yeah, I'm going to bathe. I'll let you in on strategy that works better. Get on your knees to begin with, and you can reach the water and your body parts."

"How often does your family bathe?"

"Ordinarily, once a week. A special occasion might require an additional bath. You will notice that they wash often and more thoroughly than we do."

She sat down on the edge of the bed. "Your mother knew something was wrong. I told her about our situation at home and why we came. She was so calm, like it wasn't unusual to have a family move in with you, who you would need to support, at least for the time being. She actually seemed pleased with the added responsibility. How will your dad react?"

"I'm not surprised at Mother's response. I don't know about my dad. If it was twenty years ago, it would be totally opposite of Mother's. I guess we'll find out soon enough." I got up and moved over to the one chair in the room. "What happened, Effie? You've changed overnight. Don't get me wrong. It's a positive change."

"I know. At first, I was confused. Later, after thinking about it, I believe this is the first time that anyone ever needed me—truly needed me. Everybody waited on me and did things to make me comfortable. I did not contribute anything to anyone, not even my own children. Of course, that meant I had no responsibility except to do things that made me happy. Suddenly, my family needed me. I didn't even have time to think about it. I prayed for strength and was able to do things that I would not have thought possible. At first, I thought—where is the anger, the grief over losing everything? After that, I had no time to dwell on the past. I was needed."

I listened to and saw a different Effie. What if she hadn't changed? The answer is simple—we couldn't have made it.

I woke up the next morning feeling better. It was the first

time in years that Effie and I had slept in the same bed. I had slept well, not waking up but once when I thought it was raining but mistook it for Grant using the chamber pot.

I joined my mother and dad in the kitchen for coffee before my family was up. There was a small table with four chairs in the kitchen. The dining room had a larger table that would accommodate six.

"Good morning. The coffee smells good."

"Sit down. I'll get you a cup. You want sugar and cream if I remember right," Mother said.

"Sounds good."

Dad didn't waste any time bringing up why we were here. "Your mother filled me in on your problems." His next statement caught me by surprise. "You and your family are welcome here for as long as you need to stay. We're glad that you came home so that we could help you."

"Thank you." What else could I say? There was no use making excuses for going broke and needing help.

Mother put the biscuits in the oven and sat down with us. "Elliot, I told your dad about your health problems. We want you to take care of yourself and not think you have to work."

"She's right. Also, I want to take you to see Dr. Johnson tomorrow. He's a good doctor even though he does charge too much. He can make sure you have plenty of the medicine you are taking."

This wasn't the same Charlie Barlowe that I left over twenty years ago. "I appreciate it. I'm hoping that, with rest, my health improves, and it's possible for me to do more. Effie is going to look for a job in town to provide some income."

Mother rose and got the coffee pot. "There's no hurry. We'll do fine." She filled Dad's cup. "Charlie, what do you think about fixing up our old house for them? I know they would appreciate a place of their own."

"It's pretty run down. There hasn't been anyone in it for ten years or so. We'll go look it over and see what needs to be done to make it livable." He got up and started toward the door. "Gotta make a trip to the privy. Coffee does it every time."

"He's changed, Mother," I said, after he was gone.

"We all do. Hopefully, for the better. You've been away for twenty years, Elliot. I hope and pray that you and your dad can forget the past and start fresh."

I took a sip of my coffee. I'd forgotten how strong she made it. "I'm sorry, Mother, for crashing in on you with my problems. I made foolish investments that had devastating results. We had nowhere else to go."

"Sorry? I'm thrilled to have you home and to meet your wife and my grandkids. Something good always comes out of hopelessness. Grant is precious and Nichole is—well, a challenge. But we have plenty of time to work on that. The first thing we need to do after the holidays is get them back in school."

"The school Nichole attended wouldn't admit Grant. They said polio was contagious. I tried several times but was turned down."

It had been twenty years, but I recognized that look. "Just leave that up to me."

There was a knock at the back door. "Come on in, Daniel."

The young man who came in carried a bucket of milk and looked as if he could break and run at any second. "We've got company, Daniel. This is my son, Elliot. They'll be with us for a while." She turned to me. "Elliot, this is our hand, Daniel. He's been with us for over two years and is part of the family."

I stood and offered my hand. "Pleased to meet you, Daniel." The handshake was firm, but he didn't look at me.

"I am sorry for interrupting," he said, and sat the bucket on the counter.

"You're welcome any time in our house, Daniel. Now, sit down and have a cup of coffee with us."

"I better be going." He was out the door before either of us could object.

I could tell he was of mixed race, probably a Mexican. "Is he always like that?"

"No. He has been much better the last few months." She laughed. "Y'all may be a setback for him. He's a good boy, and we're quite fond of him. When he showed up at the ranch, he reminded me of a stray dog. He needed food and shelter but was afraid of getting close enough to let you pet him. Charlie can tell you more about him. He's never told us, but we think he is part Indian—maybe more than part. We couldn't do without him. Our friends help us, also. You remember John and Jake?"

"Yeah, they were nice. Does Dad pay them for helping him, now?"

She sighed and shook her head. "Some things will never change. I've put my foot down lately and paid them myself."

"I'm surprised the weather is so nice for this time of year. I expected it to be cold," I said.

"For years we've had a bad spell between Christmas and the first of the year. It looks as if we might get by without it this year. We've had to feed little so far this winter." She got up when Dad came back in. "I need to start breakfast. Charlie always wants bacon and eggs. Will that be all right with your family?"

"That will be wonderful. I haven't had homemade biscuits since I left home. I don't think Effie or the kids ever have."

While Mother moved around the kitchen fixing breakfast, Dad and I sat there and talked about the ranch—the smell of bacon frying mixed with cigar smoke brought back a flood of memories. I quickly put them out of my mind to concentrate on my dad and listen to what was going on in his life.

The next day, on the drive to town, I compared the ride on the dirt roads to my Rolls gliding along the pavement in New York. I smiled, thinking *there would probably be many other comparisons in the future.* Dr. Johnson's waiting room was full when we arrived. Dad registered for me, and the next two hours we waited. I was about to give up when they called my name.

I followed the nurse, with Dad right behind me. We only

had a short wait before the doctor came in. He looked the same as when I had last seen him, slender and tall, with glasses that looked half an inch thick. He stopped abruptly and looked at me. "It's been a long time, Elliot. Are you back for a visit?"

I had already decided to be honest. "No, I came back to stay. I needed help and brought my family home."

"Well, I'm glad you're back. Maybe you can do something with Charlie. He's getting old and feeble."

That started an exchange that lasted several minutes. Finally, Dr. Johnson directed his attention back to me. "I assume you're the patient. What's the problem?"

I told him about my heart attack and the pain, with shortness of breath. He took my blood pressure, listened to my heart, and conducted the step test. He had me step up and down on some portable steps. I gasped for breath after only a few ups and downs. He took my vitals again after I had to stop. I rested for several minutes, and we repeated the process. After we finished, he said that we needed to talk in his office.

We followed him and sat down at a small table. He leaned forward with his elbows on the table and his hands clasped in front of him. "I imagine you have been examined by doctors who were on the cutting edge of treating disease. I know they have access to procedures that have not reached us. I don't know how much they told you. I can only give you my opinion based on over fifty years' experience. The one advantage you have in me treating you is that I will tell you the truth. Your heart is not pumping enough blood. The extensive damage that you suffered with the heart attack has weakened it greatly. The result is chest pain and extreme shortness of breath. I'll give you a prescription for the dynamite pills. That's what I call them. I'm sure you have found them to help. As far as treatment is concerned, I'd encourage you not to exert yourself. When you experience shortness of breath or pain, stop whatever you're doing and sit down. After a meal, you should rest for at least one hour, and if it's a large meal, two hours. I wish I had a better diagnosis for you. I don't expect you to get any better—hopefully, I'll be wrong."

I thanked him and we left. The doctors in New York had never given me that kind of news. They weren't positive but it was nothing like this. We waited in the office while the nurse went back to inquire about how much the bill would be. She came back a few minutes later, smiling. "You're good to go."

Dad asked, "How much we owe?"

"Nothing. There's no charge for this visit." She handed me a note. "Here's your prescription."

We rode home in silence and didn't arrive until almost lunch. Effie met us at the door. "We have a problem. Nichole will not come out of her room. I have begged and pleaded with her. She has the door locked. Your mother is looking for the key but hasn't found it."

Maybe Dad knows where the key is. I looked around, and he was gone. I could try anyway. I knocked before speaking. "Nichole, you need to come out of there, at once. Did you hear me?"

"Go way! Leave me alone! I want to go home."

"Just come out and talk to us. You can't stay in there forever."

She screamed, "I hate it here! It's uncouth and dirty and gross."

My dad tapped me on the shoulder before I realized he was there. He motioned for me to follow him. He sat down at the kitchen table and pointed at a chair for me. I didn't understand. Were we just going to give up?

Mother and Effie came into the kitchen with Mother holding up a key. "I found it. We can unlock the door now."

"Leta, let's wait a little bit. There's no hurry. She's been in there all morning. She may change her mind," my dad said.

Mother remained standing. "I'm going to unlock the door and get her out of there. If we don't do something, she may stay in there all day."

"Leta, just trust me. She needs to decide to come out on

her own. If you'll just be patient and give it half an hour. If she's not out by then you can unlock the door."

Mother finally sat down and the four of us waited, maybe as much as ten minutes. She was running out of patience. "Charlie, what's going on? You're up to something and it's probably no good. I've seen that look too many times."

My dad smiled. "Listen. Hear those footsteps on the roof. That's Daniel." He looked at Effie. "There's a chimney in Nichole's room. We have a rat snake that stays in the woodshed. We leave him alone because he gets mice. Daniel has caught him and is climbing up on the roof. We need to just sit back and see what happens."

I could hear footsteps on the roof. It wasn't long until we heard a blood curdling scream and Nichole came running out of the room, through the kitchen, and out the back door.

30

TEXAS WEATHER

Leta

After Nichole flew through the kitchen and out the back door, we heard the collision, and her screams became louder. We all crowded around the door to see what happened. Nichole was on top of Daniel beating him with her fists, screaming bloody murder. Evidently, he had been coming back into the house to remove the snake when she ran over him, knocking him down. He was covering his face with his hands to protect himself.

Effie rushed to his rescue and pulled Nichole off him. She continued to scream but managed to include words. "Grabbed me—attacked me!"

Effie was trying to calm her. "Nichole, listen to me." She had her by the shoulders gently shaking her. "You are not hurt. You are okay. Now calm down."

Poor Daniel. He looked as if he could bolt and run at any second. He kept slowly backing up as if trying to put as much distance between us as he could.

Effie managed to stop Nichole from screaming, which now was replaced with crying, or maybe squalling would be a better description. In between the outburst she kept saying, "I want to go home! Please take me home."

"Let's go back inside and get you cleaned up," Effie said.

That was the wrong thing to say. "No!" she screamed. "I am

never going back in that house again. There's a snake in there. I saw it! It came after me!" She jerked away from her mother. "We cannot stay here!"

"Just calm down, Nichole. Go with me back into the kitchen. I will explain everything to you."

She had calmed down enough to notice Daniel. "Who is that?"

"That's Daniel, he works for your granddad and grandmother." Effie was talking softly.

"He attacked me. He should go to jail," she said, in her calmest voice yet.

"No, Nichole. You ran over him. It was not his fault. Now, we need to go back into the house and get the dirt off you."

She started shaking her head. "That snake is still in there."

"Daniel, go get the snake and put him back in the woodshed," Charlie said.

Daniel made a wide circle around us and went into the house. While he was gone, Effie continued to try and reason with Nichole. "We cannot go back home. You have to accept that. We are staying, and you are going to school here after the holidays. You agreed to stay until you were eighteen. After that, you can go where you please."

It looked as if she was making some progress and then Daniel came out of the house carrying the snake. The screams started again. Effie grabbed her before she could run and held her until Daniel passed. I didn't realize the snake was that big. It must have been at least three feet long.

I thought it might be best to go back into the house and leave Effie and Nichole. I motioned for Charlie and, followed by Elliot and Grant, we went back inside. All this had happened when I was trying to get something together for dinner. I had to reheat my grease and finish peeling the potatoes. I had already sliced enough ham for sandwiches to go with the fried potatoes.

Elliot and Grant went on into the living room. "Well, Charlie, you really made a mess out of things. We have a hysterical girl on our hands. She may never get over this."

"I'm not worried about her. What about Daniel? He got the worst of it." He laughed. "We couldn't get her out and now we can't get her inside. You have to admit, Leta—my plan did work. I bet she won't lock herself in her room again."

I couldn't be mad at him. It did serve Nichole right for being unreasonable. Evidently, she had never had to make any sacrifices for others and always got her way. That was going to change.

By the time I had dinner on the table, Effie and Nichole had come into the house. Nichole was a sight. She'd probably never had dirt on her face or wore clothes in the condition hers were in. She was a pretty girl, but at that moment that would not have been an accurate description. When we all sat down to eat, she said she wasn't hungry, but she didn't leave the dining room.

I said the blessing and then made an announcement. "We're going to pass the blessing around so each of you will have a turn. Who's going to volunteer for supper tonight?"

"I will do the blessing tonight," Effie said.

"I also need a volunteer to do the dishes after supper."

Grant raised his hand. "I can do that."

I was pleased but not surprised that Grant volunteered. We were late eating because of all the excitement provided by Nichole and the snake. Of course, Daniel didn't show up. I would have Charlie deliver his meal to him. That's the least we could do after what he'd been through.

"We need to go shopping for clothes. I know you couldn't get much in the one suitcase each of you brought. I kept Chisum's clothes, and Elliot can wear some of those. I'm afraid they're not going to be as fancy as what you're used to," I said, looking at Effie.

"That will be fine. I brought a couple of nice dresses." Effie glanced at Nichole, who was sitting with her head down, like she was praying. "Nichole will be fine with that, also. Isn't that right, Nichole?"

"I guess," she murmured.

We left the next morning to go shopping, with Effie in the front seat with me and my grandchildren in the back. It was a beautiful day to be late December.

Grant leaned forward to allow us to hear better. "Gram, Nichole and I traded rooms last night. I wasn't afraid of that old snake."

I smiled. "That was nice of you to trade with your sister."

"I don't mind using the pot in my room. It is much easier than having to go all the way down a hall to the water closet."

"Good. I'm glad you're adjusting to the changes, Grant."

There were two dry good stores in town but, in my opinion, one was much better than the other. It was early, so there weren't many customers. Before we got out of the car, I suggested what we should buy. "I think everyday clothes would work best. Maybe one pair of overalls for each of you. Also, a pair of jeans. We may have to buy them in the men's department. I know few women wear pants, but on the ranch, they work better than dresses. We need to buy several outfits that would be appropriate for school clothes. Of course, Nichole will need dresses. Girls are not allowed to wear pants at school."

We were in the store for over two hours. Everything went pretty well except Nichole complaining about the overalls. She tried them on and looked at herself in the full-length mirror. "I am not wearing these."

We didn't argue with her but bought them anyway. She did better with the jeans because they did look good on her. They were a little snug, but we didn't press the issue. We found a heavy coat for all three plus work boots, which they would need. When we checked out, the bill came to over fifty dollars. Charlie was going to be livid.

As we left the store, the owner followed us to the car, thanking us at least a dozen times. It was probably the biggest bill for the entire year. The weather had changed drastically since we had gone into the store.

"It's colder," Effie said, as we loaded our purchases.

"Welcome to Texas. It looks as if we might have our New Year storm after all." We didn't have much room with our packages. "I need to buy some groceries but that'll have to wait. There would be no place to put them."

On the way home, something began to fall. At first it was rain, but it turned to sleet by the time we had unloaded and were in the house. Charlie had a fire going in the living room and had turned on the stove in the kitchen. When he saw the packages, he put into words what I knew he was thinking. "Looks like y'all bought out the store."

"They had to have clothes, Charlie. It's wintertime and from the looks of it, we're in for some bad weather. I thought we might miss this annual spell that comes between Christmas and the new year."

"We need more wood, Leta. Daniel usually keeps the wood box full. He's probably going to stay away from the house for a while."

Now was as good a time as any for Effie and Nichole to put their new clothes to use. "Effie, do you think you and Nichole could bring some wood into the house?"

"Sure. We need to change."

Nichole had been silent up until now. "Where do we get the wood?"

"It's in the woodshed," I said.

"That is where the snake lives. I am not going in there."

Effie solved the problem. "You will not need to go inside. You can stand outside the door. I can bring the wood out to you."

They went right to work and within half an hour had the wood box full. It sat right inside the back door in a small room. I was impressed that they didn't hesitate to carry armloads of wood from the shed. Effie had worn her overalls, but Nichole put on her jeans.

The next three days we stayed in the house most of the time. We got along fine with card games, dominos, and the radio. Charlie estimated that it snowed between six and eight inches, which made for good winter moisture. Effie and Nichole kept the wood box full, and we stayed warm. Grant's little dog was never far from him. Evidently Grant had not had much of a life in New York. He seemed to be enjoying himself and said a number of times how much fun he was having.

Daniel continued to stay away from the house. Effie volunteered to take him food twice a day. When we were alone, I asked Charlie what we should do. "Leta, let's just wait until the weather clears, then I'll talk to him. You know how he was with us when he first came to our house. Now, he has a whole new group of strangers to deal with."

"I'm a little worried, Charlie, about groceries. I canned enough vegetables from our garden and fruit to last the three of us. We also have some canned meat that will help. But I don't know if it's enough to last the winter with the four extra places at the table. I need to buy some groceries as soon as the weather clears."

"We'll do fine. I'll have Daniel kill a couple of deer and that will help. I've been hungry for some of your fried venison steak, with biscuits and gravy. It's good to have Elliot and his family with us. Isn't Grant something? To be crippled, he has such a good outlook on life. We could all learn something from him. Now, Nichole is a different matter. I'd say she might be a lost cause."

"I don't think so, Charlie. She has a way to go but, with time, she might change. I'm not going to give up on her. You just have to imagine the kind of life she's lived. Anyway, our family is back together."

31

SHEEP AND GOATS

Effie

I lay in bed thinking of the past ten days we had been in Texas. With the exception of Nichole, we had adjusted as well as could be expected. Nichole had withdrawn into herself, not talking and staying in her room much of the time. Her room was our room since she refused to go back to where the snake had been.

Grant was as happy as I had ever seen him since he developed polio. He had Rose with him constantly. He had become the resident dishwasher, but we continued the rotation for the mealtime blessing. Nichole still refused to take her turn at saying the blessing.

Elliot had not gotten any better, even with rest. When he walked from one room in the house to another it brought on shortness of breath. He took at least three pills a day for chest pain. I was sorry for being so angry with him and resorting to having an affair, but that was in the past, and I tried not to dwell on it.

Within a month I had become a different person. Did I like the new person? Would I go back to being the other person if given the chance? The questions I asked myself were easy to answer. Yes—I liked myself better, now. No—I would not go back to my old life if given the chance. Did I miss the conveniences of New York? Of course, I did. The outhouse was cold and crude by any standard. Using the chamber pot in the same room we slept was gross, as Nichole said. I was cold most of the time since the only really warm place was in front of the fireplace. Because of not having a regular bath, I felt dirty. But I was more alive here than I ever was in New York.

We were taking Nichole and Grant to school today. It had not opened the day after New Year's because of the weather. I hoped that Grant would be allowed to enroll but doubted it, because of what we faced in New York.

I was astonished at what Leta and Charlie could do at their age. They did not seem to realize they were old and supposed to be limited in their physical tasks. Both had been kind, and I had not for one moment felt unwelcome.

Leta and Charlie both insisted that I call them by their first names. Leta was an amazing cook with meals consisting mostly of fried foods. I tried to help but just seemed to get in the way. Nichole tried to extend her rebellion to not eating but could not resist the pancakes and sausage at breakfast.

I was anxious to have our own place but had not seen the house where we might live. With the weather improved, we should be able to start work on it soon. Of course, Elliot wouldn't be able to help, and Charlie would be limited. Most of the work would have to be done by Nichole, Daniel, and me, which brought up another problem. Daniel had stayed away since the episode involving his run-in with Nichole, which was an appropriate description. Somehow, we needed to make him comfortable around us. It was going to be up to me to make that happen. I threw back the covers and got out of bed. Now was as good a time as any to get started.

I was holding two cups of coffee and had to put one down to knock on Daniel's door. He opened it quickly and looked surprised. Before he could say anything, I said, "I brought you some coffee. Could I come in?"

He stepped back but said nothing, so I went in. The little

room had a small kitchen with a table and two chairs. In another corner was a bed across from the only other furnishing, a small wood burning stove. It was actually warmer than the other house. I presented him with the coffee and sat down at the table without an invitation. "I need to talk with you. Is that all right?"

"Yeah, I guess." He took a sip of coffee. "What about?"

"We need you. I know you had an unpleasant experience with us. My daughter was just a frightened little girl when she ran over you. I do not blame you in the least. We are going to do some repairs on the old house to make it livable. We cannot do it without your help."

He took longer to answer than I would have liked. "I will do what I can. The ranch takes up a lot of my time."

"We have not even looked at the house yet. I have no idea what is needed before we can move," I said.

I studied him as I waited for a response. He was a handsome young man. The long hair did not take away from his looks. In fact, it looked normal. He was dark but not that much, with high cheekbones and a broad forehead. His nose sloped downward, and his mouth was thin but wide. I had never seen him smile. I had seen pictures with his features. He was at least part Indian and probably full blood. I had a feeling that he could be a good friend or a dreaded enemy.

"I will talk with Charlie and see what he wants me to do."

I sighed. Not the answer I would have liked. But Charlie would tell him to help us. "Thank you." Then I took a chance. "Would you tell me something about yourself—where you grew up—how you got here?"

He looked away. "I do not have time. I have work that needs to be done. Thank you for the coffee." He got up, which was a not-so-subtle message that I should leave.

I took his cup and left, hoping for more and realized he was going to be a challenge. The walk back to the house through the mud was not easy. I had on my work boots but took them off before entering. Leta was at the stove cooking breakfast. She turned as I came into the kitchen. "How'd it go?"

I told her about my effort to ask Daniel for help and his response. "I do not believe anything was accomplished by my visit."

She continued to stir the gravy. "Don't be too sure of that. Something in the past made that boy suspicious of everyone. It took months for him to warm up to Charlie and me. Just be patient."

She continued to stir the gravy. I had never heard of gravy for breakfast—in fact, I had never seen white gravy. It was delicious, poured over her biscuits. In ten days, I had gained several pounds and at least two inches in my waist. I smiled. The work that waited for us on the old house would probably take care of that. "How do you do it, Leta? I mean—cooking, washing clothes, your outside chores."

She laughed and turned around. "You mean at my age, don't you? I never think about my number of years on this earth. I do what needs to be done—what I've always done."

"You are amazing. I want to be able to help you. We owe you so much, taking us in."

She took the gravy off the stove. "Thank you. But you owe us nothing. Your presence is worth more than anything. Have you noticed the relationship between Elliot and his dad? It is a prayer that was answered. Elliot left here angry and for a reason. Charlie didn't treat him right when Elliot was growing up. Now, they seem to have forgotten the anger and treat one another as a father and son should." She wiped a tear away. "Don't you think for a minute that you owe us anything. I will allow you to help me, though. You can start by getting everyone to the dining room. Breakfast is ready and will be on the table in a few minutes."

We were about to leave for town to get Nichole and, hopefully, Grant enrolled in school. Leta suggested that we wear our best clothes. I was surprised to see her dressed as if she was going to church. She had on hose with her dress and was wearing a hat and was holding what was probably her best pair of shoes. She insisted that we wear our work boots to the car to keep from getting our shoes muddy. We would change before going into the school office. Grant wore his best pants and shirt we had brought from New York. I had made sure Nichole brought a nice dress when she packed. She looked beautiful and, more important, decent.

The road to town was muddy, and several times it looked as if we would not get through some of the mud holes, but we made it. Before we got out of the car, Leta announced that we were to let her do the talking. We entered the school and went into an office with a sign on the door reading superintendent.

"We would like to see Mr. Avery," Leta said to the woman behind the desk.

The woman left and returned, escorting us to a door down a short hallway. When we went in, a man dressed in a suit and tie stood. "Mrs. Barlowe, what can I do for you today?" He motioned for us to sit down.

"I have my two grandchildren with me to enroll." She nodded toward them. "This is Nichole and Grant. They will be staying at the ranch and need to get into school. This is their mother, Effie Barlowe."

When he looked at Grant, I expected the worst. "Well, I-I think t-there might be a p-problem. You see, we have certain rules set up by the school board."

Leta had not accepted the invitation to sit, so we followed her decision to stand. "What do you mean?" she asked.

He shifted around in his chair as if trying to find a comfortable seat. "We must l- look after the i-interest of all our students. We can't afford to endanger the children."

"Yes, and as their grandmother I am going to do what is best for my grandchildren. You are a Christian, Mr. Avery, are you not?"

More squirming around in his chair. "Yes, certainly."

"Let me remind you of what the Bible says in Matthew 25:40. And this is from the King— 'Truly I say to you, as you have done it to the least of these brothers and sisters of mine, you did it for Me.' Matthew 25:45 The King goes on to say—'Truly I tell you whatever you did not do for the least of these you did not do for Me.' Now, I don't need to remind you of what happens to the goats, do I?"

He threw up his hands in surrender. "All right—all right. I'll go with you to the principal's office and tell him to enroll them. Please wait outside for me."

While we waited in the hall, Leta filled us in on what would happen. "The principal goes to the same church as we do. He was never going to be a problem. I knew the superintendent was going to give us trouble. That's just the way he is. We're home free now."

Our visit to the principal went just the way Leta said it would. We left the school with Nichole and Grant enrolled. They would be able to ride the bus to and from school, but we would have to meet it at the road. Impressed is not a strong enough word to describe Leta's appeal to Mr. Avery. It was like Jesus was standing right alongside her when she was insisting that Grant be allowed to attend school.

The mood was good on the drive home. Even Nichole joined the conversation. We changed into our work boots before getting out of the car. We followed Leta into the house, and I heard her gasp. I moved around her and saw Elliot lying on the floor.

32

APOLOGIES

Elliot

I came to, looking up at Effie. "What happened?"

She pulled a quilt over me. "We found you on the living room floor when we came home."

"Now, I remember. The fire needed wood. Dad was gone, and I went to the wood bin and got an armload. The last thing I remember was putting it on the fire."

"You are not supposed to lift anything," she kindly scolded.

"It wasn't that heavy. I went slow. Could you get me a pill? My chest hurts."

She brought me my medicine. "Your mother called Dr. Johnson. He's on his way."

I took the pill with the glass of water she handed me. "I'm all right, now. I shouldn't have tried to lift anything. Did you get the kids enrolled in school?"

She smiled. "Yes, thanks to Leta. She is a remarkable lady. I would like to have her confidence. The superintendent was no match for her." She bent and kissed me on the forehead. "You need to rest. It may be a while until the doctor gets here." She left after putting another quilt on me.

The pill had already begun to work its magic. I would be pain free for at least a couple of hours. The pills used to last for a full day but were effective less and less time.

My life had changed so much since October, which was

only a little over two months ago. My major concern had been making more money so we could move to Florida. Now, I am broke and not able to perform the most minimal task. There was no doubt that stress caused by the market crash resulted in my heart attack. My lifestyle probably had something to do with it, also. Now, the money seemed unimportant compared to not being able to breathe after the slightest physical effort, such as walking across the room.

I was able to relax and doze off since the pain was gone. Dr. Johnson came into the room talking and woke me. "How're you feeling?"

"Better. I took a pill. I must have passed out."

He took a stethoscope out of his bag. He listened to my heart but continued to talk. "You were carrying wood? That was too much for your heart." He told me to roll over and had me take deep breaths as he listened to my lungs. He put his stethoscope back into his bag and sat down on the edge of the bed. "You're going to need to be careful."

"I thought rest would help me improve. I only carried a small amount of wood."

"You have a weak heart brought on by a severe heart attack. Your heart is pumping at no more than twenty-five percent of what it should. I was truthful with you when you came into my office earlier. I don't expect you to get any better. I'm sorry to have to give you that kind of news. I suggest that you get a wheelchair and have someone push you to get around."

"There is no good news, is there?" I asked.

He reached and squeezed my arm. "Yes. Your family is here with you, and you will be well cared for. Charlie Barlowe is my friend. I've known him for over forty years. We argue back and forth because we're both stubborn old men. But he's a good man and will do what is right with your wife and kids. And Leta—well she is a strong woman with a strong faith. That is the good news. Your family is in good hands."

"So, you're telling me I am dying?"

"Elliot, we're all dying. You may live several months, several weeks, or several days. I don't know. In fact, you may outlive me. But you have one of the weakest hearts that I've seen. Now, I need to get back to my office. I brought you some more of the dynamite pills. Try to do as little as possible."

"Thank you," I said, as he left. I lay there a few more minutes before getting up. There was something I wanted to do before the pain returned. My dad was sitting in front of the fire.

"You should be resting," he said.

"Could we go for a ride around the ranch, or is it too muddy?" I asked.

"We might be okay if we stay on the road. I haven't been stuck lately, so I'm overdue anyway."

It was my first time to be outside today, and it was typical Texas weather. The sun was shining—a beautiful day—totally different from two days ago. We were able to drive over a large portion of the ranch. Toward the back of the place at the bottom of a mountain was a small hill that had two markers. I pointed to the spot. "Could we stop over there for a few minutes?"

Dad removed his cigar. "Sure. That's where your brother is buried and Pete our hand who died during the flu epidemic. You remember him? He was with us from the time we left New Mexico and came to Texas. He was my best friend and more of a partner than a hired hand."

"Yes, I don't see how you and Mother did it after Chisum and Pete died. It must have been a hardship. I should never have gone off and left you."

"Our neighbors were a tremendous help. We were younger then, too. Your mother was amazing. She could outwork any two men. We were able to hire dayworkers when we couldn't handle the challenges ourselves."

I got out and walked over to the headstones. My brother's read: John Chisum Barlowe— 1880-1915—A Loving Son. I had never grieved when my brother died, having nothing but resentment for him. All I could think of at the time was how Dad loved him and didn't even like me. I mumbled, "I'm sorry, Chisum. Please forgive me."

I looked around before returning to the pickup. It was a beautiful spot and would be even more so in the spring. You could see a large part of the ranch from here. It was only a quarter mile or so to the creek that bordered our place on the south. One of my few good memories was the days spent swimming and fishing there.

Dad had remained in the pickup, allowing me time alone at my brother's marker. He was silent when I got back in. "I should have gotten to know Chisum better. I was so full of resentment. If I hadn't left home so quickly, I might have changed. I was young and thought only of myself."

"There was too much difference in your ages. By the time you were twelve, Chisum was in his twenties, and we had you doing a man's work. It wasn't right. We took your childhood away from you. I didn't treat you the way a father should treat a son. Chisum didn't treat you the way an older sibling should treat his young brother. There's plenty of blame to go around. I wish I had it all to do over again." He started the pickup. "Let's see if we can get back to the house."

By the time I managed to get inside the house, I was exhausted. Cold, I sat as close to the fireplace as possible. Grant joined me, excited about going to school Monday.

"Dad, you should have seen Grams. She would not take no for an answer. She made the superintendent feel about this high." He measured at his knee with his hand. "I think he was just glad to get rid of us. The principal was really nice. I hope we never go back home. I do miss Sofia. Maybe she can come visit us some time."

Dr. Johnson's words came back. "They will take care of your family." It was already happening.

Dad came in with two cups of coffee and gave me one, then turned to Grant. "What about you? You want a cup?"

He looked surprised. "I've never had coffee."

"Well, you're in Texas, now. We start our young on coffee early." He went back into the kitchen and returned with a cup, giving it to Grant." I put a little cream and sugar in it."

Grant took a sip. "That's good! Thanks, CK. Now would you tell me about when you were young and saw Indians and buffalo?"

"That was a long time ago. Maybe I can remember some of what happened." Dad talked for the next two hours about his youth, even before he married Mother. He described the cattle drives and seeing buffalo by the thousands. He told about being attacked by Indians and stampedes where they chased the cattle for miles. Grant didn't move and was mesmerized by the stories. They fascinated me as well, since this was the first time I'd heard them. He took the time to give details of how the Indians dressed and the weapons they used. He gave us a lesson on the buffalo that would have been a credit to any college or university history class.

"It's time for a break," Dad said, getting up and going toward the door. "Nature calls."

"What do you think, Grant?" I asked after Dad was gone.

"I cannot believe it. In New York people go to the Talkies to see make believe cowboys and Indians. CK has lived and actually done these things."

I smiled and thought, *my dad will always be his hero.* And then the next thought surprised me—*there are worse people to have as a hero.*

33

THE CHICKEN PEN

Nichole

Disgusting—that was my life. I left my friends, servants, and a modern house with all the conveniences to move out here to this horrible place. I could not decide what was worse—the outhouse, chamber pot, the tub for bathing, or sleeping in the same room with my parents. If there was just some way to get back to New York, I could live with one of my friends. I had no money for train fare and no way of getting it. I was in a panic at having to stay here for another year and a half.

I was trying to get up the nerve to move back into my room. At least, I would have a little privacy. I had not been back in there since the snake had frightened me out of my mind. My mother told me about the man putting the snake down the chimney to get me out of the room. I could not believe my parents would allow such a thing. I kept telling myself the snake was gone from the room but so far could not move back.

No one believed me when I told them the man grabbed me when I went outside, running from the snake. I had never seen a man with hair that long, which made him almost as scary as the snake. I had no doubt but what he was mean and would hurt me if given the chance.

I had never known old people like my grandparents. Old people that I knew sat around all day and had someone wait on them. My grandparents were doing something all the time, especially my grandmother. My granddad did spend some time sitting around talking and smoking those stinking cigars. I have to admit that my grandmother was a good cook.

What confused me the most was my mother. She had accepted the change in our life without complaining. At home, she used to get angry at anything that happened having to do with us, especially Dad. Now, she was nice to everyone—strange.

I understood Grant and why he could be happy. He is treated more like a normal person. He even volunteered to do the dishes. To my grandparents' credit, they could see that Grant just wanted to be treated like everyone else and not as a cripple. I do not believe that my parents ever realized that.

We were going to school tomorrow. I tried to imagine what it would be like. At least I would be able to get away from here. Maybe they would have indoor toilets and inside water. I tried to visualize what the other students would be like. Certainly not like the ones I was used to going to school with. For one thing, they would probably be dirty, like I felt, after not bathing but once a week. I know they would not be as smart as the students in my New York private school. It would not be a surprise if they were three or four years behind me. In my English class we had been reading Julius Ceasar, whom I doubt they had ever heard of.

The dresses my grandmother had bought me were terrible. Something that was probably worn twenty years ago in New York. I wouldn't have been caught dead in them. What kind of teachers could they get out here in nowhere? I would probably be better educated than they were.

It was cold Monday morning, which required me to wear the work coat that Grams had bought. I inspected myself in the mirror after getting dressed and looked like I felt—ugly. At least my friends from New York would never see me like this. I would probably look like the other students—gunky.

I had sneaked a headband in my suitcase when packing for Texas. I would wait until I got to school to put it on. It fit into the little purse I was carrying. The headband was one of my favorites and included a feather. If I had my flapper outfit to go with it, I could really show this school what fashion was about.

Grams—what a silly name—took us to school. Mom went with us also and gave instructions all the way on how to be polite and nice to everyone. At home, she never mentioned school to me. When we arrived, I was surprised to see so many students standing around outside. Grant was out of the car before me.

"Go to the office and get your schedule," Grams said. "The principal will show you where your classes are."

I followed Grant who was moving faster than I had ever seen him. The principal's office was just inside the front door. A lady behind a desk greeted us. "Good morning, Mr. McNalley is out today, but I have your schedule. I have asked a student who has the same classes to help you find your way around today. She looked at Grant. "I'll take you to your building after the bell rings."

It was not long before the bell rang, and the girl came into the office. "Hi, my name is Louise. I hope you like our school. I'll be glad to show you where your classes are." She was nice but looked nothing like my friends. I left my coat in a locker that was next to hers. My schedule showed a math class first period on the second level of the three-story building.

Every desk was filled when class started. The teacher surprised me by asking that I stand, introduce myself, and tell where I was from. "My name is Nichole Barlowe, and I am from New York City." A murmur went through the class which pleased me. They were impressed, which did not surprise me.

"We are pleased to have you, Nichole," Mr. Jenkins said. He had a name plate on his desk.

The class, which was plane geometry, began with students being called on to work a problem at the blackboard. The class was forty-five minutes long, and I didn't understand one thing the students were doing. I was going to take plane geometry next year. Evidently, they assumed I was already taking it. I would need to be placed in an algebra class.

The bell rang, and on our way to the second period I stopped off in the bathroom and put on my headband. When Louise saw me, she looked surprised. "That's neat. I haven't seen anyone wear one to school."

"All I my friends in New York wear them." Maybe I could educate some of these girls on fashion.

Second period was an English class, and the teacher was an older lady, probably at least fifty. She passed a sheet of paper around and had everyone sign their name. When the paper was given back to her, she looked at it and said, "Miss Barlowe, could I see you a minute?"

Surprised, I followed her out into the hall. What was going on?

"You will need to remove your headband before returning to class. It is a distraction and not allowed." She stood there with her arms folded reminding me of a statue.

The surprise turned to anger. "I always wore a headband to school in New York."

"You're not in New York now. We have a dress code and anything that distracts violates it."

"That is ridiculous. What kind of school is this anyway?"

"You come with me, young lady."

I followed her and we ended up in the office. I stood silent as she explained what had happened to the secretary. "I will not allow her back in class with that headband and feather."

"Mr. Mobley is not in today. Coach Medford is to take care of any problems which arise in his absence. I'll go get him."

She must not have had to go far since they were back in a couple of minutes. The coach was big and tough looking. He did not waste any time. "What's the problem, Mrs. Parsons?"

She nodded in my direction. "She needs to remove her headband before coming back to my class. It is a distraction. Besides that, she was rude."

"What about it?" he asked, moving closer.

"I think it is unfair. The way I dress is my business. I wore a headband every day at my school in New York," I repeated.

He turned to the secretary. "Do you have the phone number where she is living?"

"Yes."

"Call her parents and tell them to come get her." He left without another word.

I waited for over an hour before my mother came into the office. "What is it, Nichole?"

"I am not going to school here. You can get me a tutor like you did Grant." I had taken off the headband and put it back in my purse before she arrived.

"We have no money for a tutor," she said.

I managed to shed a few tears. "Please, Mother, I cannot go to school here. Let me go back to Grams. I will do whatever you tell me there."

I think the tears worked. She took me back to the car, where Grams was waiting. "What was the problem, Nichole?"

"I am not going to school here. They are not fair and do not treat me right. I believe it is because I am from New York."

"Leta, she said she would do whatever we asked her at home if she didn't have to go to school." I didn't want to argue with her at school. "I have no idea what started the problem," my mother said.

I was afraid they were going to demand to know what caused me to get into trouble and be sent home; however, nothing was said the rest of the way. The first thing I did when we arrived was to move my possessions back to my room. I was not going to stay another night with my parents. I would rather face the fear of the snake reappearing.

I had just finished moving when Grams came to my room. "I appreciate you volunteering to help us out. You need to put on your overalls for a little job I have for you."

After she left, I changed into the overalls. I could not bear to look at myself in the mirror. At least no one would see me but my family, and anything was better than going to that horrible school.

Grams was in the kitchen showing Mother how to make a pie crust. I watched as my mother took in everything she said. I was still finding it hard to believe that my mother had changed so much in such a short period of time. Grams stopped and turned. "Come with me."

I followed outside to the pen where the chickens were kept. It was empty now since they were running around the yard. She went to a storage shed and came out with a shovel and a cart you push. "This is a job I've been putting off for some time. The chicken coop needs cleaning out in the worst way. Just shovel the chicken manure in this wheelbarrow and take it away from the house to dump it. It's smelly so take it a good way from the house. Don't come back in the house until you've cleaned your boots off good. You have any questions?"

I could not believe this. Wading around in chicken poop. "No, I guess not."

When she was gone, I eased myself into the chicken pen, trying to watch where I stepped, which was useless. It was everywhere, with the smell being the worst I had ever experienced. I began to shovel it into the cart, but the stench was too much, causing me to gag. I went outside the pen and finally was able to stop gagging. My stomach was turning flips as I stood there staring at the pen, not knowing what to do. I had agreed to do what was asked of me. But this was too much.

A voice behind me caused me to jump. "Somebody must be mad at you to give you this job."

It was him! I started to run, but he was between me and the house. I backed up pointing the shovel at him. "Stay away from me!"

He smiled and those evil black eyes stared at me. "I am not going to hurt you." He pulled a red handkerchief out of his back pocket and held it up to his face. "It will help if you put this around your face to help block the smell. That is what I do when cleaning the chicken coop." He took a step forward offering me the handkerchief.

I lowered the shovel. "You must be joking. I'm not going to put something on my face that you probably blew your nose with."

"This is a bandana that I wear around my neck to keep out the cold. I do not blow my nose on it. I washed it yesterday."

I hesitated. He took another step toward me. "Go ahead—take it. It will help. I promise."

I had to do something. I could not go back into that pen. I reached as far as possible and took the rag or whatever it was called.

"I need to show you how to fold it and tie it on."

He came another step closer, causing me to back up. "Stay away from me."

"Okay, have it your way." He turned and left, saying, "Wash it before you give it back."

Of all the gall, to insinuate that my face had germs. I had been to enough of the Talkies that were westerns to see outlaws with masks. I was able to tie it around my face in a similar fashion. I went back into the chicken pen and started putting poop in my cart and was able to tolerate the smell without gagging.

I worked the rest of the morning and then spent more time trying to get the sticky, smelly, chicken stuff off my boots. I have to admit that without the rag it would have been impossible to go back into the chicken pen. What was surprising was that the rag had a pleasant smell to it.

After getting my boots as clean as possible I went back into the house, still a little nauseated, dreading what my next job would be. Maybe I should rethink my decision not to go back to school.

34

A STRONGER WORD NEEDED

Leta

Nichole didn't look happy when she came in from cleaning the chicken coop. She was going to her room when I stopped her. "Nichole, I have another little job for you. We're having fried chicken for supper, and you can help me get it started."

She held up the red bandana. "That man let me use this when I was cleaning the chicken pen. He wants it washed before I return it."

"You mean Daniel? I'm glad you got a chance to see how nice he is?"

"How long is it going to take to start the chicken dinner," she asked. "I'm tired."

"Not long." I didn't have much patience with her. I got her enrolled in school and then was embarrassed that they had to call us to come get her. Effie finally told me what caused the problem, which made the whole ordeal even worse.

I found the small piece of rope and my other tool and went out to the chicken pen with Nichole following me. The pen where the hens were kept was empty, but the fryers were still in their pen. I turned to Nichole. "Go in there and get one of those chickens and bring it to me."

She looked confused and hesitated. "I thought we were going to start dinner."

I smiled and pointed. "We are. Now bring me a chicken."

She went into the pen and finally was able to catch one. She was squeezing both wings to keep it from getting away. I took the chicken and tied the rope to its feet. I went over to the clothesline and tied the other end of the rope to the line, so the chicken was hanging from its feet.

"What are you going to do?" she asked.

I took hold of the chicken's head, stretched out the neck, and with one motion, sliced his head off. Blood went everywhere.

Nichole screamed, and ran into the house. I followed her inside and put a large pot of water on to heat and then went to her room. She had the door shut but not locked. "What's the matter, Nichole?"

Her face was as white as the sheet on the bed. "You killed that chicken. It was horrible. How could you do such a thing to that poor chicken?"

"Where did you think our fried chicken supper was coming from?" I asked.

"I don't know. I never thought about it."

The poor girl had probably never seen a live chicken before coming here. "That bacon we had for breakfast came from one of our pigs. We raise the animals that we eat and most of the vegetables. I do buy a few items from the grocery store in town. Now, come help me. I have one other chore for you."

"No, I am not going to watch you murder another chicken."

"The one chicken will be enough for supper with the other side dishes. I'm not going to murder another chicken."

"Okay, then." She followed me back to the kitchen where the pot of water was boiling.

I wrapped a towel around the handle and took it off the stove. "We need to go outside." I put the pot down, took the chicken off the line, and dipped it in the hot water. Nichole, you need to pluck the feathers off the chicken, like this." I pulled a handful of feathers off the chicken.

"It stinks," she said.

"You'll get used to it. Now, let me see you pull some feathers off." I handed her the chicken.

She timidly picked a feather off.

"It'll take you all day at that rate. Grab a handful of feathers and pull. It's not hard."

She did a little better this time. "Okay, you're getting the hang of it. I'm going inside and start the side dishes. Bring the chicken in when you finish."

I was at the back door when she squealed. "Something's crawling up my arm! What is it? They are all over me!"

"Nichole, settle down. It's just lice. They're leaving the chicken because of the hot water. You can get them off after you finish plucking the chicken." I went inside and started peeling potatoes.

It was only a few minutes until Nichole came through the kitchen, crying. "I cannot do it. They're all over me!"

I finished peeling the potatoes before going out and plucking the chicken. Effie missed all the excitement since she was sitting on the front porch with Elliot. When she came into the kitchen, I told her she might want to check on Nichole.

She came back a few minutes later, laughing. "What happened? She has taken her clothes off and is in bed with her head covered up."

I told her what happened. "I was probably too hard on her. This is a whole new world for her. But I was disappointed at her being sent home. I wanted to let her know what was in store for her if she didn't go to school."

"Nichole was already giving us problems in New York. The move to Texas came at a good time. Can I help you get dinner ready?"

With Effie's help, we had supper at the usual time. Nichole stayed in her room, saying she wasn't hungry. After we finished, I took a plate to her room. I included fried potatoes, a biscuit and gravy, and peas but left off the chicken.

The next morning Nichole was at breakfast wearing a dress. She didn't mention yesterday, but when Charlie took Grant to the road to catch the school bus she went, too.

After we washed and put up the dishes, Effie and I went to look at our old house to see what needed to be done to make it livable. It was located about a quarter of a mile northwest of our house and did have a good well with a pump in the yard. Underground water was plentiful since we were close to the creek which ran most of the year. The outhouse in the back was going to need some major work.

I tried to prepare Effie before entering by telling her the house had only about 800 square feet and would be in poor condition since it had been ten years since anyone lived in it. I was still surprised at the inside when we entered. The front door was only hanging by one hinge and would not close completely. Of course, it was filthy with at least an inch of dirt covering the living room floor. A couch was covered with a sheet that had mouse droppings all over it. The kitchen was no better with the chimney from the wood kitchen stove broken in half, soot covering the floor and ceiling.

It was too much for Effie. She started crying. I guided her to one of the cane bottom chairs and eased her down, which caused it to break, crashing her to the floor. She began to laugh through the tears and soon both of us were laughing uncontrollably. It was so pathetic that it was funny. I pulled her to her feet.

"I'm sorry, Leta. All of a sudden, I felt it was hopeless. That we could never make this a place to live. And then—God must have given me a shock to bring me back to reality. We have no choice but to make it work."

"The first thing we need to do is clean. We'll get Daniel to do the lifting for us. Nichole and Grant can help us on the weekends. Charlie wouldn't be much help except to give orders, which we can do without, so we'll just let him keep Elliot company. Are you ready to look at the two bedrooms?"

"Yes, I am ready for anything after seeing the living room and kitchen."

A small hall separated the two bedrooms which were the same size. They were dirty but not as much as the living room and kitchen. The big problem was the mice pills which were everywhere. Evidently, they had moved in, stayed, and multiplied. "We'd never be able to set out traps and get rid of these nasty little critters. What we need are cats. And I know just where to get them. Our friend, Jake has a litter of kittens that should be ready to wean. We'll take about four of them off his hands and shut them up in this house."

"When do you think we need to get started?" Effie asked.

"As soon as possible. I'd say it is going to take us at least a month and maybe more. The first thing we are going to do is clean up the kitchen and put in a kerosene stove. We'll need some heat in the house even though we won't be cooking. There is no telling what has taken up residence in the living room fireplace chimney. We'll worry about that later. We'll make a list of priorities and get started as soon as possible."

A bench on the porch looked sturdy enough to hold us, so we sat and talked about the future. Effie expressed her concern about Elliot's condition and said that he seemed to be getting worse. "He wakes me up almost every night gasping for breath. I want to do something for him but feel helpless."

"I don't know what to tell you, Effie. We have not seen a doctor other than Johnson since we bought the ranch almost forty years ago. You could ask Elliot if he'd be willing to go to Houston or Dallas and see if doctors there could help him."

Before we could continue, Charlie and Elliot drove up. We went out to the pickup. "How does it look?" Charlie asked.

"Like an old house that hasn't been lived in for over ten years. Did y'all decide to go for a ride?" I asked.

Elliot held Rose, who would bark occasionally. "Mother, she hasn't quit barking since Grant left for school. I hadn't thought about it, but she's never been away from him. She's better now compared to what she was at the house. We thought taking her for a ride might calm her."

"Leta, Daniel went hunting this morning and hasn't come back. We're going up to the area he usually hunts and see what's keeping him. He rode that bronc we bought him so anything could have happened."

After they left, we walked back to the house to start dinner.

I was enjoying having someone to talk with other than Charlie, especially a daughter-in-law.

By the time we had dinner ready, Charlie and Elliot came in. Elliot was carrying Rose who was still barking. He put her down, and she started through the house looking for Grant.

Elliot plopped down in a chair. "I don't know what we're going to do. She still hasn't settled down. If we let her outside, she would probably take off looking for Grant. I guess all we can do is tolerate her until Grant gets home."

I asked Charlie if they had found Daniel. "Yeah. He had a nice buck hanging in a tree, he was skinning. I've never seen anyone as skilled with a knife as he is. That hide came off so easily. It would have taken me at least three times longer. He was gone so long, because after killing and field dressing the buck, he had continued hunting. I had told him we needed two deer. It's probably better that he only got one. It should last us quite a while. He can go hunting again after it's gone. We brought the deer in the back of the pickup. I'm going to wait until he gets home to help us hang it in the barn. He's riding Roany back to the house. I still have a tough time believing what he's done to that outlaw. I wouldn't get on him if you paid me."

"Where do you put the deer?" Effie asked.

"We hang him from a rafter in the barn. It's cool enough this time of year to let him hang for a couple of days. The meat is better after that. Then we'll cut up the backstrap and hindquarters for steaks. We'll smoke some of the better cuts and make jerky out of the rest. Very little is wasted."

Charlie was saying *we* when I did most everything that he described except hanging up the deer.

"It's been a long time since I had venison steaks. I am looking forward to them with the biscuits and gravy. I remember that Chisum liked to hunt, and we had venison often. I was more of a fisherman than hunter."

It was the first time that Elliot had mentioned Chisum in my presence since getting here. There was no anger in his voice—for that I was thankful.

We were late eating, and by the time we had done the dishes and listened to Rose bark for two hours it was time to go pick up my grandkids. The school bus was supposed to be there at four o'clock.

Effie went with me, and the bus was right on time. Grant got into the car talking about what fun he had. Nichole said nothing and was puffed up like a big bullfrog.

Her mother finally asked about her day. "I hated it," she said.

I couldn't resist. "Was it better than cleaning out the chicken coop?"

She didn't answer me. Maybe I underestimated her when I said she was going to be a challenge. Maybe a stronger word was needed.

I was surprised the next morning when Nichole came to breakfast dressed for school. She may have thought about the chicken pen. We took them to meet the bus with Grant excited about his day. Nichole stayed silent.

At mid-morning Effie and I were in the kitchen making a list of what we needed to get our old house livable. Charlie and Elliot were on the front porch. I heard a car drive up and went to see who was visiting. The sheriff's deputy got out of the car and started toward the house. *Oh, no,* I thought. Charlie liked the sheriff but despised his deputy.

I stood in the door and listened as the deputy came on the porch. He didn't offer a greeting or a handshake. "Charlie, I need to talk to your hand. I think his name is Daniel."

I could already hear Charlie popping his teeth from where I stood. "What do you need to talk with him about?"

The deputy straightened up to his full height. "I really don't see how that's any of your business, Charlie."

I went out and stood next to Charlie—afraid of what was coming next. Charlie's teeth reminded me of a woodpecker. "You damn right it's my business. Now tell me what you want to talk with Daniel about or get off my property."

"Okay, have it your way. Your hand has been accused of attacking a young teenage girl, and I'm going to have to take him in for questioning."

35

DODGING A BULLET

Effie

I listened to the deputy say the complaint came from a teenage girl and knew at once it was Nichole. How could she do such a thing? I had to do something— quickly. I went over to where they were standing and told the deputy. "I can clear this up. I am sure that the teenage girl was my daughter, Nichole. Was the girl in school that lodged the complaint?"

The deputy looked surprised. "Yes, in fact, she was. She had gone to the principal and told him about the incident. The principal then called me. The sheriff is out of town, and I'm in charge."

I went on and told him about the incident with the snake and Nichole accusing Daniel of attacking her. "Nichole was frightened and was the one on top of Daniel when I pulled her off him. Daniel was not at fault."

"Just the same, I need to take Daniel in for questioning. It shouldn't be a problem if what you are saying is true."

"What do you mean if what she is saying is true?" Charlie asked. "That girl who brought the complaint is her daughter. I was there, also, as well as Leta, and my son. You are not taking that boy anywhere. Now, you get off my place, and I'll talk to the sheriff when he gets back in town."

"That won't work. A complaint has been lodged against your boy. It's my duty to arrest him and take him in."

Charlie turned and left, going back into the house.

"You need to leave—now!" Leta said.

"Where'd he go? I wasn't through talking to him."

Leta stepped forward. "Young man, he's gone after his gun. I know Charlie. Leave, now!"

The deputy opened his mouth but didn't speak. He left and was almost to his car when Charlie came out, wearing his pistol. I stepped in front of him. "Just calm down, Charlie. He's gone."

"I need a drink," he said, turning and going back into the house.

Leta explained to me and Elliot. "I haven't seen him put on his gun in over thirty years. It scared the daylights out of me when he left. I knew where he was going."

"What would have happened if the deputy had not left?" I asked.

Leta shook her head. "I hate to think about it. Charlie was not bluffing. He's really fond of that boy. Thank the Lord, the deputy had the good sense to leave."

Now, to confront the real problem. "I am so sorry, Leta, for the conduct of my daughter. I don't know what else to say."

"This is serious. It's not like refusing to come out of her room or being angry about moving here. She endangered Daniel and caused Charlie to do something I hadn't seen in years, but it could have been much worse. I'm going to leave it up to you and Elliot to deal with your daughter. Charlie and I will stay out of it."

I did not know what to do with Nichole. Elliot was not able to help me. He was becoming weaker and could not deal with the stress of confronting Nichole. As far as punishment, I could think of nothing that would be severe enough for what she did.

Leta and I were waiting when the school bus arrived that afternoon. I was not going to confront Nichole until we were alone. She was in a good mood when she got in the car, talking more than she had since we arrived in Texas. Grant was unusually quiet.

When we stopped at the house, I told Nichole to stay in the car, that we needed to talk since we had more privacy in the car. "Why did you do it, Nichole?" I asked after Leta and Grant were gone.

"Do what?"

I was going to try and stay as calm as possible and not get into a screaming match. "Tell the principal that Daniel attacked you. The deputy sheriff came out here to arrest Daniel. The principal had called him."

"Nobody cares about me or my feelings. I finally found someone who would listen to me. The principal asked me how everything was going in my new home. I told him the truth. That man put a snake in my room and attacked me."

"You lied, Nichole. I pulled you off Daniel after you had run over him. You were beating him in the face."

The anger showed before she spoke. "I hate it here! I will do anything to get away! That man tried to hurt me. He deserves whatever happens to him."

I was determined not to raise my voice. "You keep referring to that man. His name is Daniel. He has worked for Charlie and Leta for several years. He is like family to them. Do you know how old Daniel is?"

"No, and I don't care!"

"Leta told me he's nineteen. Does that surprise you? He is little more than a boy who had been forced to assume the responsibility of a man."

She responded in a normal tone. "I thought he was older."

"He is only a couple of years older than you, Nichole. I am sure he had a much different life though. You have no idea what the reaction to your lie could have done. It might easily have led to violence and somebody getting hurt or killed. I am at a loss as to what to do with you."

"I want to go home. I can live with my other grandparents," she said.

"You have to understand, Nichole. Everything has changed in New York—for my family as well. My dad is struggling to keep his business because of the stock market crash. They would not want the responsibility of taking care of you. You told me you would stay here until you were eighteen and had graduated."

"That was before I knew how terrible it was here. Why do you even care what I do? In the past you never paid attention to me or Grant. Why the change?"

That was not an easy question. "I was wrong not to take more interest in you. I realized when your dad became ill that I had to take care of my family. I agree with you—I have changed but for the better."

She opened the door to get out. "I liked it better when you didn't care."

"Just a minute, Nichole, I am not finished. You are going to apologize to Daniel today. You will also apologize to Charlie and Leta. Tomorrow you will tell the principal the truth about Daniel. Furthermore, you are not going anywhere until you turn eighteen and have graduated from high school."

She got out of the car and slammed the door. *Now what?* I thought. She was in her room when I went into the house and did not come out until dinner. She would only give one-word responses anytime we tried to include her in the conversation. She returned to her room after dinner and did not come back out for the rest of the evening.

That night when we were alone, I asked Elliot if he had any suggestions. "No, I've thought about it all afternoon, trying to come up with something, but drew a blank. She created a serious situation by not being truthful. She needs to be held accountable and punished—but how? We are years late in having Nichole take responsibility for her actions. She's always done what she wanted. Now, she is in a situation where that is not possible. What I worry about the most is when she turns eighteen and leaves here. She has no idea about the outside world."

"Your mom and dad have been so gracious to us, Elliot.

I hate the fact that Nichole is making trouble for them. After all, we are guests in their house. Do you think that if we let her return to New York, she could live with my parents?"

"No, with your dad's financial problems and your mom being the way she is, it wouldn't work. She would be a burden on them, which they don't need. A few months ago, I would have never said this, but now—all we can do is pray about it. You're better at that than I am."

"It is strange, Elliot, when everything else fails that is the last resort, when it should be the first. But you are right. It is all that is left."

When the weather allowed it, January and February were spent working on what would be our new home. We would have a couple of days when the weather was warm, usually followed by miserable, wet, and freezing days. Most of the time was spent cleaning. Leta and I did most of the work with Daniel helping us move the furniture. Grant also insisted on helping and had become stronger since he was more active. Nichole never apologized for her actions to anyone. If anything, her attitude became worse. The only time she helped us at all was when we demanded it. She spent most of her time in her room. I thought she might eventually become tired of being angry, but that wasn't the case. I tried to remember myself at her age and wondered if I was anything like her.

Elliot was not able to do anything to help. He stayed in the house most of the time. He went with his dad occasionally to feed but remained in the pickup. Some days would be better than others.

By the end of February, we had the house cleaned and installed a new kerosene cook stove. Daniel had cleaned out the chimney in the living room and removed a family of raccoons. We aired the mattresses out on a couple of sunny days, and the cats had done a thorough job on the mice population. The two bedrooms were small, and there was only room for one bed in each. The only solution was to put Grant's half bed in the living room. The outhouse had not been repaired, which was going to be a major undertaking. When the weather improved, John and Jake were going to reconstruct that necessity.

I was becoming more and more impressed with Daniel. He was friendly and came around more often. Grant had taken up with him and, at every opportunity, was by his side. Daniel had promised Grant that in the spring he would teach him to ride. It was a joy to see him so happy. Nichole could not wait to get away, and Grant had found a home, which he loved.

What worried me the most about moving into the other house was cooking meals for my family. I had done so little cooking in my lifetime. I shared my concern with Leta, and she did not waste any time teaching me to prepare some of the basic meals for this part of the country. Biscuits were one of the first lessons since they were a staple. Frying sausage, bacon, and ham came next. Some types of potatoes were a side for most noon and evening meals. The hardest was the baking, especially making a pie crust. After several attempts, I gave up, admitting it would have to come later. I would never be able to put a meal together as quickly and efficiently as Leta.

"It looks good, Effie. Y'all have done an amazing job," Elliot said, as we toured our new home. "I'm sorry that I couldn't help you."

It was mid-April, and we were ready to move into Charlie's and Leta's old house. I admit it did look much better than when we started. Suddenly a vision of what we had left in New York appeared. I quickly erased it. That was the past— this was the future and a new beginning.

36

ESCAPE

Nichole

I had no idea what awaited me in Texas when I agreed to go, with the promise upon graduation to be set free. It was ten times worse than expected, and I was not going to stay here for another year. Some way, somehow, I would get back to New York. I could get a job, rent an apartment, and be able to see my friends.

To be truthful, I remembered little of what happened when the snake appeared in my room. I was so terrified that I panicked, just wanting to get away. The man I saw when I first realized what had happened was the focus of my fear. It did not matter if I told the truth to the principal. I was not going to apologize to anyone. Everyone was against me—making me against everyone.

It had been a horrible three months. I hated everything about my life. Going to a water closet outside in the cold and having to use a pot in my room was the worst. Adding to my misery was the weight I had gained. The meals were good and, having nothing else to do, I ate everything and more. The clothes I had brought from New York were too small as well as the school clothes bought here. Even the jeans my grandmother brought me were difficult to button. The only thing that fit were those hideous overalls that I would die if anyone saw me in.

I had never had a problem with Grant—in fact, I felt sorry for him until we moved. Now, I detested him for liking it here. Everyone bragged on him and said how sweet and helpful he was. It made me sick.

School was not any better than living in this house. I expected to be ahead of everyone in the basic subjects, only to find the opposite was true. I was at least a year behind in math, probably more like two. The kids here studied more and tried harder than my classmates. They took school much more seriously than we did in New York. The result was that my grades were poor. I hid my anger and disappointment by pretending not to care.

I finally found something in this nothing place that interested me and might allow me to survive. Larry was a senior and in two of my classes. It had started with him staring at me, progressed to talking at lunch, and now had advanced to the stage that he was walking me to class. Larry was not that good-looking, but he paid attention to me and made me feel better about myself. It was strange that other students had little to do with him. I had not made any friends either, so maybe that was how we found one another.

The relationship advanced further when we sneaked out of a school dance and left in his car. Leta and my mom had taken me and planned to pick me up when the dance was over. Larry and I made it back in time with no one missing us.

We left during lunch several times before getting caught, which meant I had to go to the principal's office and receive a lecture about my conduct. "Nichole, I'm disappointed in you. You have a loving home and supportive parents and grandparents, yet you continue to be angry and rebellious. I feel sure that your parents don't know about Larry. Did you know that he is twenty-one years old? He dropped out of school and got into trouble with the law. He agreed to come back to school rather than go to jail. I imagine that you've noticed that other students have little to do with him. There is a reason for that."

I did not need a lecture from anyone. "I could care less about his past. He likes me, and we have fun."

"I want you to tell your parents about Larry. If you refuse, then I will do it for you. They need to know what you're getting into. I will contact your mother in a couple of days to see if you've told them about him."

"You have been nice to me. I thought you liked me, but you are like everyone else here," I said.

He leaned forward in his chair. "I do like you, Nichole. But you're incredibly angry and are on the verge of making some bad decisions that will hurt you and your parents. I want to help you, but you have to let me."

I stood. "I do not need help. Just leave me alone. Is that all? Can I go back to class now?"

He made a motion toward the door, and I left, glad to get away. People did not understand what I was going through. I was not going to tell my parents about Larry. I would get another lecture from my mother. Maybe the principal was bluffing about telling them.

A couple of days after getting caught leaving school during lunch, Mother approached me about Larry, saying the principal had called. I told her that he was just a friend that had been nice to me. She insisted that I have him come out to meet them. That was not going to happen.

"Why are we moving into that cramped up old house?" My mother had just informed me we were moving tomorrow.

"It will be ours, Nichole. We will have more privacy and give your grandparents more room. I imagine they will be glad to get us moved."

"Why can't I just continue to stay here? It would give you, Dad, and Grant more room," I said.

"We are still a family and will be together. Do not argue with me about this. You are moving with us."

I went to my room and slammed the door. I had to get away from here. If I only had money for a train ticket—any way to get back to New York. I had one person who might help me—Larry. I stayed in my room the rest of the evening and missed dinner, which might help me lose some weight. I came up with a plan to get out of here that might work.

On Saturday, April 12, we moved into our house. Of course, all we had to move was our clothes. We had only been in our residence a couple of hours before an incident happened that proved it had been a mistake to leave my grandparents'. My mother tried to fry some ham for lunch. The grease caught fire and before she could put it out the entire house was filled with smoke. We opened the doors and windows and still had to go outside and wait for the smoke to clear.

I could not resist saying, "I told you so. We should not have moved." It was the wrong thing to say at the time.

Mother glared at me. "I am tired of you, Nichole! You have made everyone around you miserable. I have tried to ignore you, but that is going to stop. You are going to help me and your dad. We are all in this together, including you. From now on, you are going to do your part. You can start by walking up to your grandparents' and getting some more ham. What I was cooking is burned."

I decided now was not the time to refuse. I had never seen her so angry. I started walking to my grandparents' which was not that far. When I was about halfway, I saw CK's truck coming. Good, I thought. I can get a ride to the house and back. I changed my mind when the truck stopped.

"Would you like a ride?" Daniel asked.

I kept walking, not looking at him. I was not about to get in the truck with him.

He drove alongside me. "Riding beats walking."

I continued to walk, not looking at him.

He drove ahead and stopped, got out, and opened the passenger door. "Get in," he said, when I reached the truck.

Now, what? I was afraid of him. He was probably still angry because I had gotten him in trouble with the law. He might take me somewhere out of sight and beat me. He just stood there blocking my way and stared at me with those dark eyes. He was not giving me a choice. I got into the truck but left the door partially open to allow me to escape.

Nothing was said on the short drive to my grandparents. I went into the house and told my grandmother what happened. She gave me another package of ham.

"Tell Effie she had the grease too hot. It's a common mistake and has happened to me before."

Daniel was waiting for me. I hesitated, not knowing what to do. He leaned over and opened my door. "Get in. I'll give you a ride back."

I did what he said—afraid not to.

"Why are you so mad?" he asked.

"I hate it here. I want to go home."

"From what I hear, that is not possible. Your dad lost all his money and is sick. Charlie and Leta must take care of you."

I knew what he said was true but was not going to admit it, so I remained silent for the rest of the short drive. When we arrived, to my surprise, he followed me into the house.

My mother and dad gave him a warm welcome, and Grant was excited to see him. "Are you going to eat lunch with us?"

"I've already had lunch, but thank you. It's a nice day, Grant. I was going down to the creek and set out some lines. Maybe the catfish will be biting. I thought you might like to go with me."

Grant was up at once, reaching for his cane. "Is it okay, Dad?"

My dad smiled. "I don't see why not. Be careful. The bank is steep at places." He turned to Daniel. "There is a deep hole about a mile west, surrounded by large oak trees. Is that still a good fishing spot?"

"Yeah. That is where we are headed. I seldom put out lines there that I do not catch a mess of fish."

"You need to eat lunch before you leave, Grant."

"I'm not hungry." He was already moving toward the door.

"Something good has come out of all of this," my dad said after they had left. "Grant is a different person."

I took it as long as I could. "What about me? Nothing good has come out of it for me! All I hear is Grant this and Grant that. Grant is so good! You don't care what I think. I hate it here!"

I was ready early and sat looking at the walls of the tiny room which was like a prison. No more after tonight. We had it all planned. There was an end of school dance tonight, and we would leave soon after it started and be miles from here before anyone knew we were gone. Larry had agreed to take me back to New York. He was as anxious to get away from this place as I was.

It had been my idea, and I was surprised when Larry agreed so quickly. I had no money, but he said that would not be a problem. I wondered if anyone would miss me—probably not. Everyone hated me and would be glad I was gone.

A knock and my mother said it was time to leave. I wore my best dress but could not take any other clothes. On the drive to town, it was impossible to sit still. I was getting away from here and going home and never coming back.

They let me out in front of the school. "Have fun, Nichole. We'll be waiting for you here when the dance is over," Mother said.

I smiled, thinking, *you are going to be surprised.*

Larry was waiting for me just inside the door. "Are you ready?"

"Yes. But maybe we should at least be seen before we leave," I said.

He seemed nervous. "No, that's not necessary. We need to get out of here. I parked behind the school. It's dark enough that people won't see us leave." He grabbed my arm. "Let's go."

When we drove away in his car, I was uneasy for the first time—something was not right.

37

MISSING

Leta

"Did you ever see anyone as rotten as she is, Leta?" Charlie asked. We were sitting on the porch enjoying a beautiful late spring day having our mid-morning cup of coffee. "No doubt, she's her daddy's girl, Leta. Remember how rebellious Elliot was at that age? I admit she is worse than he ever was. At least he would mind us even though he stayed angry most of the time. She's going to the dance tonight. I keep hoping that she will meet some of the local girls and make friends. I worry about this guy she is involved with now. From what I hear, he's trouble."

"We need to look at the positive, Charlie. Isn't Grant a sweet little boy? He has all these problems, yet he tries so hard to help us any way he can. Can you believe how he's taken up with Daniel? I think that's one reason Daniel has become so much more social. He comes around more than he ever has."

He took a cigar out of his shirt pocket and examined it. "I need to cut back on these. They're up to a nickel." He lit it and blew out a smoke ring. "It's nice to have the house back to ourselves. Y'all did an excellent job getting that old house fixed up. I'm surprised it came out as good as it did."

He continued, "The bad news, Leta, is that the cattle market continues to go down. I'm afraid we're going to take a beating this fall when we sell our calves. We've spent more money this year with the added expenses of Elliot and his family. I can't help but worry about our money. I have no doubt but what we're headed toward a depression, the likes of which we've never seen. We're not apt to get any help either, with a Republican president."

Bound for Charlie to look at the negative. "We'll make it, Charlie. We always have. You remember the years we didn't get rain. You kept worrying, but it finally rained. What about the winter when it was so cold, and we ran out of feed? You said we wouldn't make it—but we did. I'm glad we have our family with us, so we can take care of them, especially Elliot. He's in poor condition and continues to get worse. It's a helpless feeling not being able to do anything for him. It's fortunate that he has a wife like Effie. She is a strong lady and a fine daughter-in-law."

He groaned as he struggled to get out of his chair. "You know, I hear people all the time say they're getting old. Well, I'm already old. You want some more coffee?"

"No, thanks." I watched him as he limped inside. We were old but blessed to be in as good a health as we were. Many our age were already gone or bedridden. Charlie tended to always look at the dark side of everything. I did share his concern, even though I wouldn't tell him, about our finances. We had spent a lot on Elliot's family, and I believed what Charlie said about the Depression being bad. We had always just hunkered down during the tough times but now there was Elliot and his family to think about. The smokehouse only had enough food for the next couple of months when it should have lasted until fall. The garden that Effie and Grant helped me plant was doing good but needed rain. With their help, I had expanded it to allow for the extra mouths to feed.

The change in Daniel had come quickly and unexpectedly. Since Elliot and his family had moved, he had eaten every meal with us. He talked more, but still avoided anything about his earlier life. I shudder every time the incident with the deputy sheriff comes to mind. Daniel was part of the ranch now, and

Charlie was going to do whatever necessary to protect his belongings. I try not to think what would have happened if the deputy had not left when he did. I was the only one who knew how dangerous Charlie could be when he or his was threatened.

Charlie came back with his coffee, talking on a more positive subject. "Most of our calves have been born. We probably have twenty or twenty-five cows who haven't calved. We have twelve or so dry cows, so we'll keep fifteen heifer calves for replacement. We'll need to replace several bulls that are getting some age on them. I'm thankful we didn't buy any stockers this fall. Hopefully, the rest of the cows will calf by next month. I want to work the calves as soon as possible."

We stayed on the porch another hour talking about the future. I tried to keep everything positive.

"She should be coming out by now." The after-school dance was over. Effie and I were waiting in the car for Nichole. Only a few students were leaving the gym. "What should we do?" I asked.

"Go in and see if we can find her. If not, maybe someone will know where she is."

The gym was almost empty with just a couple of teachers cleaning up trash. We approached them and asked if they had seen Nichole. They looked at one another, waiting for the other to answer. "I haven't seen her all evening," the older one said.

"Me neither," the other one said.

"You mean she has not been here at all?" Effie asked.

The older one shrugged. "I haven't seen her."

"What about Larry? Have you seen him?" I asked.

She looked at her colleague before answering. "No. I haven't seen him either."

Further questioning would be useless, so we went back to the car. "What now?" I asked.

"Let's wait a few minutes," Effie suggested. "Maybe she will show up." We stayed half-an-hour before giving up and starting home. "Should we go to the police?"

"No, not yet, Effie. Maybe he will bring her home. If she's not home by morning, we'll turn it in to the police." We rode the rest of the way in silence, my mind rushing in several directions. Did they run off to get married? Maybe he forced her to leave with him—not likely. Would she show up later tonight, or were they gone for good? I dreaded Elliot finding out. It was the last thing he needed in his condition.

I stopped in front of Effie's house and killed the engine. "Let us know if she shows up tonight. If she's not here in the morning, we'll contact the sheriff. Charlie and I have a lot more confidence in him than the police."

"I am sorry, Leta. We have been so much trouble for you and Charlie—now this. We can never repay you for all that you have done for us."

"You are family, and the problems that you have are our problems as well. That's what families do. There is no way to tell you how much y'all being here means to Charlie and me. We'll get through this together." I reached and held her hand. "Now, let's hope she shows up tonight."

Charlie was asleep when I went in. I decided not to wake him. Nothing would be accomplished except to upset him. With all that they had gone through—Nichole had to do this. I should not be surprised; in fact, it should have been expected.

It had begun to rain, which was the one good thing that happened tonight. I made a pot of coffee and sat down at the kitchen table. There was no use going to bed. I couldn't sleep anyway. I took my coffee out on the porch, hoping to see a car coming up the road to our house. A car would have to go by our house to get to our old place. By two in the morning, I knew there was little chance of Nichole coming home. I went to bed, hoping to get a few hours' sleep.

I dozed off and on until Charlie woke me rattling around in the kitchen. He was pouring water in the coffee pot when I went in. "You made coffee last night when you came home?"

"Yes, I've been up most of the night. Sit down and let me tell you the latest on our granddaughter."

He listened without interrupting, but did begin popping his teeth before I'd finished. I told him about going to the sheriff this morning. "I guess that's the only thing we can do."

"No, we could just let her go. She's made it plain that she doesn't want to be here. Let her get a taste of the real world. Maybe she would appreciate what she had. She's been nothing but trouble since they came here almost five months ago."

"I doubt if that would be acceptable to Elliot and Effie. Would you go with us to see the sheriff?"

"The way it's raining, I doubt if we could get to town. I can call him later this morning and tell him about Nichole. I doubt if he can be much help, though. He doesn't have any authority outside of this county. They may be miles from here by now. Of course, they could be shacked up somewhere close, practicing the honeymoon."

"Don't be crude, Charlie. It's not funny."

I got up and poured him a cup of coffee. "Thank you. Leta, you have to admit Nichole has done nothing that would endear her to us. Quite the contrary, she has been a pain in the butt. And Grant—what a pleasure he's been. How could two kids be so different? I'd like to live long enough to see him grow up. You know, he could still do a lot, even with polio. Look at Roosevelt, he's probably going to run for president next year. I hope he does and is elected. We need a Democrat in the White House. Republicans have been starving us poor people for years."

Maybe it would be good to get him on politics and his mind off Nichole.

Charlie called the sheriff later that morning and told him about Nichole running off with Larry Felts. The sheriff's response did nothing to encourage us.

I stood close so I could hear the conversation. The sheriff asked how old Nichole was. Of course, Charlie had no idea, so I whispered, "She'll be seventeen next Wednesday."

Charlie relayed the information to the sheriff who gave us the bad news. "We may have a problem. If she has left with Larry Felts. There were several stores broken into last evening. He is our number one suspect. Nichole will be seventeen soon and is not considered an adult until she's eighteen. But—and it's a big but—if involved in a crime she will be prosecuted as an adult at seventeen. She's in bad company. I expect Felts will continue to be involved in criminal activity. I don't usually go after seventeen-year-olds that leave home, but I would make an exception in this case. Of course, I doubt if they're still in the county. I would bet they are miles from here. He has a little money from the break-ins. When that runs out, he will steal again."

"What can you do?" Charlie asked.

"Make some phone calls to law enforcement in this part of the state and tell them to be on the lookout for a man and young girl. We do have a description of his car. It's a long shot that they will be found until Larry does something stupid, involving a serious crime. I'm sorry I can't offer you more. There's no use sugar-coating it. It's a dangerous situation for Nichole."

"With your experience, where would you expect them to go?" Charlie asked.

"Probably the city. There's more opportunity for crime there. Fort Worth-Dallas area would be my guess. He didn't get a lot of money from his crime spree here. It won't last long. Maybe Nichole will come to her senses and get away from him."

Charlie turned to Effie. "Do you have any questions, Effie?"

She murmured, "No."

We thanked the sheriff and ended the call.

Three days after we talked with the sheriff, he called and told us he had news that wasn't good.

38

RANCH HAND

Effie

I had not been home from the dance long before it started raining. It continued throughout the night, coming in torrents. I was sitting at the kitchen table when Elliot came in at five. I told him what happened.

"I can't believe she just up and left," Elliot said.

"Elliot, I have never felt so helpless. We have no idea where to look for her. All we can do is hope that she gets in touch with us, which is unlikely. This man she is with is trouble."

"We're to blame, Effie. I ignored her and Grant. She was allowed to do what she pleased without any direction from us. Now it's too late. All I was interested in was making more money. I can see how foolish that was. Even with Nichole running away, we are still more of a family than when we were in New York. Look at Grant. He is enjoying life much more than he ever has. I think you are more satisfied with yourself than you have been in years. I now realize that my health is worth more than money. Of course, it took a heart attack to convince me."

"I know. I was just as guilty as you of ignoring both our children. I do have more respect for myself now than in the past. What bothers me, too, is that we have been a burden on your parents. We have depended upon them for everything—food, shelter, clothing, and now they are involved in our family problems. We have not been able to do anything for them. Oh, I helped some in the garden but that didn't amount to much. I am determined to do more. I know you are not able but that shouldn't keep me from contributing in some way."

"The biggest need is someone to help with the ranch. I could do that if able. Grant can actually do more than I can in the way of physical work. My dad is becoming more limited by the day and, with his age, can't be expected to hold up much longer. Neighbors have their own ranches to look after. I'm afraid we are in for some tough times with the economy going into a depression. It's going to affect almost everyone except the very rich. The cattle market will be hit hard like all other commodities. People in large cities will suffer the most because of unemployment. Farmers and ranchers will fare better, simply because they are more self-sufficient."

A large clap of thunder shook the house and rattled the windows, causing me to jump. "Does it always storm like this?"

"It's not unusual this time of year. About the time school is out, it's not uncommon to have storms and rain. We need the moisture, and if we don't get it now, the summer is almost always dry. If it continues, the creeks will get up and cause flooding. That's the way this country is—too much or too little—you never know which is coming."

The shadows cast on the wall by the one lamp were eerie. "Grant will be up soon. Maybe bacon and eggs will make us feel better. Toast will have to do. I'm not up to biscuits this morning."

It rained for the next two days and nights. We had several roof leaks where I placed buckets. We didn't leave the house except to visit the outhouse, which due to the remodeling was dryer than the house. Thank goodness we did have enough food in the house to last.

Monday, May 19, dawned clear with sunshine. It was beautiful after having been confined to the house since Friday night. We were sitting on the porch when we saw Daniel coming on his horse. Grant was with us as well as Rose, who started barking, warning us that we had a visitor.

He dismounted and led his horse up to the porch. "Good morning. Did y'all make it all right?"

Elliot stood and offered his hand. "No problem. We're glad to see the sun, though. How much did it rain?"

Daniel smiled. "A bunch. The rain gauge only holds five inches, and it ran over, so there is no way of knowing. It may have been twice that. Charlie sent me horseback since it was too muddy to drive. I have a message for you. The sheriff called early this morning and said a gas station was robbed at Weatherford by a man fitting the description of Felts. There was a young girl with him. I'm sorry for having to bring bad news, but Charlie thought you needed to know. He did say that the sheriff had talked with Felts' grandparents but couldn't get anything out of them. That's all the information I have. It's going to be a bad day for me. We have a water gap that always washes out in this kind of rain. It's strange since the water goes down quickly but destroys the fence. The cattle seem to know and will be out on the neighbor's if I don't get it fixed."

That was the most Daniel had talked in one setting. "Is Charlie going to help you?"

"No, he's not getting around good enough. I'll get any word to you that we receive from the sheriff." He got back on his horse.

"Wait just a second, Daniel. I could help you with the fence repair."

"Ma'am, that's no job for a lady. It's hard and dirty work."

"I insist. We need to start helping out on the ranch. Right now, I am the only one able. I will change my clothes and come to the house."

Daniel frowned, shaking his head. "It's about two miles to where the work needs to be done. It would be too long a walk in the mud. I can do the job by myself."

"Do you have a horse I could ride? I am determined to help you."

He took so long answering, I thought he was going to ignore me. "Have you ridden before?"

"No, but I can learn."

Again, he hesitated. "We have an old-retired gelding. All you have to do is sit on him. I'll saddle and lead him down here." He turned his horse and rode off before I could thank him.

"Effie, from the first time I saw him, he reminds me of someone. I can't put my finger on it. But there is something familiar about him."

"Can you and Grant cook your breakfast?" I asked.

"Sure. That won't be a problem. Are you sure that you're up to this kind of work? I've had quite a bit of experience with water gaps. It was one of my most unfavorite jobs."

"I have got to try, Elliot. We cannot continue to just take without giving something back. Maybe I can be a little help."

I went into the house and put on my overalls. Staying busy today would at least be a distraction from worrying about Nichole. In two more days, on the twentieth, she would be seventeen. The news about the robbery added more worry. Surely, she would realize her mistake and contact us.

By the time I had started the stove, cooked, and eaten a piece of toast, Daniel was back, leading a horse. Could I do this? I had always been afraid of horses.

"His name is Chester. He's a nice, gentle horse and doesn't have a mean bone in his body."

He dismounted and helped me get on Chester. I patted him on the neck. "Good boy."

Daniel showed me how to hold the reins and gave me some basic instructions. "Just follow me and don't pull on him unless you want to stop. Then say 'whoa' and gently pull back on the reins."

All I could do was nod. I thought, *what would my friends in New York think if they could see me now?*

Elliot and Grant were out on the porch when we left. "Bye, Mom. You look like a real cowboy!" Grant yelled.

Just like Daniel had said—Chester stayed right behind

him. We had to go through water several times that was up to his knees. It was scary, but he didn't hesitate. It seemed to take hours before the downed fence came into view. I had no idea what a water gap was before seeing it. It was simply a small little valley with a fence across it. The wire was down and tangled, but the posts were standing. I managed to get off Chester and suddenly, standing on the ground, felt small.

Daniel worked for several hours getting the fence untangled and back together. I was able to hand him tools and hold up the wire, so he could attach it to the post with staples. He could have probably done it by himself, but hopefully I made it a little easier. He talked little during the entire time, occasionally giving me instructions. When the fence was put back together to his satisfaction, he placed his tools back into a sack and tied them on his horse.

He turned to me. "I appreciate your help."

"I tried. Maybe it made your job a little easier."

"It did," he said, swinging onto his horse.

That meant I was going to have to get on Chester without assistance. I was able to get my foot in the—whatever you call it—and pull myself up. Chester didn't move. The ride back seemed shorter.

Charlie met us when we arrived at the house. "Y'all get'er done?"

"We did. I had some good help," Daniel said.

The compliment made my efforts worthwhile. "Have you heard anything else, Charlie? Daniel told me that the sheriff had talked with the grandparents of Felts but got nowhere."

"Yeah, he thinks they could help find him if they cooperated. Larry's been living with them for years. I don't know her that well. Her husband and I go back a long way," Charlie said. "It wouldn't hurt to talk to them and maybe get some information. We could give it a try if you'd like. Of course, the creek is out of its banks and the road to town is blocked. It'll be at least another day until the water goes down. You might talk it over with Elliot and see what he thinks."

"It would beat sitting around here and waiting. I am sure

Elliot will agree."

"Okay, it's settled then. We'll go in as soon as the road is open. And thank you, Effie, for helping Daniel. I just wasn't up to it."

After Charlie left, I told Daniel that I could walk to my house, and he could put the horses up. "It's been quite an experience. I appreciate your patience with me."

He smiled, showing him for what he was—a handsome young man. "You and Chester got along fine."

I left feeling good but tired. By the time I was halfway home, I was sorry about my offer to walk. I had to stop and rest before going on. The mud on my boots made my feet heavy. I finally reached the house with Elliot and Grant welcoming me like a hero and wanting to hear all about my day. It was already late afternoon, and all I wanted was a hot bath.

While my water heated on the stove, I told them about my adventure, maybe even exaggerating a little as to my contribution.

We were finally able to get to town on Wednesday. Charlie thought we would be more effective if only he and I went. When we stopped in front of the Felts' house he said, "They're not the friendliest people you'll ever meet. Don't be surprised if we receive a rude welcome. Not being the law, we may do some good."

Charlie knocked on the door, and we were greeted by Mr. Felts. "Charlie Barlowe. Now, why am I not surprised to see you?"

"Do you have a few minutes to visit with us, Douglas?" Charlie asked.

"Not really. I'm taking my wife to visit her sister today."

I was not going to be brushed off like that. "Mr. Felts, my daughter is missing. She is seventeen today and by all accounts is with your grandson. The sheriff has told us a person fitting his description has robbed a gas station. A young girl was with him, who would be my daughter. We are not representing the law and don't care about the criminal activity of your grandson. We are frightened out of our mind for Nichole. Your grandson is an adult, while my daughter is just a child. We want to get her back home and out of danger. Now, are you going to help us?"

He just stood and stared at me. A voice behind him said, "Ask them in, Douglas."

He stepped aside, revealing a slender woman with her hair up in a bun and dressed to go out.

Seated in the living room, I spoke directly to Mrs. Felts. "Please help us to get Nichole home. She is angry at having to move to Texas." I continued on and told her about moving from New York and Elliot's condition. Maybe I talked too long and too much, but I was driven by desperation.

"Larry has had a tough time. He's a good boy, and we're not about to help the law find him." I looked at Mr. Felts and thought for sure we would not receive any help.

Mrs. Felts sat up straighter in her chair. "Will you agree not to pass any information we give you on to the law?"

Charlie answered. "You have my word."

"Violet!" Mr. Felts shouted and stood.

One look from Mrs. Felts caused him to sit back down.

"Okay, here is what we know," she said.

39

REALITY

Nichole

"How many days do you think it will take for us to get to New York?" We had just left the dance and were on our way out of this dreadful place.

"I don't know."

"Have you looked at a map to see what roads we will take?" All I knew was that New York was northeast of Texas. We should be able to make it faster in a car than on the train. A few days from now I would be home.

"No, I have not," he replied angrily. "There're more important things to consider. Right now, I just want to get away from here."

What was going on? He had never talked to me this way. Every time we talked of leaving, New York was mentioned. Now he was avoiding it. I was depending on Larry for everything. I had no clothes except what I was wearing and only a couple of dollars. I moved over closer and put my hand on his leg. "What's the matter? You seem upset."

He stared straight ahead. "I have a lot on my mind. At the moment it's not New York."

Suddenly—panic. "What do you mean? That is why I agreed to leave. You were going to take me home. I want to go to New York and never see Texas again."

"Things change. I have to get my hands on some serious

money. How do you think we're going to eat, buy gas, and pay for a place to stay?"

"I thought you had money. You told me you did."

"Only for a few days." He moved my hand off his leg. "There'll be time enough for that later. It's beginning to rain. I have to concentrate on the road. The last thing we need to do is have a wreck."

For the next hour nothing was said. Doubt grew stronger until I began to realize that I was dumb for believing him. He had said nothing during the time we had been together that would make me not trust him. Now, it was different. I looked out the window into the darkness and shuddered—fear gripped me.

The rain came down so hard it was impossible to see the road. We finally had to pull off to the side and stop. "Where are we headed?"

"Weatherford. I have a cousin there where we can stay a few days. He's expecting me."

I was afraid to mention New York again. "After that, what are we going to do? Is he going to give you some money?"

He grabbed my arm and squeezed it until it hurt. "You ask too many questions. Just watch and learn. I got you out of that place you hated, didn't I? You need to be thankful."

The rain did not let up, and we spent the first night of our getaway on the side of the road. The rain continued the next day as we crawled along the deserted highway in silence. Larry had brought some bologna and bread, which was all we had to eat. At mid-morning, we came to the edge of a town identified as Cisco by a sign. We went through the business section but stopped at a gas station on the other side of town.

Larry reached under the seat and came out with a gun. "You stay here. I'm going to get gas and some cash."

I was too frightened to think straight. He was going to rob these people! Should I get out and run? I knew that would be dangerous. He would hurt me again.

A man came out of the station and asked Larry what he needed. "Fill'er up," he said.

I watched as Larry disappeared into the station. The man finished putting gas in our car and went back inside. I could see through the window that he was standing at a cash register. I saw Larry pull his gun and say something to the man, who took a wad of bills out of the register and gave them to Larry. Suddenly the man lunged at him, and Larry struck him in the head with the gun. He then came running to the car. "We're getting out of here." As we drove away, he handed me the roll of bills. "Here, count this and see how much we got."

I was crying. "No. You stole that money and hurt that man. I want no part of it."

Then with his right hand he backhanded me. "Do what I say! Now! And stop crying. You'll get used to it."

It hurt, and I tasted the blood from my busted lip. I started counting the bills through the tears. "There is sixty-two dollars."

"Not bad. Got a full tank of gas to get us down the road a good way."

I looked out the window. It had stopped raining, and the sun was out.

The next two days were the worst of my life. Larry's cousin lived by himself in a house which was dirty and stank. They spent the day drinking and planning ways to steal money. I thought constantly of trying to escape and get back to the safety of my parents but was afraid. I kept asking myself, "How could I be so wrong about someone?" The answer that kept coming back that I did not want to accept was, you only saw what you wanted to see—a way to get back home to New York. Look at what it got you. Larry was bad and cared nothing about me. Why did he bring me along? "Stupid," I murmured. "You know the answer to that." Would he eventually tire of me and turn me loose? No, of course not. He knew I would identify him as a thief.

The fifth day I decided to take a chance. I could not go on like this. The days were terrible and the nights worse. I was living in filth, wearing the same clothes, and not even having adequate water to wash. When I asked him to buy me some clothes he just laughed and said, "You look fine to me." The outhouse was almost unbearable. I had to put a cloth over my face to use it. I know it was not my imagination—something was crawling around in my hair.

I waited until it was dark to give me a better chance of getting away. Larry had demanded that I tell him before going to the outhouse. They were in the kitchen on the way to getting drunk. "What you want?" he asked, slurring his words.

"I need to go to the outhouse."

He laughed. "You need any help?"

I went out the back door and, when out of sight, began running. I had no idea about the direction or a destination. I just wanted to be away from here. It was dark, but I saw lights in the distance. I ran until I gave out and then started walking in the direction of the lights. Maybe I could find a policeman or someone to help me. I came to a road which made walking easier. I was getting closer to the lights when a car came up behind me. Maybe I could stop them and get help. I stood in the middle of the road and waved both arms.

The car stopped and someone got out and came toward me. "What do you think you're doing?" And then he hit me. He dragged me back to the car and shoved me into the back seat. "If you try that again—I'll fix you where you never walk again."

I was still dizzy when we got back to the house and fell, trying to get back inside. He reached down, grabbed my arm, and dragged me. "See what you get by trying to run away."

I lay on the floor trying to recover. Larry went back into the kitchen where they began discussing plans for a robbery. They took no precaution to keep what they were saying from me. Why would they? I was no threat to them.

"Are you sure he has money?" Larry asked.

"I told you—old man Lawler is loaded," his cousin said. "He told me he is afraid to keep his money in the bank. He lives by himself. It's perfect. We should get enough to last us years in Mexico. He lives just three houses down from me and seldom goes out. He won't be missed for days. We couldn't ask for anything better."

Larry laughed. "It sounds too good to be true. Are you sure he won't be missed for several days? We need at least three days to get out of the country."

"You got to trust me, cousin. The old man seldom comes out of his house. No one ever visits him. We'll be drinking tequila in Mexico before anyone finds him."

I listened in horror. They were going to rob and murder the man. I tried to get up but was dizzy and too weak. I don't know how long I lay on the floor before Larry helped me stand, guided me to the car, and put me in the back seat.

"I'll be back in a few minutes, and I better find you here." He slammed the door shut.

I tried to blank out everything. If I could sleep maybe this nightmare would go away. Later, I felt the car moving and heard them talking. "How much did we get?" Larry asked.

"Hold your horses. I'm counting it," came the reply. "Guess how much?" "Just tell me." Larry said.

"Would you believe $2,640? I told you the old man was loaded."

"That should let us live in style for at least a year in Mexico," Larry said. "We need at least three days before the law gets involved. They're going to suspect you when they find you're gone."

"Told you not to worry, cousin. The old man sure ain't gonna be talking."

They had murdered the man. I had to get away. I was able to sit up and noticed we were going through town. We stopped at a red light, and I saw a police car sitting on the side of the road. We drove past the police when the light changed.

Larry looked in his rear-view mirror and slowed. "Can't take any chances. He's not coming." He sped back up.

I made a desperate decision. I grasped the door handle, pulled up, and pushed the door open, jumping out. I felt pain when I hit the road—then nothing.

40

ST. JOSEPH HOSPITAL

Effie

I sat on the edge of my chair focused on Mrs. Felts. "Larry has a cousin that lives in Weatherford. They stay in touch. He's as sorry as they come." She looked at her husband. "It's his family. I've tried to keep Larry away from him but have not been successful. I imagine that's where he's gone. I'll give you the address, but after he leaves there, I have no idea where he'll go. I didn't tell the law anything because I don't trust them. I'm hoping that he comes back home before he gets into serious trouble. It scares me to think of the two of them together."

"Thank you. We will not give the address or any information to the police," I said.

When we left, Mr. Felts followed us to the car. It was clear that he was angry. Before we got into our car, he started in on Charlie. "I don't agree with my wife, Charlie. That girl is probably the reason he left. If it hadn't been for her, none of this would have happened. I told Larry not to get mixed up with her."

Charlie ignored him as we drove away with Mr. Felts still mouthing off. "I wouldn't have tolerated him saying those things ten years ago. As you get older, it's necessary to make some adjustments. Anyway, we got the information we came for. What're your plans now?"

"Go to Weatherford and, hopefully, find her and bring her

home. After that, I don't know what we'll do with her. She has been a pain for all of us since we came to Texas."

"You don't need to give up on her, Effie. Elliot had a terrible attitude when he was Nichole's age. I didn't have any patience with him and have regretted it since he left home. I'm sorry Elliot experienced a financial disaster and a heart attack, but that is what gave me another chance. As far as Nichole being a problem, it has been worth it to have your family here with us."

"I cannot imagine what would have happened to us if you had not taken us in. We had no money and no place to live. I hope to be able to repay your kindness."

"I have a suggestion. Take Daniel with you when you go after Nichole. Elliot is not able, and I wouldn't be of much use. If you have any trouble, Daniel would be there to help. Don't let his age fool you. He is more than capable of handling himself in a confrontation."

"Tell me about Daniel. When I spent the day with him repairing the fence, he talked little. He seemed determined not to become personable."

He laughed. "I can't help you there. I misjudged Daniel for a long time—another one of my many mistakes. He is a fine young man. I believe he has a past that he's afraid we'll discover. He hides it by being determined not to develop a personal relationship with us. That's just my opinion. Whatever his past, I don't believe it involves anything that he did that was wrong. He's not that kind of person."

"Elliot has mentioned several times there is something familiar about Daniel— like he has seen him previously."

We drove up and parked in front of our house before he responded. "I don't know where he could have seen him. All I know is that he came from Oklahoma."

"Thank you for going with me to see the Felts. I would like to leave as soon as possible and take your advice. Do you think Daniel will be willing to go?"

"Yeah, I don't have any doubt."

We left at noon on Wednesday and Charlie was right. Daniel agreed to go with me. Daniel might be competent in a confrontation, but he was not good company. I tried to talk to him but gave up, since one-word responses were all that he came back with.

Before we drove into Weatherford, it was dark. It took us another two hours to find the address, but we only found an empty house. It would do no good to wander around in the dark, so we found a hotel. I asked, encouraged, and finally begged Daniel to allow me to get a room for him. He refused and said he would sleep in the car. I finally gave up, frustrated at how stubborn he could be.

There was a small café beside the hotel. I took a burger back to the car for him and was glad that he accepted it but would not have been surprised if he refused.

I slept little, worried about Nichole, and afraid they were miles from here by now. If only I had found out sooner where they had gone. Maybe they hadn't come here at all. They could be in another state by now.

I was up early. I probably should have slept in the car, also. I could have saved some of the money that Charlie had given me for the trip. I took two cups of coffee back to the car.

Daniel smiled and thanked me. "What now?"

"Back to the house, I guess. Maybe we can talk with the neighbors and find out something. Did you sleep any?" I asked.

"Yeah, some."

It still took us an hour to find the address. Everything looked different in the light. When the house came into view there were several police cars parked along the street. "Oh, no. Something bad has happened."

A police officer met us as we approached. "You can't come any closer. We have a crime scene. Are you any relation to Mr. Lawler?"

"No, we are interested in the person who lives in that house." I pointed to where Larry's cousin lived.

"Are you related to Felts?" he asked.

"No." I explained in as few words as possible why we were

there. "We are worried about my daughter and only want to find her and take her home."

"Did your daughter go with this guy voluntarily, or was she taken against her will?"

I hesitated. "I am not sure. She probably agreed to go with him."

"She may be in a lot of trouble. We're investigating a homicide." He pointed to a house three down from the address we had. Mr. Lawler was murdered last night, and Felts is a suspect. He and another guy were caught last night and are being held in jail. A girl, probably your daughter, was with them and was severely injured. I don't know the details. You might find out more about your daughter at the St. Joseph Hospital in Fort Worth.

It was almost too much. A man murdered—Nichole possibly involved and injured—Larry and his cousin in jail. I panicked and couldn't think. Daniel asked the police officer for directions to the hospital and, with Daniel driving, we left.

I identified myself to the nurse behind the counter, who said she would get a doctor. It wasn't but a few minutes until a doctor appeared and introduced himself. "The young lady who was injured last night is your daughter?"

"Yes. We have no idea what happened. How bad are her injuries?"

"She has severe injuries. Jumping out of a moving car on the pavement will cause that type of damage to the body. She has several lacerations, broken bones, a concussion, and undetermined injuries that only time will reveal. Frankly, I don't see how she survived."

I took a deep breath, trying to remain calm. "Is she conscious?"

"In and out," he said.

I did not know what to say and was thankful when Daniel asked, "How long do you think it will be before she can be moved?"

"With her severe injuries, I could not say," he quickly said.

"Could we see her?" Daniel asked.

"Yeah, but don't try to talk with her and only stay a few minutes." He pointed to the hallway and said a nurse would show us to her room.

Nichole's room was right across from the nurse's station. I stepped inside the door and wasn't prepared for what I saw. Her face was swollen. The hair had been shaved on the left side of her head and a three-to-four-inch gash had been stitched. There was also a long cut from below her eyebrow down her cheek that had been sewed together. The hide had been scraped off her other cheek and her right arm. I would not have recognized her. I stood and stared, thinking, *this was my little girl, not the obstinate rebellious teenager that had caused us so much grief the last several months.* What was I going to do now? How was I going to take care of her? We had no money. The medical bills would be high.

I felt someone take my arm and realized Daniel was guiding me out of the room. We took seats in a lobby at the end of the hallway. "I have no idea what to do, Daniel."

A man in a suit interrupted us and introduced himself as Detective Parker. "Are you the mother of the young lady that was injured last night?"

"Yes, we just looked in on her. She's not able to have visitors."

"I'll need to talk with her as soon as she's able. She was with the two men who we suspect robbed and killed Mr. Lawler."

I was at a loss as to what to say but not Daniel. "From what we know, Nichole jumped out of the car and was injured. It sounds like she was trying to get away from the two men you suspect."

The detective's response frightened me. "We'll just have to see. At the moment it looks as if she would, at least, be an accomplice." He left after dropping that on us.

I was confused and about to panic. What would we do now? We couldn't leave Nichole here alone. If I stayed, who would take care of Elliot and Grant? Daniel couldn't stay—he was needed on the ranch. I told Daniel my thoughts and asked him if he had any suggestions.

"You have no choice. There is no one else to stay. Charlie and Leta can look after Elliot and Grant. I can also help take care of them. How much money do you have?"

I opened my purse and counted. "Twenty-two dollars. I can ask to stay in Nichole's room at night. Maybe they will furnish me a cot."

"That should be enough until Charlie and Leta can come back," he said.

"I need you to do something for me, Daniel. Check on Elliot and Grant first thing every morning and each night. Will you do that?"

"That will not be a problem."

I reached out and touched his arm. "Thank you, Daniel, for everything. I could not have made it without you."

I watched him as he left. He was a strange person. I remembered what Charlie had said about him, "He would be a loyal friend but a dreaded enemy."

With all the terrible events, I found an unexpected friend in the nurse who was on night duty. She treated me like a guest and gave me a cot, pillow, and blankets. You would have thought I was a grandchild the way she fussed over me. Besides the bedding she insisted I eat the evening meal provided to patients, saying it shouldn't go to waste.

Nichole did not come fully awake until late in the evening on the second day. I was reading a magazine when I heard a soft, "Mother."

I rushed to her bed. "How do you feel?"

"I hurt all over," she whispered. Her voice reflected the pain.

"Do you want me to get a nurse to give you something?" I reached for her hand.

I had to move closer to hear her. "What happened? I can't remember."

"They said you jumped out of the car while it was moving. Do you recall if Larry and his cousin were in the car? You were probably trying to get away."

She closed her eyes. I thought she had gone to sleep but there were tears when she opened them. "They were horrible. I had to get away from them." Tears filled her eyes. "It hurts."

I left and returned with a nurse who gave Nichole a shot for the pain. Within a few minutes, she was asleep. I stayed by the bed, held her hand, and prayed.

41

ABRAHAM AND ISSAC

Leta

Daniel returned and told us about the situation in Weatherford and that Nichole was in a Fort Worth hospital. I had expected Larry and his cousin to commit some type of crime but not robbery and murder. The frightening part was that Nichole was involved by association even if she didn't take part.

After a discussion it was clear that Charlie and I needed to go to Fort Worth as soon as possible. The situation was further complicated because Charlie had found two calves that had died. They were only about a month old, and he suspected the dreaded disease blackleg, although it didn't usually strike calves that young. Most of the cows had already calved, but we didn't usually vaccinate and work the calves until August.

"Leta, we're in a world of trouble." Daniel, Elliot, and Grant had left, and we had a chance to talk about our problems. "We're going to need a lawyer for Nichole, which will be expensive. Effie will have to stay with Nichole for no telling how long. We're looking at having to spend a lot of money, which we can't afford."

"That's just a part of it, Charlie. The medical bills are going to be huge."

I had suspected his response. "We don't need to worry about the medical bills. Surely, they won't demand that we pay them now. Maybe later when we sell the calves in the fall."

"Charlie Barlowe, we have always paid our bills. Nichole is family, which means we will pay the bills when they are due. I assume that will be when she leaves the hospital."

Teeth popping, "Leta, be reasonable. The cattle market is going down by the day. We're going to have to watch our spending, or we'll run out of money. Then what?"

"Doesn't matter. We'll pay our bills when they are due."

He ducked his head and left—mumbling something I couldn't understand— which was good.

I planned on spending the next few days weeding my garden. After the rain had given the weeds a head start, my vegetables were no match for them. We depended on the garden for summer vegetables as well as canning for the winter. I depended on Effie to help me but now that wouldn't be possible. Grant would be willing to help, which I appreciated. I hoped and prayed that Elliot would improve, but Dr. Johnson was right—Elliot wasn't going to get any better. The garden would just have to wait until we got back from Fort Worth.

We made plans to leave the next morning, but there was more bad news. Daniel came in that evening and said he'd found three more dead calves.

I wasn't surprised at Charlie's reaction. "Of all times to have a problem. I should have known something like this would happen. We get good rains and have grass for grazing. The abundant grass encourages the development of blackleg. But it's not supposed to attack calves this young."

"Maybe it's not blackleg, Charlie."

"What else could it be? I'll call the vet to come out to make sure. If it is blackleg, we have to gather the cattle and vaccinate the calves at once." He hesitated. "I can't afford to leave now. Can you go to Fort Worth by yourself?"

I turned to Daniel. "How are the roads?"

"Just fair. There are places where you may have some problems because of the recent rains."

I didn't know what to do. "Charlie, if I wait a couple of days, could you get away?"

"Probably not. More than likely, we'll need to pen the cattle and vaccinate the calves. It'll take as much as four days—maybe more. There's no need to get in a hurry. There's not anything we can do when we get there."

That was just like a man. "We can be there for Effie and our granddaughter. They need us now, not in a week. I'm leaving early in the morning."

"Leta, I wish you'd wait a couple of days and let me go with you. That's a long drive, and the roads are not that good, according to Daniel." Charlie had followed me to the car.

"I told you, Charlie—they need me."

Charlie wasn't much for sweet talk, but he surprised me. "Dammit, Leta, I wish you weren't so stubborn. I love you and don't want anything to happen to you. I couldn't do without you."

I couldn't bring myself to scold him for cursing. "Don't worry, Charlie. I'll be fine. I love you too, even though you are an ornery critter sometimes." I laughed and kissed him before getting in the car.

I drove away and wondered if I was a fool for going by myself. Here I was sixty-seven years old and driving 150 miles alone. I kept my speed under thirty miles an hour. The worst part of the trip would be to Cross Plains and then to Cisco. If I could reach Highway 80 at Cisco, it would be a breeze on into Fort Worth.

I had no problems the first two hours except to get behind some cowboys who were driving cattle. I slowed down to a crawl for several miles. Halfway between Cross Plains and Cisco I increased my speed to thirty miles an hour. My confidence had grown since the road was good. Suddenly, I hit a slick spot and applied my brakes. I realized my mistake too late when my car turned sideways and went into the ditch. I was stuck good, with half my wheels buried. My car wouldn't budge when I accelerated. Now what? All I could do was hope for someone to come along and pull me out.

I got out and stood in the road. I didn't have long to wait until a car stopped and offered to help. They had no chain to pull me out but offered to push if I thought that would help. I thanked them but knew that would be useless and ruin their clothes. They left and again I took my position in the road. It wasn't long until a pickup stopped and offered to pull me out. They had a chain.

The two men were confident that they could get me out of the ditch. I expect they were a father and son. After hooking on to my car and making half a dozen tries, it was no use. The pickup didn't have enough power to move my car. They finally gave up and apologized, asking me if I wanted to ride back to Cross Plains and hire a tow truck.

While I was trying to decide what to do a Negro man in a wagon pulled by two mules arrived. "Looks like y'all got sum problems. My name's Josh—short for Joshua."

"She's stuck good," the dad said. "We couldn't get her out."

The new arrival stroked his chin. "You wants me to give it a go. Old Abraham and Issac can pulls a mite."

The son laughed. "We couldn't do it with a new pickup. It'd be a waste of time to try with the mules."

"I'm desperate. It wouldn't hurt anything for him to try." I wasn't about to hurt the man's feelings after his offer of help. "Could he use your chain?"

"Sure," said the dad.

Joshua turned his wagon around and backed it up to my car, talking to the mules the entire time. "Come on, Abraham, git back. Issac, you being lazy. Git back."

When he had them in place, the men hooked the chain to my bumper and the wagon. "All right," said the father, "Let's see what your mules can do."

"I gots to pray first. We goin' need sum help." He looked up. "Lord, we needs help. This lady stuck bad. I ask that yous put more strong in old Abraham and Issac so theys can do this here job. Amen"

I got in my car, started it, and was ready to give it some

gas. The wagon started moving, and when the chain tightened, I pushed down on the accelerator. I could feel the car move slightly and then Joshua reached behind him and brought out a buggy whip. When he popped one of the mules twice on the rear, my car moved slowly out of the ditch onto the road.

Joshua laughed when I got out of the car and thanked him. "I hav'ta give Issac a swat or twos. He lazy."

"Thank you so much, Joshua. I really appreciate it."

He waved it off. "Awe shucks, it tweren't nothing. Yous be safe. Keep outs of the ditch."

The man and his son had the strangest look but said nothing. They unhooked their chain and left. After they were gone, I gave Joshua two dollars. He didn't want to take it, but I insisted, telling him again how much I appreciated his help. I watched him leave thinking, *I couldn't wait to get back home and tell Charlie about being rescued by Abraham and Issac.*

I was at the hospital a few minutes past four. When I found the room, Effie jumped up and hugged me. "I am so glad to see you. She is hurt really bad, Leta. They give her pain pills, which cause her to sleep. I have been able to talk with her a little. She remembers what happened and keeps saying, 'I had to get away from them.' The detective insinuated Nichole was involved, and it scares me."

"Don't worry, Effie. We'll get a lawyer. Now, you need to get out of here for a little while. I'll stay with Nichole. Go walk around—get something to eat."

"I just need some fresh air and maybe something to drink. I won't be gone long.

If she wakes up, try to find out what happened."

After she left, I stood by the bed shocked at Nichole's appearance. A nurse came in and took her vitals, ignoring me until she finished. "I bet you're her grandmother."

"Yes, I came a long way today to be with her. How is she doing?"

"There's not much change. More than likely, it will take several days before we can see any improvement. Most patients they bring in that have the damage she has are not breathing. So, you can be thankful she survived. She's young, which is an advantage."

After she left, I continued to stand beside the bed. That beautiful face with a flawless complexation would never look the same. The cut down her cheek would leave an ugly scar. I didn't know whether the damage to the other cheek with the hide scraped would return to normal or not. Her right arm was immobilized, which meant it was probably broken. I pulled the covers back and her right leg was in a cast to the knee. A pretty young girl now damaged for life.

Effie was back within an hour and looked more relaxed. "That helped, Leta. Has she been awake?"

"No, she mumbled something several times, but I couldn't understand what she said. The nurse came in and took her vitals."

"The day nurse is all business and not very friendly. But the night nurse is an angel and treats me like a patient." She went over to the bed and held Nichole's hand. "She seems to rest easier when I hold her hand. I cannot imagine what she's been through. If Larry and his cousin did rob and kill that man, there is no telling what they did to Nichole."

A knock directed our attention to the door. "Yes," said Effie.

A man in a suit and tie came in. "Mrs. Barlowe, I'm here to question your daughter."

"She's not able, detective." She turned to me. "Leta, this is Detective Parker." He went over to the bed. "Has she been awake?"

"Only for a few minutes at a time. They have her drugged for the pain," Effie said. "I have no idea how long it will be before she can talk to you."

"It's important I talk with her as soon as possible. She was with those guys that robbed and murdered Mr. Lawler. I need to find out just how involved she was."

I'd heard enough. "Detective, my daughter-in-law told you Nichole wasn't able to talk with you. My granddaughter jumped out of a moving car to get away from those guys—that should tell you something. Look what it did to her. Being a detective, I would think you could draw a conclusion from that."

He started toward the door, reached it, and turned, "We'll just have to see about that."

He shut the door behind him, and Effie burst into tears.

42

FEELING SPECIAL

Nichole

I relived my nightmare through dreams. I would wake up for a few minutes, go back to sleep, and dream. I couldn't get away from them. I would run, and Larry would catch and beat me. But the nights were the worst. I had never felt so dirty and cheap. Over and over, it happened.

I knew my mother was there beside the bed. I could not understand why she was so nice and held my hand. Why was she not angry with me for running away?

Gradually, I was able to stay awake longer with less pain. My grandmother was there. She wasn't angry with me either. She would hold my hand, also, and tell me everything was going to be okay. The nurses and doctor were nice to me, too, with encouraging words about my recovery.

A man came and asked me questions about what happened from the time I ran away. I told him everything I remembered even though some of it was hazy. He seemed determined to force me to remember even when I could not. I was glad when he left.

After several more days, my thoughts cleared. It was boring just lying there looking at the ceiling. My grandmother or my mother was with me all the time. I was glad to have one of them with me. I was still terrified that Larry would come and get me.

I expected them to say how disappointed they were and tell me what a terrible person I was for running away and causing so much trouble. I kept waiting for it, but it never came.

I think it was my fifth day in the hospital when two nurses came into my room and said it was time for me to get up. They brought a wheelchair and helped me sit on the side of the bed. When they lowered me to the floor to sit in the wheelchair, I never had such pain. I could not keep from crying. I hurt in so many places it was impossible to tell which was the worst. One of the nurses pushed me down the hallway. We passed a door which had a mirror, and I saw my face for the first time since the accident. "Stop! Take me back to the mirror."

"Honey, you don't need to see yourself yet. Wait a few more days until the doctor removes the stitches." We continued down the hallway.

I burst into tears. "Take me back to the room! Please. I don't want anyone to see me." After being helped back into bed, I pulled the sheet up over my head. I was ugly and wanted to hide. I knew my face was cut but not the way it was. My hair was gone on one side, which caused me to look like some kind of freak.

My mother tried to pull the sheet down. "Nichole, listen to me. You are fortunate to be alive—be thankful for that. Your body will heal with time."

"Please leave me alone. I wish I had died."

I heard the door open and close and assumed my mother had left. A few minutes later a nurse pulled my arm out from under the sheet and gave me a shot. I was out within minutes.

The next day my grandmother convinced me to uncover my face. I did it to please her—why? I have no idea. Something inside me wanted her approval. Before, it had never made any difference what she thought of me.

The man came back to question me that afternoon. My mother and grandmother stayed in the room. I realized by this time that he was a detective. He started out being nice when he asked me questions. "Nichole, how long had you been seeing Larry?"

"Several months," I said.

"Was he nice to you?"

I hesitated. "Yes, I wanted to leave and go home to New York. We talked about it all the time."

"Did he agree to take you to New York?"

"Yes."

He moved closer to the bed. "So, you left town with him on your own accord."

"Yes, but I didn't know what he was really like."

"When did you discover the real Larry?" he asked.

"He treated me differently, almost at once after we left town. I really saw how he was when he robbed the gas station."

"Why didn't you try to get away from him?" he asked.

"I did. He caught me and beat me. He said if I did it again, he would fix it where I would never walk."

"Were you with them when they robbed and killed Lawler?"

"I was in the car."

"That would have been a good time for you to escape," he said.

Something was not right. The tone of his voice had changed. "I was scared."

He moved a step closer to me. "It just doesn't seem right. You were too scared to run away while they were robbing and killing Lawler. Yet, you jumped out of a moving car. Didn't that frighten you?"

"I had to get away from them. Larry hurt me."

He smiled, which was more of a smirk. "Larry tells a different story, and his cousin backs it up. They said you were a part of the robbery and murder. It was actually your idea to kill the man so he couldn't identify you. They said you agreed to help with the robbery if they would give you the money to get to New York. They said you were sitting right next to the door, and it came open when they went around a corner at high speed."

My heart raced, and it was difficult to breathe. "That is a lie!"

He shrugged. "I'm just telling you what they said."

My grandmother moved up beside him and took his arm. "You need to leave and let us know before you come question Nichole again. We'll have a lawyer present."

He started toward the door but stopped and turned. "I will be back."

Then I understood. He believed I was involved in the robbery and murder. He was going to take the word of Larry and his cousin. I had been kept against my will and abused, yet I was going to be accused of taking part in this horrible crime. How much worse could it get?

Mother came over to the bed and took my hand. "Don't worry, Nichole. We are going to get a lawyer."

My grandmother said, "Let's change the subject and talk about something else. Effie, why don't you go get some fresh air and let Nichole and me have some grandmother time? I need to go back home tomorrow. I can't imagine how those men have been doing without me to cook for them."

After my mother left, Gram sat on the edge of my bed. "You know little about me, Nichole. Believe it or not, I was young like you once." She laughed. "Of course, that was a long time ago, in a different world. I met Charlie in Roswell, New Mexico when I had just turned seventeen. I had already graduated from high school and worked in a general store. I was sassy and thought I knew everything. I was taller than most women and, even if I do say so myself—attractive." Gram went on to tell me of Charlie rescuing her from the two men, after which he was rude to her.

"But you married him anyway?" I said in the form of a question.

"Of course. I discovered he was kind and considerate, yet brave."

Gram continued her story, telling of Mr. Chisum and her experiences at his ranch. She told me of their trip to Texas driving the cattle and lastly the incident involving the cattle rustlers.

"You mean you went into their camp, knowing how dangerous it was? They would have killed you when they discovered your purpose."

"I had to do something to help Charlie get our cattle back. I never gave it a second thought. I was frightened, terribly so." Gram went on to tell about Charlie shooting the man who was about to hurt her. "There are times when I can still feel his blood on me after all these years. But we did get our cattle back."

"You mean CK killed the man and saved you again? It's hard to believe he did that."

"You see us as being old, and it's hard to realize we were young once. Charlie was fearless and would do whatever was necessary to protect me and our property."

"You were only seventeen when you married?"

"That's right, and Charlie was nineteen. We came to Texas after we married. Charlie wanted to buy a ranch. Mr. Chisum encouraged us—more like insisted that we come. There was a war going on in that area, and he was afraid for Charlie.

I sat up, my interest growing. "How far was it?"

"It was over 300 miles and took us almost six weeks to get here. We faced hardships including lack of water, Indians, and of course rustlers. I was even snake bit. You are the only other person besides Charlie and me who knows all of our story. Oh, we've told parts of it to your dad and his brother. We didn't tell anyone about the rustlers and Charlie killing that man."

"Why are you telling me?" I asked.

"Nichole, you are full of life, like I was at your age. You have your whole future ahead of you. You have to understand that we all suffer hardships and have to make sacrifices. I wanted you to know what was going on in my life when I was your exact age. I expect you will find your hero to share your life with, someday."

"I never thought about you and Charlie being young," I said.

"I know. Most young people only think of their grandparents

as always being old. I wanted you to know Charlie and me better and understand that we will be there for you. Of course, Charlie is old now, but I still feel safe with him. I want you to feel safe with us, too."

"What happened when you got to Texas?"

"We had little money. Charlie found a job with a rancher about twenty-five miles southeast of our ranch. We had a small house, which was so bad it's hard to imagine. My first baby was born in 1880. Of course, we named him John Chisum after the man who had done so much for us. You probably haven't heard of him, but he's becoming famous. The toughest time for me was after my baby was born. Since Charlie was gone every day, I lived in constant fear of something happening to the baby. The Indian danger was still present even though most of them were on reservations. I had no one to talk with or who I could ask for help. We saved every dime we could for the next ten years. In 1890 we were able to buy this ranch."

"What has been the worst thing to happen?" I asked.

"In 1915 our son, your dad's brother, died suddenly. He was only thirty-five. He wasn't married and lived with us on the ranch. To lose a child is something so terrible it's beyond description. Charlie cried for the first time since I'd known him. It was hard on me but devastating for him. They were inseparable and worked together side-by-side every day."

"How long did it take you to get over it?"

"I don't believe you ever get over it. We both still grieve in our own way. We talk about it from time to time and that helps. What bothers me is that Charlie is still angry at God for taking Chisum away from us. Oh, we go to church, even Sunday school, but Charlie has never gotten over his anger. My one hope is that someday before I die it happens."

"Why are you not angry?" I asked.

"Nichole, I don't blame God for Chisum's death. Certainly, he could have prevented it, but he didn't cause it. Does that make sense? Probably not. It all comes down to faith—a belief that God is there for us in difficult times and even suffers with us. My faith provides comfort and knowing He's there with me is everything." She reached and took my hand, squeezing it.

I squeezed back and felt special for the first time since coming to Texas.

43

BIG WELCOME

Leta

The lawyer's words offered no encouragement. "From what you have told me, Mrs. Barlowe, this could be a difficult case. It's going to be the word of the two men against your granddaughter."

I had little patience with this man. "Do you want to represent my granddaughter or not, Mr. Ouster? I don't have time to waste. I've been gone a week and need to get home."

"Sure, I'll represent your granddaughter. I want you to understand, though, that it's not going to be easy. This ambitious district attorney will use anything to get another conviction on his record."

I was at a loss as to what to do—talk to another lawyer or hire this one. I was anxious to get home, and it was already ten. I'd taken too long with Nichole this morning. "Okay, I want you to represent Nichole. I'm not impressed with your attitude. You're not very sure of yourself."

"Realistic, Mrs. Barlowe—that's what I am. I'll go right to work on the case. I will need a $100 deposit. Your deposit will cover my initial work on the case. After that I charge six dollars an hour."

I wrote him a check, and thought, Charlie will be livid. I left Ouster's office—not sure I made the right decision.

I was on the way home by eleven. It had not rained, and

the roads had dried out, so I made good time and was home by six in the evening. Elliot met me in the yard. "Mother, am I glad to see you. Dad has been a wild man. Twenty-three more calves have died. I've been expecting him to have a heart attack at any minute. How's Nichole?"

"She's gotten much better since I called you three days ago. Did they get the calves vaccinated?"

"Yeah, the vet came out and verified it was blackleg and blamed it on the good grazing this spring. He thinks the disease is spread through the grass. I'm worried about Dad. I don't think he's slept two hours a night since you left. Of course, our diet has not been good. We survived on bologna sandwiches and boiled eggs. That's about all we know how to cook."

I couldn't help smiling, even with the bad news. Maybe they'd learn to cook something, now. "Where's Charlie?"

"He and Daniel are in the pasture checking on the calves we vaccinated. Grant is with them. He goes everywhere they do. He is really getting attached to Dad and Daniel. Tell me something, Mother. How in the world do you do it? I mean cook, wash, clean, milk the cow, take care of the chickens, and anything else that comes up."

I smiled. "I don't think about it, Elliot. I have always done it. It never crosses my mind to do anything else.

"Are you home to stay?"

"At least until Nichole is released from the hospital." I then told him about the visits from the detective and getting a lawyer. "I'm worried about this, Elliot."

"Surely they wouldn't believe the word of two men who robbed and killed a man."

"I'm not so sure." I noticed that Elliot looked better. "How have you been doing?"

He shrugged. "I think—better. I've been careful not to do much. Actually, I haven't had to take as many pills the last week."

"Do you feel like going to town for me?" I asked.

"Sure, I would like to feel useful."

"Let me make you a grocery list. I'll cook a decent meal

tonight."

He laughed. "That will probably be the most appreciation you have ever received."

I made the list and included T-bone steaks. It kind of pleased me to be missed.

<hr>

Potatoes were frying, and the steaks were in the oven when Charlie came in. "You finally made it home. I'd about given up on ever seeing you again."

"Glad to see me?" I asked wiping my hands on my apron.

He helped himself to several of the French fries I'd taken out of the skillet. "Yeah, almost as glad as I am to see something besides bologna." He grabbed me around the waist and pulled me to him. "I missed you, Leta. That bed is too big without you in it."

That was about as romantic as I'd seen him. "You might appreciate me more now?"

He still hadn't let go of me. "I always appreciate you, Leta. I just don't tell you."

I pulled away. "You better let me finish cooking supper. Is Daniel going to eat with us?"

"I'd hate to try to keep him away. That boy has been starving like the rest of us. Did Elliot tell you about the calves we lost?"

I checked the steaks in the oven. "Yes, but let's wait until after supper and everyone is gone to talk about it."

For once Charlie was patient and went to the living room and let me finish supper. My list had included five pounds of T-bones, which was a lot of steak. I had planned on having enough left for breakfast. When supper was finished all that was left of the steak was bone. I only took a small piece of one of the steaks. Grant ate just as much as the men.

The praise was generous, to the point of being embarrassing. Even Daniel, who was usually quiet, joined in. Charlie took Elliot and Grant home while I cleaned off the table and washed the dishes. I accepted Daniel's offer to help.

"Do you think this will change Nichole?" he asked.

I washed and he dried. "Yes, I think so. It was a terrible experience. She's going to have scars, inside and out, which she will have to deal with. I'm hoping that she'll take responsibility for what happened to her. Time will tell."

"Charlie is really taking the loss of the calves hard. It's more than the money. When we placed the dead calves in a pile to burn, he just stood for the longest and stared at them without moving. When I asked him if he was okay, he muttered something I didn't understand and started pouring kerosene on the pile."

I handed him another plate to dry. "Daniel, you would never know it by how he acts. Charlie is tender-hearted, especially toward animals. It's not uncommon for ranchers to treat their horses badly. They leave them tied all day or neglect to feed them regularly and sometimes don't treat their injuries. Charlie has never mistreated a horse or any of our animals. Even being around him as much as you are, I doubt if you realize that. He would die if anyone thought he was tender-hearted."

We finished the dishes just as Charlie returned. "Y'all already through. I planned on helping."

That was good for a laugh from Daniel and me.

After Daniel left, I made coffee, and we went out on the screened-in porch. It was a beautiful summer night. I told Charlie about Nichole with all the details, including the accusations from Larry and his cousin. I dreaded telling him about the lawyer and giving a check for $100. He took it better than I expected.

"I don't guess we have a choice. We can't just sit by and let her go to jail. I do worry about money. Of course, that's nothing new. Maybe Elliot got his obsession with money from me. I really never cared about being rich, though. All I want is to have enough to live comfortably. This depression is real, and the cattle market is going to continue to go down. That is our only source of income, which scares me. The added responsibility of Elliot and his family is another concern. Don't get me wrong—I'm glad they're here. But it's going to mean that more income will be needed."

"We'll be all right, Charlie. We always have. Our first concern now has to be getting our granddaughter home. I was thinking that maybe I should go back to Fort Worth in a week or so to help Effie."

He sat up, quickly, his cigar falling onto his lap. "Hell no!" He went to quickly brushing ashes off his pants. "I don't want you to leave again. I aged ten years while you were gone. If you think someone needs to help Effie, Daniel can go. We have plenty of grazing and won't have to feed. We can do without him."

His reaction surprised me. I hadn't given it much thought, but this was the longest I had been away from home. "I wouldn't think you could do without Daniel."

After picking up his cigar, he leaned back. "That's not a problem. How long do you think she'll be in the hospital?"

"I'm hoping for another two weeks at the most. Of course, there is the legal matter."

"I'll go into town tomorrow and talk to the sheriff. I don't know if it'll do any good, but it can't hurt anything. He knows Larry and the trouble he's had with the law."

<hr>

I spent every free minute the next week working in the garden. Everything was doing well except the tomatoes. A late freeze had killed them, causing me to have to replant. The onions would be ready by the middle of next month, and it wouldn't be long after that for the squash and okra. The peas and corn would be a little later. By mid-July it would require several hours a day of harvesting. After that, the work really started with the canning. I was hoping for some help. Maybe when Effie and Nichole got home, they would pitch in. Grant was like Daniel's shadow, going everywhere he went, so he hadn't been any help. They had lines set out on the creek and checked them each morning. We had fried catfish last night, one of Charlie's favorite meals.

A week after I was home, Effie called and said Nichole was doing well and was getting up each day and sitting in a chair. Effie had asked the doctor when she could be released, and he thought it would only be a matter of days. She said the detective had not been back to question Nichole. I asked her about the lawyer that I'd hired. She had not seen a lawyer and was surprised we had one. I became so angry it was necessary to pause before continuing. I then told her about giving the lawyer a deposit to begin working on the case.

Before I ended the call, I told her that Daniel would be there in a day or two and would stay until Nichole was released. I needed to go back to Fort Worth instead of sending Daniel. Evidently, the lawyer had done nothing in the way of gathering information needed to defend Nichole in case she was charged with a crime. But I agreed to send Daniel, and Charlie wasn't going to let me leave again.

I had a chance to talk with Daniel at supper. "Daniel, we need you to go to Fort Worth to bring Effie and Nichole home. You may have to wait a few days after you get there, but that will be okay." I went on and told him about hiring the lawyer and him not even questioning Nichole.

"Fort Worth is a big place. I don't like to drive in traffic," he said.

"You are a good driver. You have already been to the hospital, so you shouldn't have any problem." I could tell by his reaction that he didn't want to go.

"I'll go with you, Daniel. I can help you," Grant said.

Charlie laughed. "Who's going to help me? I can't do without both of you."

Grant ducked his head. "Okay, I'll stay. You will have to take me to check the fishing lines, though."

As I sat there listening to the back and forth between them, I thought—*what a difference in our lives a few months had made.*

44

RED

Effie

I was ready to get out of this place. Day in and day out it was the same thing. This was the sixteenth day. Nichole continued to improve and could actually hobble around on a crutch, but she refused to look in a mirror. After the removal of the stiches, there was still an ugly red scar running from the corner of the left eye down her cheek, almost to the corner of her mouth. The right side of her face had scabbed over where the skin had been scrapped off, but the doctor thought that would heal without leaving any evidence.

I was able to get Nichole to talk by reminiscing about our life in New York. Anytime I mentioned something about our current life in Texas, she clammed up. Eventually, I was able to convince her to write to some of her friends in New York. It gave her something to do and, after getting started, she seemed to enjoy it. With Amara's new address, we could send the letters to her, then she would make sure Nichole's friends received them. I would have liked to read the letters but was never given a chance.

I thought of my parents often and wondered what they were doing. I had not heard from them or my brothers since we moved. We kept up with the news on a radio that was in the hospital room. The economy continued to worsen with the stock market not recovering. A lot of people were out of work. Had it only been a little over five months since we left New York? What was the future going to bring? Somehow my family, no matter the challenges, had to contribute to the cost that Charlie and Leta were incurring. We could not go on living off them forever. Elliot could not work, and Grant's disability left only Nichole and me. Nichole would be unable to do much for several months and then it would be time for her to go back to school. The big question in my mind—would Nichole's attitude improve, or would the anger and rebellion continue after this experience?

Today was June 10, and Daniel was coming tomorrow to take us home when Nichole was released. Leta had given me a signed check to pay the hospital bill. Daniel was the first person Nichole knew who would see her besides Leta. She was going to be self-conscious about her appearance but, eventually, she was going to have to accept it and get on with her life.

My thoughts were interrupted by the doctor. "How's the patient today?"

Nichole was sitting up in bed, working on one of her letters. "I'm ready to get out of here."

He laughed. "It may be sooner than you think. What would day after tomorrow look like to you?"

"Great," she said.

He examined the casts on her arm and leg before taking her vitals. "When you get home you will need to visit your family doctor first thing. I will have some prescriptions for you. He touched her cheek. "That's healing nicely."

"Is there something you can do about the mark on my face. It's terrible and makes me ugly."

He sat down on the side of the bed. "I can give you some suave to apply to it. That will take some of the red out. With time, the scar should become more like the color of your skin, but it will not go away." He took her hand. "Nichole, you are a beautiful young lady and will always be. The scar will not take that away from you unless you let it. You just need to consider it a beauty mark and show the same amount of confidence in how you look that you always have. So much beauty can be attributed to confidence. The worst mistake you can make is to change the way you feel about your appearance and think others see you differently. Now, I'm out of my profession—giving advice as a psychologist. I'll see you tomorrow."

Daniel surprised me by smiling when he strode into the room, his hat in his hand. "I made it, finally. How is everyone doing?"

"Good news." We're going home tomorrow. Both of us are ready to get out of here." I was curious as to how Nichole would react to him. She said nothing, looking downward.

"You're looking good, Nichole." He moved over to the bed. Grant said to tell you hello."

She remained silent and continued to look downward.

"Well, I hate to do it, Nichole, but maybe it will help get you to talk to me. I brought the snake from home that I put in your room. It's in a box outside in the car. I'll be back in a minute." He turned and went toward the door.

"Wait! Come back. I will talk."

He returned to her side. "That's better. Where was I? Oh yeah—you're looking good. Now what do you say?"

She raised her head. "Thank you. But I don't believe you."

I found Daniel's humor hard to believe. I had never seen that side of him. Nichole had no doubt believed that he really did have the snake. After she thought about it, she would probably realize it was not true. Anyway, it worked. I was seeing an entirely new side of Daniel, socially and physically. I had never realized how handsome he was. His complexion was dark but more of bronze. His nose sloped downward, and he had a wide thin mouth. His forehead was broad. The black eyes were alarming at first, but when he smiled they changed to mysterious. What set him off from other men was his long hair, which fit him perfectly. To have been so shy and reluctant to be around us at the beginning, he had now become like family. The change was phenomenal.

Daniel told us what was going on at the ranch, including the loss of the calves. Nichole took part and would ask questions about topics Daniel introduced. It was the most social she had been since we came to Texas.

The knock interrupted our visit. A man entered and introduced himself as Mr. Ouster, our lawyer. "I have some information that you need to consider." He stopped as if confused. "I'm sorry. I should have asked how you're doing, young lady. That was callous of me."

I answered for Nichole. "She's better. We're going home tomorrow."

He coughed, as if what I said choked him. "That's why I'm here. We do have an issue that could be a problem. The district attorney has an arrest warrant for Nichole and will serve it when you leave the hospital. He is charging Nichole with being an accomplice to the robbery and murder. He has compiled some damaging evidence."

My face flushed with anger. "What have you been doing? You are our lawyer."

"Well, I-I have been e-extremely busy w-with some other cases that are in court. I have given your case a lot of thought. After studying the compelling evidence against Nichole, a plea deal might be the way to go. After all, the district attorney's main interest is conviction. I do believe it would be possible to get Nichole off with six months jail time." He stopped and waited for a reply.

"Go to jail!" Nichole exclaimed. "I did nothing wrong. That's crazy."

"You were with the men who did the crime. You did nothing to stop them. The DA has a convincing case against you. Both men said you encouraged them." Ouster had gained confidence and seemed sure of his recommendation.

I didn't know what to do. Leta had hired Ouster and already paid him a hundred dollars. Evidently, he had done nothing to prove Nichole's innocence.

Daniel came to my rescue. "Have you gathered evidence to show that Nichole was innocent? That's what I thought a lawyer was supposed to do."

He glared at Daniel. "Young man, there is no evidence I see that would indicate that she is not guilty."

Daniel moved closer to him. "We don't need your service anymore. If you were honest, you'd return the money Leta gave you. You have done nothing to earn it."

"I was hired by Mrs. Barlowe. You have no authority to dismiss me."

"You can leave now and don't come back. I do have the authority to remove you from this room and keep you away from Nichole. Now what's it going to be—leave on your own or be thrown out?" Daniel moved toward him.

Ouster whirled and left, slamming the door.

I was again surprised by Daniel's actions but grateful. "Daniel, I appreciate you speaking up for us. I had no idea what to say since Leta had hired Ouster."

"I just said what Leta would have, only nicer. If she'd been here, he would have been fortunate to get out of the room alive."

"What now, Daniel?" I asked. Maybe he would have an idea.

He shrugged. "Just wait and see what happens. You might call Leta and tell her about Ouster."

I kept thinking about what Leta had said about Daniel and the confidence she had in him. She was right.

The doctor came in early the next morning, examined Nichole, and said she was good to go. After he left, we waited on a nurse to bring the prescriptions and a wheelchair. A knock and a surprise when a large lady carrying a briefcase waltzed in. "I'm sorry to barge in. My name is Roselyn Sinclaire—most people shorten that to Red. I thought you might need my services. I'm an attorney and expected you might need one." She was tall and large with fiery red hair.

It caught me by surprise and took me a minute to recover.

"You are a lawyer?"

She laughed. "Yes. We ladies currently make up two percent of the attorneys in this wonderful country, which only gave us the vote eleven years ago." She spoke quietly, which did not fit her size. I would have expected a loud, gruff voice from someone as large.

"Yes, we do need a lawyer. How did you find out about our situation?"

More laughter. "I have a tough time getting clients for the obvious reason. I follow Ouster around and try to salvage what he screws up. I pick up quite a bit of business that way. I probably don't need to tell you what kind of attorney he is."

I explained our situation to her and that we had no money available. Her response was shocking. "No problem. You can pay me later. My fee is fifty dollars, no matter what the outcome. The most pressing problem is the warrant for Nichole's arrest, which will be forthcoming when she's released. We need to demand a bail hearing, so she doesn't spend one night in jail. After that, I'll go to work gathering evidence to prove her innocence. Is that agreeable?"

"Yes. And thank you." She must have been sent straight from heaven.

Two police officers stood near the counter where I paid the hospital bill. They informed me that Nichole was under arrest. I was thankful that Roselyn or Red was there with us. She didn't waste any time. "What are you doing with those handcuffs?" Her voice had changed, loud and gruff.

One of the police officers pointed to Nichole. "We have a warrant for her arrest."

She put one hand on her hip and stepped forward, towering over the police officers. "So, you think she's a flight risk? Look at her! You got to be kidding me. We're taking her in our car and will meet you at the station."

They didn't argue, retreating back outside to their car. The change in Red was amazing. It was like the Dr. Jekyll and Mr. Hyde story.

The hospital and doctor bills came to $852, which I paid

with the check Leta had given me. Red rode in the car with us to the police station. Nichole was able to get in the car without help but needed aid getting out. When we entered the station, we were met by whom I suspect was the police chief.

"We need to get you booked and then transferred to a cell," he said.

"Just hold your horses, Chief. We want a bail hearing. Not next week, not tomorrow, and not this afternoon. We want it now!" I couldn't help flinching when she spoke, hoping she never got upset with me.

The chief appeared confused. "I have no idea when the judge will be available." "We're not moving until you find him, and we get a bail hearing. This girl is innocent. She's been assaulted by those terrible men and now harassed by the police—especially that two-bit detective. Now get on with it."

We helped Nichole over to a bench and waited. The police chief returned an hour later and told us the judge would see us in the courtroom, which was across the street. It took us awhile to navigate the distance, having to help Nichole. I was surprised that the judge was a younger man. I expected judges to be old and grey headed. This judge was probably in his forties. The district attorney had been summoned and was in the courtroom, also.

Red approached the bench. "Judge, my client had a ridiculous charge brought against her. She has been through a terrible experience and needs to rest at home. I am asking that she be released on bail on her own recognizance."

"Ms. Sinclaire, I need to hear evidence from the district attorney before I decide bail," the judge said.

"That's fair enough. I'm anxious to hear what bogus charges he came up with."

The DA presented the evidence which just accused Nichole of being with Larry and his cousin during the robbery and murder. He did emphasize that both had said she was a willing participant. He asked that she be held without bail.

Red took her place in front of the judge. "Judge, if you took part in a robbery and murder and were running from the law would you jump out of a car going thirty miles an hour onto the pavement? Look at my client! See the results of her escape. That was the price she was willing to pay to get away from those goons. They had kept her against her will and assaulted her. She was willing to maybe die to get away from them. I'm asking you to allow her to go home and recover from this horrific experience. When, and even if, she has to go to trial she will return. We will then prove her innocence."

"I'm going to grant your request, Ms. Sinclaire, that your client be released on her recognizance. I will require that once home, she report to the local law enforcement in that area and let them know of the pending charges."

"Thank you, Judge."

We left the court, feeling much better than when we entered. I assured Red that we would send her a check at once for her services. Nichole accepted the hug from her and thanked her over and over.

We were on the way home, with Daniel driving, by early afternoon—thankful.

45

HOME

Nichole

I stared at the back of his head—my thoughts as jumbled as the pieces of a puzzle. I had been terrified of him in the beginning and considered him evil and a threat. Next, I began to see that he was none of these, but I was too stubborn and angry to admit it. Now, I was indebted to him, which bothered me almost as much as being afraid of him.

My mother turned around. "Are you comfortable, Nichole? If you start hurting, we can stop and let you get out for a few minutes. It might have been better for you to ride up front."

"I'm doing okay. How much further do we have?"

"We're about halfway. We probably will be after dark getting home," Daniel said, staring ahead.

Why did he wear his hair that long? Maybe I would ask him. He might tell me it was none of my business. Why would I think that? He had never been rude to me. What would my friends in New York think of him? Would they laugh and make fun of him? No, they would be afraid of him just as I was. Those black eyes seemed to look right into your soul.

Ouster, our first lawyer, left the room at once when he told him to. No doubt, Ouster was afraid of him. Daniel was only nineteen but seemed older. That was not an Indian name. If not, what was his real name?

I still did not understand why everyone was being nice to

me after all the trouble I caused. Maybe when we got home, they would all unload on me. Should I apologize for running away? I hated to admit wrongdoing. It was not in my nature. One thing for sure—I would not do it again. I would stay in Texas for another year and then leave. I owed my grandparents, my parents, and Daniel. When able, I would do more to help out on the ranch.

I came close to going to jail. I would have been a prisoner put in with criminals. The thought brought horrible images. My case would go before a grand jury later in the summer, so jail might still be in my future. I had been fooled so badly by Larry, who knew he was not going to take me to New York. I was only baggage that he took along for his pleasure. My mother had not asked me about that part of my captivity, afraid I'm sure of what she would find out. Hopefully, she would never ask me. I was ugly and dirty because of him. I had fought him at first but gave in when he hit me. If I had continued to fight him, I have no doubt that he would have killed me.

We were at Cisco by late in the afternoon. I needed to use the toilet and told my mother. We stopped at a small café, which we thought might have a facility. I waited in the car for Mother to help me but instead Daniel opened my door and offered his hand. It was rough but felt strong and, when I struggled, he put his hands under my arms and helped me to a standing position. I had never been that close to him and was surprised at his pleasant scent, which I am sure was much better than mine. When he released me, my good leg gave way, and I fell into his arms. I was embarrassed and struggled to stand. "I-I am sorry."

He laughed. "No problem. Just stand still for a minute and get your balance."

I did as he asked and was able to hobble into the café. Unfortunately, they only had an outhouse. As my mother went with me to the outhouse, I was tingling all over, which I attributed to the long ride in the car.

"I wish you could come in!" Grant yelled. "The water feels great."

I was sitting under a big tree, watching Daniel and Grant swim. Large trees created shade along the creek, and the breeze made it cool. I still had the cast on my leg but not the one on my arm.

It was a Monday, the last day of June. Daniel and Grant had invited me to go with them to the swimming hole in the creek. Grant was right at home in the water, his handicap not visible. He was standing in water up to his shoulders and coming to Daniel's waist. Both were wearing cut-off jeans. I was determined not to look at Daniel but was losing the battle. His dark skin with the rippling muscles kept drawing my gaze. Splashing around with Grant brought several bursts of laughter which changed him into a beautiful young boy that posed no threat to anyone. At those times, I just gave up and stared.

The last several weeks had passed slowly. The summer days were hot, and most days were spent sitting on the porch trying to stay cool. I did whatever I could to help my mother in the kitchen and was able to do more when the cast was removed from my arm. Nothing was ever said by my parents or my grandparents about the trouble I caused by running away. I could never bring myself to apologize even though it would have been the right thing to do.

I envied Grant seeing him on the go from morning until night with either Daniel or CK. He had grown several inches and gained weight. He was getting around better and being out in the sun his skin had darkened, giving him a healthier look. I was not angry at him anymore, having experienced the limited movement that he had dealt with a large part of his life.

I inspected the scar on my face each day and hoped it would become less noticeable. Some of the redness was gone, but it still made me ugly. When people looked at me their eyes would focus on the scar.

Last week I was able to help gather the vegetables from the garden. I actually enjoyed having something to do that would help pass the day. I could not imagine what Gram was going to do with all the vegetables that filled the large baskets.

Laughter drew my attention back to the creek. Grant was riding on Daniel's shoulders as he moved around in the water. Suddenly, Daniel threw him over his head into the water. Grant came up spitting water and laughing. "You fooled me! Watch me. I can swim." He leaned forward, moved his arms, and started splashing.

Amazing. He was actually going forward. When did this happen? I clapped when he stopped and stood. "That was great, Grant. When did you learn to swim?"

"Daniel taught me. You should see him swim. He can go fast." He took off again, this time going further before stopping.

Daniel came out of the water and sat down beside me. His hair was wet and dripping. He shook his head, spraying me with water.

"Hey, what are you doing?"

"You need to get wet. Are you going swimming with us when you get your cast off your leg?"

"Probably." I was aware of his closeness and started to panic. He was sitting to my right and couldn't see the scar. I felt the need to thank him for everything— Grant, helping me get home, and for all he did for my mother, dad, and grandparents. But how to go about it was confusing.

He gave me an opening. "What are you thinking about? You look serious."

"I need to thank you," I said.

"What for?"

"For helping everyone. You have been so good for Grant. You helped me get home, and you have been there for my parents and grandparents."

"That was just part of my job," he said.

I shook my head. "No. Others would not have done as much. I was afraid of you and still am—a little. But I see what a good person you are. There! That was what was on my mind. Now, I have said it and feel better."

"Have you said the same to your parents and grandparents?"

"No. I should but have not been able to. Maybe now I can.

Can I ask you a personal question?"

"Sure, but I may not answer it," he said. "Why do you let your hair grow long?"

He smiled. "I will answer that. It is an important part of my culture. My people consider long hair a sign of strength and power."

"Who are your people?"

He hesitated. "I will tell you but no more questions. My people are the Comanche—the greatest and most fearless warriors of all tribes."

I knew better than to ask him anything else. We sat in silence and watched Grant practice his swimming. Then he reached and touched my arm. "You need to tell your parents and grandparents what you told me. You will feel better about yourself."

I knew he was right.

Several weeks after my trip to the swimming pool, I found out what Gram was going to do with all the vegetables from her garden. Mother and I helped bring dozens of glass jars from a cellar back of the house. After that, we started filling the jars with the vegetables. Gram had placed a large pan on the stove filled with water that was boiling. She melted candles and let the wax drip on top of the vegetables before putting the lid on the jars. When that was done, she placed the jars in the boiling water.

She explained. "The boiling water seals the jars and prevents contamination. The vegetables will last a long time. Of course, we will eat most of them this winter. We will still have plenty of vegetables from the garden to eat before frost, which is usually around the first of November. We will put up onions before frost, and they will keep through most of the winter. Our fruit trees died a couple of years ago. We have a neighbor who lets us gather peaches and apples from her trees. It will only be a few more days until we can start canning them. We have a large growth of wild plums along the creek that will be ready soon. They make wonderful plum jelly. With the spring rains, we are having a bountiful harvest for which we need to be thankful."

I had no idea that so much food was put up for the winter. In New York, Amara went shopping and bought everything from a store. I never thought about how it got to the store.

I was able to do more now since the cast had been removed from my leg. It was already the middle of July and halfway through the summer. School would start in six weeks, meaning only nine more months, then I could leave and return to New York. Strange, but I didn't think of leaving as often now. I had grown to see my grandparents in a different way since I returned from the hospital. My Gram was so strong and independent. I could never imagine my grandmother in New York doing any of the things she did. CK was funny, always making jokes, and keeping everyone laughing. My mother, though, told me about him running off the deputy that came to arrest Daniel. She admitted that seeing that side of him frightened her. His action didn't surprise me now that Gram had told me about the incident involving the rustlers when they were coming from New Mexico.

I had come to accept the change in my mother and realized that it was lasting. She would never return to the person she was in New York. I had not sympathized with my dad when he became ill. I was sorry for that. I think he is doing better, now.

And then there is Daniel. I went swimming with him and Grant last week after my cast was removed. The swimsuit Gram bought me was terribly outdated and made me feel even uglier; however, I had a wonderful time. The cool water in the creek was soothing to my arm and leg. Each time I was around Daniel, I became more comfortable and less afraid of him. We had no time alone since Grant was always with us. I wanted to know more about him but knew it would be useless to ask and might make him angry. I had begun to think he was hiding something from his past.

On July 17, which was a Thursday, the sheriff came to our house late in the afternoon and told me that my case would go before the grand jury next Wednesday.

46

GOOD NEWS-BAD NEWS

Leta

"I'd like to get ahold of that lawyer. He cheated us out of a hundred dollars."

"Now, Leta, you're always quoting the Bible to me. Remember—the peacemakers inherit the earth."

That was just like Charlie talking about something he knew nothing about. "It's the meek that shall inherit the earth, Charlie. Peacemakers will become children of God."

"Well, anyway, you sure don't sound much like a peacemaker, Leta."

I never knew what to expect from Charlie. Here he was quoting the Bible. But he was right. I was guilty, but quoting the Bible was a lot easier than living by it. I might as well forget the money and Ouster. It was my mistake for ever giving him an advance. The best thing for me to do was change the subject. "I should've gone with them to Fort Worth. Daniel could have stayed home with you in case you needed him."

"Daniel can't cook, and he's not as pretty as you." That little crooked smile meant he thought he'd said something smart. "Remember, when we came all the way from New Mexico to Texas, driving those heifers, Leta? What an adventure that was! We were so young we didn't know any better. It's a wonder we didn't get scalped by Indians."

"Yes, I remember trying to cook you breakfast that first morning on an open fire. The bacon and eggs were both full of ashes. You ate them anyway and said how good they were. That was the first lie I ever heard you tell, Charlie Barlowe, and I've loved you ever since for that. I will say though, that those were not the good old days. The scariest part of the trip was not worrying about Indians but the rustlers. Also, just as frightening, was almost running out of water after we left the Pecos."

He took a cigar out of his shirt pocket. "I agree that those were tough times, but I wouldn't take anything for the memories." He continued after putting a match to his King Edward. "You know, a guy asked me the other day why I didn't smoke Roi-Tan cigars since they were cheaper. I told him, 'I'd as soon smoke a mare's tail.'"

"The mare's tail would probably be better for you. One of these days they're going to find out that smoking is bad for your health."

"Well, it won't matter. I'll be gone by then, but if I was still around it wouldn't stop me from smoking. It relaxes me and, besides that, I enjoy smoking."

It was no use arguing with him. "What do you think will happen to Nichole?"

"It could go either way. The key is how believable Larry and his cousin are. Me—I wouldn't believe anything they said. We can hope for a no-bill from the grand jury, so she doesn't have to stand trial. At least we should know something tomorrow."

"She's changed, for the better, Charlie. I do wish she had apologized, but I guess that was too much for her. You do know the main reason for the change, don't you?"

He put his cigar in the ash tray. "Sure. She had the fright of her life."

"That could be a small part of it. I don't guess you noticed the way she looks at Daniel. Most men wouldn't be aware of that."

"What do you mean?" he asked.

"She looks at him sort of like you look at a piece of warm apple pie topped off with a large gob of whipped cream."

He was silent for at least a minute. "Are you sure? I would

have never guessed she was the least bit interested in Daniel." He struggled to his feet. "I've got to think about this." He started toward the door but turned. "She could do a lot worse."

He finally said something with which I agreed. Nichole was a beautiful girl, even with the scar. I didn't know how Daniel would respond and if he even realized she was attracted to him.

At least Charlie didn't get started on money today. That was what happened each time we talked for the past several weeks. Thirty-one calves had died, which was only going to leave about 140 to sell in the fall. Lightweight calves were already down to four dollars a hundred. That would mean we would only get about $1600 before expenses. Charlie had already decided we wouldn't send them to Fort Worth but sell them to a contractor who would pick them up here in trucks.

Of course, Charlie always looked at the bad side of everything. My garden was producing more than in years. Effie and Nichole had been helping, and we had already gotten a lot done with the canning. Another positive was Elliot, who had been doing better the last several weeks. He went with Charlie every day and was not experiencing the extreme shortness of breath that was present earlier. He was going in to see the doctor tomorrow and get more of his pills.

It was already nearly eleven and time to start lunch. Even though Grant was just a boy he ate as much or more than a man. He had grown and changed so much since coming here. He no longer used his cane even though he still limped badly. He had gained weight and thickened up in his shoulders. Charlie had mentioned several times how strong he was. The next time Charlie started in on what a dire situation we were in, I would remind him of our blessings.

"I don't understand it. It's one time I'm pleased about being wrong. No doubt about it—your heart is stronger. Have you been doing anything differently?"

Charlie butted in, unable to resist the temptation. "I'm

surprised you can admit you were wrong. That's a first."

"I was talking to Elliot, Charlie. Let him answer my question," said Dr. Johnson.

"Not much," Elliot said. "I have been walking the quarter mile to Dad's each day and back home after we finish whatever we're doing. I have noticed that my shortness of breath is much better. Some days, I don't even have to take a pill."

Charlie and I had gone in with Elliot to see the doctor and were in his office, listening to his report after the exam was completed.

"Well, whatever you're doing—keep doing it. I have no idea why you have improved. The human body is a remarkable machine, and it's not uncommon to be surprised by the way it responds to disease. I do believe that we get help sometimes by divine intervention. I know that's strange coming from a doctor whose profession generally likes to take all the credit. But I do believe there is a Healer greater than all of us." Dr. Johnson rose from behind his desk. "I will warn you not to overdo it. You can get to feeling so well that you forget about having a bad heart. Increase your activity gradually. Whatever you do, don't let Charlie put you to work. He has a habit of working people and not even paying them."

That started an argument which would last longer than I was willing to listen. Elliot followed me out of the room and on to the pickup. "Do they always argue that way?" he asked.

"Short answer—yes. For over forty years. You'd think they'd get tired of it." I asked him what he thought about his report.

"You know, Mother, I never thought about my health until the heart attack. I took it for granted, thinking nothing would change. All I thought about was making more money. Now, I realize nothing comes close to good health. I guess in order to appreciate it you have to be sick. Every day I spend feeling good I am thankful."

Charlie came out sooner than I expected. "You know what he charged for that short visit?"

"No, but I'm sure you're going to tell us," I said.

"I timed how long we were in there. We only took up

twenty-seven minutes of his time and the bill was five dollars. That's outrageous!"

I stopped him before he lit the cigar. "Wait until we get home. You'll suffocate us crammed into this pickup."

"I hope we hear something from Fort Worth today. It would be good to get this behind us," Elliot said.

Charlie had put his cigar back in his shirt pocket. "I don't see how anyone could believe those guys. It's a mystery to me why they want to testify against Nichole. I can't see how they think that would help them."

When we got home Grant came out to meet us. He had stayed since we didn't have room in the pickup. He had bad news. "Daniel called and said they had indicted Nichole for conspiratory to commit murder and robbery. They will be home tomorrow. What does that mean?"

Elliot explained. "The grand jury believes there is enough evidence against her for a trial. It is an accusation, not a conviction. The trial will decide whether she is innocent or guilty."

"But she didn't do anything," Grant said.

It was going to be hard for Grant to understand. "It's time for me to start supper. Do you want to help me, Grant?"

"Sure."

Now what, I thought? Is there a chance they will convict Nichole and send her to jail? I was anxious to hear what Effie thought. The good news about Elliot was forgotten with the verdict from the grand jury.

47

QUESTION ANSWERED

Effie

"It's clear now why the two defendants have accused Nichole of being involved in their crime. With information they provide to the district attorney, who is an ambitious little snot, they are hoping for a deal. The DA made it known he will seek the death penalty, and their lawyer is doing what he can to avoid that verdict. Their lawyer believes he can get the death penalty off the table in exchange for Larry and his cousin's testimony against Nichole."

We had just received the grand jury's verdict of an indictment, meaning Nichole would stand trial. Red, our lawyer, was explaining what happened. "Will they be tried together?" I asked.

"Over my dead body! I'm looking forward to getting Nichole on the stand. Of course, the grand jury only heard the evidence presented by the prosecution. We'll have our chance at the trial. Another thing, an indictment from the grand jury only requires nine of the twelve votes. A conviction in a criminal trial must be unanimous. I am glad the charge was conspiratory rather than accessory to the crime."

She continued before I could ask a question. "I'll need some character witnesses for Nichole. Teachers would be preferable. Another would be her minister."

I had a sinking feeling. None of her teachers would walk across the street to say something good about Nichole. We had not attended church since moving to Texas. Who could I recommend? I would not worry about that now. There were enough problems—the bail money was at the top of the list. Since Nichole was indicted, the judge had set bail at $10,000. I had gone to a bail bondsman and given him a check for $1,000 to post the remaining bail. Leta had signed several checks for me in case we had expenses. The $1,000 was non-refundable, and I dreaded giving them the news. Nichole or Daniel had said nothing during the exchange.

"When will a trial date be set?"

Red looked at Nichole. "I'd like to have it as soon as possible, so Nichole would not miss school. That is unlikely though. I would say that it could be as late as Thanksgiving. Is there anything I need to know about Nichole's past that might hurt her?"

This was getting worse by the minute. I looked at Nichole who had her head down. Thank goodness for Daniel. "We need a little time to talk with her dad and put something together. We can get back with you within a few days either by letter or phone."

Red was too savvy for that. "Okay, what's going on here? Nichole, talk to me. We are trying to keep you out of jail. I need some truth here."

Nichole started crying.

"Effie, what's going on? I need to know my client. Tell me what you're hiding."

Red was right. We were withholding information from her. "Nichole has not always been a model citizen. She got into trouble in New York and was arrested at a speakeasy. No charges were brought. I don't know if it will be public record or not."

Red glared at me. "Well, I'll tell you one damned thing. That DA will find out about it and use it against us. You've got to be honest with me. Evidently, Nichole was anything but a sweet, respectful child during her first seventeen years. Now tell me more about this problem child."

Nichole had gotten herself together by now. "I made mistakes. I'm sorry for being the way I was. My past will not help me in the trial. In fact, it will hurt my case. I've changed, but it might be too late." She started crying again.

I believe she meant what she said. I felt sorry for her. Maybe it took this to change her.

Red took a deep breath and exhaled. "I need a drink. What have I gotten myself into?" She moved over closer to Nichole and put her hand under Nichole's chin, lifting it up. "Listen carefully to me. You go home and be a perfect little angel. Start attending church every time the wind blows the door open. That includes Sunday School. When school starts you find a seat in the front row of every one of your classes and smile. Can you do those things?"

Nichole nodded. "I'll try."

Red grabbed Nichole's chin again and moved closer. "Try? That doesn't get it. If you can't do better than that—I'm through. You can get yourself another lawyer. You have no idea what that DA will do with your past. Young lady, there is a good chance that if you are not able to make some changes in your behavior, you are going to prison—not jail—prison. Now, let me ask the question again. Can you do these things that I have suggested?"

This time Nichole spoke up. "Yes, I can do what you asked."

"This changes everything. I'll postpone the trial as long as possible to be able to get some good character witnesses for Nichole. It'll be up to Nichole to do the rest. Now, I need some more money. I had no idea this was going to turn into so much work. I'll need to make a trip to the defendants' town to gather information on them. I imagine their past will reveal a great deal about their ability to tell the truth."

"How much?" I asked, dreading the answer.

"A hundred dollars will get me started. I'll need more later. Most attorneys would charge three times that for the amount of work involved."

I filled out a check and gave it to her. I tried not to think about Charlie's reaction when he discovered how much this was costing. "What else can we do to help Nichole?"

She shook her head. "I imagine, from what little information you have given me, that you've tried about everything with her and got nowhere. It's up to Nichole now. I'll be in touch with you to let you know how everything is going. I'll want a report on Nichole, also."

The first thing I did when getting home was to tell Charlie and Leta about the money spent on bail and the attorney. Charlie started to say something but a look from Leta silenced him. I noticed he was popping his teeth.

"That's no problem, Effie. Our first priority is getting Nichole out of this mess. What else can we do?" asked Leta.

"I think we've all done everything we can. Just like our lawyer said—it's up to Nichole." Elliot was with me, and we were sitting on the porch with Leta and Charlie. I was surprised when Nichole appeared. I guessed she had been listening from the door.

She stood as she spoke to her grandparents. "I am going to do everything our lawyer asked me to. I am sorry for being so much trouble for you and costing all this money. Someday, somehow, I will repay you." She left quickly before anyone could reply.

I hope everyone understood how much effort it required for her to apologize. I can't remember that ever happening. It was a good start. Now if she could just follow up on what she promised.

Elliot and I walked home after we finished talking to his parents. Charlie offered to drive us, but Elliot insisted on walking, saying that he thought that was part of the reason for his improvement. It seemed natural for him to take my hand as we walked. It gave us a chance to visit alone for the first time since I returned. "Did it surprise you that Nichole apologized?"

"It did, Effie. But pleased me that she did."

"Red, our lawyer, was straightforward with her and did not mince words. I could tell that it frightened Nichole. It did me as well. If the trial were held today, there would be a good chance she would be convicted. I believe she will change."

"Something else, Effie, that I need to ask you. What's going on with Daniel and Nichole? He seems to have assumed the role of her protector. It's like a dog that is with its master. He doesn't bark or growl at you, but you know he would not allow you to hurt his master. You have been around them more than me. Am I imagining things?"

I laughed. "No, you have been observant. I can't tell you about Daniel and what his feelings are. Nichole though is enamored with him. I'm not sure she even realizes it. At some time, it occurred to her that he would be there for her. It is easy to see why she would get that impression. He is young, strong, and fearless, plus, if you haven't noticed, a good-looking young man. I do not believe that him being an Indian has entered her mind. I have no doubt that he has been a positive influence on Nichole."

"That gives me a better understanding of their relationship. It's about to drive me crazy trying to remember why Daniel is so familiar—like I have seen him before. Of course, that's impossible. Anyway, I can't think of anyone I would trust more than him to look after Nichole. Grant thinks the sun rises and sets on Daniel. That is easy to understand. Just look at the way he treats Grant."

When we reached our house, rather than going inside we sat on the porch. "I'm hoping that my health continues to improve. We have been here for over six months and have been totally dependent on Mom and Dad. Maybe I can eventually help out on the ranch." He stopped and stared off into the distance. "Effie, do you ever think about our life in New York and what we gave up living here?"

I laughed. "Not as much as during the winter when I had to visit the outhouse. What about you?"

"New York seems like a long time ago. My biggest regret is being dependent on Mother and Dad. If I had just a small part of the money lost in the market, I could pay our way. Of course, if not for going broke, we wouldn't even be here. Short answer to the question—yes, I think about New York but with few regrets. I was confused about what was important. I never dreamed Dad and I would have the kind of relationship we do. He actually likes me now. We can talk to one another, laugh and joke, occasionally even bring up the past. I am not in the best of health but feel more alive than in New York. We are a family now, unlike when we were living separate lives in New York. I wanted to die in the hospital when I discovered the extent of my losses in the market. When we left New York, I did not expect to live. Now, I want to live and see Nichole and Grant grow to adulthood and have families. I want to be healthy enough to play with my grandkids." He hesitated. "Now I'm rambling. That wasn't a short answer to the question."

I took his hand with both of mine and looked into his handsome, but thin face. "Just think, if we still lived in New York, and were rich, what our lives would be like. None of us were really happy then. Why would it be any different now? I like myself much better here in Texas, and I believe you do. Somehow, we will repay your mother and dad for what they have done for us."

"You deserve credit, Effie, for holding our family together after my heart attack. Had it not been for you, we couldn't have made it. I would have never opted to come back home if not for you. I don't know what would have happened without you stepping up to take over the decision making for our family."

I squeezed his hand. "You see, sometimes things do happen for a reason. Maybe we were supposed to come back to your home in Texas."

48

TRIAL

Nichole

"Would you tell us what kind of student Nichole has been this school year." Red, our attorney, asked of the high school principal who was testifying.

"She has been an exemplary student," Principal Mobley replied. "She has been an office aide which makes me aware of her conduct. She is polite, courteous, and a credit to our school. Her teachers have nothing but good things to say about her. She has made nothing lower than an A on her report cards this school year."

"Thank you, Mr. Mobley, that is all," said our attorney.

When Red sat down, she reached and patted my hand. I was on the edge of my seat as the prosecuting attorney approached Mr. Mobley. At least I was going to get it over with. I thought this day would never come. Our attorney's delay of the trial had worked, and it had been almost seven months since Larry and his cousin had robbed and killed the man. I had done everything possible to be a good student and attended church regularly as well as Sunday School.

Mr. Watson, the man who wanted to send me to prison, approached the bench. "Mr. Mobley, your description of Miss Barlowe was impressive. Has it always been that way from the first time you met her? I remind you that you are under oath."

"Nichole had some problems when she enrolled in our

school. She had recently moved from New York into an entirely different environment. I imagine it would have been the same for anyone in her situation."

Mr. Watson smiled. "I did not ask for your opinion, Mr. Mobley—only the facts. I want a more detailed description of Miss Barlowe's first semester as a student in your school. Did she cause trouble? A simple yes or no will suffice."

Mr. Mobley hesitated and looked at the judge. "Answer the question, Mr. Mobley."

"Well, of course, I was not around her that much, being the principal. She did have a few minor confrontations with her teachers. She was not accustomed to attending a school with a dress code. She was confused at first."

I scooted down in my seat, ashamed of putting Mr. Mobley in such a difficult position. He should just tell him how terrible my behavior was. I was scared and wished Daniel was here. He had refused to come, which confused me. I felt safe around him.

Mr. Watson raised his voice. "Let me remind you of a few of these minor confrontations. She refused to follow the dress code, was rude to her teacher, and sent home. She was constantly a problem in the classroom. In fact, several of the teachers came to you, asking that she be removed from their class. Her conduct became even worse when she became involved with the man whom she robbed and killed a man with."

Red jumped to her feet. "Objection! She has not been convicted of anything, your honor."

"Sustained," the judge said.

Mr. Watson said that was all and returned to his seat.

Red called the pastor of our church for the next witness. His questioning and response were similar to Mr. Mobley's. On cross examination by Watson, my pastor admitted that I didn't attend his church until after being charged.

After his testimony, Red asked for a fifteen minute recess, which was granted. I followed her outside where she explained the reason for requesting a recess. "It's not going well, Nichole.

I need to put you on the stand. Can you handle it?"

"I-I don't know."

"The jury needs to see that you are truly sorry for ever getting involved with these guys."

"That man scares me. He's mean."

"If his questioning gets too aggressive, I'll stop him. It may be the only chance we have to keep you from being convicted. I watched the jurors. They have shown no sympathy toward you. Your witnesses did well, but it's clear that you did not change until after the crime was committed."

"I'll try."

"You can do it, Nichole. You have too."

I was still confused. "I don't understand why my trial is first."

"Nichole, it was vital that we had a separate trial. I agreed to have yours first to ensure that would happen. You have got to convince the jurors that you were not involved in this crime."

Red approached the bench and said that I would be her next witness.

I sat down after taking the oath. Red went right to the point. "Nichole, tell me what happened from the time you left with Mr. Felts until you jumped out of the moving car to escape them."

I started from the time we left the dance. I gained more confidence the longer I talked and went into detail about being beaten and abused by Larry from the time he robbed the gas station. I described my attempted escape and being dragged to his car and into the house.

Red interrupted me and asked, "Why didn't you try to escape again?"

"Larry told me if I tried to escape again, he would fix it where I never walked. I believed him."

"It must have taken a lot of courage to jump from a moving car," she said.

"I had to get away and did not consider the danger. I would do it again without hesitation. I made a horrible mistake becoming involved with Larry. I did want to go home to New

York, but I had no idea what kind of person he was."

"Thank you, Nichole, for describing this terrible ordeal that you suffered through. You are a brave young lady." Red returned to her seat.

Terrified, I watched the prosecutor approach me smiling. "So, Miss Barlowe, you became a changed person after the robbery and murder of the victim?"

Red jumped to her feet. "He is again implying my client took part in the crime, your honor."

"Sustained," the judge said.

"Okay, let me rephrase the question. Miss Barlowe, what made you change after you voluntarily left your home with the accused?"

My voice quivered as I started to speak, which caused me to start over. "I saw what kind of person he was after we left. He treated me differently before then. I realized what a terrible mistake I made when he robbed the gas station in Cisco. I tried to object, and he hit me."

Mr. Watson continued to smile, as if he knew something no one else did. "I find it hard to believe that you didn't see some of the evil in the accused during your relationship before leaving with him."

Again, Red was on her feet. "Your honor, my client has answered that question."

"Sustained," said the judge.

"Miss Barlowe, did you have intimate relations with Mr. Larry Felts?"

I panicked and wanted to run and hide. Before I could answer, Red interrupted, "Your honor, I object! The question is not relevant."

The judge nodded at Mr. Watson. "I will allow it."

Mr. Watson's smile turned to a glare. "Do I need to repeat the question, Miss Barlowe?"

"No, I understand the question. The answer is yes." I ducked my head and spoke softly.

"So, you were intimate with Mr. Felts before you ran off with him?"

"Yes." I was ashamed and embarrassed for everyone to know, especially my mother and grandmother, even though they probably knew it.

"After you left with Mr. Felts, did the intimacy continue?"

Would the humiliation never end? "Yes."

Mr. Watson's smile had returned as he stepped closer. "Were you forced or was it mutual?"

"After we left, and I saw what kind of person he was, it was forced." Maybe that would end it.

"So, it was a mutual relationship before you left with him?"

Before I could respond Red stood. "Objection, your honor! She has answered the question. He is trying to shame my client."

"Sustained," said the judge.

"I understand that you left with Mr. Felts because he promised to take you back to New York. Is that correct?"

I was relieved to move on. "Yes. I wanted to go home."

"You were desperate to leave Texas because you hated it. Is that correct?

Remember, you are under oath."

"Yes. But I have changed since then and don't feel the same way now."

He stared at me. "We are not talking about now. Were you willing to do anything to get out of Texas at the time you left home with Larry Felts?"

"I guess so."

His voice rose. "Yes or no, Miss Barlowe!"

"Yes." I felt trapped by my own words.

"Were you not warned about Larry Felts—about his character and the kind of person he was? Didn't your parents try to discourage you from seeing him after talking to the principal?"

"Yes," I said.

"Yet, you testified that you had no idea he was so evil before you left with him." He hesitated, shaking his head. "I am sorry, Miss Barlowe—it confuses me. Surely, your judgement cannot be that poor. After all, you seem to be an intelligent young lady. It just makes more sense to me that you did not care what kind of person Larry Felts was and that you were willing to do anything to get out of Texas, including being part of a terrible murder."

"Objection!" screamed Red.

Mr. Watson immediately turned to the judge. "I withdraw the statement, your honor." He went back to his seat.

"We will recess until tomorrow morning at ten o'clock." The judge lightly tapped his gavel to show court was adjourned.

Mom, Gram, and I met with Red in a small room in the courthouse. I was relieved but disappointed that it didn't go well. "I am sorry for not doing better. I was scared."

"You did fine, Nichole." Red patted me on the arm. "Tomorrow, we get Larry on the stand. I'm anxious to get a crack at him."

"It doesn't look good, does it?" Mother asked.

"It was a tough day. It will go better tomorrow. Let's meet at nine in the morning and go over some things before we begin."

"That prosecutor is something else," said my grandmother.

"You're right, and he's not above pulling some shady deals to get a conviction. He's ambitious, which sometimes gets in the way of honesty and the law." Red told us she would see us tomorrow and left.

"Are you going to call Daddy and tell him about the trial today?" I asked.

"I am thankful he didn't come. It stressed me out, and I have a strong heart." Mother turned to Gram. "What do you think about reporting back home on what happened today?"

Gram shook her head. "Let's wait until we have more positive news. Maybe tomorrow things will be looking up."

I went for a walk when we got back to our hotel, giving me time to think. Mother and Gram had still not shown any anger toward me, nor had they expressed disappointment in my actions. I know they must be embarrassed and disappointed at the truths that were brought out in court today. I was ashamed and felt cheap and dirty. Maybe I deserved to go to prison. After all, it was my doings that got me into all this trouble.

I was glad Daniel was not here to see what happened today. He would find out eventually how terrible I was. Would he be mad or disappointed? It probably didn't make any difference to him if I was a slut.

Was it too late to care what people thought about me? I had already messed up so bad it might be too late.

The next morning, I watched as Larry took an oath to tell the truth, hopeful that he would abide by it. Mr. Watson questioned him first. "Do you know the defendant?" He pointed toward me.

Larry looked at me and smiled. "Of course, she's my girl."

"How long have you known Nichole?"

"Let's see. I guess it would be about ten months or so. Of course, I haven't seen her since June of last year. I thought she might visit me, but she didn't."

"When was the last time you saw her," Mr. Watson asked.

"I haven't seen her since she fell out of the car before I was arrested. I was worried she might have been killed but found out later she was only hurt."

"Tell me what part Nichole played in the robbery and murder of the victim." Mr. Watson looked back at me.

"Nichole was set on going to New York. She agreed to help us if we shared the money with her from the robbery. I didn't want to kill Mr. Lawler and my cousin didn't either. Nichole insisted that if we left him alive, he could identify us." He shrugged. "We did what she said. I really felt badly about the whole thing."

"Nichole said she jumped out of the car to get away from y'all."

Larry laughed. "That's crazy. We were going at least forty miles an hour. She wasn't going to jump out of the car going that fast. The door came open, and she fell out. I wanted to go back and see about her. My cousin was driving, and he kept going."

"That's all I have for the witness." Mr. Watson returned to his seat. I looked at the jurors and saw nothing but anger.

49

VERDICT

Effie

We were exhausted. The trial had dragged on for a week and had now gone to the jury. Our attorney, Ms. Sinclaire or Red, had done everything she could to defend Nichole. She had been aggressive in her questioning of Larry and his cousin, accusing them of lying but had not been able to break them. The prosecuting attorney, Mr. Watson, had questioned Nichole to the point that I thought she might fall apart, and insisted that she was part of the crime. I was proud of her for holding herself together and answering the accusations that were relentless. I tried to read the jury and at times felt good, but that feeling would disappear when their expressions reflected scorn.

Both our attorney's and the prosecution's closing arguments were emotional, loud, and convincing. I have to admit the prosecution was confident and made valid points about Nichole and her past conduct leading up to the crime. He repeated the sworn testimony of the other two defendants a number of times. Our attorney's presentation was just as strong, portraying Nichole as a confused little girl who was fooled by Larry and saw in him her only way to get back to New York. She reminded the jury of the positive testimony of the principal and how she had turned her life around. At times, I thought that it would be impossible for the jury to find her guilty; however, I could not help but think, watching the all-male jury, that we were at a disadvantage having a female attorney. Maybe I was wrong. Now, it was just a waiting game.

We had been in a room in the courthouse several doors down from the courtroom. Nichole couldn't sit still, getting up and moving around every few minutes. "What is taking so long? How long has it been?"

"A little over three hours," I said. "Maybe that is a good sign."

Nichole looked at Red. "Is it a good sign?"

"I can't say. I have seen jurors take several days to reach a verdict."

"I can't stand it any longer in here. I'm going outside and walk around," Nichole said.

"What about it, Red? You must have some kind of idea how it's going," Leta asked.

She took too long to respond, throwing up her hands. "I'm hopeful. The problem is Nichole's conduct prior to running away with Larry. If the jurors can just get by that. I have no doubt but what those two guys are lying about Nichole being part of the robbery and murder. I'm sure that Watson has made a deal with their lawyer. I could be wrong, but why else would they lie if they had nothing to gain? I better check on Nichole," Red said, and left the room.

I hadn't even asked Leta about her phone call home last night. "Was everything all right at the ranch?"

"Yeah, I guess. After listening to Charlie, you wouldn't think so, though. It's been dry this winter, and he's had to feed more than usual. On top of that, he's complaining about the cattle market, predicting we'll have to give our calves away this year. On the positive side, Elliot continues to improve, and Grant is doing well in school. He said that Daniel asked about Nichole after every call. I imagine they've all lost weight without having a cook."

"Leta, we have cost you and Charlie so much money. How are your finances holding out? I know Charlie worries, but you never say anything."

She smiled. "Charlie would worry no matter how much money we had. I think he probably likes to worry. I just try to stay positive and believe everything will be okay. Thus far that has worked out. We have been through some tough times and come out of them. At the moment finances are the least of our concerns. We have to get Nichole out of this mess, so she can get on with her life. I am praying that this will be a lesson well learned for her and turn out to be something positive in her life."

I had no doubt that Leta was hiding the fact they were in financial trouble because of us. The only thing we could do was come to Texas. If Nichole had not gotten into trouble, everything would have been fine. I tried to concentrate on something positive. Elliot was better, which Dr. Johnson described as a miracle. He had to take a pill occasionally but sometimes went days without the need. Grant was a different young man, now involved in life and not just a spectator.

When this was over, I had to get a job—somewhere. It did not matter where or how much it paid. I had to provide something to Charlie and Leta for what they were doing for us.

Red and Nichole came back into the room. "Something is happening. People are stirring in the hallway." Red motioned for us. "Let's see what's going on."

We met an officer in the hall who told us the jury had reached a verdict. We entered the courtroom with Red and Nichole taking their seats at the front. Leta and I sat as close to them as we could.

Everyone stood as the judge entered and took his seat. He looked at Nichole. "Please stand, Miss Barlowe." He turned his attention to the jury. "Have you reached a verdict?"

A man stood holding a piece of paper. "Yes, we have, your honor. We find the defendant guilty of conspiracy to commit murder and robbery."

A murmur went through the crowded courtroom. Nichole fell to her knees— sobbing. Red picked up her and held her. I had tried to prepare myself but couldn't hold back the tears. Leta put her arm around me. "She'll be all right, Effie. We have to be strong for her."

The judge banged his gavel several times. "Order." The

room quieted. "It is unusual, but I will pass sentence at once. Miss Barlowe, you are to spend five years in the Women's Huntsville Unit of the Texas Prison System, which is located on the Johnson Farm. You are to be taken to the county jail and transferred to Johnson Farm in one month. Court is adjourned." He banged his gavel.

I stood in disbelief as two officers approached Nichole, handcuffed her, and practically carried her out of the courtroom.

Red walked over to us. "Let's go somewhere and talk."

Neither Lena or I had eaten anything today, only having coffee this morning. I couldn't eat but Leta was probably starved. "Could we go somewhere and get something to eat?" I asked Red.

"Sure, there's a place a few blocks from here. Just follow me."

On the short drive to the café, Leta said, "I need to get back to the ranch. I know it's going to be hard for you to leave."

I was still in shock at seeing my little girl in handcuffs. "I don't know what to do. I know that Elliot and Grant need me, but how can I leave Nichole?"

Red already had a table when we entered the little café, which had only a few customers, since it was mid-afternoon. "This place doesn't have a lot of atmosphere, but the food is excellent."

I couldn't eat but ordered a coke, hoping it would settle my stomach which felt like it had turned upside down. "What now?" I asked Red.

"We appeal. I'm anxious to see what happens in the other trial. It won't start for another ten days. I'm sorry for the guilty verdict. I've already been going over in my mind what I could have missed. One thing in our favor—the sentence was lenient. I know it may not seem like it to you. But it could have been much worse. Also, the charge of conspiracy instead of accessory was good."

At first, I was angry at her comments. How could five years be lenient? "Five years seems like a lifetime for an eighteen-year-old."

"I know. Maybe I should have put it another way. Nichole will be eligible for parole in half of that time—probably less. I'm not saying it will be easy on you or her. I'm just trying to look at the positives. I do believe we have a good chance for a new trial on appeal."

Leta broke her silence. "We understand what you're saying and appreciate your effort on behalf of Nichole. We knew it was going to be a tough go when both Larry and his cousin testified as to Nichole's part in the crime. I don't know what you could have done differently." She looked at me. "What we need help with now is deciding what Effie should do. I need to go home. Do you think that Effie should remain here for the next month to be close to Nichole? Would she be allowed to visit her if she did remain here?"

Red toyed with her glass of tea. "Visitation varies, but most of the time only weekend visits are allowed. The decision is going to be up to Effie." She nodded at me. "Personally, I wouldn't recommend it. It might be better to come back in a couple of weeks to visit. I know this sounds cruel, but Nichole must get used to this life. I can't see it helping if her mother is here. It's your decision though. I'm not comfortable recommending anything—one way or the other."

Could I leave Nichole here alone? I made a decision. Elliot and Grant needed me. I would go home and return in two weeks. Hopefully, Elliot and Grant can come back with me.

I waited the next morning in a small room at the jail. I had been granted a visit to say goodbye to Nichole. I spent a sleepless night trying to decide what to say. The door opened and an officer appeared with Nichole. Her eyes were red and swollen. She moved into my outstretched arms, crying softly. "Please get me out of here, Mother."

I pushed her back, still holding on to her. "Let's sit down." Several chairs surrounded a small table. "Nichole, our attorney is going to appeal and believes we have a chance for a new trial."

"I-I am s-scared. T-he other w-omen are mean."

My eyes pictured a different person—one I had never seen. "I know. I wish there was something we could do."

"P-lease take me h-home." She broke down again, burying her head in her hands.

"I can't. You have to stay." I moved over to her, taking her hands in mine.

"Listen to me, Nichole. When I discovered your dad was deathly ill, and we had no money—I prayed for strength. I was able to continue and do the things that needed to be done. I felt my strength increase and a feeling came over me that I could do this. When there was nowhere else to go, I was given the ability to survive and care for our family. I am not preaching to you, only telling you what helped me through my challenges. You cannot go home. You have been found guilty and sentenced to prison. I have to go back to the ranch and be with your dad and brother. You have to understand—I have no other choice. I will come back in two weeks with Grant and your dad."

She grabbed me with both arms. "No! You cannot leave me here! Please, Mother. Don't leave me!"

We held one another until the guard returned and took her arm as she cried and begged me not to leave her. As she was taken down the hallway to her cell, I stood and listened to her pleading.

50

MORE PROBLEMS

Leta

"I'm afraid we are going to run into some bad weather before we get home." I expected no response from Effie since she had been silent for the first hour of our trip home. I tried to make conversation but only received one word replies and sometimes nothing. I was afraid she was going to ask me to turn around and take her back to Fort Worth.

"She was so helpless and fragile. I had never seen her like this even when she was a small child." Effie turned away and looked out the window.

I chose my words carefully. "Effie, there was nothing more you could do. I know you feel terrible leaving Nichole. I promise you though that young people are resilient, and she will come out of this a better person. Nichole is learning a lesson the hard way—there are consequences for your actions. At this time that is a lesson that many young people do not experience."

Effie said nothing and continued to gaze out the window. By the time we drove into Cisco, the dark cloud in the north was close. It was a blue norther and was bringing colder weather and who knows what else. It was mid-January, and the winter had not been that bad. Charlie complained about how little winter moisture we had received. I didn't stop in Cisco since we had plenty of gas. I was anxious to get home ahead of the weather. We were only about twenty miles out of Cisco when the north wind caught up with us. At least it was behind us. It started raining and within minutes I could feel the cold seep into the car. Thank goodness the car had a heater but was not efficient enough to warm the car, even though it did do some good. It wasn't but a few minutes until sleet began to hit the windshield.

"Effie, we're going to have a problem. The windshield is going to freeze over."

"What can we do?" she asked.

"There's a piece of flat metal under your seat that we use for a scraper. We're going to need it in a few minutes." I had to bend to see through the small opening in the windshield. When the small hole disappeared, I pulled off to the side of the road.

"I'll try to clear the windshield." Effie opened the door with help from the wind. "Just clean off my side of the windshield." Our only chance to get home is if the sleet stops or is replaced with snow, which is easier to clean.

Effie was shaking as she got back in. "I thought it was cold in New York. Never have I experienced anything like this freezing wind. Can you see now?"

There was a small opening. "A little. Maybe we can make it a few miles." I was only able to go a short distance before we had to stop again. "This is no good. The best thing for us to do is cover the windshield and wait until it stops sleeting." I had an old blanket over the back seat placed there to protect it.

"Let me do that." Effie got out and covered the windshield. "Mercy! That is brutal. It's a good thing we have our heavy coats. Have you ever seen anything like this?"

"Oh, yeah. This is just Texas. Anything can happen here. Charlie will be worried out of his mind, knowing we're caught out in this storm." It was positive that our situation had gotten Effie's thoughts away from Nichole.

"I thought it would be warmer in Texas; it is so far south. Do these storms usually last long?"

"There's no way of knowing. I've seen them last a week and, then again, just a day or so." We spent the next hour talking about various things but stayed away from Nichole. The sleet stopped, and it started snowing. Effie removed the blanket and scrapped the windshield, which allowed us to go further without stopping. With this strategy we were able to get home just after nightfall.

Charlie met us before we reached the house. "I'd given up on you. I had already imagined we'd find you in three or four days frozen to death in the car." He took my arm to help me, but it was more like we were helping one another get inside out of the wind.

Elliot and Grant were relieved to see us, also. We sat as close to the fireplace as possible and told them the details of the trial and what had happened. Elliot and Grant interrupted often to ask questions, but Charlie remained quiet. I knew him well enough to know something was wrong—something that had nothing to do with Nichole or our trip home.

Elliot, Effie, and Grant decided to stay with us rather than confront the storm to get home. After they had gone to their rooms, I had a chance to ask Charlie what was wrong.

He had half an unlit cigar that he'd been chewing on for the past hour. He removed it. "How'd you know something was wrong?"

"Charlie, for crying out loud, I've been living with you over fifty years. Now what is it?"

He reached into his pocket and brought out a crumbled-up letter. "We're overdrawn, Leta, for the first time in—I don't remember when. The bank didn't turn down the check. With the storm it's going to be at least several days before I can get to the bank. The only thing I can do is take out a loan to cover the check and provide money for us to get through the year. Our next source of income will be in the fall when we sell the calf crop unless we sell some cows. It wouldn't be selling as much as giving them away with the market the way it is. The expenses caused by Elliot and his family have drained our bank account. Of course, most of it went to Nichole after her arrest, including medical and legal expenses. Also, our last calf crop only made enough to pay the feed bill. I tell you, Leta, it makes me sick. I thought these times of being broke were behind us."

I actually felt sorry for him. He was taking it better than I expected. He always worried about money—justified or not. This time it was definitely justified. "How much do you think we need to borrow to get by until we sell our calves in the fall?"

He popped his teeth several times before answering. "It depends on how much feed we need to buy. We're getting some snow now, but it's been dry. Have you given any checks the last week?"

"Yes. A forty-dollar check for our hotel and another $100 to our attorney. That should be all the checks to come in." I expected an outburst but was surprised.

He lit his cigar stub. "How are we for groceries?"

"Good. We have plenty of canned vegetables and fruit. Since we butchered two hogs last fall that will help. We need to buy some chicks for broilers but that can wait until spring." I reached and took the letter from him. The check for insufficient funds was for seventy-five dollars that I'd given to our attorney. "Will $1,000 be enough to get us through until we have calves ready to sell?"

"That's what I had in mind. After all these years we think alike," he said.

"We'll make it, Charlie—we always have. If Elliot, Effie, and our grandchildren had not come to us for help, we wouldn't have this problem. I would rather have the problem and our family together. I believe that you feel the same way."

The storm lasted three days, ending on a Thursday, with snow measuring at least six inches. We were eating breakfast that morning when the sheriff called and wanted to talk with Charlie.

He returned to the table. "He wants to see me as soon as possible. Now what could the sheriff want?"

"It must be about Nichole," Effie said. "Maybe it's good news."

When we finished our breakfast Charlie went outside. He returned a few minutes later. "It's bitter cold. The snow is frozen, which should allow us to get into town. I need to go to the bank too, besides finding out what the sheriff wants."

I knew it was useless but thought it wouldn't hurt to try. "Charlie, let's wait until tomorrow. The roads will be better, and one more day won't make any difference."

"No, I don't want to put it off," he said.

"Effie and I will stay here to keep the fire going. Since school is out, Grant has informed me he is going with Daniel to feed. I hope you find out good news about Nichole," Elliot said.

The sun was shining when we left for town. Like Charlie thought, the roads were slick but driving slowly we had no trouble. Charlie was anxious to see what the sheriff wanted that required urgency, so we went there first.

The sheriff was in his office, sitting at his desk, holding a cup of coffee. "Morning, Charlie—Leta. Would y'all like coffee?" He motioned for us to sit down.

"Not me," Charlie said.

"No, thanks," I said, sitting down.

The sheriff sipped his coffee. "Is it cold enough for you? My thermometer said 10 this morning." He glanced at Charlie. "How much snow did you get?"

"What ta hell, Fincher? You get us out in this weather asking us silly questions. What was so important that you needed to see me? I think you said, 'As quickly as possible.'"

He leaned forward. "I'm sorry, Charlie. I was just trying to be sociable before putting this on you." He looked off to one side. "Let's see—where do I start? I guess Daniel is still working for you?"

"Yeah, an hour ago he was leaving the house to feed some cold cattle." The teeth popping began.

"Charlie, do you and Leta know anything about Daniel and his past?"

"No, Daniel has been very private about his past," I said.

"I got a call from a friend of mine who works at the Fort

Worth Stock Yards. He told me that three men had been there recently asking about Daniel. They had heard about him through word that had spread clear to Oklahoma. That didn't surprise me since there was a lot of talk about the incident. After I visited with him I called the sheriff of the county they were from and asked about them. He gave me more information than I expected." He paused and rose. "You sure you don't want some coffee? I've got to have another cup."

I thought Charlie was going to come out of his chair. I reached and squeezed his arm, made eye contact, and shook my head. Maybe it helped, since he stayed put.

The sheriff sat back down, with his fresh cup of coffee. "Let's see now, where was I? Oh, yeah. The sheriff in Oklahoma knew Daniel, as well as the three brothers. He provided a detailed description of what happened. There was another brother, also, who made unwelcome advances toward Daniel's mother. Daniel was only seventeen and just a boy or that's what the assailant thought. A fight occurred and the brother ended up dead. The sheriff arrested Daniel, but a grand jury did not indict him. It was somewhat unusual since an Indian killed a white man. The white man, though, was well known for his disrespect for women and had been accused on numerous occasions of assault. The Oklahoma sheriff said the three brothers made it known to everyone that they would not rest until Daniel was dead.

"Charlie, there is every reason to believe that the brothers found out information that would lead them to you. You are going to need to tell Daniel about this threat to him and to your family since you are in the way of their revenge."

"Daniel has told us nothing of his past," Charlie said. "He's a good boy and has become like family."

"Is there nothing you can do, Sheriff Fincher?" I asked.

He sat his cup down. "Not unless they break the law. All they've done is talk."

This was the last thing we needed now, with our situation. I couldn't believe this was happening, with Nichole in jail and on our way to the bank to borrow money. I looked at Charlie and knew the answer before it came.

"I won't run Daniel off my ranch. I'll give him the information and let him decide." He repeated. "He is like family."

"Another bit of information, Charlie. You made a trail drive to New Mexico, across the plains. That was fifty or so years ago when things were different. What Indians were the most feared?"

"Comanche, no other tribe came close."

"Another question. Who was the most feared leader of the Comanche?" "Where's this going, Fincher. You're wasting our time."

"Just answer the question, Charlie."

"Everybody knows it was Quanah Parker, that half-breed who killed white men and went on to become a respectable rancher and friend of Teddy Roosevelt."

The sheriff leaned back, with his hands behind his head and smiled. "His grandson works for you. Now, if that is not enough—there's more. Daniel was born the day the great chief died. There has always been a belief among the Comanche that Quanah Parker returned in the form of his grandson. The story has grown since the boy is the spitting image of his granddad. Isn't that something? Crazy, isn't it? As you know, Quanah Parker was popular among most of his people but not all. Some hated him. That boy is in extreme danger. I hate to lay this on you, Charlie, but you needed to know. It probably would have been better if you had never laid eyes on this boy."

"Can you believe that, Charlie? A grandson of that famous Indian Chief."

He didn't answer my question until we were parked in front of the bank. "I knew something wasn't right. I'm to blame for sending him to Fort Worth with our cattle. That's how he was discovered. I guess they would have found him eventually, anyway. Now, the tough part is telling him. I have no doubt but what he will leave. I don't know how we'll do without him. We can't afford to hire anyone, and with cattle to feed in midwinter, we'll be in more trouble than we are now—if that's possible. Well, it's one problem at a time. I need to see the banker now for a loan." He opened the door to get out.

"Charlie, be careful, that sidewalk is slick."

I don't know whether he didn't hear me or just ignored the warning. Probably the later. He took a step up onto the sidewalk and his feet went out from under him. I was out of the car and bent over him within seconds. His face was scrunched up in pain as he tried to talk. "Hip—leg. S-Something's b-broken."

51

BIG DECISION

Daniel

I was cutting wood when Elliott came out and told me Charlie was in the hospital. He did not provide any details. Within minutes, we were on the way to town, driving slowly on the slick roads. We made it to the hospital and were met by Leta in the lobby.

"He slipped and fell on the way into the bank. He's in a lot of pain. I know he's hurting because he didn't even argue with Dr. Johnson. They're taking some x-rays now. I warned him about the ice, but he paid no attention to me. All he had on his mind was talking to the banker. His feet just went out from under him. It was a hard fall." She wiped away a tear.

Leta went back to be with Charlie, leaving Elliot and me in the lobby. He took a small bottle out of his pocket, removed a pill, and swallowed it. "I feel badly about this. It's my fault this happened. I know Dad was on the way to the bank to borrow money. If not for Nichole this would not have been necessary. And if I hadn't made stupid financial decisions, we wouldn't have been a burden on them in the first place. Now, Dad is hurt, and I'm not even able to help with the ranch."

"Charlie is worried about the cattle market. Do you think it will get better?" I asked.

He shook his head. "No, definitely not. In fact, the economy is probably going to get much worse. The cattle market may not recover for years. This country is in for some tough times."

It was some time before Leta came back with a report about Charlie's injuries. "He has a broken leg and will be in the hospital indefinitely. Dr. Johnson wouldn't even commit to how long." She was interrupted by Dr. Johnson who came into the lobby.

"Leta, what in the world were y'all doing out in this weather. You should have known better even if your hard-headed husband didn't."

Leta ducked her head. "Charlie had to go to the bank on urgent business."

"Well, it wasn't so important that it couldn't have waited for a better day," he said, turning and leaving.

We waited until Charlie was moved to a room before going in to see him. Dr. Johnson had given him something to help with the pain, and he was not alert. Charlie sounded like he had too much to drink and slurred his words. "S-Should have been m-more c-careful. Wanted to g-get i-it over w-with. Hate to ask for m- money." He closed his eyes, and I'd thought he'd gone to sleep. "Tell him, Leta."

I thought he was talking out of his head until Leta answered, after reaching for his hand. "Don't worry, I'll take care of it. We'll be all right, Charlie." She bent and kissed him on the forehead. "We better leave so he can rest."

We followed her out of the room and to the car. She asked us to get inside so we could talk. "We have a problem. You need to hear it, too, Elliot."

We listened as she told us about their meeting with Sheriff Fincher. He told them about me being a grandson of Quanah Parker and the men who vowed revenge. She paused—expecting a response.

"I knew that sooner or later they would find me," I said. "There is no choice but to leave. If I stay it would put your family in danger. The men who are after me will not hesitate to kill anyone in their way. I should have told you. I wanted to hide from everybody and live my life without conflict. The man I killed was hurting my mother. When I tried to stop him, he turned on me with a knife. I was protecting Mother and myself."

"Don't get us wrong, Daniel. We know you weren't at fault," Leta said. "We just want you to know that you're in danger. With you leaving, it will put us in an impossible situation. It would take two or three men to replace you, and we don't have the money to hire them. That wouldn't make any difference since no one could replace you and do the things that you do on the ranch. Charlie will be unable to do anything for—who knows how long."

"But you will be in danger if I stay," I said.

"The thing about it, Daniel, these men who are looking for you will come to the ranch," Elliot said. "They will not believe us when we tell them you are gone. There will be trouble anyway. At least, if you're here you can help with whatever happens. Maybe, they won't show up at all."

"It has been almost three years since I left home. My mother went to live with her sisters where she would be safe. I have no brothers or sisters, and my dad died when I was young." I wanted to give them more information which they deserved. "I will stay if that is what you want. I will do what I can to not put you in danger. You have been good to me, and it saddens me that this has come upon you."

Elliot exclaimed, "I knew you looked familiar, Daniel! There was a painting of Quanah Parker in one of the restaurants where we ate. It's amazing how much you favor your granddad. I racked my brain trying to think where I'd seen you."

"Yeah, that's what everyone has told me. He was my mother's father. He died the day I was born. That was a problem for the men that are looking for me. They think that because of my family, I was not punished for killing their brother. Also, my grandfather is still hated by some of the white families who have not forgotten that he killed many of their kind."

"Your grandfather went to a reservation a few years before Charlie and I made the trip across the plains from New Mexico. His reputation was still present, and the mention of his name brought fear like I'd never seen. It is amazing what he did for his people after becoming peaceful."

"I guess so. About all my people talk about is the battles he won and what a great warrior he was."

"I'm going to stay with Charlie, at least for a while," Leta said. "I know the weather is bad, but we need to build a gate at our entrance that we can lock as soon as possible. At least, that would discourage anyone from just being able to drive in."

I left the hospital in sadness, knowing the danger that my being here had brought upon this family.

I sat in front of the stove, which had gone out. It was cold but warmth was not important. The first thing I remembered about my dad was him beating my mother. I was no older than four or five. I grew to hate him as his treatment of my mother continued until he drank himself to death when I was ten. I never touched liquor because I had seen what it did to my people. One of my uncles told me about my dad after he died. He said that my dad married my mother, thinking he would have the influence of her father, Quanah Parker, who owned much land. It turned out that the great chief ignored my dad. We had 160 acres of land, which my dad leased to an adjoining rancher. He used most of the money to buy liquor, which caused us to go hungry at times. I started working for area ranchers, breaking horses for them after my dad died. My mother made blankets and sold them. This brought in enough money for us to survive.

I was able to attend a white school for several years due to being a grandson of the last Comanche chief. I was one of the few Indians that went to the school. I was ridiculed at first, but as I grew older and stronger that changed.

I arrived home from work one Saturday night after dark and heard screams coming from the house. I jumped off my horse, ran to the house, burst through the door, and saw a man struggling with my mother. He turned on me and took out a knife. "Get out of here! Me and this here Injun squaw have business."

I reached into my boot and pulled out my knife.

He laughed. "Look-ee here. I'm going to have to teach this pup a lesson." He looked back at my mother. "I'll deal with you later, squaw." He was overweight and drunk, which caused him to be slow. He came toward me swinging his knife from side to side. "I'm gonna cut you for messing up my fun."

I waited until he was close before blocking his arm on one of his wide swings and sinking my knife to the hilt in him. He staggered to the door, opened it, and fell outside. As I think back, I felt no guilt. I know that hatred of my dad and the image of him beating my mother with me being helpless to do anything was the reason. I had finally been able to protect her.

I went for the sheriff who put me in jail for my own protection. A grand jury was formed a couple of weeks later. With my mother's testimony and the reputation of the victim, the grand jury ruled that I did not have to stand trial. I left town the day of my release from jail and have not seen my mother since.

I had put this family in danger by coming here and should have known this would happen. Now, they needed me—more than they feared what they might face because of me. I was only seventeen when I left home, not old or wise enough to make good decisions. I was frightened and lonely when I found this refuge. I knew at once that this would be a safe place. Charlie and Leta were good people and treated me fairly. I admired Charlie and knew that in his early life he was a warrior. I grew up not having a father or a grandfather to look up to, and Charlie filled that need. He didn't trust me at first but after Fort Worth that changed.

I was confused about Nichole. She was rotten and had done terrible things. But I did not believe she was an evil person. I was angry when I heard she had run off with that boy. She was stupid, but I still hoped she would not go to prison and would come back here to live. It was a strange feeling—not knowing why I wanted her close.

It was foolish to sit here and think about the past. It could not be changed. I took the next few minutes to get my fire going and then went to check on Roany. I went into his stall, gave him some feed, and brushed him while he ate. He was a good horse—a little onery, but still what I wanted in a horse. He was independent, but as the years passed he would become more loyal. I smiled, thinking of the horse trader. I was surprised at how he lied. My people are known for their truthfulness.

My thoughts kept going backward. The men who were coming to kill me were evil. They made whiskey and sold it to my people. Because of the hardships and poverty of my people, many of them drank. Our land had been taken from us in 1903 when a treaty was broken, which allowed the government to buy most of the 2,000,000 acres for $1.25 an acre. My people were given 160 acres for each man, woman, and child. What followed was poverty for my people.

"What is wrong with you?" I muttered. "Thinking backward." I left Roany and went to get the post hole diggers to get started on the gate at the entrance.

52

THE VISIT

Effie

After Elliot had come home and told me everything that had happened, I went to find Daniel. He was loading something in the back of the truck. "Could I talk with you?"

"I need to do something right away. You can help me. We can talk later." He continued to put other items in the back of the truck, including a long piece of pipe and several logs. "You need to put on your work clothes and big coat."

I went back into the house and told Elliot I was going to help Daniel with something but didn't know what. Grant insisted on going with us and, not feeling like arguing with him, I didn't refuse. First Nichole and now Charlie being injured. On top of that, Daniel was being hunted by dangerous men. I kept thinking—this could not all be happening at once.

We joined Daniel and found out on the drive to the road what we were going to do. I had put on my overalls and heavy coat but was still cold. Daniel unloaded the truck and gave Grant his job. "Gather up some small wood and build us a fire. There is a box of matches in the compartment of the pickup. We are going to be here for some time and need the fire to warm up."

With a tape we measured two feet on each side of the cattle guard. Daniel went to work digging a hole where we had put a mark. He surprised me by asking about Nichole.

"She's terribly upset, which is understandable. It was difficult to leave her."

He stopped digging and leaned on the diggers. "We can all do more than we think. She will suffer but be okay. She will be a stronger person because of it. She is not a bad person. I am sorry she has to go through this." He went back to digging.

I was surprised at his compassion and the kind words about Nichole. Maybe the feeling between them was mutual. "I can only hope," I muttered silently. I went over to the fire.

Grant put another piece of wood on it. "I built a good fire. It smells good. CK said it was mesquite and was good to cook with, too."

I hugged him. "You did build a warm fire. It feels good."

Daniel didn't stop digging until he was satisfied with the depth. He took a huge post out of the bed of the truck. "You can come help me, now." He dropped the end of the post in the hole. "This is a crosstie which is used to build railroad tracks. It is strong and will not rot. If you will hold it straight, I can fill in and pack the dirt around it."

I did what he asked. He repeated the process on the other side of the cattle guard. When he finished, he took a strange tool out of the pickup. He must have noticed my confused look. "This is a tool to drill a hole in the crosstie. It will take some time to make it big enough for the pipe."

I stood by the fire with Grant and watched as he worked the tool in a circular motion. After at least half an hour he moved to the other post and did the same. When he finished, he brought the pipe from the truck and ran it through the hole in one of the posts. I saw that the end of the pipe was larger. He pushed the pipe through the hole in the other post. After doing this, he stopped and looked with satisfaction at his work. "I will bring a chain and fix it to the end of the pipe and around the post with a lock. We can slide the pipe out when we use a key to unlock the chain. It will not be easy for someone to get through the gate without a key."

"Won't whoever is trying to get through the gate, just cut down the post?" I asked.

"That will not be easy. These men are lazy, and it would take work."

"Aren't you afraid?" I asked.

"Yeah, for all your family—not for myself. You are in danger because of me. If I had my way, I would leave. But I am needed here. I hope to kill them before they harm your family."

I couldn't believe how he said this. Like it was nothing out of the ordinary. I had wanted to find out if he was going to stay. He answered my question without me having to ask.

"I don't know what to do, Elliot. It has been two weeks since I left Nichole. I promised her to return, but the current situation makes it hard for me to leave. What if those men show up?"

"Effie, I've about decided it was a false alarm. If those guys were coming, they would have been here by now. Besides, what could you do if they did show up?"

It was an unusually warm day for mid-winter, and we were sitting on the porch. "I would never forgive myself if something happened to you and Grant with me gone to Fort Worth. But I promised Nichole to return in two weeks."

"My suggestion, Effie, would be for you to go see Nichole at least for a day. You could leave early in the morning, be there by early afternoon, and after visiting with her, stay the night. You can leave the next day after spending a couple of hours with her. That way you would not be gone but two days. We'll be fine. I have a lot of confidence in Daniel. I'm sure you've noticed that he stays close to the house most of the time."

I lowered my voice even though there was no danger Charlie and Leta could hear me. "Your dad is a terrible patient. I admire your mother more all the time for how she is able to cope. I'm afraid my patience would not last with what she has to go through."

Elliot laughed. "That's just how he is. I never knew him to be able to sit still. Now he's forced to stay in the house, unable even to move around."

"I guess my decision is made. I will leave first thing in the morning and do as you suggest."

"Good, we'll be fine. You probably noticed that my dad keeps his pistol close by, usually covered up by his blanket. My dad is not afraid of anything. He and Daniel will be a match for any danger that comes along. Who knows? Maybe I could be of some help."

Having made my decision, I put in a phone call to our attorney. Long distance was always iffy, but this time was successful. She was glad that I had called.

"Effie, I've been busy and haven't been to see Nichole. It would be good for you to come. The men's trial starts next week. It was delayed for some reason. I'm looking forward to it and think that something might come out of it that helps our appeal."

After telling her that I was coming tomorrow, we ended the call.

I left at daylight the next morning. The weather looked promising with it not being that cold and the sun shining. In fact, it was a problem driving into the sun and forced me to shade my eyes with my free hand. There was little traffic, giving me plenty of time to think. Elliot continued to improve. He told me yesterday that he'd only had to take one pill for the last two weeks. I guess it could be called a miracle since the diagnosis of his condition had been so poor. I encouraged him not to try and do too much.

Had it only been a little over a year since we arrived in Texas? So much had changed in those thirteen months. What would have happened if Elliot had not lost everything when the market crashed, and we had remained in New York? The answer was simple—we would be divorced and the family split. At least our family was together even with the problems we faced. Elliot, Grant, and I were all better off in Texas. I actually believed that eventually Nicole would look back and be thankful we moved.

In the brief time here, I had come to love Charlie and Leta. I had not known anyone like them in New York. No one would have done as much for us, including my mom and dad. At this moment, I would not return to New York even with electricity and indoor toilets. I smiled—the outhouse wasn't that bad.

I only stopped once for gas in Weatherford and was at the jail a few minutes after two. When I told the jailer the purpose of my visit, he showed me to a room and said he would get Nichole.

It was only a few minutes until the door opened and Nichole appeared. She stumbled into my arms, crying. I held her for several minutes until she could talk. I stepped back and looked at her. She had lost weight and was filthy with the shapeless dress just hanging on her. She had bruises up and down both arms.

"Did you come to get me?" she whimpered.

I took her arm and guided her to one of the chairs in the room. "What happened to your arms?"

She looked at one arm and then the other. "They pinched me." She started crying again.

I held her until she was able to talk. "T-They h-ate me. P-Please t-take me h- home."

"I came to visit, Nichole. You cannot leave. Who hates you?"

"The others. They say mean things and hurt me. They take my food. I am hungry. Please, Mother, take me home."

"You wait here. "I will be back in just a minute. I am going to talk with the jailor."

The jailor was sitting with his feet propped up on his desk. He looked up and asked, "Is there a problem?"

"Yes, you could say that. My daughter has been abused and mistreated. Why have you allowed this to happen? Did you not see the bruises on her arms?"

He smiled. "This is a jail. What do you expect?"

"I expect you to protect your prisoners. I want her put in a cell by herself. She has lost weight and said the others take her food."

He scooted back and put his feet on the floor. "Sorry. Can't do that. I don't have an empty cell. She'll have to learn to take up for herself."

I glared at him before leaving and going back to Nichole. She rushed into my arms. "Mother, I cannot stay here. I will die. Please take me home."

I explained again that it was not possible. She finally calmed down enough for me to tell her what was going on at the ranch. She seemed concerned when I told her about Charlie breaking his leg. She asked me about her dad and Grant. Talking about our lives moved her thoughts away from her present situation, which calmed her even more. She asked about Daniel and a hint of a smile appeared. I told her about him asking about her and that he seemed concerned as to how she was doing.

The smile became noticeable. "I would like to see him. Daniel makes me feel safe. I hope he does not think badly of me because of going to jail."

"No, I promise you, Nichole, that he will not." She had improved so much in the last few minutes talking about the ranch that I told her about the danger facing Daniel.

"Oh, Mother! Are you frightened out of your mind?"

"No, not really. Your dad believes that Daniel and Charlie will provide protection for us. I am glad Daniel decided to stay rather than flee from these men."

"I could not imagine coming home and Daniel not being there," she said.

"Nichole, I have to leave for a while. I need to find Red and see if she can help me get you to a single cell and away from the abuse you are suffering. I should be back shortly. You will have to return to your cell."

She broke down again, begging to go with me.

I checked for Red at her office but found her at the

courthouse. I described Nichole's condition and asked for her help.

"Sure. I know the jailor, he's a piece of work. I have some time, so let's go now." I left the courthouse with her following. When we arrived and went into the jail, Red changed her demeanor and became aggressive. "What in the hell is going on, Horace? My client's mother said she was being abused."

He looked up in surprise from his magazine. "It's what it is, Red. This is not a nursery."

"Stand up, Horace! Women are present. Didn't your mother teach you any manners?"

He stood, slowly, looking around the room. "Who do you think you are, coming in here making demands and insulting me?"

"I'm Roselyn Sinclaire, an Attorney at Law. You are no match for me. If I leave this room without you finding a private cell for Nichole, I will prove that. I will file a suit against you immediately and nail your sorry ass to the wall. That's who I am. Now, tell me who you are?"

He blinked and looked confused. After a minute of awkward silence, he mumbled, "I'll see what I can do."

Red took a step toward his desk. "What did you say? Speak up!"

"I'll see what I can do," louder this time as he rose and left the room.

"What do you think?" I asked.

"He'll find a private cell. He's afraid of losing this job. He's too lazy to work at a real job."

I said goodbye to Nichole the next day a little before noon. She had a private cell, and I was able to provide her with magazines and several books to read. She only cried a little after I promised to return before she was taken to the women's prison at Huntsville in two weeks.

53

INTERESTING NEWS

Leta

"Leta! I can't get this radio to work."

I was in the bedroom getting clothes together to wash. I had a large pot of water boiling outside. It was the first pretty day we'd had, and I wanted to take advantage of it. Should I pretend not to hear him?

"Leta! Where are you? I need some help."

It was no use. I might as well fix the radio. It was difficult to get anything done with having to wait on him. He was working the knobs when I went into the room. "What's the problem?"

"All I can get is static. You think the battery pack is weak?"

"No, it shouldn't be." I moved the knob slowly and picked up a station at once. "Charlie, you can't move the knob fast—you have to go slow and allow time to pick up the station. You're too impatient."

"Thank you. I don't know what I'd do without you. Could you get me a glass of water? Are there any of those cookies left you made for Grant? It seems kind of stuffy in here or is it just me?"

I started to leave but stopped and sat down.

"I'm a lot of trouble, ain't I?"

"Yes, Charlie. You are. I'm trying to get some washing done, which is impossible with having to stop and wait on you. It is kind of stuffy in here with all the cigar smoke. And there are some cookies left. I'll get you a couple and some water." I went to the kitchen and returned with his cookies."

"Thank you. I'll leave you alone now."

I went back to my washing but knew it wouldn't be long before another interruption. Charlie was not used to sitting in one place. He had been home from the hospital for a week and was getting more restless by the day. I was hoping that within another week he could get around good enough to go with Daniel to get him out of the house.

As I put bundles of clothes in the wash pot, I thought of the last two weeks. I had returned to the bank after his accident and borrowed $1000 to get us by until fall.

We might be able to make it unless we had some unexpected expenses. We had spent several thousand dollars on Nichole but that should be finished. We had plenty to eat with the two hogs we killed in the fall and the vegetables I'd put up. Daniel had killed two deer to supplement our diet with venison. A wagon came selling beef once a month, and we splurged and bought steak occasionally. I have to give Charlie credit—he had handled being broke better than I expected.

The problem now was that the price of cattle continued to drop. The sale of our calves in the fall would not raise enough cash to sustain us and pay off the loan. Unless something changed, we would be forced to pay the interest and renew the loan.

Elliot was convinced that the men looking for Daniel were not coming. I wasn't so sure but hoped he was correct. Daniel still checked on us several times a day.

While the clothes soaked, I went back inside and put on the large pot of stew I'd cooked yesterday. It was going to be leftovers for lunch. I had too much to do to stop and cook a meal. Effie would be back later today from Fort Worth and could help me catch up.

I hadn't heard from Charlie in half an hour, which was a record. When I checked on him, he was leaned back in his chair asleep with a cigar dangling from his mouth. I smiled and removed the cigar. For all his faults. . .

"Leta, I appreciate you going with me."

"No problem. It'll be good to get away for a while. Charlie is able to get around good enough to take care of himself. Besides, Elliot and Grant are going to stay with him. Goodness knows, I need a break after two weeks of waiting on him."

It was early February, and we were on the way back to Fort Worth. Effie had not been home from her previous trip but ten days. Our attorney had called Effie late yesterday and told her some interesting news. Larry and his cousin had been given the death penalty for the robbery and murder of Mr. Lawler. Red had discovered that the district attorney had promised Larry and his cousin life sentences instead of seeking the death penalty, in return for their testimony against Nichole. He went back on his word, not able to resist a death sentence conviction, which would be good for his political career. Now, Red thought there was a chance that Larry would tell the truth about Nichole. She was going to meet with him and his cousin today.

We left by sunrise and were at the jail by early afternoon. We waited in a vacant room while the jailer brought Nichole to us. Nichole was glad to see us, hugged her mother and then me. She cried but not anything like the last time. She was filthy but looked better, and the sores on her arm had healed. Effie asked her how she was doing.

"Better than when I was with those mean people. My room is cold and dark. I have trouble reading the books you gave me. I do get enough to eat now. I try to be brave and strong but it's hard." She started crying. "I want to go home. Please take me out of here."

Her mother told her about the call from our attorney and the possibility that Larry might change his story. "We are going to Red's office when we leave here."

The excitement showed in her voice. "You mean, I might not have to go to prison?"

"We are hoping and praying for a new trial that would reverse your sentence," I said. "We'll find out more when we talk to Red. We'll come back after we visit with her."

The jailer was surprised at the short visit, but we assured

him we would be back soon.

We were fortunate to find Red at her office. She was mad and didn't waste any time telling us about it. "I couldn't get in to see Larry and his cousin. Larry went crazy when the judge pronounced sentence and had to be carried out of the courtroom in a strait jacket. They put them in a cell and denied anyone access to them. I imagine the district attorney was responsible for that. I argued with the jailer for an hour but didn't get in to see them."

She finally stopped long enough to allow me to ask, "Is there not anything else we can do?"

She bolted out of her chair. "Yeah! Let's go see the district attorney."

We went with Red who talked constantly about how sorry the guy was that we were going to see. She called him about everything that I scolded Charlie for saying. When we entered his office, the secretary informed us that "Mr. Watson was not seeing anyone this afternoon." Red stood with her hands on her hips and stared at her.

The secretary repeated. "I have strict orders that he's not available this afternoon."

"Well, is he here?" asked Red.

"It doesn't matter. You cannot see him today," The smirk couldn't hide her satisfaction at being in control.

Red went past the secretary and marched right into Mr. Watson's office. Effie and I didn't follow, but it was no problem to hear the exchange.

"You can't come barging in here! I'm not doing any business this afternoon." Red's voice was even but grew louder. "Oh, yes you are, you scumbag! You double crossed the two defendants who are now headed to the electric chair. You couldn't resist it, could you? Two death sentences would look good on your resume. Now, an innocent girl is going to prison because of your lies. I want to talk with the defendants."

He was speaking softly now, and we had to move into his office to hear him. "I'm afraid that may not be possible. No one is allowed to see them. They're considered dangerous. The conviction of the girl is not my problem—a jury found her guilty."

Red moved up next to the desk. I expected her to attack him at any time. Her voice was hoarse but quieter. "You are a sorry piece of shit and a disgrace to this profession." She turned and bumped into Effie. "Oh, I'm sorry. Let's get out of here."

When we returned to her car, Red sat quietly behind the wheel for several minutes. "We have a problem. I would go to Larry and his cousins' lawyer, but that would be useless. The court-appointed lawyer to represent them is none other than Ouster. He's probably in on it. We have to go talk to the judge."

We had no problem getting in to see the judge. After Red went over everything with him, the news was not much better. He agreed to have detectives question the defendants and see if they wanted to change their testimony. If they did a new trial could be in order; however, that would take time. Enough time that Nichole would be in prison before the new trial was scheduled.

We returned to the jail and visited with Nichole for several hours. I was surprised at how calm she was. She was interested in the happenings at the ranch, asking about everyone, including her brother. It was obvious that her greatest interest was in Daniel, which caused her to smile when he was mentioned.

Before we started home the next morning, we went by the jail to say goodbye to Nichole and discovered we had a message to see the judge. We debated as to whether to visit with Nichole or see the judge immediately. We decided on the latter, thinking he might have some news.

Seated in the judge's office, he went right to the point. "Detectives talked with Larry yesterday, and he confessed that he lied about Nichole being involved in the crime. He lied in return for a promise from the district attorney that he would not seek the death sentence for him and his cousin."

Effie interrupted. "Can Nichole get out of jail?"

The judge raised his hand to quieten her. "Not so fast. A jury convicted Nichole, which means a jury must find her innocent. She cannot be released until that happens. I know that your attorney will request a new trial which, in all likelihood, will be granted. I would predict that she will be found innocent this time, but there are no guarantees." He hesitated.

With the opening Effie, blurted, "It's not fair that she goes to prison while she waits for another trial. She's innocent, and no telling what will happen to her in prison."

The judge didn't respond for several uncomfortable minutes while Effie rambled on about the unfairness of the situation. He finally stopped her by raising his hand again. "Okay, you've made your point. I may have a solution. It's not the best but better than prison. I'll give the order, pending a new trial, that she be transported to the jail in your hometown until her new trial date. That way she will be close and make it easier on her and you."

I couldn't believe it. That was more than fair. Hopefully, Effie would see it. I didn't wait for her response. "Thank you, Judge, we appreciate that."

Effie realized how fortunate we were, too. "That is exceedingly kind of you. We do appreciate it. When will she be sent to our jail?"

"Within the week," he said. "I know it's been tough on her and y'all, but it's going to work out. I'm sorry we have a dishonest DA but, believe me, he will not be in the position for long. I imagine, due to his dishonesty, that the defendants' death sentence will be changed to life imprisonment."

We thanked him again and left, anxious to get back to the jail and tell Nichole the good news.

The middle of February, Nichole was brought back to Coleman County to spend the time before her trial. All of us were there to meet her when they arrived at the courthouse. Although we expected her to spend the time in the county jail,

Sheriff Fincher surprised us and released her to Charlie and me as a trustee until her new trial.

Three months later Nichole received another trial. The jury deliberated only half an hour before returning a verdict of innocent, overturning the guilty conviction.

54

CHANGING PLANS

Daniel

"It's a hell'va note, Daniel. We've had plenty of moisture, good grass, a mild winter and a ninety percent calf crop—the best in years. Now it's July and turned off hot and dry. We still have enough grass to last until we sell the calves. The sad news is that if they average 300 it looks like we won't get but about $4 a hundred weight when we sell them or $12 a head. With about 180 to sell that would be less than $2,200. That's a third of what we got a couple of years ago."

Charlie repeated this to me a number of times. I had learned that the white man worried about the future—the Indian lived each day. I did not tell this to Charlie. I had been thinking for some time that I should leave. I decided this was a good time to talk about it. "I might need to leave, Charlie. You are able to work again. Elliot is improving and can do more, now. Grant is able to help some, as is Nichole. You could get by without me."

"Why? It's been months since the threat from the men that the sheriff said were coming for revenge. We'll probably never hear from them again."

I shook my head. "No, they will come. I know them and the hate they carry. These past months have been a busy time for them. They use crops which are harvested in the spring and summer to make their whiskey. I promise you—they have not forgotten me. If I leave, maybe the word will get back to them. They will leave you alone then."

"Daniel, you'll hurt all of us if you leave, especially Grant and Nichole. What about Nichole? Since she was released y'all have spent a lot of time together. Also, I know how hard it is to run from someone. I had to do it fifty years ago. To this day, it still bothers me. Talk to Nichole about this and see how she responds."

We had been driving over the ranch looking at the cows with their calves. Charlie let me off at the barn. I took Roany out of his stall, brushed, and saddled him. I still had to be careful. If given an opportunity he would bite me or try to get in a position to kick me. His stamina was amazing. I could ride him all day, and he would continue to be fresh.

I rode him west, giving him his head to go at his own pace. I could think better while horseback. Was I going to leave? It would be the right thing to do. Charlie did not understand. These men would show up one day and put everyone in danger—grave danger. I had no doubt about that. Could I leave and come back later or just leave? The truth was, I wanted to stay. I had always tried to be honest with myself. The weight holding me here was Nichole. Charlie reminded me how much time we had spent together. Up until now, it had been more of a friendship relationship. Most of the time we were together, Grant was present. Maybe Charlie was right—I should include Nichole in my decision. I turned Roany in the direction of her house.

Grant met me as I arrived. "Are we going fishing?"

"Not today. Would you get your sister for me?"

He went back into the house. It was amazing how much better he was getting around. I stayed on Roany as Nichole came out of the house, wearing her jeans. "Are you busy?"

She smiled. "Not really. What are you doing?"

"Just riding. Want to go with me?" I kicked my foot out of the stirrup and held out my hand.

She looked confused. "That's scary. Would it be safe?"

I shrugged. "Don't you trust ole Roany?"

"No, he's mean."

I held my hand out again. "Come on. It will be a first for

Roany."

She hesitated, took my hand, and put her foot in the stirrup. I pulled her up behind me. Roany jumped forward, almost losing her before she wrapped her arms around me. After that he took several crow hops before settling down.

"You still there?" I asked.

She was almost squeezing the breath from me. "Y-Yes—barely. Will he do that again?"

"Maybe. You better keep holding on."

She continued her grip on me. "Where are we going?"

"Nowhere in particular. I'll just let him go where he wants to. I needed to talk with you. I do better on my horse, not looking at you. It's easier that way."

"What do you mean?" she asked.

I told her about leaving. She didn't say anything until I finished. "I don't want you to leave. You make me feel safe." She put her head against my back.

"I thought you were going back to New York after you graduated and reached eighteen."

She squeezed harder. "Not if you stay here."

Now, the decision became harder.

For the next several days, I thought of nothing but whether I should leave or not. Finally, I made up my mind. I knew it was the right decision and should have been made months ago. I would go at once without telling anyone, to avoid having to go through the goodbyes. I would leave tonight and ride my horse to town. I would sell him in the morning and, along with the money I had saved, use it for train fare. Where would I go? I would need to see how far the money would take me. I might get as far as Montana. It really didn't matter as long as I was gone from here. It would be a safer place without me.

That night, I was packing when there was a knock. I opened the door. Effie marched right in without an invitation. She looked around. "What are you doing?"

It was no use trying to hide it. "I am packing—getting ready to leave."

"Without even saying goodbye? That's not very nice." She sat down at the table and pointed to the chair across from her. "I had a suspicion that you had something on your mind at supper. Nichole had told me earlier that you were thinking about leaving."

"It is for the best. Everyone will be safer."

"It will break Grant's heart, and Nichole will be devastated. She is a different person since returning from Fort Worth. I'm afraid your leaving will be a setback for her. Will you put off leaving until September? Maybe that will help since she will be involved in school then. You have no idea what you mean to Grant and Nichole."

I was not comfortable disagreeing with this woman that I respected. "Every day I stay the danger increases."

"You are probably right. I have accepted the danger that your being here poses for us. I have weighed that with you leaving, and I am beginning to accept the danger. I believe that is the lesser of the two evils. Simply put—we need you, Daniel, physically and emotionally. Please stay until September at least."

"Okay, I will stay until September. It is not a good decision. I am afraid someone will be hurt because of me."

"Thank you." She hugged me before leaving.

I gave in because I was weak. It was not something of which to be proud. I would pray to the white man's God that he keeps this family safe.

55

QUESTIONS

Nichole

I had done everything possible to help on the ranch since coming home. It was the last week in July, and we had put up dozens of canned vegetables and fruit. I had also helped my mother clean and cook to the best of my abilities. I had never tried to cook anything. My mother was patient and passed on to me what she had learned from Gram.

When Daniel told me about leaving, I panicked. He made me feel safe. I couldn't imagine my life without him and tried not to think about it but was not successful. That wasn't all of it by any means. I cared about him in another way that was hard to describe. I didn't know if he had feelings similar to mine or not. I tried to get up the nerve to ask him but couldn't. Confused, I didn't know what to do.

I was still self-conscience about the scar on my face and continued to check daily to see if it was less visible. Some days it was red, other days almost the color of my skin. The doctor's words kept coming back to me, each time I looked in the mirror. "You just need to consider it a beauty mark." I always had the same thought, *some beauty mark.*

A week after Daniel told me about leaving, I decided to do something. I made sure Gram was alone and went to talk with her. She was outside feeding the chickens and seemed surprised to see me. "Hi, Nichole. How are you today?"

"Good, I guess. Could I talk with you about something personal?"

She threw out the rest of the feed from the bucket. "Sure, come on in. Let's go sit on the porch, it's cooler."

I followed her through the house and settled into one of the chairs. "I don't know what to do. Please don't tell anyone about this."

She made a zip motion across her mouth. "What's on your mind?"

"Daniel. I am afraid he will leave. He makes me feel safe. What can I do to get him to stop thinking of leaving?"

Leta smiled. "Are you being completely honest with your old grandmother?"

"What do you mean?"

"Nichole, is that the only reason you want him to stay—so you will feel safe?"

I should have known she would see through me. "Uh—no—I guess not." I looked down and mumbled, "I like him."

"Have you told him that you like him? *Like* seems a little weak for your feelings. Would that be correct?"

I continued to look at the floor. "I guess so. He probably doesn't feel the same way about me."

She repeated, "Have you told him about your feelings?"

I looked up. "No, every time I try it just won't come out. What can I do?"

She laughed. "Please don't get me wrong. I'm not making fun of you. I think it's wonderful that you have strong feelings for Daniel. He's a fine young man. Now, has he kissed you yet?"

"Oh, no! We don't even hold hands. I did get to put my arms around him when we rode his horse last week. He didn't seem to mind. It was special to me. I didn't even worry about getting bucked off Roany."

She leaned forward. "You want me to give you some advice—right?"

"Yes, I am afraid he will leave without knowing how I feel.

And I will never see him again."

"I'm guessing that Daniel has little experience with girls. I know he hasn't for the last several years. He's probably more than a little shy. It doesn't bother you that he's an Indian?"

At first, I was confused. "No, I've never thought about that. I don't see Daniel as being any different. Should it bother me?"

"It would be an issue for a lot of people."

"Well, it's not for me."

"Okay, that's settled. The first thing you need to do is tell him how you feel. After that, you need to show him. I gave up on Charlie, so I had to tell him to kiss me. You'll have to be more aggressive. After all, you don't have that much time to change his mind about leaving."

"I'm afraid he will think I'm a slut. I did run away with Larry."

"You have to forget about the past—that is history. If you want a future with Daniel, then you must not worry about what he thinks until you know for sure. I think you're going to be surprised."

I was not expecting Gram to tell me to be aggressive. Could I do that? "Is there anything else?"

"You have made such a change, Nichole, since coming here less than two years ago. I am proud of you. Let me know how it goes with Daniel. I want him to stay, too."

"Thank you for our talk." I left, hugging her on the way out.

Now what? The problem was that anytime I was with Daniel, so was Grant. He was like Daniel's shadow. For me to tell him how I felt, we had to be alone. I thought about it on the walk from Gram's back to our house and came up with nothing. Mother was making sandwiches when I went into the kitchen. "Where have you been?"

"Grams. Visiting with her. Can I do anything to help?"

"Yes, you can put some chairs on the porch. It is so hot we are going to eat outside," she said.

Picnic! I would invite him to go on a picnic. We could go down to the creek and be alone. Why hadn't I thought about that?

"What are you smiling about?" Mother had turned around and saw the reaction to my idea. "Surely, putting chairs outside doesn't make you smile like that."

"I just had a thought."

She smiled. "I don't imagine you would want to share it."

"No, not now. Maybe later."

I didn't waste any time. The next day was Saturday and Daniel usually came over to get Grant to go fishing. I was going to take advantage of the opportunity. He would always come in my grandad's truck, so I watched for him since he came at about the same time. When I saw him, I beat it out to the truck before Grant and went around to his side. "Good morning."

"Morning, Nichole. How are you today?"

"Good. I have a question for you. Would you like to go on a picnic after church tomorrow?"

Before he could answer, Grant hobbled out of the house and jumped into the truck. "You ready? I bet we catch a monster today."

My hopes sank. Why couldn't he have waited just a minute longer?

Daniel turned to Grant. "Nichole invited us to go on a picnic tomorrow after church. What do you think about that?"

"That's awesome! Maybe we can go to the creek and swim after we eat."

It went from bad to worse. I backed away and told them to have fun. I watched as they drove away, probably discussing the picnic.

I went to my room and plopped down across my bed. I might as well give up. It wasn't long before my mother came in. "Are you feeling bad, Nichole? I noticed you were watching for Daniel and went out to meet him."

I told her what happened. "Now, Grant is going with us. I wanted it to be a picnic just for Daniel and me."

She sat down on the edge of the bed. "You had it all

planned, didn't you?"

I shook my head. "Now it's ruined."

"Not necessarily. I'll have a talk with Grant tonight. He understands more than you think he does. It's only a guess, but I imagine that Grant will not feel well enough tomorrow afternoon to go on a picnic."

I raised up. "You would do that for me?"

She reached and stroked my hair. "Of course. I guess you and Daniel might like to go swimming after your picnic, right?"

"I don't know. That swimsuit is yucky. It's for an old person. The skirt comes down to below my knees. I look terrible."

She smiled. "Let me see now—your Gram can sew. I'll take it up to her tonight, and maybe we can make some alterations."

I jumped up and hugged her. "Thank you! Thank you!"

"We need to plan your meal. Leta usually has fried chicken on Sunday. Would that be okay? Instead of eating with us, you and Daniel could take a picnic lunch to the creek."

"Perfect," I said.

I spent the rest of the day rehearsing what I would say and how to express my feelings. Everything I came up with sounded dumb and childish. I thought writing it down might help—it made it worse.

That night when Mother returned from Gram's with my swimsuit, I went to my room and tried it on. I couldn't believe it. My grandmother had done this and was going to allow me to wear it? It had no skirt and was as revealing as any of my friends in New York would wear. I stood and stared for the longest. I giggled— maybe I wouldn't need to say anything.

I went to bed early but hardly slept any. I was up right after daylight and helped cook breakfast. I thought it would never be time to go to church and, when we did get there, it seemed to last for hours.

After we got home, I put my swimsuit on under my jeans and waited for Daniel on the porch. I thought he would never come, and all kinds of thoughts entered my mind—maybe he decided not to come—maybe my granddad had found something important for him to do that couldn't wait. I was about to give up when I saw the truck. I breathed a sigh of relief.

"I've got the fried chicken. It smells great. Where's Grant?" he asked when I opened the door to get in.

"Grant is not feeling well." I took a chance and moved over a little closer to him. He had on his cutoffs and looked great.

"Maybe we should wait and go some other time when Grant is feeling better," he suggested.

"No, that is okay. It's just going to be the two of us." I inched a little closer. He drove as close to the creek as possible. We found a grassy spot under a large oak tree to spread a quilt. My grandmother had included a container of potato salad with the chicken as well as a jar of tea.

"I hope Grant gets to feeling better. I cannot imagine him being too sick to attend a picnic." He opened the basket of chicken and passed it to me.

I guess he was going to spend all afternoon feeling bad because Grant wasn't able to come. Should I just confess and tell him the truth about why Grant didn't come? No, not yet.

I wasn't hungry but was able to force down a chicken leg and a small portion of potato salad before asking, "Are you ready to go swimming?"

"Give me a few more minutes. This chicken is good."

"Well, I might as well go on. You can come when you finish eating." I had worn my jeans and a blouse over my swimsuit. I removed my shoes before standing and taking off my jeans and blouse.

Suddenly, Daniel started choking. Alarmed, I asked, "Are you okay?"

He was hard to understand, but it sounded like, "Something went down wrong." I went on to the creek. Evidently, he recovered and didn't finish his chicken because he joined me a few minutes later. The water was nice—cool but not too cold. We didn't get close to one another. I couldn't understand why everything seemed so awkward. It wasn't that way when Grant was with us.

I was becoming more frustrated by the minute. I had to do something even if it was desperate. I moved over closer to him. When I was within arm's reach, I screamed, "Snake," and jumped into him grabbing him around the neck. He put his arms around me, and we were locked in an embrace.

"Where's the snake?" he asked.

"Oh, Daniel, I'm sorry. It was just that old stick over there." I pointed behind him to a spot he couldn't see. "I'm still a little shaky. Do you mind holding me for a minute until I calm down?"

After more than a few minutes he pushed away from me. "Are you okay, now?"

"Yes, I guess so." Now what? Then I remembered what Gram had said about my granddad. I moved back closer to him. "Would you like to kiss me?" I held my breath.

He didn't hesitate, pulling me to him. Gram was wrong—he did have some experience.

56

IMPOSTER

Leta

"I tell you, Leta, we're going under. We only have a couple of hundred dollars in the bank and no way of paying off the note. After we sell the calves and pay our feed bill, there won't be anything left. I knew when we elected a Republican president this would happen and . . ."

"Stop it, Charlie!" I'd heard enough. "We're going to have plenty to eat, unlike a lot of people in this country. Be thankful for what we have. Look at our blessings—Nichole is a different person—Elliot has improved dramatically when we thought there was no hope. We could be a lot worse off than we are."

He left the room, mumbling. I was pretty hard on him, but I had all I could take of his negative outlook. I knew we were in financial trouble but had faith that we would come out of it just like we had done in the past.

I continued to think of the positive. The change in Nichole had been remarkable. Since her release from jail, she had done everything possible to help out on the ranch. I prayed that her experience would change her attitude but never dreamed it would be to this extent. From mid-February to the first of August, she had been a different person.

My garden had done well, and we harvested and canned a record number of vegetables. I could never have done it without help from Effie, Elliot, and Nichole. Elliot continued to improve and volunteered to help with the garden. It was becoming harder and harder to get Grant away from Daniel and Charlie.

The sheriff called Charlie early in the morning, on August 10, while I was cooking breakfast. I heard part of what Charlie said but couldn't understand what they were talking about.

Charlie came into the kitchen and sat down at the table after he got off the phone. "It looks like something good might have happened. The sheriff got a call from a couple of guys from a town in East Texas. They found out I worked for Mr. Chisum and knew Billy Bonney. There's a man who lives in their town who claims to be Bonney. They're excited over the prospect of having him in their town. Isn't that something? Bonney, a thieving killer, who has become famous as Billy the Kid. Now people actually want him to live in their community. They want to bring him out here for me to identify and prove that he really is Bonney. Now here is the good part—they're willing to pay me for my time."

"Charlie, he threatened you and Mr. Chisum. That's the reason we left New Mexico. Why would you want anything to do with him?"

He held up his hand clicking his thumb and finger together in the sign of money. "It's been over fifty years. He's probably not even Bonney. Besides, it's kind of interesting that people come to me for information."

"How much are they going to pay you?"

He held up two fingers. "Two hundred dollars. That money will come in handy."

I was skeptical of the whole thing. "When are they coming?" I asked.

"Leaving at once. They'll be here in a couple of days. "It's going to be a cash deal. I'm not taking a check."

"Do you think you'll recognize him if it is Bonney?" I asked.

"Probably. If not, I can ask him questions about what was going on at the time in New Mexico. I can tell if he's the real deal or not."

It all seemed kind of shady to me. Of course, when the sheriff mentioned money, Charlie was all in. I often wonder what would have happened had we stayed in New Mexico. I made three trips back to Roswell. One was five years after we married, to show off Chisum, who was four. The other was six years after that when my mother passed. Charlie didn't go with us since we had just bought the ranch. I tried to get my dad to come and live with us, but he wanted to stay in Roswell. My dad passed in 1900, and this time Charlie went with us. It wasn't a bad trip by train, not anything like the time we came in '79 trailing cattle.

Charlie was right about one thing. During my time in Roswell, most of what I heard about Bonney was not good. Evidently, he did have some friends that helped hide him from the law. I had heard Charlie say that Mr. Chisum was largely responsible for Pat Garrett running and being elected sheriff of Lincoln County. He would go on to kill Bonney later. Or maybe Bonney was still alive—and was coming to see us.

Two days later the sheriff called and said the men were on the way out. He was not coming but had given them directions. I asked Charlie if we needed Daniel to be here for the meeting. He acted insulted. "Why would we need Daniel here? I can take care of myself."

We decided to stay on the porch for the meeting. I moved a couple of chairs out there to provide seating. Charlie insisted on sitting in the swing by himself, with his gun hidden under a pillow beside him. I told him how ridiculous it was and hoped they didn't see the gun.

We were waiting on the porch when the car drove up and three men approached the house. I opened the screen door and invited them in. It wasn't difficult to tell which one was supposed to be Bonney. He was shorter and had on a hat and boots while the others were wearing clothes fit for church.

The older of the men introduced his companions. Charlie stayed seated but told them our names. I invited them to sit and asked if they'd like water or coffee.

"No ma'am," the larger man said. "We are not going to take much of your time. As you've been told, this man," he pointed to the little cowboy, "insists that he is Billy the Kid—that Garrett killed the wrong man in 1881. We have brought a sworn statement that, if Mr. Barlowe agrees, he can sign, testifying that it is Billy the Kid. We can then go back to our town and advertise we are the home of William Bonney. Needless to say, it will bring quite a lot of notoriety to our little community."

I could see that Charlie was staring at the little man as if trying to decide if he was familiar. He didn't say anything for several minutes.

The older man must have grown tired of waiting. "Well, what do you think, Mr. Barlowe?"

"It's been over fifty years. Give me a little more time." After another few minutes he asked the man claiming to be Bonney, "How old are you?"

"Seventy-one. Born in 1860 in New York. I killed my first man when I was twelve. Garrett killed my friend that night in Fort Sumner. I escaped and went to Old Mexico where I stayed for years before moving back to Texas. I got tired of eating frijoles. Course, those Mexican senoritas were nice."

That was a long answer to the question of his age. Charlie started popping his teeth. He asked him several questions about the Lincoln County War, including the people involved. The little man spit out the answers and included much more detail than Charlie asked. His next question surprised me. "Why did you steal cattle from the Jinglebob?"

He blinked and hesitated before answering. "Chisum owed me money and wouldn't pay up."

I was surprised that he didn't provide more details this time. "Just how many men did you kill, Mr. Bonney?" Charlie asked.

The little man sits up straighter. "It's common knowledge that I killed twenty-one. History says that I killed one for each year of my life. Of course, that's not true because I'm still living."

"So, you killed twenty-one?" Charlie said in the form of a

question.

He smiled, "Yep, give or take a few. I actually didn't keep count." He held up his left hand. "This left hand was fast and true when it came to gun play."

Charlie started popping his teeth. "So, you're left-handed?"

"Yep, there's a picture of me to prove that. I understand it's worth quite a lot of money." He leaned back as though pleased with his answer.

Charlie looked at the older man who had done the talking. "Well, it's settled. He's lying. Billy Bonney was right-handed. He probably didn't kill over half a dozen men—none in a fair fight. Bonney is in a grave at Fort Sumner if you want to find him."

"But the photo does show Billy the Kid to be left-handed," said the older man. "That doesn't matter. He was right-handed." He nodded at the imposter. "I was hoping he was Bonney. I still have a score to settle with him. He threatened me, and I ran away. I have always regretted that."

The imposter stood. "I resent you calling me a liar."

"I've always considered someone who doesn't tell the truth a liar. That fits you." He looked back at the older man. "Now y'all can leave after you pay me my two hundred dollars."

"Just a minute, Mr. Barlowe. The deal was—if you signed the sworn statement confirming this was Billy the Kid. Now, if you sign this piece of paper, we can give you your money." He took a folded piece of paper out of his shirt pocket.

His teeth popping increased until I was afraid he might spit them out. "So, you want me to lie in order to get my money."

"I wouldn't say that, Mr. Barlowe. You can't be sure this isn't Billy the Kid." He gestured toward the imposter. "After all, as you said, it has been over fifty years."

I had to do something to keep this from going any further. I saw Charlie's hand easing toward the pillow. I stood and got between Charlie and the man doing the talking. I took several steps toward him. "Mister, it's time for you and your friends to leave before there's trouble. If my husband says this is not Bonney, then you better believe him."

He seemed surprised but didn't move. I took another step toward him until I could have touched him. "Do you understand? Leave. Now!"

He motioned for his friends and within seconds they were gone.

Now I had to deal with Charlie. "Leta, you ruined it. I was going to get my money."

"I know what you were going to do, Charlie. That's why I got rid of them. We can do without the two hundred dollars. More than likely, they'll look long enough to find someone who swears that guy is Bonney. That's not our problem, is it?" I went over to him and sat down on the pillow, forcing him to remove his hand from the gun.

57

EMPLOYED

Effie

I didn't have to ask Nichole how it went when she came back from the picnic. Her mood told it all. She moped around the house and had nothing to say. I finally gave up and asked her how it went.

"Oh, Mother, it was disappointing. He does like me. No, it's more than that. He has strong feelings for me and told me so. Of course, it took a little encouragement on my part. I told him that no one wanted him to leave, especially me. I promised him if he would stay, I would not go to New York after graduation."

"Did he say that he wouldn't leave?" I asked.

"No, in fact, he plans on leaving the first of the month. I don't want him to go, but nothing is going to stop him. He thinks that leaving is the only way to keep us safe."

"He's doing what he believes is right, Nichole. That shows what a good person he is. I predict that he will come back eventually."

"But when is eventually? It could be years. I could be an old maid by then. I can't just wait and wither away."

I laughed. "I can't imagine you withering away. Things have a way of working out when two people care deeply for one another."

School was going to start in a few weeks, and I had an idea. I paid a visit to the dry goods store where we had bought school clothes and asked about a job. Maybe it was because we had been good customers, or it could have been because he was short-handed and approaching a busy time of year. Regardless, I had a job with income. He did say that he wouldn't guarantee the job to last past September. He offered me two dollars a day and five percent of what I sold. I accepted it before he could change his mind. Working six days a week, that would be at least forty-eight dollars a month if I didn't sell anything.

I was finally going to be in a position to repay Elliot's mom and dad some of what they had done for us. It wasn't going to be much but at least something. Also, it would be a little money to buy school clothes for Nichole and Grant. Grant had grown so much he needed clothes badly.

I started to work on Monday, August 16, which was several weeks before school started. I had three nice dresses, which I could rotate wearing. I wasn't going to buy anything for myself. Since I worked at Macy's I did have some experience. I discovered quickly that the customers dressed and talked differently but were still the same. Most were nice and polite—a few were rude. We were busy the first week and, with my salary plus the five percent, I received $14 in cash at the end of the day Saturday. I was thrilled to be taking home money. I was going to work another week before buying school clothes.

We celebrated by having supper with Charlie and Leta. The menu was fried fish that Daniel and Grant provided. Salad, peas and corn on the cob all from the garden were also on the table. The highlight, at least for me anyway, was that Nichole said the blessing. I was surprised when she volunteered, especially since Daniel was present.

Fish was one of Rose's favorites, and she made the rounds, receiving bites from everyone, even Charlie. After the meal, we moved out onto the porch. The heat was almost unbearable inside.

"Grant, are you looking forward to school?" I asked.

He scrunched up his face. "No, I'm having too much fun

on the ranch. CK's going to have a hard time doing without me. Daniel will miss me, too. I'll have weekends though and holidays. I'll be glad when I graduate, so I can be a full-time rancher. CK can teach me everything he knows about cattle, and Daniel can teach me everything he knows about horses."

I glanced at Charlie, who was smiling. "That sounds good to me, Grant."

It was a wonderful evening, listening to stories of the early days from Charlie and Leta. Even though they downplayed the hardships, I was amazed at what they had gone through. Grant was quiet the whole evening as was Nichole. I imagine both were afraid the subject of Daniel leaving would come into the conversation. In the future someone would have to tell Grant, which would devastate him.

When it came time to leave, Charlie offered to take us home, but Elliot wanted to walk. Grant asked if he and Rose could stay with Charlie and Leta and, of course, everyone agreed. Nichole and Daniel followed behind us a good distance. The full moon offered plenty of light with the night becoming much cooler.

Elliot took my hand. "I'm proud of you for getting a job."

"It's such a relief to be able to contribute something. It's not much but at least it will help a little. Just to bring in a few dollars makes me feel good."

He squeezed my hand. "I continue to get stronger. I can even help out some on the ranch. I've tried to figure out what caused the improvement. I don't guess it makes any difference. I do believe walking has helped and having less stress. I've prayed about it, too. At first, I was ashamed to ask for help, the way I have been most of my life. Now, it doesn't bother me, which I can't explain. I think my biggest question is how so much can change in less than two years. We have given up much in the way of material things, yet all of us are happier. You made $14 working forty-eight hours this week and were thrilled, yet two years ago I would pay that much for a meal at a restaurant and think nothing about it. Our friends in New York would consider that crazy."

"Let me ask you a question, Elliot. How much is having a

positive relationship with your dad worth in regard to money?"

He didn't answer for several minutes. "I never thought about it. It seems terrible to even compare money to our relationship. I would never have thought that we could be close. Two years ago, I never expected to see my dad again, much less be able to sit down and have a normal conversation with him."

I brought up something that was not so positive. "When are we going to tell Grant that Daniel is leaving?"

"Oh me. I have been dreading that. It has to be done and soon. I keep hoping that Daniel will change his mind and stay. That's not going to happen but, at least, it gives me an excuse to put it off."

When we reached our house, we sat on our porch and waited for Daniel and Nichole. The porch was small and only had room for a table and two chairs. We heard laughter before we saw them. When they came into view, Nichole was riding Daniel piggyback, who was trotting. They stopped abruptly and grew quiet when they saw us on the porch, with Nichole getting off Daniel. They walked the rest of the way to the house. Evidently Nichole thought we needed some kind of explanation. "I was tired, and Daniel gave me a ride."

Elliot laughed. "It's been a long time, and your mother probably doesn't remember. We were on the beach and returning to our car when she insisted that I give her a ride. She claimed to be too tired to walk, but to this day I believe she was faking it."

I reached and squeezed his arm. "I do remember and even where we were— Coney Island. It was my birthday. I confess. I just wanted to feel those muscles carrying me."

Even with so little light, I could see Nichole's face turn red. "It is a pretty long walk."

They sat on the edge of the porch and, with the mood becoming more relaxed and even festive, we talked until midnight.

For the next two weeks, Elliot took me to work and picked me up when my day ended. He was up early each morning and cooked breakfast and performed most of the household chores as well as doing what he could to help his dad. The last week in August we finally were forced to tell Grant about Daniel leaving. It was even worse than we expected. At first, he denied the information, saying that Daniel would never leave. I think the news was so devastating to him that he wouldn't accept it. We finally convinced him that he was leaving in order to protect us.

"But he is my best friend," he said, with tears rolling down his cheeks. "I didn't believe he would ever leave."

"Don't you understand, Grant, he's afraid we will be hurt by those men who are coming to kill him?"

"I don't care about those men. I'm not afraid of them. If Daniel leaves, I will never see him again," he said, trying to wipe away the tears.

I knew it was useless to try and reason with him now. Maybe time would heal his hurt. I hugged him. "I am sorry. I know how special Daniel is to you."

He went to his room, carrying Rose, still crying.

We discussed it on the way to work the next morning. "Will he ever get over it, Elliot?"

"Sure. It's going to take time. Starting school will help. Dad will keep him busy on the ranch. He may recover more quickly than Nichole. I assume Daniel told her before he left."

"I had been so concerned about Grant, I hadn't thought that much about Nichole," I said.

Elliot stopped in front of the store. "We're all going to miss Daniel. Frankly, I don't see how we are going to manage the ranch without him. Dad is able to do less and less. I can do more but not enough to cover what Daniel does. It's going to be a challenge."

58

LAWTON

Daniel

I was going to leave early in the morning. I had made up my mind after the picnic to change my plans. I was going back to Oklahoma and face the men who were determined to kill me. If I ran now, there was a good chance of never being able to return. I wanted a future here on this ranch—with this family—with Nichole.

I took a few of my meager possessions including one change of clothes, a couple of relics my mother had given me, a package of deer jerky, and my old Henry repeating rifle. My uncle gave it to me when I was seven or eight years old. The stock was broken and held together with wire.

I had not told Nichole that I was leaving in the morning. She had asked me many times not to go. I saw no reason to tell her. I could not promise her that I would return. I was going to face the men who wanted to kill me, and they might be successful. Grant was another matter. I could not bring myself to tell him. The sadness would have been too much. I know that his mother and dad would be there for him.

I finished my packing and went to tell Charlie and Leta. I had tried to come up with words to express my thanks to them for all they had done for me. What I came up with did not seem to be enough.

Leta led me to the front porch where Charlie was smoking his evening cigar. He put it in the ash tray. "Well, from the look on your face, Daniel, it's bad news."

I might have known it would be evident. "I am leaving in the morning. I wanted to tell you goodbye and thank you for everything. Words are not enough. Maybe someday I can repay you."

"I'm sorry. We will miss you greatly," Leta said. "Where are you going?"

I was expecting the question and had given it much thought. "Just far away so that your family will not be in danger. It is better that you do not know since the men who come for me will demand the information from you. You can honestly say that you have no idea where I am."

Charlie picked up his cigar and relit it. "You're running away, Daniel. I did that once and still regret it. If you stay here, you'll be safe. You're like family to us, and we need you."

"We've been over this. It is too big a risk for everyone if I stay."

Leta left and came back carrying a rifle. "Daniel, this is a gun that Mr. Chisum gave me for a wedding present. It's like new, only having been fired a few times. I want you to have it, and you can leave that old gun of yours with us." She handed it to me.

"That's a Winchester 73, and the best gun ever made. It holds fifteen shells and will not fail you. It's over fifty years old but is more dependable than any gun on the market today." Charlie turned to Leta. "You better get him some shells. The 44-40 may be hard to find today. I think we have a couple of boxes."

She left and Charlie continued. "Daniel, come back if it's at all possible. There's a lot of future for you here on this ranch. Of course, I don't need to tell you that. As far as you leaving—you're probably right. I shouldn't let my experience affect you. Looking back, I know Mr. Chisum was right in forcing me to leave New Mexico for my own safety. I just never got over the fact that I ran from danger." He smiled. "You need to come back and take care of that ornery horse that no one else would even consider riding."

Leta returned and, after a hug from her, I left with Charlie, who would take me to town to catch the early morning train.

It took me two days to get to Lawton, Oklahoma which was only about six miles from my home. As I stepped from the train, it was clear that Lawton had grown in the last four years. I was glad that Leta had provided me with a quilt case for the gun, which would attract less attention. I went directly to the sheriff's office, which was located in the center of town. He was the first person I saw when I went through the door.

"Daniel! What are you doing back here?" He motioned for me to follow him to his office. He shut the door behind us and offered his hand. "I should say it's good to see you, but that would be a lie. You're about to make my job a lot harder. Now, back to my first question—what are you doing back?"

"They found out where I was and are coming after me. I would not put the family in danger where I was living. I was not going to run. The only thing to do was come back and face them."

He went behind his desk and sat down, motioning to the chair by me. "They're as bad as ever, Daniel. Still selling whiskey to your people and creating trouble. I can't get enough evidence to arrest them, and people are too afraid to testify against them. I've talked with them about you but have gotten nowhere. I'm surprised they haven't showed up before now since they discovered where you lived. Your sheriff called me and asked about you. I told him the whole story. What is your plan?"

"Just to be seen around the area and at my home. They will come for me when they find out I am here."

He leaned forward in his chair. "You shouldn't have come back, Daniel. There are three of them, and there is nothing they won't do."

"I know that. It's better than running away and not knowing when they will show up. Also, I have found a home in

Texas and a future. I want to return without causing a danger to them. The only way is to settle it here."

"Your sheriff told me about this family. Charlie Barlowe was raised by John Chisum and left New Mexico to come to Texas. I don't blame you for not wanting to put them in danger, but your chances of surviving here are not good. I can see that nothing I say will change your mind, so maybe I can help you a little. I'll give you a ride out to your place. We can stop and get you some groceries."

"Thank you. I am going to need a horse. Can you help me with that?"

"Maybe. There's a horse trader that has moved in about halfway to your house. We'll stop there and see what he has to offer. We might as well get moving."

I followed him out to his car, which had a sign on the door—Sheriff, Comanche County. I thought, *what a joke. The county is named for us and what else do my people have? Our land has been taken from us, and we have been starved.* That did not make every white man bad. The sheriff had been good to me and probably saved my life. Charlie and Leta had never treated me any different because I was an Indian.

We stopped at a grocery to buy food, a couple of blankets, and some coal-oil. I bought mostly canned goods since they would keep. The food should last me at least two weeks. I would need the coal-oil for the lamps if they were still there. I had saved enough money to last me for several months. It should be settled by then—one way or the other.

We stopped at the horse trader's place, but he had nothing but old, worn-out horses and yearling colts. We looked them over and left. As we approached my home, a wave of sadness came over me. It had been almost four years since I'd seen my mother. I thanked the sheriff, got out of the car, stood and remembered.

"Daniel. Be careful and watch for trouble. I'll check on you in a week or so." The sheriff drove away.

The house looked small from what I remembered. The inside was just like I had left it, except for the dust which covered everything. Even though it was mid-day it was dark since the windows were boarded up. I found a lamp, which still had coal- oil and lit it. I did find a broom in the closet and went to sweeping up dust. I used a piece of thin wood I found on the porch to pick up the dirt. When I quit sometime after dark, the house was so full of dust I could hardly breathe. I took a can of beans and ate on the porch.

After eating, I took my gun, blankets, and lantern to the small barn back of the house. It only had two stalls and a small room for my supplies and feed. It had been a long day, and the soft sand in one of the stalls made a comfortable bed. I went to sleep thinking—*it should be at least a couple of days until word got around that I was back home.*

I dreamed throughout the night of a time long ago when we were at war with the white men. There were no faces, only images, and when one battle ended another began. The dreams would wake me and return when I went back to sleep. I woke sometime in the early morning to a cold nose pressed against my face and a pair of black eyes staring at me. I bolted up and saw a huge black and silver dog standing by me. It looked more like a wolf than a dog. He did nothing but stand there and look at me. "Where did you come from? You must belong to someone." The only response was a continual stare.

The dog followed me to the house and lay down on the porch when I went inside. I built a fire in the stove and put on a pot of water to boil for coffee. The dust had settled and made it possible to stay inside while my coffee made. I took my coffee back outside and sat down in the one cane-bottom chair. The dog moved over beside me. Now what, I thought? I needed a horse, but where could I get one? I needed to get ready for the men who were coming for me. How long would it be? I needed to be patient and stay alert.

I wanted to see my mother but that would have to wait. She was staying with two of her sisters only about twenty miles from here. After this was finished, I would go see her before returning to Texas. I looked down at the dog. His behavior was strange. He showed no affection, yet he stayed close to me. He was not a stray since he was in good shape. Someone had taken care of him. Where did he come from and why did he show up here now?

I spent the next couple of days doing some repairs around the house and barn. I also took the time to walk over the 160 acres. There were hills and gulleys and a few trees. The sight of the Wichita mountains brought back memories. It was a place where I had hunted many times. At the back of the place there was an area that was high enough to offer a view of the entire place with some large rocks that would offer protection. I decided to spend most of my time there watching for visitors. The dog followed me everywhere. I would feed him some of whatever I ate at mealtime. At times he would brush up against me when we were walking but never showed any affection. He definitely had a master, but it was not me. I kept thinking he would disappear.

The third morning as I watched my house from the hill a horse appeared, walking toward me from the west part of the place. He seemed to come out of nowhere and showed no fear of me when I went to meet him. I took off my belt, put it around his neck and led him back to the barn. Like the dog, he was well cared for and must belong to someone. He was solid white with no markings. He stood as I saddled and got on him. I was not surprised that he responded well to my commands as I rode him away from the barn. Unlike Roany, my horse at the ranch, he was well trained—a strong and seasoned horse. I could feel the power when I nudged him off into a gallop.

I made a circle around my property and ended up back at the barn. The dog stayed with us and showed little interest in the horse, like it was normal for him to be with us.

I decided it was getting risky to stay even close to the house. I set up a make-shift shelter at my look-out spot. It only amounted to a pile of brush and an old tarp I had in the barn, but it did provide some protection from the wind and sun. I was about a good distance from the house but could see everything clearly.

My hut was actually pretty comfortable with the straw I had brought from the barn. I staked out my horse in an area close to me that had some grazing and, with the dog beside me, went to sleep that night feeling good about my set up.

The low growl of the dog woke me sometime after midnight. The moon gave off enough light to see the truck that had driven up to my house. I could make out figures as they got out and moved toward the house. Within seconds a flame leaped out from the building and shots were fired. From what I could make out, a couple of the figures were firing at the front door while someone had gone to the back and was pumping bullets into the back door. They were going to make sure I had no way of escaping the blaze. The wind picked up, and it was only minutes until the whole house was in flames. It was sad watching my home burn, but I had left nothing of value inside. I had taken all my food with me.

The truck did not leave until only ashes remained of the house.

59

HELP FROM THE PAST

Daniel

The next morning, I sat and watched the smoke rise from the smothering ruins of my house. The three men who did this were celebrating this morning, thinking I was dead. Now what? The advantage was mine now if I could find a way to use it.

I had not slept after midnight and leaned back with the warm morning sun making me drowsy. I drifted off to sleep and dreamed. I was dressed in war paint, riding the white horse with the dog running beside us. I had no rifle, only a bow and arrows. My enemies scattered before me, not choosing to stand and fight. Why were they running when I was only one? The dog woke me, with his nose pressed against my face and staring at me, like he was trying to tell me something. "What is it?" I asked. "Where did you come from? Who is your master?" All I received was that stare from those knowing eyes—then I knew.

At midday I saw a car drive up to the ashes of my house. A man got out of the car and walked up to the ruins. Even from a distance, I recognized the sheriff. I made my way down to the house with the dog at my side.

The sheriff came to meet me. "You're alive."

I pointed to my lookout. "I was up there when it happened about midnight. There were three of them. They fired into the front and back door while it burned. They think I'm dead."

He nodded toward my companion. "Where did you get the dog or whatever it is? It looks like a wolf."

"He just showed up. Came out of nowhere."

He pushed his hat back. "What are you going to do now?"

"I need you to take me to where my mother is staying. It is not that far, only about twenty miles."

"Sure, I can do that," he said.

"That is not all. They think I'm dead. Let everyone continue to think that. Go to the newspaper and report my death. Would you do that?"

He shook his head. "That would be an outright lie. Why would you want people to think that you're dead?"

"I have a plan that might work. It depends on you helping me. Would you like to get rid of these men who are trying to kill me? These are men who sell whiskey to my people when they do not have money to feed their families. They are men who believe they murdered me. They are evil. You have not been able to do anything to stop them. Does that bother you?"

He turned and started toward his car. "Come on if you want a ride."

I opened the back door for the dog and got in the front seat. I told him the way to my mother's and waited for an answer to my question. Nothing was said until we stopped in front of where my mother lived.

He killed the car and turned to me. "I'm going to help you—against my better judgement. Comanche County will think you died in a house fire. I hope I'm doing the right thing as sheriff. I'm not comfortable with lying."

"Thank you," I said, getting out of the car and opening the back door to let the dog out. I asked him if he could come back for me in three days, and he agreed.

I knocked on the door of the little house. It was opened by an older woman who shouted, "Tabemohats!" and started talking excitedly in Comanche. She threw her arms around me and pulled me in the house, yelling, "Chonie."

My mother came into the room and hugged me, crying.

"My son, you came home."

Another one of my aunts arrived, extending the reunion. After several minutes they settled down enough for me to begin and explain why and how I got here. My mother spoke English, but my two aunts did not. A scratching on the door reminded me I forgot the dog. I let him in, and he went straight to the older woman and jumped on her nearly knocking her down. She held his head in her hands as he began to lick her face. What was going on? He showed no affection for me but could not give my aunt enough attention.

My aunt asked me where I got the dog. I explained that he just showed up at my place the day after I arrived.

I did not have time to think about this because my mother's questions came quickly. It took much time for me to tell my story since we had to translate it to my aunts.

During the three days I stayed with my mother, the meals we ate came from their garden and had no meat. I had noticed that Mother and my aunts were thin, which meant they weren't getting enough to eat. I did not ask her about this because it would have embarrassed her.

During my stay, I was able to get my grandfather's possessions from the time he waged war on the white man. They included his weapons—lance, bow and arrows, war bonnet and other things.

When the sheriff came to get me the afternoon of the third day, I promised my mother I would see her again soon. I asked her not to tell anyone of my visit. I expected the dog to stay, but he followed me to the car and waited while I opened the door for him.

"What are you doing with all that Indian stuff?" the sheriff asked. "That lance is too long to go in the car."

"I need it for something I am going to do. Maybe we can tie the lance to the side of the car. Did you speak with the newspaper in Lawton?"

The sheriff reached under his front seat, brought out a paper, and gave it to me. It was on the front page.

Daniel Parker, grandson of the famous Quanah Parker,

died in a fire that destroyed his home, three days ago. It is believed that foul play was involved, and arson was suspected, but no one was arrested. Daniel was born in 1911 on the day that his grandfather died.

The page included a picture of my grandfather dressed as a warrior. The article went on to list my mother as a survivor and that no funeral arrangements were planned.

"Thank you." We left, after securing the lance to the car with pieces of rope."

The sheriff kept his attention on the road. "I'm still not happy about lying. I don't know what you have in mind. I just hope it works. I know your plan includes the Blackstone brothers, which scares me. I don't need any more killing in my county."

"Do they still live west of town?" I asked.

"Yeah. I told you—they're still as mean as ever." He glanced over his shoulder. "That dog makes me nervous. He could tear a man up in no time."

When we stopped at my place, I thanked the sheriff again. After he left, I went up to my lookout, carrying my grandfather's possessions and hoping the horse was still around. I had not gone far until he met me.

My shelter was still there and had not been disturbed. I had enough canned food to last me for several more days. The Blackstone brothers lived about thirty miles from me but less than half that as the crow flies. The good thing was a large ranch separated us, and I could reach them without having to travel on the road.

The dog had returned to his normal self and showed no affection toward me. If he bumped up against me, he quickly moved away.

During my youth, I was good with the bow and arrow but years had passed since then. I chose a target of a clump of sage brush and practiced until I was satisfied. That evening, I sat beside a small fire since the nights were becoming cooler and planned my attack.

After two days of waiting there was a full moon. I began preparing at sunset. I painted the lower part of my face black and put on a breechcloth. I remained naked from the waist up. I put on the war bonnet that came down to my waist and gathered my bow, arrows, and the war lance. I placed a blanket on the horse and tied it. I waited until dark and started my journey.

I had no problem staying out of sight until I reached the ranch. The horse had such power and stamina that I was at the home of the Blackstone brothers before midnight. I rode up to within a few yards of the door, stuck the lance in the ground beside me, took my bow and shot three arrows into the door. I retreated but remained within sight of the house, holding the lace, spotlighted by the full moon. I let out a Comanche war cry.

A lantern came on in the house, and the door opened. I sat still on my horse, so they could get a good look at me, before turning and galloping away.

I was home several hours before daylight, tired but satisfied with my night's work. The horse or dog showed no sign of the long journey. I ate a can of beans and slept until noon. Awakening, I thought of my early years. My mother, after my dad died, took her maiden name and insisted that I be called Daniel Parker. My Indian name had been Tabemohats which means Bright Sun. I had to do something to make my mother and aunts' lives better. That would come after this was over.

The next night, I repeated the previous evening. This time, a lantern was left burning in the brothers' house and on the porch. I stopped about thirty yards from the house, fitted an arrow in my bow and let out a Comanche war cry again. This time the door flung open, and the brothers came out with their rifles. Before they could shoot, I let the arrow fly. It struck the brother who was leaning against the house, went through his shoulder, and penned him to the house. I could hear his screams mixed with the rifle shots as the big white horse took me away.

I was back at my shelter before dawn. The attack had been

even more successful than expected. I was surprised that my first arrow found its mark, and the shots fired at me had not come close.

I stayed at my shelter for the next two days. I left after dark on the second day and about an hour from the Blackstone place stopped to get ready for my attack. I had brought a small bottle of kerosene and some cloth. I wrapped four arrows with strips of cloth and soaked them in kerosene. After I finished I continued on. When I was within a couple of hundred yards of the house, the dog, without making a sound, took off to my left. Within minutes, I heard a shot and a scream. I stopped and waited until the dog returned, panting with his tongue hanging out. Evidently one of the brothers had been a lookout, expecting me to return.

When I reached their house, I circled around to the side but stayed within arrow range of the house. From there, I lit an arrow with matches I brought and shot it onto the roof. I followed that with the three other arrows, spacing them so they would cover the entire roof. The house was old with a wooden roof and within minutes it was engulfed in flame. The one brother ran out of the house but was helpless to do anything but watch. I rode down at full speed, surprising him. Before he could bring his rifle up, I struck him with my hand—counting coup as my grandfather had done many years ago. I expected shots as the horse took me away, but none came.

I was back at my place even earlier on this raid. The big horse was amazing. He seemed to never tire. I was asleep in my shelter before daylight and did not wake up until late in the morning. I sat up and looked around. The dog and the horse were gone.

Late the next afternoon the sheriff came out. It took me several minutes to reach him. He was smiling as he greeted me. "Well, you look okay. I half expected you to be all shot up." He looked around. "Where's the dog and horse?"

I shrugged. "They are gone."

"Strange, isn't it. It's almost like they came to help you." He took off his hat and wiped his forehead. "I have some news for you. I was out at the Blackstone brothers this morning after a fire was reported. The house was only ashes, and they were loading a truck with their whiskey making equipment, which was all they had left. I have never seen more frightened grown men. The older brother was the only one able to do anything. One brother's arm was in a sling, the middle brother looked like he had been run through a meat grinder. He needed stiches badly on his face, neck, and arms. If I didn't know better, I'd have thought he had a run-in with a grizzly bear."

The older brother was doing all the talking. "He's back! We saw him! Quanah Parker is back! He came to our house three nights. He shot my brother, burned our house, and his wolf attacked my brother. We're gettin' out'a here! We have kin in Montana. Sheriff, you need to warn people about this Indian! He's come back from the dead."

The sheriff burst out laughing. "The Blackstone brothers won't sell no more whiskey around here. What are you going to do now?"

"I need a ride to my mother's. I would like to stay with her a week and then—I am going home to Texas."

Five years later, I received a package from the Lawton sheriff. It contained a calendar with each month portraying an Indian painting. The month of January depicted Quanah Parker, sitting on a white horse. Standing beside the horse was a huge black dog which resembled a wolf.

EPILOGUE

Leta

I was sitting on the front porch, watching my great-grandchildren play. I smiled. Charles Elliot, who was eight, was giving orders to his two younger sisters, Leta May and Effie Fay. The girls were five and three and were addressed as May and Fay. It was only natural that Charles Elliot was called Charlie. I continued to be amazed at how much Charlie was like his Poppa. Of course, he had been inseparable from his Poppa for the first six years of his life. Charlie had already received several spankings for cursing—a result of his great-granddad's influence.

I lost my beloved husband and hero in 1940, two years ago. I know it was my imagination, but at times I would still catch the aroma of cigar smoke in the house. The sixty-one years of memories still occupied much of my time.

The ranch was doing well, with high cattle prices, even without Daniel, who had joined the army after Pearl Harbor. All the pleading from Nichole and myself to keep him home had done no good. He was being used in communication as a Code Talker along with a dozen other members of the Comanche nation. The messages in their language were impossible for the Germans to interpret. His safety was a constant worry for all of us, especially Nichole.

Most of the decisions concerning the ranch were made by Grant, who at twenty-three was dedicated and capable of addressing any issue which might arise. Elliot was of some help but still had to be careful with what he did. Nichole, even though she was busy with her family, still did all she could to help out on the ranch. Help was not that much of a problem since we had a ranch hand. Elliot and Effie had moved in with me after Charlie passed, so their little house was where our hand lived.

Daniel was able to build a new home on the ranch for his family in 1935 with the income he received from the two producing oil wells on his property in Oklahoma. He was also able to have a home built for his mother and aunts to replace the one that burned.

The Barlowe family had a lot for which to be thankful. I missed Charlie but was grateful that he had made his peace with God the last few years of his life, saying, "I lost one son but gained another plus two grandchildren and three great-grandchildren."

Three days before he died, we were sitting on the porch when he started laughing. "Leta, I know what I want on my tombstone." He had that mischievous look, which I had seen so many times. "The old son-of-a-bitch didn't amount to much, but he sure had a lot of fun." He knew that was never going to happen.